Eb search
smile left

"You don't know what my life was like in those days," he said, and for once his eyes were unguarded.

"Aunt Jessica told me," she said slowly.

His eyes darkened. His face hardened. "All of it?"

She nodded.

He released her to gaze off into the distance.

"I'm not sure that I wanted you to know."

"Secrets are dangerous."

"More dangerous than you realize. I've kept mine for a long time."

He looked down at her, his eyes intent on her softly flushed cheeks. She lifted his heart. Just the sight of her made him feel welcome, comforted, cared for. He'd missed that. In all his life, Sally had been the first and only person who could thwart his black moods. She made him feel as if he belonged somewhere after a life of wandering. He'd always expected that she'd come back to him one day, or that he'd go to her, despite the way they'd parted.

Love, if it existed, was surely a powerful force.

A prolific author of more than one hundred books, **Diana Palmer** got her start as a newspaper reporter. A *New York Times* bestselling author and voted one of the top ten romance writers in America, she has a gift for telling the most sensual tales with charm and humor. Diana lives with her family in Cornelia, Georgia.

Delores Fossen, a *USA TODAY* bestselling author, has written over a hundred and fifty novels, with millions of copies of her books in print worldwide. She's received a Booksellers' Best Award and an RT Reviewers' Choice Best Book Award. She was also a finalist for a prestigious RITA® Award. You can contact the author through her website at deloresfossen.com.

MERCENARY'S WOMAN

NEW YORK TIMES BESTSELLING AUTHOR
DIANA PALMER

Harlequin

BESTSELLING AUTHOR COLLECTION

Harlequin®
BESTSELLING
AUTHOR
COLLECTION

Recycling programs
for this product may
not exist in your area.

ISBN-13: 978-1-335-47485-8

Mercenary's Woman
First published in 2000. This edition published in 2025 with revised text.
Copyright © 2000 by Diana Palmer
Copyright © 2025 by Diana Palmer, revised text edition.

Safety Breach
First published in 2019. This edition published in 2025.
Copyright © 2019 by Delores Fossen

Harlequin Enterprises ULC
22 Adelaide St. West, 41st Floor
Toronto, Ontario M5H 4E3, Canada
www.Harlequin.com

HarperCollins Publishers
Macken House, 39/40 Mayor Street Upper,
Dublin 1, D01 C9W8, Ireland
www.HarperCollins.com

Printed in U.S.A.

CONTENTS

Also by Diana Palmer

Long, Tall Texans

The Wyoming Men

Visit her Author Profile page
at Harlequin.com for more titles.

MERCENARY'S WOMAN

Diana Palmer

For the Habersham Co. (GA) Sheriff's Department, and the Habersham Co. Emergency Medical Service, with thanks.

CHAPTER ONE

Ebenezer Scott stood beside his double-wheeled black pickup truck and stared openly at the young woman across the street while she fiddled under the hood of a dented, rusted hulk of a vehicle. Sally Johnson's long blond hair was in a ponytail. She was wearing jeans and boots and no hat. He smiled to himself, remembering how many times in the old days he'd chided her about sunstroke. It had been six years since they'd even spoken. She'd been living in Houston until July, when she and her blind aunt and small cousin had moved back, into the decaying old Johnson homestead. He'd seen her several times since her return, but she'd made a point of not speaking to him. He couldn't really blame her. He'd left her with some painful emotional scars.

She was slender, but her trim figure still made his heartbeat jump. He knew how she looked under that loose blouse. His eyes narrowed with heat as he recalled the shocked pleasure in her pale gray eyes when he'd touched her, kissed her, in those forbidden places. He'd hoped to frighten her so that she'd stop teasing him, but his impulsive attempt to discourage her had succeeded all too well. She'd run from him then, and she'd kept running. She was twenty-three now, a woman; probably an experienced woman. He mourned for what might have been if she'd been older and he hadn't just come

back from leading a company of men into the worst
bloodbath of his career. A professional soldier of fortune was no match for a young and very innocent girl.
But, then, she hadn't known about his real life—the one
behind the facade of cattle ranching. Not many people
in this small town did.

It was six years later. She was all grown-up, a schoolteacher here in Jacobsville, Texas. He was...retired,
they called it. Actually he was still on the firing line
from time to time, but mostly he taught other men in
the specialized tactics of covert operations on his ranch.
Not that he shared that information. He still had enemies from the old days, and one of them had just been
sprung from prison on a technicality—a man out for
revenge and with more than enough money to obtain it.

Sally had been almost eighteen the spring day he'd
sent her running from him. In a life liberally strewn
with regrets, she was his biggest one. The whole situation had been impossible, of course. But he'd never
meant to hurt her, and the thought of her sat heavily
on his conscience.

He wondered if she knew why he kept to himself
and never got involved with the locals. His ranch was
a model of sophistication, from its state-of-the-art gym
to the small herd of purebred Santa Gertrudis breeding
cattle he raised. His men were not only loyal, but tight-
lipped. Like another Jacobsville, Texas, resident—Cy
Parks—Ebenezer was a recluse. The two men shared
more than a taste for privacy. But that was something
they kept to themselves.

Meanwhile, Sally Johnson was rapidly losing patience with her vehicle. He watched her push at a strand
of hair that had escaped from the long ponytail. She

kept a beef steer or two herself. It must be a frugal existence for her, supporting not only herself, but her recently blinded aunt, and her six-year-old cousin as well.

He admired her sense of responsibility, even as he felt concern for her situation. She had no idea why her aunt had been blinded in the first place, or that the whole family was in a great deal of danger. It was why Jessica had persuaded Sally to give up her first teaching job in Houston in June and come home with her and Stevie to Jacobsville. It was because they'd be near Ebenezer, and Jessica knew he'd protect them. Sally had never been told what Jessica's profession actually was, any more than she knew what Jessica's late husband, Hank Myers, had once done for a living. But even if she had known, wild horses wouldn't have dragged Sally back here if Jessica hadn't pleaded with her, he mused bitterly. Sally had every reason in the world to hate him. But he was her best hope of survival. And she didn't even know it.

In the five months she'd been back in Jacobsville, Sally had managed to avoid Ebenezer. In a town this size, that had been an accomplishment. Inevitably they met from time to time. But Sally avoided eye contact with him. It was the only indication of the painful memory they both shared.

He watched her lean helplessly over the dented fender of the old truck and decided that now was as good a time as any to approach her.

Sally lifted her head just in time to see the tall, lean man in the shepherd's coat and tan Stetson make his way across the street to her. He hadn't changed, she thought bitterly. He still walked with elegance and a slow arrogance of carriage that seemed somehow for-

eign. Jeans didn't disguise the muscles in those long, powerful legs as he moved. She hated the ripple of sensation that lifted her heart at his approach. Surely she was over hero worship and infatuation, at her age, especially after what he'd done to her that long-ago spring day. She blushed just remembering it!

He paused at the truck, about an arm's length away from her, pushed his Stetson back over his thick blond-streaked brown hair and impaled her with green eyes.

She was immediately hostile and it showed in the tautening of her features as she looked up, way up, at him.

He raised an eyebrow and studied her flushed face. "Don't give me the evil eye," he said. "I'd have thought you had sense enough not to buy a truck from Turkey Sanders."

"He's my cousin," she reminded him.

"He's the Black Plague with car keys," he countered. "The Hart boys wiped the floor with him not too many years back. He sold Corrigan Hart's future wife a car that fell apart when she drove it off the lot. She was lucky at that," he added with a wicked grin. "He sold old lady Bates a car and told her the engine was optional equipment."

She laughed in spite of herself. "It's not a bad old truck," she countered. "It just needs a few things…"

He glanced at the rear tire and nodded. "Yes. An overhauled engine, a paint job, reupholstered seats, a tailgate that works. And a rear tire that isn't bald." He pointed toward it. "Get that replaced," he said shortly. "You can afford a tire even on what you make teaching."

She gaped at him. "Listen here, Mr. Scott…" she began haughtily.

"You know my name, Sally," he said bluntly, and his eyes were steady, intimidating. "As for the tire, it isn't a request," he replied flatly, staring her down. "You've got some new neighbors out your way that I don't like the look of. You can't afford a breakdown in the middle of the night on that lonely stretch of road."

She drew herself up to her full height, so that the top of her head came to his chin. He really was ridiculously tall...

"This is the twenty-first century, and women are capable of looking after themselves..." she said heatedly.

"I can do without a current events lecture," he cut her off again, moving to peer under the hood. He propped one enormous booted foot on the fender and studied the engine, frowned, pulled out a pocketknife and went to work.

"It's *my* truck!" she fumed, throwing up her hands in exasperation.

"It's half a ton of metal without an engine that works."

She grimaced. She hated not being able to fix it herself, to have to depend on this man, of all people, for help. She wouldn't let herself think about the cost of having a mechanic make a road service call to get the stupid thing started. Looking at his lean, capable hands brought back painful memories as well. She knew the tenderness of them on concealed skin, and her whole body erupted with sensation.

Less than two minutes later, he repocketed his knife. "Try it now," he said.

She got in behind the wheel. The engine turned noisily, pouring black smoke out of the tailpipe.

He paused beside the open window of the truck, his pale green eyes piercing her face. "Bad rings and

valves," he pointed out. "Maybe an oil leak. Either way, you're in for some major repairs. Next time, don't buy from Turkey Sanders, and I don't give a damn if he is a relative."

"Don't you give me orders," she said haughtily.

That eyebrow lifted again. "Habit. How's Jess?"

She frowned. "Do you know my aunt Jessie?"

"Quite well," he said. "I knew your uncle Hank. He and I served together."

"In the military?"

He didn't answer her. "Do you have a gun?"

She was so confused that she stammered. "Wh... what?"

"A gun," he repeated. "Do you have any sort of weapon and can you use it?"

"I don't like guns," she said flatly. "Anyway, I won't have one in the house with a six-year-old child, so it's no use telling me to buy one."

He was thinking. His face tautened. "How about self-defense?"

"I teach second grade," she pointed out. "Most of my students don't attack me."

"I'm not worried about you at school. I told you, I don't like the look of your neighbors." He wasn't adding that he knew who they were and why they were in town.

"Neither do I," she admitted. "But it's none of your business..."

"It is," he returned. "I promised Hank that I'd take care of Jess if he ever bought it overseas. I keep my promises."

"I can take care of my aunt."

"Not anymore you can't," he returned, unabashed. "I'm coming over tomorrow."

"I may not be home…"

"Jess will be. Besides, tomorrow is Saturday," he said. "You came in for supplies this afternoon and you don't teach on the weekend. You'll be home." His tone said she'd better be.

She gave an exasperated sound. "Mr. Scott…"

"I'm only Mr. Scott to my enemies," he pointed out.

"Yes, well, Mr. Scott…"

He let out an angry sigh and stared her down. "You were so young," he bit off. "What did you expect me to do, seduce you in the cab of a pickup truck in broad daylight?"

She flushed red as a rose petal. "I wasn't talking about that!"

"It's still in your eyes," he told her quietly. "I wish I hadn't left so many scars, but the whole damned thing was impossible, you must have realized that by now!"

She hated the embarrassment she felt. "I don't have scars!"

"You do." He studied her oval face, her softly rounded chin, her perfect mouth. "I'll be over tomorrow. I need to talk to you and Jess. There have been some developments that she doesn't know about."

"What sort of developments?"

He closed the hood of the truck and paused by her window. "Drive carefully," he said, ignoring the question. "And get that tire changed."

"I am not a charity case," she said curtly. "I don't take orders. And I definitely do not need some big, strong man to take care of me!"

He smiled, but it wasn't a pleasant smile. He turned on his heel and walked back to his own truck with a stride that was peculiarly his own.

Sally was so shaken that she barely managed to get the truck out of town without stripping the gears out of it.

JESSICA MYERS WAS in her bedroom listening to the radio and her son, Stevie, was watching a children's after-school television program when Sally came in. She unloaded the supplies first with the help of her six-year-old cousin.

"You got me that cereal from the TV commercial!" he exclaimed, diving into bags as she put the perishable items into the refrigerator. "Thanks, Aunt Sally!" Although they were cousins, he referred to her as his aunt out of affection and respect.

"You're very welcome. I got some ice cream, too."

"Wow! Can I have some now?"

Sally laughed. "Not until after supper, and you have to eat some of everything I fix. Okay?"

"Aw. Okay, I guess," he muttered, clearly disappointed.

She bent and kissed him between his dark eyes. "That's my good boy. Here, I brought some nice apples and pears. Wash one off and eat it. Fruit is good for you."

"Okay. But it's not as nice as ice cream."

He washed off a pear and carried it into the living room on a paper towel to watch television.

Sally went into Jessica's bedroom, hesitating at the foot of the big four-poster bed. Jessica was slight, blond and hazel-eyed. Her eyes stared at nothing, but she smiled as she recognized Sally's step.

"I heard the truck," she said. "I'm sorry you had to

go to town for supplies after working all day and bringing Stevie home first."

"I never mind shopping," Sally said with genuine affection. "You doing all right?"

Jessica shifted on the pillows. She was dressed in sweats, but she looked bad. "I still have some pain from the wreck. I've taken a couple of aspirins for my hip. I thought I'd lie down and give them a chance to work."

Sally came in and sat down in the wing chair beside the bed. "Jess, Ebenezer Scott asked about you and said he was coming over tomorrow to see you."

Jessica didn't seem at all surprised. She only nodded. "I thought he might," Jessica said quietly. "I had a call from a former colleague about what's going on. I'm afraid I may have landed you in some major trouble, Sally."

"I don't understand."

"Didn't you wonder why I insisted on moving down here so suddenly?"

"Now that you mention it—"

"It was because Ebenezer is here, and we're safer than we would be in Houston."

"Now you're scaring me."

Jessica smiled sadly. "I wouldn't have had this happen for the world. It isn't something that comes up, usually. But these are odd circumstances. A man I helped put in prison is out pending retrial, and he's coming after me."

"You...helped put a man in prison? How?" Sally asked, perplexed.

"You knew that I worked for a government agency?"

"Well, of course. As a clerk."

Jessica took a deep breath. "No, dear. Not as a clerk."

She took another deep breath. "I was a special agent for an agency we don't mention publicly. Through Eb and his contacts, I managed to find one of the confidants of drug lord Manuel Lopez, who was head of an international drug cartel. I was given enough hard evidence to send Lopez to prison for drug dealing. I even had copies of his ledgers. But there was one small loophole in the chain of evidence, and the drug lord's attorneys jumped on it. Lopez is now out of prison and he wants the person responsible for helping me put him away. Since I'm the only one who knows the person's identity, I'm the one he'll be coming after."

Sally just sat there, dumbfounded. Things like this only happened in movies. They certainly didn't happen in real life. Her beloved aunt surely wasn't involved in espionage!

"You're kidding, right?" Sally asked hopefully.

Jessica shook her head slowly. She was still an attractive woman, in her middle thirties. She was slender and she had a sweet face. Stevie, blond and dark-eyed, didn't favor her. Of course, he didn't favor his father, either. Hank had had black hair and light blue eyes.

"I'm sorry, dear," Jessica said heavily. "I'm not kidding. I'm not able to protect myself or you and Stevie anymore, so I had to come home for help. Ebenezer will keep us safe until we can get the drug lord back on ice."

"Is Ebenezer a government agent?" Sally asked, astounded.

"No." Jessica took a deep breath. "I don't like telling you this, and he won't like it, either. It's deeply private. You must swear not to tell another soul."

"I swear." She sat patiently, almost vibrating with curiosity.

"Eb was a professional mercenary," she said. "What they used to call a soldier of fortune. He's led groups of highly trained men in covert operations all over the world. He's retired from that now, but he's still much in demand with our government and foreign governments as a training instructor. His ranch is well-known in covert circles as an academy of tactics and intelligence-gathering."

Sally didn't say a word. She was absolutely speechless. No wonder Ebenezer had been so secretive, so reluctant to let her get close to him. She remembered the tiny white scars on his lean, tanned face, and knew instinctively that there would be more of them under his clothing. No wonder he kept to himself!

"I hope I haven't shattered any illusions, Sally," her aunt said worriedly. "I know how you felt about him."

Sally gaped at her. "You...know?"

Jessica nodded. "Eb told me about that, and about what happened just before you came to live with Hank and me in Houston."

Her face flamed. The shame! She felt sick with humiliation that Ebenezer had known how she felt all the time, and she thought she was doing such a good job of hiding it! She should have realized that it was obvious, when she found excuse after excuse to waylay him in town, when she brazenly climbed into his pickup truck one lovely spring afternoon and pleaded to be taken for a ride. He'd given in to that request, to her surprise. But barely half an hour later, she'd erupted from the passenger seat and run almost all the half-mile down the road to her home. Too ashamed to let anyone see the state she was in, she'd sneaked in the back door and gone straight to her room. She'd never told her parents

or anyone else what had happened. Now she wondered if Jessica knew that, too.

"He didn't divulge any secrets, if that's why you're so quiet, Sally," the older woman said gently. "He only said that you had a king-size crush on him and he'd shot you down. He was pretty upset."

That was news. "I wouldn't ever have guessed that he could be upset."

"Neither would I," Jessica said with a smile. "It came as something of a surprise. He told me to keep an eye on you, and check out who you went out with. He could have saved himself the trouble, of course, since you never went out with anyone. He was bitter about that."

Sally averted her face to the window. "He frightened me."

"He knew that. It's why he was bitter."

Sally drew in a steadying breath. "I was very young," she said finally, "and I suppose he did the only thing he could. But I was leaving Jacobsville anyway, when my parents divorced. I only had a week of school before graduation before I went to live with you. He didn't have to go to such lengths."

"My brother still feels like an idiot for the way he behaved with that college girl he left your mother for," Jessica said curtly, meaning Sally's father, who was Jessica's only living relative besides Sally. "It didn't help that your mother remarried barely six months later. He was stuck with Beverly the Beauty."

"How are my parents?" Sally asked. It was the first time she'd mentioned either of her parents in a long while. She'd lost touch with them since the divorce that had shattered her life.

"Your father spends most of his time at work while

Beverly goes the party route every night and spends every penny he makes. Your mother is separated from her second husband and living in Nassau." Jessica shifted on the bed. "You don't ever hear from your parents, do you?"

"I don't resent them as much as I did. But I never felt that they loved me," she said abruptly. "That's why I felt it was better we went our separate ways."

"They were children when they married and had you," the other woman said. "Not really mature enough for the responsibility. They resented it, too. That's why you spent so much time with me during the first five years you were alive." Jessica smiled. "I hated it when you went back home."

"Why did you and Hank wait so long to have a child of your own?" Sally asked.

Jessica flushed. "It wasn't…convenient, with Hank overseas so much. Did you get that tire replaced?" she added, almost as if she were desperate to change the subject.

"You and Mr. Scott!" Sally exploded, diverted. "How did you know it was bald?"

"Because Eb phoned me before you got home and told me to remind you to get it replaced," Jessica chuckled.

"I suppose he has a cell phone in his truck."

"Among other things," Jessica replied with a smile. "He isn't like the men you knew in college or even when you started teaching. Eb is an alpha male," she said quietly. "He isn't politically correct, and he doesn't even pretend to conform. In some ways, he's very old-fashioned."

"I don't feel that way about him anymore," Sally said firmly.

"I'm sorry," Jessica replied gently. "He's been alone most of his life. He needs to be loved."

Sally picked at a cuticle, chipping the clear varnish on her short, neat fingernails. "Does he have family?"

"Not anymore. His mother died when he was very young, and his father was career military. He grew up in the army, you might say. His father was not a gentle sort of man. He died in combat when Eb was in his twenties. There wasn't any other family."

"You said once that you always saw Ebenezer with beautiful women at social events," Sally recalled with a touch of envy.

"He pays for dressing, and he attracts women. But he's careful about his infrequent liaisons. He told me once that he guessed he'd never find a woman who could share the life he leads. He still has enemies who'd like to see him dead," she added.

"Like this drug lord?"

"Yes. Manuel Lopez is a law unto himself. He has millions, and he owns politicians, law enforcement people, even judges," Jessica said irritably. "That's why we were never able to shut him down. Then I was told that a confidant of his wanted to give me information, names and documents that would warrant arresting Lopez on charges of drug trafficking. But I wasn't careful enough. I overlooked one little thing, and Lopez's attorneys used it in a petition for a retrial. They got him out. He's on the loose pending retrial and out for vengeance against his comrade. He'll do anything to get the name of the person who sold him out. Anything at all."

Sally let her breath out through pursed lips. "So we're all under the gun."

"Exactly. I used to be a crack shot, but without my vision, I'm useless. Eb will have a plan by tomorrow." Her face was solemn as she stared in the general direction of her niece's voice. "Listen to him, Sally. Do exactly what he says. He's our only hope of protecting Stevie."

"I'll do anything I have to, to protect you and Stevie," Sally agreed at once.

"I knew you would."

She toyed with her nails again. "Jess, has Ebenezer ever been serious about anyone?"

"Yes. There was a woman in Houston, in fact, several years ago. He cared for her very much, but she dropped him flat when she found out what he did for a living. She married a much-older bank executive." She shifted on the bed. "I hear that she's widowed now. But I don't imagine he still has any feelings for her. After all, she dropped him, not the reverse."

Sally, who knew something about helpless unrequited love, wasn't so quick to agree. After all, she still had secret feelings for Ebenezer...

"Deep thoughts, dear?" Jessica asked softly.

"I was remembering the reruns we used to see of that old TV series, *The A-Team*," she recalled with an audible laugh. "I loved it when they had to knock out that character Mr. T played to get him on an airplane."

"It was a good show. Not lifelike, of course," Jessica added.

"What part?"

"All of it."

Jessica would probably know, Sally figured. "Why didn't you ever tell me what you did for a living?"

"Need to know," came the dry reply. "You didn't, until now."

"If you knew Ebenezer when he was still working as a mercenary, I guess you learned a lot about the business," she ventured.

Jessica's face closed up. "I learned too much," she said coldly. "Far too much. Men like that are incapable of lasting relationships. They don't know the meaning of love or fidelity."

She seemed to know that, and Sally wondered how. "Was Uncle Hank a mercenary, too?"

"Yes, just briefly," she said. "Hank was never one to rush in and risk killing himself. It was so ironic that he died overseas in his sleep, of a heart condition nobody even knew he had."

That was a surprise, along with all the others that Sally was getting. Uncle Hank had been very handsome, but not assertive or particularly tough.

"But Ebenezer said he served with Uncle Hank."

"Yes. In basic training, before they joined the Green Berets," Jessica said. "Hank didn't pass the training course. Ebenezer did. In fact," she added amusedly, "he was able to do the Fan Dance."

"Fan Dance?"

"It's a specialized course they put the British commandos, the Special Air Service, guys through. Not many soldiers, even career soldiers, are able to finish it, much less able to pass it on the first try. Eb did. He was briefly 'loaned' to them while he was in army intelligence, for some top secret assignment."

Sally had never thought very much about Ebenezer's profession, except that she'd guessed he was once in the military. She wasn't sure how she felt about it. A man

who'd been in the military might still have a soft spot
or two inside. She was almost certain that a commando,
a soldier for hire, wouldn't have any.

"You're very quiet," Jessica said.

"I never thought of Ebenezer in such a profession,"
she replied, moving to look out the window at the No-
vember landscape. "I guess it was right there in front of
me, and I didn't see it. No wonder he kept to himself."

"He still does," she replied. "And only a few people know about his past. His men do, of course," she
added, and there was an inflection in her tone that was
suddenly different.

"Do you know any of his men?"

Jessica's face tautened. "One or two. I believe Dallas Kirk still works for him. And Micah Steele does
consulting work when Eb asks him to," she added and
smiled. "Micah's a good guy. He's the only one of Eb's
old colleagues who still works in the trade. He lives in
Nassau, but he spends an occasional week helping Ebenezer train men when he's needed."

"And Dallas Kirk?"

Jessica's soft face went very hard. At her side, one of
her small hands clenched. "Dallas was badly wounded
in a firefight a year ago. He came home shot to pieces
and Eb found something for him to teach in the tactics
courses. He doesn't speak to me, of course. We had a
difficult parting some years ago."

That was intriguing, and Sally was going to find out
about it one day. But she didn't press her luck. "How
about fajitas for supper?" she asked.

Jessica's glower dissolved into a smile. "Sounds
lovely!"

"I'll get right on them." Sally went back into the

kitchen, her head spinning with the things she'd learned about people she thought she knew. Life, she considered, was always full of surprises.

CHAPTER TWO

EBENEZER WAS A MAN of his word. He showed up early the next morning as Sally was out by the corral fence watching her two beef cattle graze. She'd bought them to raise with the idea of stocking her freezer. Now they had names. The white-faced Black Angus mixed steer was called Bob, the white-faced red-coated Hereford she called Andy. They were pets. She couldn't face the thought of sitting down to a plate of either one of them.

The familiar black pickup stopped at the fence and Ebenezer got out. He was wearing jeans and a blue checked shirt with boots and a light-colored straw Stetson. No chaps, so he wasn't working cattle today.

He joined Sally at the fence. "Don't tell me. They're table beef."

She spared him a resentful glance. "Right."

"And you're going to put them in the freezer."

She swallowed. "Sure."

He only chuckled. He paused to light a cigar, with one big booted foot propped on the lower rung of the fence. "What are their names?"

"That's Andy and that's… Bob." She flushed.

He didn't say a word, but his raised eyebrow was eloquent through the haze of expelled smoke.

"They're watch-cattle," she improvised.

His eyes twinkled. "I beg your pardon?"

"They're attack steers," she said with a reluctant grin. "At the first sign of trouble, they'll come right through the fence to protect me. Of course, if they get shot in the line of duty," she added, "I'll eat them!"

He pushed his Stetson back over clean blond-streaked brown hair and looked down at her with lingering amusement. "You haven't changed much in six years."

"Neither have you," she retorted shyly. "You're still smoking those awful things."

He glanced at the big cigar and shrugged. "A man has to have a vice or two to round him out," he pointed out. "Besides, I only have the occasional one, and never inside. I have read the studies on smoking," he added dryly.

"Lots of people who smoke read those studies," she agreed. "And then they quit!"

He smiled. "You can't reform me," he told her. "It's a waste of time to try. I'm thirty-six and very set in my ways."

"I noticed."

He took a puff from the cigar and studied her steers. "I suppose they follow you around like dogs."

"When I go inside the fence with them," she agreed. She felt odd with him; safe and nervous and excited, all at once. She could smell the fresh scent of the soap he used, and over it a whiff of expensive cologne. He was close at her side, muscular and vibrating with sensuality. She wanted to move closer, to feel that strength all around her. It made her self-conscious. After six years, surely the attraction should have lessened a little.

He glanced down at her, noticing how she picked at her cuticles and nibbled on her lower lip. His green eyes narrowed and there was a faint glitter in them.

She felt the heat of his gaze and refused to lift her face. She wondered if it looked as hot as it felt.

"You haven't forgotten a thing," he said suddenly, the cigar in his hand absently falling to his side, whirls of smoke climbing into the air beside him.

"About what?" she choked.

He caught her long, blond ponytail and tugged her closer, so that she was standing right up against him. The scent of him, the heat of him, the muscular ripple of his body combined to make her shiver with repressed feelings.

He shifted, coaxing her into the curve of his body, his eyes catching hers and holding them relentlessly. He could feel her faint trembling, hear the excited whip of her breath as she tried valiantly to hide it from him. But he could see her heartbeat jerking the fabric over her small breasts.

It was a relief to find her as helplessly attracted to him as she once had been. It made him arrogant with pride. He let go of the ponytail and drew his hand against her cheek, letting his thumb slide down to her mouth and over her chin to lift her eyes to his.

"To everything, there is a season," he said quietly.

She felt the impact of his steady, unblinking gaze in the most secret places of her body. She didn't have the experience to hide it, to protect herself. She only stood staring up at him, with all her insecurities and fears lying naked in her soft gray eyes.

His head bent and he drew his nose against hers in the sudden silence of the yard. His smoky breath whispered over her lips as he murmured, "Six years is a long time to go hungry."

She didn't understand what he was saying. Her eyes

were on his hard, long, thin mouth. Her hands had flattened against his broad chest. Under it she could feel thick, soft hair and the beat of his heart. His breath smelled of cigar smoke and when his mouth gently covered hers, she wondered if she was going to faint with the unexpected delight of it. It had been so long!

He felt her immediate, helpless submission. His free arm went around her shoulders and drew her lazily against his muscular body while his hard mouth moved lightly over her lips, tasting her, assessing her experience. His mouth became insistent and she stiffened a little, unused to the tender probing of his tongue against her teeth.

She felt his smile before he lifted his head.

"You still taste of lemonade and cotton candy," he murmured with unconcealed pleasure.

"What do you mean?" she murmured, mesmerized by the hovering threat of his mouth.

"I mean, you still don't know how to do this." He searched her eyes quietly and then the smile left his face. "I did more damage than I ever meant to. You were seventeen. I had to hurt you to save you." He traced her mouth with his thumb and scowled down at her. "You don't know what my life was like in those days," he said solemnly, and for once his eyes were unguarded. The pain in them was visible for the first time Sally could remember.

"Aunt Jessica told me," she said slowly.

His eyes darkened. His face hardened. "All of it?"

She nodded.

He was still scowling. He released her to gaze off into the distance, absently lifting the cigar to his mouth. He

blew out a cloud of smoke. "I'm not sure that I wanted you to know."

"Secrets are dangerous."

He glanced down at her, brooding. "More dangerous than you realize. I've kept mine for a long time, like your aunt."

"I had no idea what she did for a living, either." She glared up at him. "Thanks to the two of you, now I know how a mushroom feels, sitting in the dark."

He chuckled. "She wanted it that way. She felt you'd be safer if she kept you uninvolved."

She wanted to ask him about what Jessica had told her, that he'd phoned her about Sally before the painful move to Houston. But she didn't quite know how. She was shy with him.

He looked down at her again, his eyes intent on her softly flushed cheeks, her swollen mouth, her bright eyes. She lifted his heart. Just the sight of her made him feel welcome, comforted, cared for. He'd missed that. In all his life, Sally had been the first and only person who could thwart his black moods. She made him feel as if he belonged somewhere after a life of wandering. Even during the time she was in Houston, he kept in touch with Jessica, to get news of Sally, of where she was, what she was doing, of her plans. He'd always expected that she'd come back to him one day, or that he'd go to her, despite the way they'd parted. Love, if it existed, was surely a powerful force, immune to harsh words and distance. And time.

Sally's face was watchful, her eyes brimming over with excitement. She couldn't hide what she was feeling, and he loved being able to see it. Her hero worship had first irritated and then elated him. Women had wanted

him since his teens, although some loved him for the danger that clung to him. One had rejected him because of it and savaged his pride. But, even so, it was Sally who made him ache inside.

He touched her soft mouth with his fingers, liking the faint swell where he'd kissed it so thoroughly. "We'll have to practice more," he murmured wickedly.

She opened her mouth to protest that assumption when a laughing Stevie came running out the door like a little blond whirlwind, only to be caught up abruptly in Ebenezer's hard arms and lifted.

"Uncle Eb!" he cried, laughing delightedly, making Sally realize that if she hadn't been around Ebenezer since their move from Houston, Jessica and Stevie certainly had.

"Hello, tiger," came the deep, pleasant reply. He put the boy back down on his feet. "Want to go to my place with Sally and learn karate?"

"Like the Teenage Mutant Ninja Turtles in the movies? Radical!" he exclaimed.

"Karate?" Sally asked, hesitating.

"Just a few moves, and only for self-defense," he assured her. "You'll enjoy it. It's necessary," he added when she seemed to hesitate.

"Okay," she capitulated.

He led the way back into the house to where Jessica was sitting in the living room, listening to the news on the television.

"All this mess in the Balkans," she said sadly. "Just when we think we've got peace, everything erupts all over again. Those poor people!"

"Fortunes of war," Eb said with a smile. "How's it going, Jess?"

"I can't complain, I guess, except that they won't let me drive anymore," she said, tongue-in-cheek.

"Wait until they get that virtual reality vision perfected," he said easily. "You'll be able to do anything."

"Optimist," she said, grinning.

"Always. I'm taking these two over to the ranch for a little course in elementary self-defense," he added quietly.

"Good idea," Jessica said at once.

"I don't like leaving you here alone," Sally ventured, remembering what she'd been told about the danger.

"She won't be," Eb replied. He looked at Jessica and one eye narrowed before he added, "I'm sending Dallas Kirk over to keep her company."

"No!" Jessica said furiously. She actually stood up, vibrating. "No, Eb! I don't want him within a mile of me! I'd rather be shot to pieces!"

"This isn't multiple choice," came a deep, drawling voice from the general direction of the hall.

As Sally turned from Jessica's white face, a slender blond man with dark eyes came into the room. He walked with the help of a fancy-looking cane. He was dressed like Eb, in casual clothes, khaki slacks and a bush jacket. He looked like something right out of Africa.

"This is Dallas Kirk," Eb introduced him to Sally. "He was born in Texas. His real name is Jon, but we've always called him Dallas. This is Sally Johnson," he told the blond man.

Dallas nodded. "Nice to meet you," he said formally.

"You know Jess," Eb added.

"Yes. I...know her," he said with the faintest empha-

sis in that lazy Western drawl, during which Jess's face went from white to scarlet and she averted her eyes.

"Surely you can get along for an hour," Eb said impatiently. "I really can't leave you here by yourself, Jess."

Dallas glared at her. "Mind telling me why?" he asked Eb. "She's a better shot than I am."

Jessica stood rigidly by her chair. "He doesn't know?" she asked Eb.

Eb's face was rigid. "He wouldn't talk about you, and the subject didn't come up until he was away on assignment. No. He doesn't know."

"Know what?" Dallas demanded.

Jessica's chin lifted. "I'm blind," she said matter-of-factly, almost with satisfaction, as if she knew it would hurt him.

The look on the newcomer's face was a revelation. Sally only wished she knew of what. He shifted as if he'd sustained a physical blow. He walked slowly up to her and waved a hand in front of her face.

"Blind!" he said huskily. "For how long?"

"Six months," she said, feeling for the arms of the chair. She sat back down a little clumsily. "I was in a wreck. An accident," she added abruptly.

"It was no accident," Eb countered coldly. "She was run off the road by two of Lopez's men. They got away before the police came."

Sally gasped. This was a new explanation. She'd just heard about the wreck—not about the cause of it. Dallas's hand on the cane went white from the pressure he was exerting on it. "What about Stevie?" he asked coldly. "Is he all right? Was he injured?"

"He wasn't with me at the time. And he's fine. Sally lives with us and helps take care of him," Jess replied,

her voice unusually tense. "We share the chores. She's my niece," she added abruptly, almost as if to warn him of something.

Dallas looked preoccupied. But when Stevie came running back into the room, he turned abruptly and his eyes widened as he stared at the little boy.

"I'm ready!" Stevie announced, holding out his arms to show the gray sweats he was wearing. His dark eyes were shimmering with joy. "This is how they look on television when they practice. Is it okay?"

"It's fine," Eb replied with a smile.

"Who's he?" Stevie asked, big-eyed, as he looked at the blond man with the cane who was staring at him, as if mesmerized.

"That's Dallas," Eb said easily. "He works for me."

"Hi," Stevie said, naturally outgoing. He stared at the cane. "I guess you're from Texas with a name like that, huh? I'm sorry about your leg, Mr. Dallas. Does it hurt much?"

Dallas took a slow breath before he answered. "When it rains."

"My mama's hip hurts when it rains, too," he said. "Are you coming with us to learn karate?"

"He's already forgotten more than I know," Eb said in a dry tone. "No, he's going to take care of your mother while we're gone."

"Why?" Stevie asked, frowning.

"Because her hip hurts," Sally lied through her teeth. "Ready to go?"

"Sure! Bye, Mom." He ran to kiss her cheek and be hugged warmly. He moved back, smiling up at the blond man who hadn't cracked a smile yet. "See you."

Dallas nodded.

Sally was staggered by the resemblance of the boy to the man, and almost remarked on it. But before she could, Eb caught her eyes. There was a look in them that she couldn't decipher, but it stopped her at once.

"We'd better go," he said. He took Sally by the arm. "Come on, Stevie. We won't be long, Jess," he called back.

"I'll count the seconds," she said under her breath as they left the room.

Dallas didn't say anything, and it was just as well that she couldn't see the look in his eyes.

IT WAS IMPOSSIBLE to talk in front of Stevie as they drove through the massive electronic gates at the Scott ranch. He, like Sally, was fascinated by the layout, which included a helipad, a landing strip with a hangar, a swimming pool and a ranch house that looked capable of sleeping thirty people. There were also target ranges and guest cabins and a formidable state-of-the-art gym housed in what looked like a gigantic Quonset hut like those used during the Second World War in the Pacific theater. There were several satellite dishes as well, and security cameras seemingly on every available edifice.

"This is incredible," Sally said as they got out of the truck and went with him toward the gym.

"Maintaining it is incredible," Eb said with a chuckle. "You wouldn't believe the level of technology required to keep it all functioning."

Stevie had found the thick blue plastic-covered mat on the wood floor and was already rolling around on it and trying the punching bag suspended from one of the steel beams that supported other training equipment.

"Stevie looks like that man, Dallas," she said abruptly.

He grimaced. "Haven't you and Jess ever talked?"

"I didn't know anything about Dallas and my aunt until you told me," she said simply.

"This is something she needs to tell you, in her own good time."

She studied the youngster having fun on the mat. "He isn't my uncle's child, is he?"

There was a rough sound from the man beside her. "What makes you think so?"

"For one thing, because he's the image of Dallas. But also because Uncle Hank and Aunt Jessie were married for years with no kids, and suddenly she got pregnant just before he died overseas," she replied. "Stevie was like a miracle."

"In some ways, I suppose he was. But it led to Hank asking for a combat assignment, and even though he died of a heart condition, Jess has had nightmares ever since out of guilt." He looked down at her. "You can't tell her that you know."

"Fair enough. Tell me the rest."

"She and Dallas were working together on an assignment. It was one of those lightning attractions that overcome the best moral obstacles. They were alone too much and finally the inevitable happened. Jess turned up pregnant. When Dallas found out, he went crazy. He demanded that Jess divorce Hank and marry him, but she wouldn't. She swore that Dallas wasn't the father of her child, Hank was, and she had no intention of divorcing her husband."

"Oh, dear."

"Hank knew that she'd been with another man, of course, because he'd always been sterile. Dallas didn't know that. And Hank hadn't told Jessica until she an-

nounced that she was expecting a child." He shrugged. "He wouldn't forgive her. Neither would Dallas. When Hank died, Dallas didn't even try to get in touch with Jess. He really believed that Stevie was Hank's child. Until about ten minutes ago, that is," he added with a wry smile. "It didn't take much guesswork for him to see the resemblance. I think we won't go back for a couple of hours. I don't want to walk into the firefight he's probably having with Jess even as we speak."

She bit her lower lip. "Poor Jess."

"Poor Dallas," he countered. "After the fight with Jessie, he took every damned dangerous assignment he could find, the more dangerous the better. Last year in Africa, Dallas was shot to pieces. They sent him home with wounds that would have killed a lesser man."

"No wonder he looks so bitter."

"He's bitter because he loved Jess and though she felt the same, she wasn't willing to hurt Hank by leaving him. But in the end, she still hurt him. He couldn't live with the idea that she was having some other man's child. It destroyed their marriage."

She grimaced. "What a tragedy, for all of them."

"Yes."

She looked toward Stevie, smiling. "He's a great kid," she said. "I'd love him even if he wasn't my first cousin."

"He's got grit and personality to boot."

"You wouldn't think so at midnight when you're still trying to get him to sleep."

He smiled as he studied her. "You love kids, don't you?"

"Oh, yes," she said fervently. "I love teaching."

"Don't you want some of your own?" he asked with a quizzical smile.

She flushed and wouldn't look at him. "Sure. One day."

"Why not now?"

"Because I've already got more responsibilities than I can manage. Pregnancy would be a complication I couldn't handle, especially now."

"You sound as if you're planning to do it all alone."

She shrugged. "There is such a thing as artificial insemination."

He turned her toward him, looking very solemn and adult. "How would it feel, carrying the child of a man you didn't even know, having it grow inside your body?"

She bit her lower lip. She hadn't considered the intimacy of what he was suggesting. She felt, and looked, confused.

"A baby should be made out of love, the natural way, not in a test tube," he said very softly, searching her shocked eyes. "Well, not unless it's the only way two people can have a child," he added. "But that's an entirely different circumstance."

Her lips parted on the surge of emotion that made her heart race. "I don't know...that I want to get that close to anyone, ever."

He seemed even more remote. "Sally, you can't let the past lock you into solitude forever. I frightened you because I wanted to keep you at bay. If I didn't discourage you somehow I was afraid that the temptation might prove too much for me. You were such a baby." He scowled bitterly. "What happened wouldn't have been so devastating if you'd had even a little experi-

ence with men. For God's sake, didn't they ever let you date anyone?"

She shook her head, her teeth clenched tightly together. "My mother was certain that I'd get pregnant or catch some horrible disease. She talked about it all the time. She made boys who came to the house so uncomfortable that they never came back."

"I didn't know that," he said tautly.

"Would it have made any difference?" she asked miserably.

He touched her face with cool, firm fingers. "Yes. I wouldn't have gone nearly as far as I did, if I'd known."

"You wanted to get rid of me..."

He put his thumb over her soft mouth. "I wanted you," he whispered huskily. "But a seventeen-year-old isn't mature enough for a love affair. And that would have been impossible in Jacobsville, even if I'd been crazy enough to go all the way with you that day. You were almost thirteen years my junior."

She was beginning to see things from his point of view. She hadn't tried before. There had been so much resentment, so much bitterness, so much hurt. She looked at him and saw, for the first time, the pain of the memory in his face.

"I was desperate," she said, speaking softly. "They told me out of the blue that they were divorcing each other. They were selling the house and moving out of town. Dad was going to marry Beverly, this girl he'd met at the college where he taught. Mom couldn't live in the same town with everybody knowing that Dad had thrown her over for someone younger. She married a man she hardly knew shortly afterward, just to save her pride." She stared at his mouth with more hunger

than she realized. "I knew that I'd never see you again. I only wanted you to kiss me." She swallowed, averting her eyes. "I must have been crazy."

"We both were." He cupped her face in his hands and lifted it to his quiet eyes. "For what it's worth, I never meant it to go further than a kiss. A very chaste kiss, at that." His eyes drifted down involuntarily to the soft thrust of her breasts almost touching his shirt. He raised an eyebrow at the obvious points. "That's why it wasn't chaste."

She didn't understand. "What is?"

He looked absolutely exasperated. "How can you be that old and know nothing?" he asked. He glanced over her shoulder at Stevie, who was facing the other way and giving the punching bag hell. He took Sally's own finger and drew it across her taut breast. He looked straight into her eyes as he said softly, "That's why."

She realized that it must have something to do with being aroused, but no one had ever told her blatantly that it was a visible sign of desire. She went scarlet.

"You greenhorn," he murmured indulgently. "What a babe in arms."

"I don't read those sort of books," she said haughtily.

"You should. In fact, I'll buy you a set of them. Maybe a few videos, too," he murmured absently, watching the expressions come and go on her face.

"You varmint…!"

He caught her top lip in both of his and ran his tongue lazily under it. She stiffened, but her hands were clinging to him, not pushing.

"You remember that, don't you, Sally?" he murmured with a smile. "Do you remember what comes next?"

She jerked back from him, staggering. Her eyes found Stevie, still oblivious to the adults.

Eb's eyes were blatant on the thrust of her breasts and he was smiling.

She crossed her arms over her chest and glared up at him. "You just stop that," she gritted. "I'll bet you weren't born knowing everything!"

He chuckled. "No, I wasn't. But I didn't have a mother to keep my nose clean, either," he said. "My old man was military down to his toenails, and he didn't believe in gentle handling or delicacy. He used women until the day he died." He laughed coldly. "He told me that there was no such thing as a good woman, that they were to be enjoyed and put aside."

She was appalled. "Didn't he love your mother?"

"He wanted her, and she wouldn't be with him until they got married," he said simply. "So they got married. She died having me. They were living in a small town outside the military base where he was stationed. He was overseas on assignment and she lived alone, isolated. She went into labor and there were complications. There was nothing that could have been done for her by the time she was found. If a neighbor hadn't come to look in on us, I'd have died with her."

"It must have been a shock for your father," she said.

"If it was, it never showed. He left me with a cousin until I was old enough to obey orders, then I went to live with him. I learned a lot from him, but he wasn't a loving man." His eyes narrowed on her soft face. "I followed his example and joined the army. I was lucky enough to get into the Green Berets. Then when I was due for discharge, a man approached me about a top secret assignment and told me what it would pay." He

shrugged. "Money is a great temptation for a young man with a domineering father. I said yes and he never spoke to me again. He said that what I was doing was a perversion of the military, and that I wasn't fit to be any officer's son. He disowned me on the spot. I didn't hear from him again. A few years later, I got a letter from his post commander, stating that he'd died in combat. He had a military funeral with full honors."

The pain of those years was in his lean, hard face. Impulsively she put a hand on his arm. "I'm sorry," she told him quietly. "He must have been the sort of man who only sees one side of any argument."

He was surprised by her compassion. "Don't you think mercenaries are evil, Miss Purity?" he asked sarcastically.

CHAPTER THREE

SALLY LOOKED UP into pain-laced green eyes and without thinking, she lifted her hand from his arm and raised it toward his hard cheek. But when she realized what she was doing, she drew it back at once.

"No, I don't think mercenaries are evil," she said quickly, embarrassed by the impulsive gesture that, thankfully, he didn't seem to notice. "There are a lot of countries where atrocities are committed, whose governments don't have the manpower or resources to protect their people. So, someone else gets hired to do it. I don't think it's a bad thing, when there's a legitimate cause."

He was surprised by her matter-of-fact manner. He'd wondered for years how she might react when she learned about what he did for a living. He'd expected everything from revulsion to shock, especially when he remembered how his former fiancée had reacted to the news. But Sally wasn't squeamish or judgmental.

He'd seen her hand jerk back and it had wounded him. But now, on hearing her opinion of his work, his heart lifted. "I didn't expect you to credit me with noble motives."

"They are, though, aren't they?" she asked confidently.

"As a matter of fact, in my case, they are," he replied. "Even in my green days, I never did it just for

the money. I had to believe in what I was risking my life for."

She grinned. "I thought maybe it was like on television," she confessed. "But Jess said it was nothing like fiction."

He cocked an eyebrow. "Oh, I wouldn't say that," he mused. "Parts of it are."

"Such as?"

"We had a guy like B.A. Barrabas in one unit I led," he said. "We really did have to knock him out to get him on a plane. But he quit the group before we got inventive."

She laughed. "Too bad. You'd have had plenty of stories to tell about him."

He was quiet for a moment, studying her.

"Do I have a zit on my nose?" she asked pleasantly.

He reached out and caught the hand she'd started to lift toward him earlier and kissed its soft palm. "Let's get to work," he said, pulling her along to the mat. "I'll change into my sweats and we'll cover the basics. We won't have a lot of time," he added dryly. "I expect Jess to call very soon with an ultimatum about Dallas."

JESS AND DALLAS had squared off, in fact, the minute they heard the truck crank and pull out of the yard.

Dallas glared at her from his superior height, leaning heavily on his cane. He wished she could see him, because his eyes were full of anger and bitterness.

"Did you think I wouldn't see that Stevie is the living image of me? My son," he growled at her. "You had my son! And you lied to me about it and wouldn't ask Hank for a divorce!"

"I couldn't!" she exclaimed. "For heaven's sake, he

adored me. He'd never have cheated on me. I couldn't bring myself to tell him that I'd had an affair with his best friend!"

"I could have told him," he returned furiously. "He was no angel, Jess, despite the wings you're trying to paint on him. Or do you think he never strayed on those overseas jaunts?" he chided.

She stiffened. "That's not true!"

"It is true!" he replied angrily. "He knew he couldn't get anybody pregnant, and he was sure you'd never find out."

She put a hand to her head. She'd never dreamed that Hank had cheated on her. She'd felt so guilty, when all the time, he was doing the same thing—and then judging her brutally for what she'd done. "I didn't know," she said miserably.

"Would it have made a difference?"

"I don't know. Maybe it would have." She smoothed the dress over her legs. "You thought Stevie was yours from the beginning, didn't you?"

"No. I didn't know Hank was sterile until later on. You told me the child was Hank's and I believed you. Hell, by then, I couldn't even be sure that it was his."

"You didn't think—" She stopped abruptly. "Oh, dear God, you thought you were one in a line?" she exploded, horrified. "You thought I ran around on Hank with any man who asked me?"

"I knew very little about you except that you knocked me sideways," he said flatly. "I knew Hank ran around on you. I assumed you were allowed the same freedom." He turned away and walked to the window, staring out at the flat horizon. "I asked you to divorce Hank just to see what you'd say. It was exactly what I expected. You

had it made—a husband who tolerated your unfaithfulness, and no danger of falling in love."

"I thought I had a good marriage until you came along," she said bitterly.

He turned, his eyes blazing. "Don't make it sound cheap, Jess," he said harshly. "Neither of us could stop that night. Neither of us tried."

She put her face in her hands and shivered. The memory of how it had been could still reduce her to tears. She'd been in love for the first time in her life, but not with her husband. This man had haunted her ever since. Stevie was the mirror image of him.

"I was so ashamed," she choked. "I betrayed Hank. I betrayed everything I believed in about loyalty and duty and honor. I felt like a Saturday night special at the bordello afterward."

He scowled. "I never treated you that way," he said harshly.

"Of course you didn't!" she said miserably, wiping at tears. "But I was raised to believe that people got married and never cheated on each other. I was a virgin when I married Hank, and nobody in my whole family was ever divorced until Sally's father, my brother, was." She shook her head, oblivious to the expression that washed over Dallas's hard, lean face. "My parents were happily married for fifty years before they died."

"Sometimes it doesn't work," he said flatly, but in a less hostile tone. "That's nobody's fault."

She smoothed back her short hair and quickly wiped away the tears. "Maybe not."

He moved back toward her and sat down in a chair across from hers, putting the cane down on the floor. He leaned forward with a hard sigh and looked at Jes-

sica's pale, wan face with bitterness while he tried to find the words.

She heard the cane as he placed it on the floor. "Eb said you were badly hurt overseas," she said softly, wishing with all her heart that she could see him. "Are you all right?"

That husky softness in her tone, that exquisite concern, was almost too much for him. He grasped her slender hands in his and held them tightly. "I'm better off than you seem to be," he said heavily. "What a hell of a price we paid for that night, Jess."

She felt the hot sting of tears. "It was very high," she had to admit. She reached out hesitantly to find his face. Her fingers traced it gently, finding the new scars, the new hardness of its elegant lines. "Stevie looks like you," she said softly, her unseeing eyes so full of emotion that he couldn't bear to look into them.

"Yes."

She searched her darkness with anguish for a face she would never see again. "Don't be bitter," she pleaded. "Please don't hate me."

He pulled her hand away as if it scalded him. "I've done little else for the past five years," he said flatly. "But maybe you're right. All the rage in the world won't change the past." He let go of her hand. "We have to pick up the pieces and go on."

She hesitated. "Can we at least be friends?"

He laughed coldly. "Is that what you want?"

She nodded. "Eb says you've given up overseas assignments and that you're working for him. I want you to get to know Stevie," she added quietly. "Just in case…"

"Oh, for God's sake, stop it!" he exploded, rising

awkwardly from the chair with the help of the cane. "Lopez won't get you. We aren't going to let anything happen to you."

She leaned back in her chair without replying. They both knew that Lopez had contacts everywhere and that he never gave up. If he wanted her dead, he could get her. She didn't want her child left alone in the world.

"I'm going to make some coffee," Dallas said tautly, refusing to think about the possibility of a world without her in it. "What do you take in yours?"

"I don't care," she said indifferently.

He didn't say another word. He went into the kitchen and made a pot of coffee while Jessica sat stiffly in her own living room and contemplated the direction her life had taken.

"YOU HAVE GOT...to be kidding!" Sally choked as she dragged herself up from the mat for the twentieth time. "You mean I'm going to spend two hours falling down? I thought you were going to teach me self-defense!"

"I am," Eb replied easily. He, too, was wearing sweats now, and he'd been teaching her side break-falls, first left and then right. "First you learn how to fall properly, so you don't hurt yourself landing. Then we move on to stances, hand positions and kicks. One step at a time."

She swept her arm past her hip and threw herself down on her side, falling with a loud thud but landing neatly. Beside her, Stevie was going at it with a vengeance and laughing gleefully.

"Am I doing it right?" she puffed, already perspiring. She was very much out of condition, despite the work she did around the house.

He nodded. "Very nice. Be careful about falling too close to the edge of the mat, though. The floor's hard."

She moved further onto the mat and did it again.

"If you think these are fun," he mused, "wait until we do forward breakfalls."

She gaped at him. "You mean I'm going to have to fall deliberately on my face? I'll break my nose!"

"No, you won't," he said, moving her aside. "Watch."

He executed the movement to perfection, catching his weight neatly on his hands and forearms. He jumped up again. "See? Simple."

"For you," she agreed, her eyes on the muscular body that was as fit as that of a man half his age. "Do you train all the time?"

"I have to," he said. "If I let myself get out of shape, I won't be of any use to my students. Great job, Stevie," he called to the boy, who beamed at him.

"Of course he's doing a great job," she muttered. "He's so close to the ground already that he doesn't have far to fall!"

"Poor old lady," he chided gently.

She glared in his direction as she swept her arm forward and threw herself down again. "I'm not old. I'm just out of condition."

He looked at her, sprawled there on the mat, and his lips pursed as he sketched every inch of her. "Funny, I'd have said you were in prime condition. And not just for karate."

She cleared her throat and got to her feet again. "When did you start learning this stuff?"

"When I was in grammar school," he said. "My father taught me."

"No wonder it looks so easy when you do it."

"I train hard. It's saved my life a few times."

She studied his scarred face with curiosity. She could see the years in it, and the hardships. She knew very little about military operations, except for what she'd seen in movies and on television. And as Jess had told her, it wasn't like that in real life. She tried to imagine an armed adversary coming at her and she stiffened.

"Something wrong?" he asked gently.

"I was trying to imagine being attacked," she said. "It makes me nervous."

"It won't, when you gain a little confidence. Stand up straight," he said. "Never walk with your head down in a slumped posture. Always look as if you know where you're going, even if you don't. And always, always, run if you can. Never stand and fight unless you're trapped and your life is in danger."

"Run? You're kidding, of course?"

"No," he said. "I'll give you an example. A man of any size and weight on drugs is more than a match for any three other men. What I'm going to teach you might work on an untrained adversary who's sober. But a man who's been drinking, or especially a man who's using drugs, can kill you outright, regardless of what I can teach you. Don't you ever forget that. Overconfidence kills."

"I'll bet you don't teach your men to run," she said accusingly.

His eyes were quiet and full of bad memories. "Sally, a recruit in one of my groups emptied the magazine of his rifle into an enemy soldier on drugs at point-blank range. The enemy kept right on coming. He killed the recruit before he finally fell dead himself."

Her lower jaw fell.

"That was my reaction, too," he informed her. "Ab-

solute disbelief. But it's true. If anyone high on drugs comes at you, don't try to reason with him...you can't. And don't try to fight him. Run like hell. If a full automatic clip won't bring a man down, you certainly can't. Neither can even a combat-hardened man, alone. In that sort of situation, it's just basic common sense to get out of the way as quickly as possible if there's any chance of escape, and pride be damned."

"I'll remember," she said, all her confidence vanishing. She could see in Eb's eyes that he'd watched that recruit die, and had to live with the memory forever in his mind. Probably it was one of many nightmarish episodes he'd like to forget.

"Sometimes retreat really is the better part of valor," he said, smiling.

"You're educational."

He smiled slowly. "Am I, now?" he asked, and the way he looked at her didn't have much to do with teaching her self-defense. "I can think of a few areas where you need...improvement."

She glanced at Stevie, who was still falling on the mat. "You shouldn't try to shoot ducks in a barrel," she told him. "It's unsporting."

"Shooting is not what I have in mind."

She cleared her throat. "I suppose I should try falling some more." She brightened. "Say, if I learn to do this well, I could try falling on an adversary!"

"Ineffective unless you want to gain three hundred pounds," he returned. He grinned. "Although, you could certainly experiment on me, if you want to. It might immobilize me. We won't know until we try it. Want me to lie down and let you practice?" he added with twinkling eyes.

She laughed, but nervously. "I don't think I'm ready to try that right away."

"Suit yourself. No hurry. We've got plenty of time."

She remembered Jess and the drug lord and her eyes grew worried. "Is it really dangerous for us at home...?"

He held up a cautioning hand. "Stevie, how about a soft drink?"

"That would be great!"

"There are some cans of soda in the fridge in the kitchen. How about bringing one for me and your aunt as well?"

"Sure thing!"

Stevie took off like a bullet.

"Yes, it's dangerous," Eb said quietly. "You aren't to go alone, anywhere, at night. I'll always have a man watching the house, but if you have to go to a meeting or some such thing, let me know and I'll go with you."

"Won't that cramp your social life?" she asked without quite meeting his eyes.

"I don't have a social life," he said with a faint smile. "Not of the sort you're talking about."

"Oh."

His face tautened. "Neither do you, if I can believe Jess."

She shifted on the mat. "I haven't really had much time for men."

"You don't have to spare my feelings," he told her quietly. "I know I've caused you some sleepless nights. But you've waited too long to deal with it. The longer you wait, the harder it's going to be to form a relationship with a man."

"I have Jess and Stevie to think about."

"That's an excuse. And not a very good one."

She felt uncomfortable with her memories. She

wrapped her arms around her chest and looked at him with shattered dreams in her eyes.

He took a sharp breath. "It will never be like that again," he said curtly. "I promise you it won't."

She averted her eyes to the mat. "Do you think Jess and Dallas have done each other in by now?" she asked, trying to change the subject.

He moved closer, watching her stiffen, watching her draw away from him mentally. His big, lean hands caught her shoulders and he made her look at him.

"You're older now," he said, his voice steady and low. "You should know more about men than you did, even if you've had to learn it through books and television. I was fiercely aroused that day, it had been a long, dry spell, and you were seventeen years old. Get the picture?"

For the first time, she did. Her eyes searched his, warily, and nodded.

His hands contracted on her soft arms. "You might try it again," he said softly.

"Try what?"

"What you did that afternoon," he murmured, smiling tenderly. "Wearing sexy clothes and perfume and making a beeline for me. Anything could happen."

Her eyes were sadder than she realized as she met his even gaze. "I'm not the same person I was then," she told him. "But you still are."

The light seemed to go out of him. His pale eyes narrowed, fastened to hers. "No," he said after a minute. "I've changed, too. I lost my taste for commando work a long time ago. I teach tactics now. That's all I do."

"You're not a family man," she replied bravely.

Something changed in his face, in his eyes, as he

studied her. "I've thought about that a lot recently," he contradicted. "About a home and children. I might have to give up some of the contract work I do, once the kids come along. I won't allow my children anywhere near weapons. But I can always write field manuals and train teachers in tactics and strategy and intelligence-gathering," he added.

"You don't know that you could settle for that," she pointed out.

"Not until I try," he agreed. His gaze fell to her soft mouth and lingered there. "But then, no man really wants to tie himself down. It takes a determined woman to make him want it."

She felt as if he were trying to tell her something, but before she could ask him to clarify what he'd said, Stevie was back with an armful of soft drinks and the moment was lost.

JESS AND DALLAS weren't speaking at all when the others arrived. Dallas was toying with a cup of cold coffee, looking unapproachable. When Eb came in the door, Dallas went out it, without a word or a backward glance.

"I don't need to ask how it went," Eb murmured.

"It would be pretty pointless," Jessica said dully.

"Mama, I learned to do breakfalls! I wish I could show you," Stevie said, climbing into his mother's lap and hugging her.

She fought tears as she cuddled him close and kissed his sweaty forehead. "Good for you! You listen when Eb tells you something. He's very good."

"Stevie's a natural," Eb chuckled. "In fact, so is your niece." He gave Sally a slow going-over with his eyes.

"She's a quick learner," Jessica said. "Like I was, once."

"I have to get back," Eb said. "There's nothing to worry about right now," he added, careful not to speak too bluntly in front of the child. "I have everything in hand. But I have told Sally to let me know if she plans to go out alone at night, for any reason."

"I will," Sally promised. She didn't want to risk her aunt's life, or Stevie's, by being too independent.

Eb nodded. "We'll keep the lessons up at least three times a week," he told Sally. "I want to move you into self-defense pretty quickly."

She understood why and felt uneasy. "Okay."

"Don't worry," he said gently. "Everything's going to be fine. I know exactly what I'm doing."

She managed a smile for him. "I know that."

"Walk me to the door," he coaxed. "See you, Jess."

"Take care, Eb," Jessie replied, her goodbye echoed by her son's.

On the front porch, Eb closed the door and looked down into Sally's wide gray eyes with concern and something more elusive.

"I'll have the house watched," he promised. "But you have to be careful about even normal things like opening the door when someone comes. Always keep the chain lock on until you know who's out there. Another thing, you have to keep your doors and windows locked, curtains drawn and an escape route always in mind."

She bit her lip worriedly. "I've never had to deal with anything like this."

His big, warm hands closed over her shoulders. "I know. I'm sorry that you and Stevie have been put in the line of fire along with Jess. But you can handle this,"

he said confidently. "You're strong. You can do what-ever you have to do."

She searched his hard, lean face, saw the deep lines and scars that the violence of his life had carved into it, and knew that he would never lie to her. Her frown dissolved. His confidence in her made her feel capable of anything. She smiled.

He smiled back and traced a lazy line from her cheek down to her soft mouth. "If Stevie wasn't so unpredict-able, I'd kiss you," he said quietly. "I like your mouth under mine."

Her caught breath was audible. There had never been anyone who could do to her with words what he could.

He traced her lips, entranced. "I used to dream about that afternoon with you," he said in a sensuous tone. "I woke up sweating, swearing, hating myself for what I'd done." He laughed hollowly. "Hating you for what I'd done, too," he added. "I blamed us both. But I couldn't forget how it was."

She colored delicately and lowered her eyes to his broad chest under the shirt he wore. The memories were so close to the surface of her mind that it was impos-sible not to glimpse them from time to time. Now, they were blatant and embarrassing.

His lean hands moved up to frame her face and force her eyes to meet his. He wasn't smiling.

"No other man will ever have the taste of you that I did, that day," he said roughly. "You were so deli-ciously innocent."

Her lips parted at the intensity of his tone, at the faint glitter of his green eyes. "That isn't what you said at the time!" she accused.

"At the time," he murmured huskily, watching her

mouth, "I was hurting so much that I didn't take time to choose my words. I just wanted you out of the damned truck before I started stripping you out of those tight little shorts you were wearing."

The flush in her cheeks got worse. The image of it was unbelievably shocking. Somehow, it had never occurred to her that at some point he might undress her, to gain access...

"What an expression," he said, chuckling in spite of himself. "Hadn't you considered what might happen when you came on to me that hard?"

She shook her head.

His fingers slid into the blond hair at her temples where the long braid pulled it away from her face. "Someone should have had a long talk with you."

"You did," she recalled nervously.

"Long and explicit, the day afterward," he said, nodding. "You didn't want to hear it, but I made you. I liked to think that it might have saved you from an even worse experience."

"It wasn't exactly a bad experience," she said, staring at his shirt button. "That was part of the problem."

There was a long, static silence. "Sally," he breathed, and his mouth moved down slowly to cover hers in the silence of the porch.

She stood on tiptoe to coax him closer, lost in the memory of that long-ago afternoon. She felt his hands on her arms, guiding them up around his neck before they fell back to her hips and lifted her into the suddenly swollen contours of his muscular body.

She gasped, giving him the opening he wanted, so that he could deepen the kiss. She felt the warm hardness of his mouth against hers, the soft nip of his teeth,

the deep exploration of his tongue. A warm flood of sensation rushed into her lower abdomen and she felt her whole body go tense with it. It was as if her body had become perfectly attuned to this man's years ago, and could never belong to anyone else.

He felt her headlong response and slowly let her back down, lifting his mouth away from hers. He studied her face, her swollen, soft mouth, her wide eyes, her dazed expression.

"Yes," he said huskily.

"Yes?"

He bent and nipped her lower lip sensuously before he pushed her away.

She stared up at him helplessly, feeling as if she'd just been dropped from a great height.

His eyes went to her breasts and lingered on the sharp little points so noticeable at the front of her blouse, the fabric jumping with every hard, quick beat of her heart.

She met that searching gaze and felt the power of it all the way to her toes.

"You know as well as I do that it's only a matter of time," he said softly. "It always has been."

She frowned. Her mind seemed to have shut down. She couldn't quite focus, and her legs felt decidedly weak.

His eyes were back on her breasts, swerving to the closed door, and to both curtained windows before he stepped in close and cupped her blatantly in his warm, sensuous hands.

Sally's mouth opened on a shocked gasp that became suddenly a moan of pleasure.

"I won't hurt you," he whispered, and his mouth covered hers hungrily.

It was the most passionate, adult kiss of her life, even eclipsing what had come before. His hands found their way under her sweatshirt and against lace-covered soft flesh. Her body responded instantly to the slow caresses. She curled into his body, eagerly submissive.

"Lord, what I wouldn't give to unfasten this," he groaned at her mouth as his fingers toyed with the closure at her back. "And sure as hell, Stevie would come outside the minute I did, and show and tell would take on a whole new meaning."

The idea of it amused him and he lifted his head, smiling down into Sally's equally laughing eyes.

"Ah, well," he said, removing his hands with evident reluctance. "All things come to those who wait," he added.

Sally blushed and moved a little away from him.

"Don't be embarrassed," he chided gently, his green eyes sparkling, full of mischief and pleasure. "All of us have a weak spot."

"Not you, man of steel," she teased.

"We'll talk about that next time," he said. "Meanwhile, remember what I said. Especially about night trips."

"Now where would I go alone at night in Jacobsville?" she asked patiently.

He only laughed. But even as she watched him drive away she remembered an upcoming parents and teachers meeting. There would be plenty of time to tell him about that, she reminded herself. She turned back into the house, her mouth and body still tingling pleasantly.

CHAPTER FOUR

Jessica was subdued after the time she'd spent with Dallas. Even Stevie noticed, and became more attentive. Sally cooked her aunt's favorite dishes and did her best to coax Jess into a better frame of mind. But the other woman's sadness was blatant.

With her mind on Jessica and not on time passing, she forgot that she had a parents and teachers meeting the next Tuesday night. She phoned Eb's ranch, as she'd been told to, but all she got was the answering machine and a message that only asked the caller to leave a name and number. She left a message, doubting that he'd hear it before she was safely home. She hadn't really believed him when he'd said the whole family was in danger, especially since nothing out of the ordinary had happened. But even so, surely nothing was going to happen to her on a two-mile drive home!

She sent Stevie home with a fellow teacher. The business meeting was long and explosive, and it was much later than usual when it was finally over. Sally spoke to the parents she knew and left early. She wasn't thinking about anything except her bed as she drove down the long, lonely road toward home. As she passed the large house and accompanying acreage where her three neighbors lived, she felt a chill. Three of them were out on their front porch. The light was on, and it looked

as if they were arguing about something. They caught sight of her truck and there was an ominous stillness about them.

Sally drove faster, aware that she drew their attention as she went past them. Only a few more minutes, she thought, and she'd be home...

The steering wheel suddenly became difficult to turn and with horror she heard the sound of a tire going flatter and flatter. Her heart flipped over. She didn't have a spare. She'd rolled it out of the bed to make room for the cattle feed she'd taken home last week, having meant to ask Eb to help her put it back in again. But she'd have to walk the rest of the way, now. Worse, it was dark and those creepy men were still watching the truck.

Well, she told herself as she climbed out of the cab with her purse over her shoulder, they weren't going to give her any trouble. She had a loud whistling device, and she now knew at least enough self-defense to protect herself. Confident, despite Eb's earlier warnings, she locked the truck and started walking.

The sound of running feet came toward her. She looked over her shoulder and stopped, turning, her mouth set in a grim line. Two of the three men were coming down the road toward her in a straight line. Just be calm, she told herself. She was wearing a neat gray pantsuit with a white blouse, her hair was up in a French twist, and she lifted her chin to show that she wasn't afraid of them. Feeling her chances of a physical defense waning rapidly as she saw the size and strength of the two men, her hand went nervously to the whistle in her pocketbook and brought it by her side.

"Hey, there, sweet thing," one of the men called. "Got a flat? We'll help you change it."

The other man, a little taller, untidy, unshaved and frankly unpleasant-looking, grinned at her. "You bet we will!"

"I don't have a spare, thank you all the same."

"We'll drive you home," the tall one said.

She forced a smile. "No, thanks. I'll enjoy the walk. Good night!"

She started to turn when they pounced. One knocked the whistle out of her hand and caught her arm behind her back, while the other one took her purse off her shoulder and went through it quickly. He pulled out her wallet, looked at everything in it, and finally took out a bill, dropping her self-defense spray with the purse.

"Ten lousy bucks," he muttered, dropping the bag as he stuffed the bill into his pocket. "Pity Lopez don't pay us better. This'll buy us a couple of six-packs, though."

"Let me go," Sally said, incensed. She tried to bring her elbow back into the man's stomach, as she'd seen an instructor on television do, but the man twisted her other arm so harshly that the pain stopped her dead.

The other man came right up to her and looked her up and down. "Not bad," he rasped. "Quick, bring her over here, off the road," he told the other man.

"Lopez won't like this!" The man on the porch came toward them, yelling across the road. "You'll draw attention to us!"

One of them made a rude remark. The third man went back up on the porch, his footsteps sounding unnaturally loud on the wood.

Sally was almost sick with fear, but she fought like a tigress. Her efforts to break free did no good. These men were bigger and stronger than she was, and they had her helpless. She couldn't get to her whistle or spray

and every kick, punch she tried was effectively blocked. It occurred to her that these men knew self-defense moves, too, and how to avoid them. Too late, she remembered what Eb had said to her about overconfidence. These men weren't even drunk and they were too much for her.

Her heart beat wildly as she was dragged off the road to the thick grass at the roadside. She would struggle, she would fight, but she was no match for them. She knew she was in a lot of danger and it looked like there was no escape. Tears of impotent fury dripped from her eyes. Helpless while one of the men kept her immobilized, she remembered the sound of her own voice telling her aunt just a few weeks ago that she could handle anything. She'd been overconfident.

A sound buzzed in her head and at first she thought it was the prelude to a dead faint. It wasn't. The sound was growing closer. It was a pickup truck. The headlights illuminated her truck on the roadside, but not the struggle that was going on near it.

It was as if the driver knew what was happening without seeing it. The truck whipped onto the shoulder and was cut off. A man got out, a tall man in a shepherd's coat with a Stetson drawn over his brow. He walked straight toward the two men, who released Sally and turned to face the new threat. Eb!

"Car trouble?" a deep, gravelly voice asked sarcastically.

One of the men pulled a knife, and the other one approached the newcomer. "This ain't none of your business," the taller man said. "Get going."

The newcomer put his hands on his lean hips and stood his ground. "In your dreams."

"You'll wish you had," the taller of them replied harshly. He moved in with the knife close in at his side.

Sally stared in horror at Eb, who was inviting this lunatic to kill him! She knew from television how deadly a knife wound in the stomach could be. Hadn't Eb told her that the best way to survive a knife fight was to never get in one in the first place, to run like hell? And now Eb was going to be killed and it was going to be all her fault for not taking his advice and getting that tire fixed...!

Eb moved unexpectedly, with the speed of a striking cobra. The man with the knife was suddenly writhing on the ground, holding his forearm and sobbing. The other man rushed forward, to be flipped right out into the highway. He got up and rushed again. This time he was met with a violent, sharp movement that sent him to the ground, and he didn't get up.

Eb walked right over the unconscious man, ignoring the groaning man, and picked Sally up right off the ground in his arms. He carried her to his truck, balancing her on one powerful denim-covered thigh while he opened the passenger door and put her inside.

"My...purse," she whispered, giving in to the shock and fear that she'd tried so hard to hide. She was shaking so hard her speech was slurred.

He closed the door, retrieved her purse and wallet from the ground, and handed it in through his open door. "What did they take, baby?" he asked in a soft, comforting tone.

"The tall one...took a ten-dollar bill," she faltered, hating her own cowardice as she sobbed helplessly. "In his pocket..."

Eb retrieved it, tossed it to her and got in beside her.

"But those men," she protested.

"Be still for a minute. It's all right. They look worse than they are." He took a cell phone from his pocket, opened it, and dialed. "Bill? Eb Scott. I left you a couple of assailants on the Simmons Mill Road just past Bell's rental house. That's right, the very one." He glanced at Sally. "Not tonight. I'll tell her to come see you in the morning." There was a pause. "Nothing too bad; a couple of broken bones, that's all, but you might send the ambulance anyway. Sure. Thanks, Bill."

He powered down the phone and stuck it back into his jacket. "Fasten your seat belt. I'll take you home and send one of my men out to fix the truck and drive it back for you."

Her hands were shaking so badly that he had to do it for her. He turned on the light in the cab and looked at her intently. He saw the shock, the fear, the humiliation, the anger, all lying naked in her wide, shimmering gray eyes. Last, his eyes fell to her blouse, where the fabric was torn, and her simple cotton brassiere was showing. She was so upset that she didn't even realize how much bare skin was on display.

He took off the long-sleeved chambray shirt he was wearing over his black T-shirt and put her into it, fastening the buttons with deft, quick hands over the ripped blouse. His face grew hard as he saw the evidence of her ordeal.

"I had a...a...whistle," she choked. "I even remembered what you taught me about how to fight back...!"

He studied her solemnly. "I trained a company of recruits a few years ago," he said evenly. "They'd had hand-to-hand combat training and they knew all the right moves to counter any sort of physical attack. There

wasn't one of them that I couldn't drop in less than ten seconds." His pale green eyes searched hers. "Even a martial artist can lose a match. It depends on the skill of his opponent and his ability to keep his head when the attack comes. I've seen karate instructors send advanced students running with nothing more dangerous than the yell, a sudden quick sound that paralyzes."

"Those two men...they couldn't...touch you," she pointed out, amazed.

His pale eyes had an alien coldness that made her shiver. "I told you to get that damned tire fixed, Sally."

She swallowed. Her pride was bruised almost beyond bearing. "I don't take orders," she said, trying to salvage a little self-respect.

"I don't give them anymore," he returned. "But I do give advice, and you've just seen the results of not listening. At least you had the sense to leave a message on my answering machine. But what if I hadn't checked my messages, Sally? Would you like to think where you'd be now? Want me to paint you a picture?"

"Stop!" She put her face in her hands and shivered.

"I won't apologize," he told her abruptly. "You did a damned stupid thing and you got off lucky. Another time, I might not be quick enough."

She swallowed and swallowed again. "The... conquering male," she choked, but she wasn't teasing now, as she had been that afternoon when he'd told her to get the tire fixed.

He drew her hands away from her face and looked into her eyes steadily. "That's right," he said curtly, and he wasn't kidding. "I've been dealing with vermin like that for almost half my life. I told you there was danger

in going out alone. Now you understand what I meant. Get that damned tire fixed, and buy a cell phone."

Her head was spinning. "I can't afford one," she said unsteadily.

"You can't afford not to. If you'd had one tonight, this might never have happened," he said forcefully. The heat in his eyes made her shiver. "A man is physically stronger than a woman. There are some exceptions, but for the most part, that's the honest truth. Unless you've trained for years, like a policewoman or a federal agent, you're not going to be the equal of a man who's drunk or on drugs or just bent on assault. Law enforcement people know how to fight. You don't."

She shivered again. Her hair was disheveled. She felt bruises on her arms where she'd been restrained by those men. She was still stunned by the experience, but already a little of the horror of what might have happened was getting to her.

He let her wrists go abruptly. His lean face softened as he studied her. "But I'll say one thing for you. You've got grit."

"Sure. I'm tough," she laughed hollowly, brushing a strand of loose hair out of her eyes. "What a pitiful waste of self-confidence!"

"Who the hell taught you about canned self-defense?" he asked curiously, referring to the can of spray on the ground.

"There was this television self-defense training course for women," she said defensively.

"Anything you spray, pepper or chemical, can rebound on you," he said quietly. "If the wind's blowing the wrong way, you can blind yourself. If you don't hit the attacker squarely in the eyes, you're no better

off, either. As for the whistle, tonight there would have been no one close enough to hear it." He sighed at her miserable expression and shook his head. "Didn't I tell you to run?"

She lifted a high-heeled foot eloquently.

He leaned closer. "If you're ever in a similar situation again, kick them off and try for the two-minute mile!"

She managed a smile for him. "Okay."

He touched her wan, drawn face gently. "I wouldn't have had that happen to you for the world," he said bitterly.

"You were right, I brought it on myself. I won't make that mistake again, and at least I got away with everything except my pride intact," she said gamely.

He unfastened her seat belt, aware of a curtain being lifted and then released in the living room. "I sent Dallas straight here as soon as I got the message," he explained, "to watch out for Jess and Stevie. You should have let me know about this night meeting much sooner."

"I know." She was fighting tears. The whole experience had been a shock that she knew she'd never get over. "There was a third man, on the porch. He said that Lopez wouldn't like what they were doing, calling attention to themselves."

He stared at her for a long moment, seeing the fear and terror and revulsion that lingered in her oval face, watching the way her hands clenched at the shirt he'd fastened over her torn bodice. He glanced at the window, where the curtain was in place again, and back to Sally's face.

"Come here, sweetheart," he said tenderly, pulling her into his arms. He cuddled her close, nuzzling his face into her throat, letting her cry.

Her clenched fist rested against his black undershirt
and she sobbed with impotent fury. "Oh, I'm so...mad!"
she choked. "So mad! I felt like a rag doll."

"You do your best and take what comes," he said at
her ear. "Anybody can lose a fight."

"I'll bet you never lost one," she muttered tearfully.

"I got the hell beaten out of me in boot camp by
a little guy half my size, who was a hapkido master.
Taught me a valuable lesson about overconfidence,"
he said deliberately.

She took the handkerchief he placed in her hands
and wiped her nose and eyes and mouth. "Okay, I get
the message," she said on a broken sigh. "There's always somebody bigger and you can't win every time."

"Nice attitude," he said, approving.

She wiped away the last trace of tears and looked
up at him from her comfortable position across his lap.
"Thanks for the hero stuff."

He shrugged. "Shucks, ma'am, t'weren't nothin'."

She laughed, as she was meant to. Her eyes adored
him. "They say that if you save a life, it becomes yours."

His lips pursed and he looked down at where the
jacket barely covered her torn blouse. "Do I get that,
too?"

"Too?"

He opened the shirt very slowly and looked at the
pale flesh under the torn blouse. There was a lot of it on
view. Sally didn't protest, didn't grab at cover. She lay
very still in his arms and let him look at her.

His pale eyes met hers in the faint light coming from
the house. "No protest?"

"You saved me," she said simply. She sighed and

smiled with resignation. "I belonged to you, anyway. There's never been anyone else."

His long, lean fingers touched her collarbone, his eyes narrow and solemn, his expression serious, intent. "That could have changed, tonight," he reminded her quietly. "You have to trust me enough to do what I tell you. I don't want you hurt in this. I'll do anything I have to, to protect you. That includes having a man follow you around like a visible appendage if you push me to it. Think what your principal would make of *that*!"

"I won't make any more stupid mistakes," she promised.

"What would you call this?" he mused, nodding toward the ripped fabric that left one pretty, taut breast completely bare.

"Cover me up if you don't like what you see," she challenged.

He actually laughed. She was constantly surprising him. "I think I'd better," he murmured dryly, and pulled the shirt back over her, leaving her to button it again. "Dallas is at the window getting an education."

"And I can tell how much he needs it," she said with dry humor as Eb helped her back into her own seat.

"That makes two of you," Eb told her. His eyes were kind, and now full of concern. "Will you be all right?"

"Yes." She hesitated with her hand on the doorknob. "Eb, is it always like that?"

He frowned. "What?"

She looked up into his eyes. "Physical violence. Do you ever get to the point that it doesn't make you sick inside?"

"I never have," he said flatly. "I remember every face, every sound, every sick minute of what I've done

in my life." He looked at her, but he seemed to go far away. "You'd better go inside. I'll take you and Stevie out to the ranch Thursday and Saturday and we'll put in some more time."

"For all the good it will do me," she managed to say nervously.

"Don't be like that," he chided. "You got overpowered. People do, even 'big, strong' men. There's no shame in losing a fight when you've given it all you've got."

She smiled. "Think so?"

"I know so." He touched her disheveled French knot. "You wore your hair down that spring afternoon," he murmured softly. "I remember how it felt on my bare chest, loose and smelling of flowers."

Her breath seemed to stick in her throat as she recalled the same memory. They had both been bare to the waist. She could close her eyes and feel the hair-roughened muscles of his chest against her own softness as he kissed her and kissed her...

"Sometimes," he continued, "we get second chances."

"Do we?" she whispered.

He touched her mouth gently. "Try not to dwell on what happened tonight," he said. "I won't let anyone hurt you, Sally."

That felt nice. She wished she could give him the same guarantee, but it seemed pretty ridiculous after her poor performance.

He seemed to read the thought right in her mind, and he burst out laughing. "Listen, lady, when I get through with you, you'll be eating bad men raw," he promised. "You're just a beginner."

"You aren't."

"That's true. And not only in self-defense," he added dryly. "You'd better go in."

"I suppose so." She picked at the buttons of the shirt he'd loaned her. "I'll give it back. Eventually."

"You look nice in it," he had to admit. "You can keep it. We'll try some more of my clothes on you and see how they look."

She made a face at him as she opened the door. "Eb, do I have to go and see the sheriff?"

"You do. I'll pick you up after school. Don't worry," he said quietly. "He won't eat you. He's a nice man. But you must see that we can't let Lopez's people get away with this."

She felt a chill go down her arms as she remembered who Lopez was. "What will he do if I testify against his men?"

"You let me worry about that," Eb told her, and his eyes were like green steel. "Nobody touches you without going through me."

Her heart jumped right up into her throat as she stared at him. She was a modern woman, and she probably shouldn't have enjoyed that passionate remark. But she did. Eb was a strong, assertive man who would want a woman to match him. Sally hadn't been that woman at seventeen. But she was now. She could stand up to him and meet him on his own ground. It gave her a sense of pride.

"Debating if it's proper for a modern woman to like being protected?" he chided with a wicked grin.

"You said yourself that none of us are invincible," she pointed out. "I don't think it's a bad thing to admire a man's strength, especially when it's just saved my neck."

He made her feel confident, he gave her joy. It had

been years since she'd laughed so much, enjoyed life
so much. Odd that a man whose adult years had been
imbued with such violence could be so tender.

"Okay now?" he asked.

She nodded. "I'm okay." She glanced toward the
road and shivered a little. "They won't come looking
for me?"

"Not in that condition they won't," he said matter-
of-factly. "And they're very lucky," he added, his whole
face like drawn cord. "Ten years ago, I wouldn't have
been so gentle."

Both eyebrows went up at the imagery.

"You know what I was," he said quietly. "Until com-
paratively recent years, I lived a violent, uncertain life.
Part of the man I was is still in me. I won't ever hurt
you," he added. "But I have to come to grips with the
old life before I can begin a new one. That's going to
take time."

"I think you're saying something."

"Why, yes, I am," he mused, watching her. "I'm giving notice of my intentions."

"Intentions?"

"Last time I stopped. Next time I won't."

Her mind wasn't quite grasping what he was telling
her. "You mean, with those men...?"

"I mean with you," he said gently. "I want you very
badly, and I'm not walking away this time."

"You and what army?" she asked, aghast.

"I won't need an army. But you might." He smiled.
"Go on in. I'm having the house watched. You'll be
safe, I promise."

She pulled his shirt closer. "Thanks, Eb," she said.

He shrugged. "I have to take care of my own. Try to sleep."

She smiled at him. "Okay. You, too."

He watched her go up onto the porch and into the house, waiting for Dallas, who came out tight-lipped with barely a word to Sally as he passed her.

He got into the truck with Eb and slammed the door.

"What happened to Sally?" he asked, putting his cane aside.

"Lopez's men rushed the truck when she had a flat. I don't know if it was premeditated," he added coldly. "They could have lain in wait for her and caused the flat. The tire was almost bald, but it could have gone another few hundred miles."

"She looked uneasy."

"They assaulted her and may have raped her if I hadn't shown up," Eb said bluntly as he backed the truck and pulled out into the road. "I want to have another look, if the ambulance hasn't picked them up yet."

"You sent for an ambulance?" Dallas asked with mock surprise. "That's new."

"Well, we're trying to blend in, aren't we?" came the terse reply. He glared at the tall blond man. "Difficult to blend in if we let people die on the side of the road."

"If you say so."

They drove to where Sally's pickup truck was still sitting, but there was no sign of the two men. The house nearby was dark. There wasn't a soul in sight.

As Eb digested that, red lights flashed and a big boxy ambulance pulled up behind the pickup truck, followed closely by a deputy sheriff in a patrol car.

Eb pulled off the road and got out. He knew the

deputy, Rich Burton, who was one of the department's ablest members. They shook hands.

"Where are the victims?" Rich asked.

Eb grimaced. "Well, they were both lying right there when I took Sally home."

The deputy and the ambulance guys looked toward the flattened grass, but there weren't any men lying there.

"Unless one of you needs medical attention, we'll be on our way," one of the EMTs said with a wry glance.

"Both of the perps did," Eb said quietly. "At least one of them has broken bones."

The EMT gave him a wary look. "Not their legs, by the look of things."

"No. Not their legs."

The EMTs left and Rich joined Eb and Dallas beside the truck.

"Something's going on at that house," Rich said quietly. "I've had total strangers stop me and tell me they've seen suspicious activity, men carrying boxes in and out. That's not all. Some holding company bought a huge tract of land adjoining Cy Parks's place, and it's filling up with building supplies. There's a contractor been hired and a plan has gone to the county commission's planning committee about a business starting up there."

"How much do you know about the men who live here?" Eb asked coolly.

Rich shrugged. "Not as much as I'd like to. But my contacts tell me that there's a drug lord named Manuel Lopez, and the talk is that these guys belong to him. They're mules. They run his narcotics for him."

Eb and Dallas exchanged quiet glances.

"What sort of business are we talking about?" Eb queried.

"Don't know. There's a huge steel warehouse going up behind Parks's place," Rich replied, and he looked worried. "If I were making a guess, and it is just a guess, I'd say somebody had distribution in mind."

CHAPTER FIVE

"A DISTRIBUTION CENTER," Eb said curtly. "With Manuel Lopez, the head of the most violent of the international drug cartels, behind it! That's just what we need in Jacobsville."

"That's right," the younger man replied. He scowled. "How do you know about Lopez?"

Eb didn't answer. "Thanks, Rich," he said. "If I hear anything about the men who attacked Miss Johnson, I'll give you a call."

"Thanks. But I'd bet that they're long gone," he said carelessly. "They'd be crazy to stick around and face charges like attempted rape in a town this size. Lopez wouldn't like the notoriety."

"My guess exactly. So long," Eb said, motioning to Dallas. Rich drove off with a wave of his hand. Eb hesitated, and once Rich was out of sight, he looked for and found a board with new nails sticking through it. It was lying point-side down, now, but the wood was new and there was a long cord attached to it. Evidently it had been placed in the road just as Sally approached, and then jerked away once Sally had run over it. That meant that there had to be a fourth man involved, besides the man on the porch and the two men who'd assaulted Sally. That disturbed Eb.

"They set a trap," Dallas guessed. "She ran over this. That's how she got the flat."

"Exactly." Eb threw the board in the bed of the truck before he climbed in under the wheel. "There were at least four men in on it, and I don't think assault was the sole object of the exercise. I think I'll go over and have a talk with Cy Parks first thing in the morning. He may know something about that new construction behind his place."

CY PARKS WAS GRUMPY. He hadn't been able to sleep the night before, and he was groggy. Even after four years, he still had nightmares about the loss of his wife and five-year-old son in a fire back home in Wyoming. He'd moved here to Jacobsville, where Ebenezer Scott lived, more for someone to talk to than any other reason. Eb was not only a former comrade at arms, but he was also the only man he knew who could listen to the unabridged horror of the fire without losing his supper. It kept him sane, just having someone to talk to. And not only could he talk about the death of his family at Lopez's henchmen's hands but also he had someone to help him exorcise the nightmares of the past that he and Ebenezer shared.

The knock on the door came just as he was pouring his second cup of coffee. It was probably his foreman. Harley Fowler was an adventurer wannabe who fancied himself a mercenary. He was forever reading a magazine for armchair adventurers and once he'd actually answered one of the ads for volunteers and, supposedly, had taken a job during his summer vacation. He'd come back from his vacation two weeks later grinning and bragging about his exploits overseas with a

group of world-beaters and lording it over the other
ranch hands who worked for Cy. Harley had become
the overnight hero of the men. Cy watched him with
amused cynicism. None of the men he'd served with
had ever returned home strutting and bragging about
their exploits. Nor had any of them come home smiling. There was a look about a man who'd seen combat.
It was unmistakable to anyone who'd been through it.
Harley didn't have the look.

None of the ranch hands knew that Cy Parks hadn't
always been a rancher. They knew about the fire that
had cost him his family—most people locally did. But
they didn't know that he was a former professional mercenary and that Lopez was responsible for the fire. Cy
wanted to keep it that way. He was through with the
old life.

He opened the front door with a scowl on his lean,
tanned face, but it wasn't Harley who was standing on
his porch. It was Ebenezer Scott.

Cy's eyes, two shades darker green than Eb's, narrowed. "Lost your way?" he taunted, running a hand
through his thick unruly black hair.

Eb chuckled. "Years ago. Got another cup?"

"Sure." He opened the door and let Eb in. The living room, old-fashioned and sparsely furnished, was
neat as a pin. So were the formal dining room—never
used—and the big, airy kitchen with not a spot of dirt
or grime anywhere.

"Tell me you hired a housekeeper," Eb murmured.

Cy got down an extra cup and poured black coffee
into it, handing it across the table before he sat down.
"I don't need a housekeeper," he replied. "Why are you
here?" he added with characteristic bluntness.

"Did you keep in touch with any of your old contacts when you got out of the business?" Eb asked at once.

Cy shook his head. "No need. I gave it up, remember?" He lifted the cup to his wide, chiseled mouth.

Eb sipped coffee, nodded at the strength of it, and put the mug down on the Formica tabletop with a soft thud. "Manuel Lopez is loose," he said without preamble. "We think he's in the vicinity. Certainly some of his henchmen are."

Cy's face hardened. "Are you certain?"

"Yes."

"Why is he here?"

"Because Jessica Myers is here," Eb replied. "She's living with her young son and her niece, Sally Johnson, out at the old Johnson place. She got one of Lopez's accomplices to rat on Lopez without giving himself away. She had access to documents and bank accounts and witnesses willing to testify. Now Lopez is out and he's after Jess. He wants the name of the henchman who sold him out."

Cy made an impatient gesture. "Fighting out in the open isn't Lopez's style. He's the original knife-in-the-back boy."

"I know. It worries me." He sipped more coffee. "He had three, maybe four, of his thugs living in a rental place near Sally's house. Two of them attacked her last night when her truck had a flat tire just down the road from them. It was no accident, either. They've obviously been gathering intelligence, watching her. They knew exactly where she was and exactly when she'd get as far as their place." His face was grim. "I think there are more than four of them. I also think they may have the same sort of surveillance equipment I maintain at the

ranch. What I don't know is why. I don't know if it's solely because Lopez wants to get to Jessica."

"Is Sally all right?"

Eb nodded. "I got to her in time, luckily. I broke a couple of bones for her assailants, but they got away and now the house seems to be without tenants—temporarily, of course. Have you noticed any activity on your northern boundary?"

"As a matter of fact, I have," Cy replied, frowning. "All sorts of vehicles are coming and going. They've graded about an acre, and a steel warehouse is going up. The city planning commission chairman says it's going to be some sort of production and distribution center for a honey concern. They even have a building permit." He sighed angrily. "Matt Caldwell has been having hell with the planning commission about a project of his own, yet this gang got what they wanted immediately."

"Honey," Eb mused.

"That isn't all of it," Cy continued. "I investigated the holding company that bought the land behind me. It doesn't belong to anybody local, but I can't find out who's behind it. It belongs to a corporation based in Cancún, Mexico."

Eb's eyes narrowed. "Cancún? Now, that's interesting. The last report I had about Lopez before he was arrested was that he bought property there and was living like a king in a palatial estate just outside Cancún." He stopped dead at the expression on his friend's face. Cy and Eb had once helped put some of Lopez's men away.

Cy's breathing became rough, his green eyes began to glitter like heated emeralds. "Lopez! Now what the hell would he want with a honey business?"

"It's evidently going to be a front for something ille-

gal," Eb assured him. "He may have picked Jacobsville for a distribution center for his 'product' because it's small, isolated, and there are no federal agencies represented near here."

Cy stood up, his whole body rigid with hatred and anger. "He killed my wife and son...!"

"He had Jessica run off the road and almost killed," Eb added coldly. "She lived, but she was blinded. She came back here from Houston, hoping that I could protect her. But it's going to take more than me. I need help. I want to set up a listening post on your back forty and put a man there."

"Done," Cy said at once. "But first I'm going to buy a few claymores..."

It took a minute for the expression on Cy's face, in his eyes, in the set of his lean body to register. Eb had only seen him like that once before, in combat, many years before. Probably that was the way he'd looked when his wife and son died and he was hospitalized with severe burns on one arm, incurred when he'd tried to save them from the raging fire. He hadn't known at the time that Lopez had sent men to kill him. Even in prison, Lopez could put out contracts.

"You can't start setting off land mines. You have to think with your brain, not your guts," Eb said curtly. "If we're going to get Lopez, we have to do it legally."

"Oh, that's new, coming from you," Cy said with biting sarcasm.

Eb's broad shoulders lifted and fell as he sat down again, straddling the chair this time. "I'm reformed," he said. "I want to settle down, but first I have to put Lopez away. I need you."

Cy extended the hand that had been so badly burned.

"I know about the burns," Eb said. "If you recall, most of us went to see you in the hospital afterward."

Cy averted his eyes and pulled the sleeve down over his wrist, holding it there protectively. "I don't remember much of it," he confessed. "They sent me to a burn unit and did what they could. At least I was able to keep the arm, but I'll never be much good in a tight corner again."

"You mean you were before?" Eb asked with howling mockery.

Cy's eyes widened, narrowed and suddenly he burst out laughing. "I'd forgotten what a bunch of sadists you and your men were," he accused. "Before every search and destroy mission, somebody was claiming my gear and asking about my beneficiary." Cy drew in a long breath. "I've been keeping to myself for a long time."

"So we noticed," came the dry reply. "I hear it took a bunch of troubled adolescents to drag you out of your cave."

Cy knew what he meant. Belinda Jessup, a public defender, had bought some of the property on his boundary for a summer camp for youthful offenders on probation. One of the boys, an African-American youth who'd fallen absolutely in love with the cattle business, had gotten through his shell. He'd worked with Luke Craig, another neighbor, to give the boy a head start in cowboying. He was now working for Luke Craig on his ranch and had made a top hand. No more legal troubles for him. He was on his way to being foreman of the whole outfit, and Cy couldn't repress a tingle of pride that he'd had a hand in that.

"Even assuming that we can send Lopez back to prison, that won't stop him from appointing somebody

to run his empire. You know how these groups are organized," Cy added, "into cells of ten or more men with their chiefs reporting to a regional manager and those managers reporting to a high-level management designee. The damned cartels operate on a corporate structure these days."

"Yes, I know, and they work complete with pagers, cell phones and faxes, using them just long enough to avoid detection," Eb agreed. "They're efficient and they're merciless. God only knows how many undercover agents the drug enforcement people have lost, not to mention those from other law enforcement agencies. The drug lords make a religion of intimidation, and they have no scruples about killing a man and his entire family. No wonder few of their henchmen ever cross them. But one did, and Jessica knows his name. I don't expect Lopez to give up. Ever."

"Neither do I. But what are we going to do about Lopez's planned operation?" Cy wanted to know.

Eb sobered. "I don't have a plan yet. Legally, we can't do anything without hard evidence. Lopez will be extra careful about covering his tracks this time. He won't want anything that will connect him on paper to the drug operation. From what I've been able to learn, Lopez has already skipped town, forfeiting the bond. Believe me, there's no way in hell he'll ever get extradited from Mexico. The only way we'll ever get him back behind bars again is to lure him back here and have him nabbed by the U.S. Marshals Service. He's at the top of the DEA's Most Wanted list right now." He finished his second cup of coffee. "If we can get a legal wiretap on the phones in that warehouse once it's operating, we might have something to take to the au-

thorities. I know a DEA agent," Eb said thoughtfully. "In fact, he and his wife are neighbors of yours. He's gung-ho at his job, and he's done some undercover work before. Good-looking devil, too. His wife's father left her that small ranch…"

"Lisa Monroe," Cy said, and averted his eyes. "Yes, I've seen her around. Yesterday she was heaving bales of hay over the fence to her horse," he added in the coldest tones Eb had ever heard him use. "She's thinner than she should be, and she has no business trying to heft bales of hay!"

"When her husband's not home to do it for her…"

"Not home?" Cy's eyes widened. "Good God, man, he was standing ten feet away talking to a leggy blond girl in an express delivery uniform! He didn't even seem to notice Lisa!"

"It's not our business."

Cy moved abruptly, standing up. "Okay. Point taken. Suppose we ride up to the boundary and take a look at the progress on that warehouse," he said. "We can take horses and pretend we're riding the fence line."

Eb retrieved high-powered binoculars from the truck and by the time he got to the stable, Cy's young foreman had two horses saddled and waiting.

"Mr. Scott!" Harley said with a starstruck grin, running a hand absently through his crew-cut light brown hair. "Nice to see you, sir!" He almost saluted. He knew about Mr. Scott's operation; he'd read all about it in his armchair covert operations magazine, to say nothing of the top-secret newsletter to which he subscribed.

Eb gave him a measuring glance and he didn't smile. "Do I know you, son?"

"Oh, no, sir," Harley said quickly. "But I've read about your operation!"

"I can imagine what," Eb chuckled. He stuck a cigar into his mouth and lit it.

Cy mounted offside, from the right, because there wasn't enough strength in his left arm to permit him to grip the saddle horn and help pull himself up. He hated the show of weakness, which was all too visible. Up until the fire, he'd been in superb physical condition.

"We're going to ride up to the northern boundary and check the fence line for breaks," Cy said imperturbably. "Get Jenkins started on the new gate as soon as he's through with breakfast."

"He'll have to go pick it up at the hardware store first," Harley reminded him. "Just came in late yesterday."

Cy gave him a look that would have frozen running water. He didn't say anything. But, then, he didn't have to.

"I'll just go remind him," Harley said at once, and took off toward the bunkhouse.

"Who is he?" Eb asked as they rode out of the yard.

"My new foreman." Cy leaned toward him with mock awe. "He's a real *mercenary*, you know! Actually went on a mission early this summer!"

"My God," Eb drawled. "Fancy that. A real live hero right here in the boonies."

"Some hero," Cy muttered. "Chances are what he really did was to camp out in the woods for two weeks and help protect city campers from bears."

Eb chuckled. "Remember how we were at his age?" he asked reminiscently. "We couldn't wait for people

to see us in our gear. And then we found out that the real mercs don't advertise."

"We were like Harley," Cy mused. "All talk and hot air."

"And all smiles." Eb's eyes narrowed with memory. "I hadn't smiled for years by the time I got out. It isn't romantic and no matter how good the pay is, it's never enough for what you have to do for it."

"We did do a little good in the world," came the rejoinder.

"Yes, I guess we did," Eb had to admit. "But our best job was breaking up one of Lopez's cocaine processing plants in Central America and helping put Lopez away. And here he is back, like a bad bouncing ball."

"I knew his father," Cy said unexpectedly. "A good, honest, bighearted man who worked as a janitor just up the road in Victoria and studied English at home every night trying to better himself. He died just after he found out what his only child was doing for a living."

Eb stared off into space. "You never know how kids will turn out."

"I know how mine would have turned out," Cy said heavily. "One of his teachers was in an accident. Not a well-liked teacher, but Alex started a fund for him and gave up a whole month's allowance to start it with." His face corded like wire. He had to swallow, hard, to keep his voice from breaking. The years hadn't made his memories any easier. Perhaps if he could help get Lopez back in prison, it might help.

"We'll get Lopez," the other man said abruptly. "Whatever it takes, if I have to call in markers from all over the world. We'll get him."

Cy came out of his brief torment and glanced at his comrade. "If we do, I get five minutes alone with him."

"Not a chance," Eb said with a grin. "I remember what you can do in five minutes, and I want him tried properly."

"He already was."

"Yes, but he was caught and tried back east. This time we'll manage to apprehend him right here in Texas and we'll stack the legal deck by having the best prosecuting attorney in the state brought in to do the job. The Hart boys are related to the state attorney general—he's their big brother."

"I'd forgotten." He glanced at Eb. His eyes were briefly less tormented. "Okay. I guess I can give the court a second chance. Not their fault that Lopez can afford defense attorneys in Armani suits, I guess."

"Absolutely. And if we can catch him with enough laundered money in his pockets and invoke the RICO statutes, we can fund some nice improvements for our drug enforcement people."

They'd arrived at the northernmost boundary of Cy's property, and barely in sight across the high-wire fence was a huge construction site. From their concealed position in a small stand of trees near a stream, Eb took his binoculars and gave the area a thorough scrutiny. He handed them to Cy, who looked as well and then handed them back.

"Recognize anybody?" Cy asked.

Eb shook his head. "None of them are familiar. But I'll bet if you looked in the right places, you could find a rap sheet or two. Lopez isn't too picky about pedigrees. He just likes men who don't mind doing whatever the job takes. Last I heard, he had several foreign nationals

in his employ." He sighed. "I sure as hell don't want a drug distribution network out here."

"Neither do I. We'd better go have a word with Bill Elliott at the sheriff's office."

Cy shrugged. "You'd better have a word with him by yourself, if you want to get anywhere. I'd jinx you."

"I remember now. You had words with him over Belinda Jessup's summer camp."

"Hard words," Cy agreed uncomfortably. "I've mellowed since, though."

"You and the KGB." He pulled his hat further over his eyes. "We'd better get out of here before they spot us."

"I can see people coming."

"They can see you coming, too."

"That should worry them," Cy agreed, grinning.

Eb chuckled. It was rare these days to see a smile on that hard face. He wheeled his horse, leaving Cy to follow.

THAT AFTERNOON, EB DROVE over to the Johnson place to pick up Sally and Stevie for their self-defense practice.

Sally's eyes lit up when she saw him and he felt his heart jump. She made him feel warm inside, as if he finally belonged somewhere. Stevie ran past his aunt to be caught up and swung around in Eb's muscular arms.

"How's Jess?" Eb asked.

Sally made a face and glanced back toward the house. "Dallas got here just before you did. It's sort of unarmed combat in there. They aren't even speaking to each other."

"Ah, well," he mused. "Things will improve eventually."

"Do you gamble?" she teased. "I feel a lucky streak coming on."

He chuckled as he loaded them into the pickup. No, he wasn't willing to bet on friendlier relations on that front. Not yet, anyway.

"How much do you know about surveillance equipment?" Sally asked unexpectedly.

He gave her a look of exaggerated patience. "With my background, how much do you think I know?"

She laughed. "Sorry. I wasn't thinking. Can a microphone really pick up voices inside the house? Jess tried to convince me that they could hear us through the walls and we had to be very careful what we discussed. I mentioned that Lopez man and she shushed me immediately."

He glanced at her as he drove. "You've got a lot to learn. I suppose now is as good a time as any to teach you."

When he parked the truck at the front door, he led her inside, parking Stevie at the kitchen table with Carl, his cook, who dished up some ice cream for the child while Eb led Sally down the long hall and into a huge room literally crammed with electronic equipment.

He motioned her into a chair and keyed his security camera to a distant view of two cowboys working on a piece of machinery halfway down a rutted path in the meadow.

He flipped a switch and she heard one cowboy muttering to the other about the sorry state of modern tools and how even rusted files were better than what passed for a file today.

They weren't even talking loud, and if there was a microphone, it must be mounted on the barn wall out-

side. She looked at Eb with wide, frankly disbelieving eyes.

He flipped the switch and the screen was silent again. "Most modern sound equipment can pick up a whisper several hundred yards away." He indicated a shelf upon which sat several pairs of odd-looking binoculars. "Night vision. I can see anything on a moonless night with those, and I've got others that detect heat patterns in the dark."

"You have got to be kidding!"

"We have cameras hidden in books and cigarette packs, we have weapons that can be broken down and hidden in boots," he continued. "Not to mention this."

He indicated his watch, a quite normal looking one with all sorts of dials. Normal until he adjusted it and a nasty-looking little blade popped out. Her gasp was audible.

He could see the realization in her eyes as the purpose of the blade registered there. She looked up at him and saw the past. His past.

His green eyes narrowed as they searched hers. "You hadn't really thought about exactly what sort of work I did, had you?"

She shook her head. She was a little paler now.

"I lived in dangerous places, in dangerous times. It's only in recent years that I've stopped looking over my shoulder and sitting with my back against a wall." He touched her face. "Lopez's men can hear you through a wall, with the television on. Don't ever forget. Say nothing that you don't want recorded for posterity."

"This Lopez man is very dangerous, isn't he?" she asked.

"He's the most dangerous man I know. He hires kill-

ers. He has no compassion, no mercy, and he'll do absolutely anything for profit. If his henchman hadn't sold him out, he'd never have been taken into custody in this country. It was a fluke."

She looked around her curiously. "Could he overhear you in here?"

He smiled gently. "Not a chance in hell."

"It looks like something out of *Star Wars*," she mused.

He grinned. "Speaking of movies, how would you and Stevie like to go see a new science fiction flick with me Saturday?"

"Could we?" she asked.

"Sure." His eyes danced wickedly at the idea of sitting in a darkened theater with her...

CHAPTER SIX

SALLY FOUND THE WORKOUTS easier to do as they progressed from falls to defensive moves. Not only was it exciting to learn such skills, but the constant physical contact with Eb was delightful. She couldn't really hide that from him. He saw right through her diversionary tactics, grinning when she asked for short breaks.

Stevie was also taking to the exercise with enthusiasm. It wasn't hard to teach him that such things had no place at school, either. Even at his young age, he seemed to understand that martial arts were for recreation after school and never for the playground.

"It goes with the discipline," Eb informed her when she told him about it. "Most people who watch martial arts films automatically assume that we teach children to hurt each other. It's not like that. What we teach is a way to raise self-esteem and self-confidence. If you know you can handle yourself in a bad situation, you're less likely to go out and try to beat somebody up to prove it. It's lack of self-confidence, lack of self-esteem, that drives a lot of kids to violence."

"That, and a very sad lack of attention by the adults around them," Sally said quietly. "It takes two incomes to run a household these days, but it's the kids who are suffering for it. Any gang member will tell you the reason he joined a gang was because he wanted to be part

of a family. But how do we change things so that parents can earn a living and still have enough free time to raise their children?"

He put both hands on his narrow hips and studied her closely. "If I could answer that question, I'd run for public office."

She grinned at him. "I can see you now, mopping the floor with the criminal element on the streets."

He shrugged. "Piece of cake compared to what I used to do for a living."

Her pale eyes searched his lean, scarred face while Stevie fell from one side of the mat to another practicing his technique. "I rented one of those old mercenary films and watched it. Do you guys really throw grenades and use rocket launchers?"

A dark, odd look came into his pale eyes. "Among other things," he said.

"Such as?" she prompted.

"High-tech equipment like the stuff you saw in my office. Plastic explosive charges, small arms, whatever we had. But most of what we do now is intelligence-gathering and tactics. And intelligence-gathering," he told her dryly, "is about as exciting as two-hour-old cereal in milk."

She was surprised. "I thought it was like war."

He shrugged. "Only if you get caught gathering intelligence," he replied on a laugh. "We were good at what we did."

"Dallas was one of your guys, wasn't he?"

He nodded. "Dallas, Cy Parks and Callie Kirby's stepbrother Micah Steele, among others."

Her mouth fell open. "Cy Parks was a mercenary?"

His eyebrows levered up. "You didn't notice that he has a hard time interacting with other people?"

"It's hard to miss. But in the condition he's in..."

"I know. That's one reason that he isn't in our line of work anymore. He was one of the group that helped put Lopez's organization away a little over two years ago—so was I. It was Jess who got to the man himself. But Lopez appealed the verdict and only went to prison six months ago. As you can see, he's out now," he added dryly.

"Two years ago—that was about the time Cy came to Jacobsville," she recalled.

"Yes. After one of Lopez's goons torched his house in Wyoming. The idea was to kill all three of them, not just Cy's wife and child," he added, seeing the horror in her eyes. "But Cy wasn't asleep, as they'd assumed. He got out."

She grimaced. "But why would Lopez burn his house down?"

"That's how he gets even with people who cross him," he said simply. "He doesn't take out just the person responsible, but the whole family, if he can get to it. There have been slaughters like you wouldn't believe down in Mexico when anyone tried to stand against him. He does usually stop short of children, however; his one virtue."

"I never knew people like him existed," she said sorrowfully.

"I wish I could say the same," he told her. "We don't live in a perfect world. That's why I want you to learn how to defend yourself."

"Fat lot of good it would have done me the night I

had the flat tire," she pointed out. "If you hadn't come along when you did…" She shuddered.

"But I did. Don't look back. It's unproductive."

Her soft, worried eyes searched his scarred face quietly.

"What are you thinking?" he asked with a faint smile.

She shrugged. "I was thinking what a false picture I had of you all those years ago," she admitted. "I suppose I was living in a dream world."

"And I was living in a nightmare," he replied. "That unforgettable spring day six years ago, I'd just come home from a bloodbath in Africa, trying to help an incumbent government fight off a military coup by a very nasty native communist general. I lost most of my unit, including several friends, and the incumbent president's office was blown up, with him in it. It wasn't a good time."

She named the country, to his surprise. "We were studying that in a political science class at the time," she said. "I had no idea what you did for a living, or that you were involved. But we all thought it was an idealistic resistance," she added with a smile.

"Idealistic," he agreed. "And very costly, as most ideas are when you try to put them into practice." His eyes were very old as they met hers. "After that, I began to concentrate on intelligence and tactics. War isn't noble. Only the resolution of it is that."

She recalled the fresh scars on his face that day, scars that she'd attributed to ranch work. She studied him with obvious interest, smiling sheepishly when one of his eyebrows levered up.

"Sorry," she murmured.

He moved a step closer to her, forcing her to raise

her chin so that she could see his face. The contact, barely perceptible, made her heart race. It wasn't so much the proximity as the way he was looking at her, as if he'd like to press her against him and kiss her until she couldn't stand up.

She moved a step back, her gaze going involuntarily to her cousin, who was giving the punching bag a hard time.

"I hadn't forgotten he was there," Eb said in a velvety tone. His pale eyes fell to her mouth and lingered. Even without makeup and with her long hair disheveled, she was pretty. "One night soon I'm going to take you out to dinner. Dallas can keep an eye on Jess and Stevie while you're away."

Until he said that, she'd actually forgotten the danger for a few delightful minutes. It all came rushing back.

He smoothed out the frown between her thin eyebrows. "Don't brood. I've got everything under control."

"I hope so," she said uneasily. "Does Mr. Parks know that Lopez is out of prison?"

"He knows," Eb replied. He ran a hand through his thick hair. "He's the one loose cannon I'm going to have to watch. Even in the old days, Cy never had much patience. He and his wife weren't much of a pair, but he loved that boy to death. He won't rest until Lopez is caught, and if he gets to him first, we can forget about a trial. You can't ever afford to act in anger," he added quietly. "Anger clouds reason. It can get you killed."

"You can't really blame him for the way he feels. Poor man," she sympathized.

"Pity would be wasted on him," he murmured with a smile. "He's more man than most."

She said genuinely. "He's very attractive."

He glared down at her. "You're off-limits."

Her eyes widened. "What?"

"You heard me."

"I'm not property," she began.

"Neither am I, but don't start thinking about Cy, nevertheless. You can concentrate on me." He took one of her hands in his and looked at it, turning it over gently to study it. "Nice hands," he said. "Short nails, well-kept. No rings."

"I have several of them, mostly silver and turquoise, but I don't wear them very much."

His lean fingers rubbed gently over her ring finger and he looked thoughtful, absorbed.

Her own fingers went to the onyx-and-gold signet ring on the little finger of his left hand with the letter *S* in gold script embossed in the onyx.

"It was my father's," Eb told her solemnly. "He was a hell of a soldier, even if he wasn't the best father in the world."

"Do you miss him?" she asked gently.

He nodded. "I suppose I do, from time to time." He touched the ring. "This will go to my son, if I ever have one."

The thought of having children with Eb made Sally's knees weak, but she didn't speak. Eb seemed about to, when they were interrupted.

"Hey, Sally, look what I can do!" Stevie called, and executed a kick that sent the bag reeling.

"Very nice!" Eb said, grinning. "You're a quick study, young man."

"I got to learn to do it real fast," he murmured, sending another kick at the bag.

"Why?" Eb asked curiously.

"So I can hit that big blond man who makes my mama cry," he said, oblivious to the shocked and then amused looks on the faces of the adults near him.

"Dallas?" Sally asked.

"That's him," Stevie agreed, and his dark eyes glimmered. "Mama was crying last night and I asked her why, and she said that man hates her."

Eb joined the young boy at the bag and went on one knee beside him, his eyes very solemn. "Your mother and Dallas knew each other a long time ago," he told him in an adult way. "They had a fight, and they never made up. That's why she cried. They're both good people, Stevie, but sometimes even good people have arguments."

"Why are they mad at each other?"

"I don't know," Eb replied not quite factually. "That's for them to say, if they want you to know. Dallas isn't a bad man, though."

"He's all banged up," Stevie replied solemnly.

"Yes, he is. He was shot."

"Shot? Really?" Stevie moved closer to Eb and put a small hand on his shoulder. "Who shot him?"

"Some very bad men," Eb told him. "He almost died. That's why he has to use a walking stick now. It's why he has all those scars."

Stevie touched Eb's face. "You got scars, too."

"Yes, I have."

"You ever been shot?" he wanted to know.

"Several times," Eb replied honestly. "Guns can be very dangerous. I suppose you know that."

"I know it," Stevie said. "One of my friends shot himself with his dad's pistol playing war out in the yard. He was hurt pretty bad, but he's okay now. Mama told

me that children should *never* touch a gun, even if they think it's not loaded."

"Good for your mom!"

"That man doesn't like my mama," he continued worriedly. "He frowns and frowns at her. She can't see it, but I see it."

"He wouldn't ever hurt her," Eb said firmly. "He's there to protect her when you're away from home," he added wryly.

"That's right, I protect her at home. I'm very strong. See what I did to the bag?"

"I sure did!" Eb grinned at him. "Those were nice kicks, but you need to snap them out from the knee. Here—" he got to his feet "—let me show you."

Sally watched them with lazy pleasure, smiling at the born rapport between them. It was a pity that Stevie didn't like Dallas. That would matter one day. But she had enough problems of her own to worry about.

Eb stopped by the local sandwich shop and bought frozen yogurt cones for all three of them, a reward for the physical punishment, he told them dryly.

While the two adults sat at a table and ate their yogurt cones, Stevie became engrossed in some knick-knacks on sale in the same store.

"He's a natural at this," Eb remarked.

"I'll bet I'm not," she mused, having had to repeat several of the moves quite a number of times before she did them well enough to suit her companion.

"You're not his age, either," he pointed out. "Most children learn things faster than adults. That's why they teach foreign languages so early these days."

"Do you speak any other languages?" she asked suddenly.

"Only a handful," he replied. "The romance languages, several dialects of African languages, and Russian."

"My goodness."

"Languages will get you far in intelligence work these days," he told her. "If you're going to work in foreign countries, it's stupid not to speak the language. It can get you killed."

"I had to have a foreign language series as part of my degree," she said. "I chose Spanish, because that's pretty necessary around here, with such a large Hispanic population. I hated it at first, and then I learned how to read in it." Her eyes brightened. "It's the most exciting thing in the world to read something in the language the author created it in. I never dreamed how delightful it would be to read *Don Quixote* as Cervantes actually wrote it!"

"I know what you mean. But the older the novel, the more difficult the translation. Words change meaning. And a good number of the more modern novels are written in the various dialects of Spanish provinces."

She grinned. "Like Blasco-Ibañez, who used a regional dialect for his matador hero, Juan Gallardo, in dialogue."

"Yes."

She finished her cone and wiped her hands. "I became really fascinated with bullfighting after I read the book, so I found a Web site that had biographies of all the matadors. I found the ones mentioned in the book, who fought in the corridas of Spain around the turn of the century."

"Until you read Blasco-Ibáñez, you have no idea how dangerous bullfighting really is," Eb agreed. "He must have seen some of the corridas."

"A number of Spanish authors did. Lorca, for example, wrote a famous poem about the death of his friend Sanchez Mejias in the bullring."

He brushed back a strand of gold-streaked brown hair and smiled. "I've missed conversations like this, although a good many of the men I train are well-educated. In fact, Micah Steele, who does consulting work for me, was a resident doctor at one of the bigger Eastern hospitals when he joined my unit."

"Why did he give up a profession that he must have studied very hard for?"

"Nobody knows, and he won't talk. Mostly what we know about him we found out from his father, who used to be a bank president until his heart attack. Micah's stepsister, Callie, looks after old man Steele these days. He and Micah haven't spoken for years, not since he and Callie's mother divorced."

"Do you know why they did?"

He shrugged. "Local gossip had it that Micah's father caught Micah and his stepmother in a compromising position and threw them both out of the house."

"Poor man."

"Poor Callie. She worshipped the ground Micah walked on, but he won't even speak to her these days."

"That name sounds familiar," she commented.

"It should. Callie's a paralegal. She works for Barnes and Kemp, the trial lawyers here in town."

"It's so nice to have a lazy day like this," she murmured, watching Stevie browse among the party decorations on a shelf. "It makes me forget the danger."

"I'm surprised that Lopez hasn't made any more moves lately," he said. "And a little disturbed. It isn't like him to back off."

"Maybe he was afraid those two men who attacked me would be arrested and they'd tell on him," she said.

He laughed mirthlessly. "Dream on. Lopez would have them disposed of before they had time to rat on him." He pursed his lips. "That could be what happened to them. You don't make a mistake when you belong to that particular cartel. No second chances. Ever."

She shivered. "We do keep all the doors locked," she said. "And we're very careful about what we say. Well, Jessica is," she amended sheepishly. "Until you taught me about surveillance equipment, I didn't know that a whisper could be heard half a mile away."

"Never forget it," he told her. "Never drop your guard, either. I'll always have someone close enough to run interference if you get into trouble, but you have to do your part to keep the house secure."

"And let you know when and where I'm going," she agreed. "I won't forget again."

He reached across the table and folded his fingers into hers, liking the way they clung. His thumb smoothed over the soft, moist palm while he searched her eyes.

"You haven't had an easy time of it, have you?" he asked conversationally. "In some ways, your whole life has been in turmoil since you were seventeen."

"In transition, at least," she corrected, smiling gently. "If there's one thing I've learned, it's that everything changes."

"I suppose so." His fingers tightened on hers and the look in his eyes was suddenly dark and mysterious

and a little threatening. "I've learned a few things my-self," he said quietly.

"Such as?" she whispered daringly.

He glanced down at their entwined fingers. "Such as never taking things for granted."

She frowned, puzzled.

He laughed and let go of her fingers. "I told you that I was engaged once, didn't I?" he asked.

She nodded.

"I never told her what I did for a living. She never questioned where my money came from. In fact, when I tried to tell her, she stopped me, saying it wouldn't matter, that she loved me and she'd go wherever my job took me." He leaned back in his chair, his expression reflective and solemn. "Her parents were dead. She and an older boy were fostered at the same time to a wealthy woman. They spent years together, but he and Maggie weren't close, so I made all the wedding arrangements and paid for her gown and the rings, everything." His eyes darkened with remembered pain. "I still felt un-comfortable about having secrets between us, though, so the night before the wedding, I told her what I did for a living. She put the rings on the coffee table, got her stuff, and left town that same night. She married two months later…a man twice her age."

She knew about his ex-fiancée, but not how much he'd cared about the woman. The expression in his eyes told her that the pain hadn't gone away. "Didn't she send you a letter, or phone you after she'd had time to think it over?" she asked.

He shook his head. "Until I ran into her in Houston a week ago, I had no idea where she was. Her adop-tive mother died just after we broke up. Tough break."

Her heart stopped in her chest. "You...saw her...in Houston?"

He nodded, oblivious to the shock in her eyes. "As luck would have it, she's a new junior partner in an investment firm I use, and widowed."

He stared at her until she looked up, and he wasn't smiling. "You're in a precarious situation, and we've been thrown together in a rather unconventional way. We're friends, but you don't have to live with what I do."

All her hopes and dreams and wild expectations crumbled to dust in her mind. Friends. Good friends. Of course they were! He was teaching her martial arts, he was helping her to survive a potential attack by a ruthless drug lord. That didn't mean he wanted her to share his life. Quite the opposite, it seemed now.

"If a woman cared enough, surely she could give it a chance?" she asked, terrified that her anguish might show.

Apparently it didn't. He leaned back in his chair with a long sigh, reflective and moody. "No. She said she wanted a career, anyway," he replied. "It suited her to have her own money and be independent."

"My parents never shared their paychecks, or anything else," she said carelessly. She glanced at Stevie. "Stevie, we'd better go, sweetheart."

He came running, smiling as he leaned against her and looked across at Eb, who was still brooding. "Can we take Mama a cone?"

"Of course we can," Sally said gently. She dug out two dollars. "Here. Get her a cup of that fat-free Dutch chocolate, okay? And make sure it has a lid."

"Okay!"

He ran off with his grubstake, feeling very adult. Sally watched him, smiling.

"I could have done that," Eb commented.

"Yes, you could, but it wouldn't help teach him responsibility. Six isn't too young to start learning independence. He's going to be a fine man," she added, her voice softer as she watched him.

He didn't comment. He was feeling claustrophobic and he didn't know why. He got up and dealt with the used napkins. By the time he was finished, Stevie came back carrying a small white sack with Jessica's treat inside.

There wasn't much conversation on the way back to the Johnson house, and even then it was completely impersonal. Sally realized that it must have hurt Eb to recall how abruptly his fiancée had rejected him. She might have loved him, but the constant danger of his profession must have been more than she could handle. Now that he was retired from the danger, it might not be such an obstacle.

That was a depressing thought. His ex-fiancée was a widow and he was in a secure profession, and they'd recently seen each other. It was enough to get Sally out of the truck with Stevie and off into the house with only a quick thank-you and a forced smile.

Eb, driving away down the road, felt a vague regret for the loss of the rapport he and Sally had seemed to share. He couldn't understand what had made her so distant this afternoon.

Eb had already contacted a man he knew in the Drug Enforcement Administration on a secure channel and told him what he knew about Lopez and his plans for Jacobsville. He'd also asked about the possibility of

having a man go undercover to infiltrate the operation and was told only that the DEA was aware of Lopez's construction project. He wouldn't tell Eb anything more than that.

Understanding government work very well, Eb had assumed that the undercover operation was already underway. He wasn't about to mention that to anyone he knew. Not even Cy.

He had Dallas monitoring some sensitive equipment that gave them direct audio and visual information from Sally's house. Nobody would sneak up on it without being noticed. He'd also had Dallas bug the telephone. That night, he was glad he had.

In the early hours of the morning, Sally was brought wide-awake by the insistent ringing of the telephone. The number was unlisted, but that didn't stop telemarketers. Ordinarily, though, they didn't call at this hour. It wasn't a good marketing strategy, especially in Sally's case. She'd hardly slept after the discussion with Eb in the yogurt shop. She wasn't in the mood to talk to strangers.

"Hello?" she asked belligerently.

"You'll never see us coming," a slow, ice-cold voice said in her ear. "But unless Jessica gives up the name by midnight Saturday, there will be serious repercussions."

Sally was so shocked that she fumbled with the phone and cut off the caller. She stood holding the receiver, blinking in astonishment. That softly accented tone had chilled her to the bone, despite the flannel gown she was wearing.

No sooner had she righted the telephone than it rang again. This time, she hesitated. Her heart was pounding like mad. She was almost shaking with the force of it.

Her mouth was dry. Her palms began to sweat. There was an uncomfortable knot in the pit of her stomach.

She wanted to ignore it. She didn't dare. Quickly, before she lost her nerve, she lifted it.

"She has one last chance," the voice continued, as if the connection hadn't been cut. "She must phone this number Saturday night at midnight exactly and give a name. One minute after midnight, you will all suffer the consequences." He gave the number and hung up. This time the connection was cut even more rapidly. Sally dropped the receiver back into the cradle with icy fingers. She stared down at it with growing horror. Surely Eb and Dallas and the others would be watching. But were they listening as well?

The phone rang a third time, but now she was angry and she didn't hesitate. She jerked it up. "Hello...?"

"We couldn't get a trace," Eb said angrily. "Are you all right?"

She swallowed, closed her eyes, took a deep breath, and swallowed again. "Yes," she said calmly. "I'm all right. You heard what he said?"

"I heard. Don't worry."

"Don't worry?" she parroted. "When a man's just threatened to kill everyone in my house?"

"He won't kill anybody," he assured her. "And he's through making threats for tonight. I'm going to find out where that phone is. Go to sleep. It's all right."

The receiver went dead. "I am sick and tired of men throwing out orders and hanging up on me!" she told the telephone earpiece.

It did no good, of course, except that voicing her irritation made her feel a little better. She climbed back into bed and lay awake, wide-eyed and nervous, until

dawn. Just before she and Stevie left for school, out of the child's hearing range, she told Jessica what had happened.

"Eb and the others are watching us," Sally assured her quickly. "But be careful about answering the door."

"No need," Jessica said. "Lopez may be certifiable, but he's predictable. He never takes action until his demands haven't been met. We have until midnight Saturday to think of something."

"Wonderful," Sally said on a sigh. "We have today and tomorrow. I'm sure we'll have Lopez and all his cohorts in jail by then."

"Sarcasm doesn't suit you, dear," Jessica said with a smile. "Go to work. I'll be fine."

"I wish I could guarantee that all of us would be fine," Sally murmured to herself as she went out the door behind Stevie.

Somehow she knew that life would never be the same again. It had been bad enough hearing Eb talk about the woman he'd loved who had rejected him at the altar, and knowing from the way he spoke of it that he hadn't gotten over her. But now, she had drug dealers threatening to kill Jessica and Stevie as well as herself. She wondered how in the world she'd ended up in such a nightmare.

It didn't help when Eb phoned again and told her that the phone number she'd been given was that of a stolen cell phone, untraceable until it was answered, and it rang and rang unnoticed now. There would be no time to run a trace precisely at midnight. It was the most disheartening news Sally had received in a long time.

CHAPTER SEVEN

EB WAS DISTURBED by the message he'd intercepted from Lopez. He knew, even better than Sally did, that it wasn't an idle threat. The drug lord, like his minions, was merciless. He'd had countless enemies neutralized, and he wouldn't hesitate because Jessica was a woman. Just the month before his arrest, he'd had the leader of a drug-dealing gang disposed of for cheating him. It was chilling even for a professional soldier to know what depths a human being could sink to in the name of greed.

He and Dallas started planning for the certainty of an attack. The Johnson homeplace was isolated, but it had plenty of cover where men could hide. Eb intended on having people in place long before Lopez's hired goons could find a safe passage to the house to carry out the madman's orders. Anything else would be impossible, since he knew Jessica would never sacrifice her informant's life, even to save herself and her family.

"I think we can safely assume that these men aren't professionals," Dallas said quietly. "Their way will be to wade in shooting."

Eb's pale eyes narrowed. "I wouldn't bet the lives of two women and a child on that," he replied. "Lopez knows I'm here, and that I have trained professionals working for me. He also knows that I'm why Jessica

talked Sally into moving back here in the first place. He's ruthless, but he isn't stupid. When he comes after Jessica, he'll send the best people he's got."

"Point taken," Dallas said heavily. "I suppose it was wishful thinking." He glanced worriedly at Eb. "We could bring all three of them over here."

"Sure we could. But it would only postpone the inevitable. Lopez doesn't quit. He'll look on it as a setback and find another way to get to them. Besides, they can't stay here indefinitely. Sally has a job and Stevie has to go to school."

Dallas stared into the distance, quiet and thoughtful. "Stevie doesn't like me," he murmured. "He told his mother he was learning karate so that he could work me over." He shot a half-amused glance in Eb's direction. "Spunky kid."

"Yes, he is," Eb agreed. "Pity he has to grow up without a father. And before you fly at me," he interrupted Dallas's exclamation, "I know Jessica didn't tell you whose child he was. But you know now."

"I know," Dallas muttered irritably, "for all the good it does me. She won't even discuss it. The minute I walk in the door, she clams up and stays that way until I leave. I can barely get her to say hello and goodbye!"

"Then she cries herself to sleep at night because you hate her."

The blond man's dark eyes widened. *"What?"*

"That's why Stevie wants to deck you," Eb said simply. "He's very protective of his mother."

Dallas seemed to calm down a little. "Imagine that," he mused. "Well, well. So she isn't quite as disinterested as she pretends." He stuck his hands into his pockets and

leaned back against the wall. "No chance she'll turn in the guy who ratted on Lopez, I gather?"

"Not one in a million." He studied the other man for a moment. "You're really worried."

"Of course I am. I've seen the aftermath of Lopez's vendettas," Dallas said curtly. "What worries me most is that if someone's willing to trade his life or his freedom to get you, he can. No protection is adequate against a determined killer."

"Then ours will make history," Eb promised him. "Let's go over to Cy Parks's place. I want to see if he's got a way to contact that guy in Mexico who used to work as a mercenary with Dutch Van Meer and Diego Laremos back in the eighties. He went on to do work infiltrating drug cartels."

"J.D. Brettman led that mercenary group," Dallas recalled, grinning. "He's a superior court judge in Chicago these days. Imagine that!"

"I heard that Van Meer lives with his wife and kids in the northwestern Rocky Mountains on a ranch. What about Laremos?" Eb asked.

"He and his family live in the Yucatán. He's given up soldiering, too." He shook his head. "Those guys were younger than us when they started and they made fortunes."

"It was a different game back then. Times have changed. So have the rules. We'd never get away with some of the stunts those guys pulled." Eb felt in his pocket for his truck keys. "All of us met them, but Cy and Diego Laremos got to know each other well several years back when Cy was doing a little job down around Cancún for a wealthy yachtsman. He may know

the professional soldier who helped a friend of Laremos's escape some nasty pothunters and a kidnapper."

"Do I know this friend?" Dallas wanted to know as they headed out the door.

"You probably know *of* him—Canton Rourke."

"Good Lord, Mr. Software?" Dallas exclaimed. "The guy who lost everything and then regrouped and now has a corporation in the Fortune 500?"

"That's him." Eb nodded. "Turns out the new Mrs. Rourke's parents are university professors who devote summers to Mayan digs in the Yucatán. It's a long story, but this Mexican agent does a little freelance work. He'd be an asset in this sort of operation."

"He might even have some contacts we could use?"

"That's so." Eb got in and started the truck. He glanced at Dallas. "Besides that, he's done undercover work on narcotics smuggling for the Mexican government and lived to tell about it. That proves how good he is. A lot of undercover people get killed."

"He'd be just what we need, if we can get him. I don't imagine the DEA is going to tell us who their undercover guy is, or what he finds out."

"Exactly. That's where I hope Cy's going to come in. He doesn't like any of the old associations very much anymore, but considering the danger Lopez poses, he might be willing to help us."

"Pity about his arm."

Eb shot him a wry glance. "Yes, but it's a lucky break it wasn't the arm he uses."

They drove over to Cy Parks's ranch, and found him watching his young foreman, Harley, doctoring a sick bull yearling in the barn. He was lounging against one of the posts that supported the imposing structure, his

hat low over his eyes, his arms folded over a broad
chest, one booted foot resting on a rail of the gate that
enclosed the stall where his man was busy.

He turned as Eb and Dallas strode down the neat
chipped bark covered floor to join him.

"You two out sightseeing?" Cy drawled without smiling, his green eyes narrowed and curious.

"Not today. We need a name."

"Whose?"

"The guy who worked with your friend Diego Laremos out near Chichén Itzá. I think he might be just
what we need to infiltrate Lopez's cartel."

Cy's eyebrows lifted. "Rodrigo? You must be out of
your mind!" he said at once.

"Why?"

"Good God," Cy burst out, "Diego says that he's
such a renegade, nobody will hire him anymore, not
even for black ops!"

"What did he do?" Dallas asked, aware that the
young man in the stall had perked up and was suddenly listening unashamedly.

"For a start, he crashed a Huey out in the Yucatán
last year," Cy said. "That didn't endear him to a certain
government agency which was running him. Then he
blew up an entire boatload of powder cocaine off Co-
zumel that the authorities were trying to confiscate—
millions' worth. In between he wrecked a few hired
cars in various chases, hijacked a plane, and broke into
a government field office. He walked off with a couple
of classified files and several thousand dollars' worth
of high-tech listening devices that you can't even buy
unless you're in law enforcement. After that, he went
berserk in a bar down in Panama and put two men in

the hospital, just before he absconded with a suitcase full of unlaundered drug money that belonged to Manuel Lopez…"

"Are we talking about the same Rodrigo that the feds used to call 'Mr. Cool'?" Eb asked with evident surprise.

"That isn't what they call him these days," Cy said flatly. "Mr. Liability would be more like it."

"He was with Laremos and Van Meer in Africa back in the early eighties," Eb recalled. "They left, but he signed on with another outfit and kept going."

"That's when he started working freelance for the feds," Cy continued. "At least, that's what Diego said," he added for Harley's benefit. He didn't want his young employee to know about his past.

"Anybody know why Rodrigo went bananas in Panama?" Dallas asked.

Cy shrugged. "There are a lot of rumors—but nothing concrete." He studied the other two with pursed lips. "If you want him for undercover work to indict Lopez, he'd probably pay you to hire him on. He hates Lopez."

Eb glanced past Cy at Harley, whose mouth was hanging open.

"Don't mind him," Cy told his companions with a mocking smile. "He's a mercenary, too," he added dryly.

Harley scrambled to his feet. "Can't I hire on?" he burst out. "Listen, I know those names—Van Meer and Brettman and Laremos. They were legends!"

"Put the top back on the medicine before you spill it," Cy told the young man calmly. "As for the other, that's up to Eb. It's his party."

Harley fumbled the lid back on the bottle. "Mr. Scott?" he asked, pleading.

"I guess we could find you something to do," Eb said, amused. Then the smile faded, and his whole look was threatening. "But this is strictly on the QT. You breathe one word of it locally and you're out on your ear. Got that?"

Harley nodded eagerly. "Sure!"

"And you'll work for him only after you do your chores here," Cy said firmly. "I run cattle, not commandos."

"Yes, sir!"

Cy exchanged a complicated glance with Eb. "I've got the last number I had for Rodrigo in my office. I'll go get it."

He left the other three men in the barn. Harley was almost dancing with excitement.

"I'll be an asset, sir, honestly," he told Eb. "I can shoot anything that has bullets, and use a knife, and I know a little martial arts…!"

Eb chuckled. "Son, we don't need an assassin. We're collecting intelligence."

The boy's face fell. "Oh."

"Running gun battles aren't a big part of the business," Dallas said without cracking a smile. "You shoot anybody these days, even a criminal, and you could find yourself behind bars."

Harley looked shocked. "But…but I read about it all the time; those exciting battles in Africa…"

"Exciting?" Eb's eyes were steady and quiet.

"Why, sure!" Harley's eyes lit up. "You know, testing your courage under fire."

The boy's eyes were gleaming with excitement, and Eb knew then for certain that he'd never seen anyone shot. Probably the closest he'd come to it was listen-

ing to an instructor—probably a retired mercenary—talking about combat.

Harley noticed his employer coming out of the house and he grimaced. "I hope Mr. Parks meant what he said. He's not much on adventure, you see. He's sort of sarcastic when I mention where I went on my vacation, out in the field in Central America with a group of mercenaries. It was great!"

"Cy wasn't enthusiastic, I gather?" Eb probed.

"Naw," Harley said heavily. "He's just a rancher. Even if he knows Mr. Laremos, he sure doesn't know what it's like to really be a soldier of fortune. But we do, don't we?" he asked the other two with a grin.

Eb and Dallas glanced at each other and managed not to laugh. Quite obviously, Harley believed that Cy's information about Rodrigo was secondhand and had no idea what Cy did before he became a rancher.

Cy joined them, presenting a slip of paper with a number on it to Eb. "That's the last number I have, but they'll relay it, I'm sure."

"You still hear from Laremos?" Eb asked his friend.

"Every year, at Christmas," Cy told him. "They've got three kids now and the eldest is in high school." He shook his head. "I'm getting old."

"Not you," Eb chuckled.

"We'd better go," Dallas said, checking his watch.

"So we had."

"What about me?" Harley asked excitedly.

"We'll be in touch, when the time comes," Eb promised him, and, oddly, it sounded more like a threat.

Cy saw them off and came back to take one last look at the bull. "Good job, Harley," he said, approving the treatment. "You'll make a rancher yet."

Harley closed the bull in his stall and latched the gate. "How do you know Mr. Laremos, sir?" he asked curiously.

"Oh, we had a mutual acquaintance," he said without meeting the other man's eyes. "Diego still keeps in touch with the old group, so he knows what's going on in the intelligence field," he added deliberately.

"I see. I thought it was probably something like that," Harley said absently and went to work on the calf with scours in the next stall, reaching for the pills that were commonly called "eggs" to dose it with.

Cy looked after the smug younger man with amusement. Harley had his boss pegged as a retiring, staid rancher with no backbone and only an outsider's familiarity with the world of covert operations. He'd think that Cy had gotten all that information from Laremos, and, for the present, it suited Cy very well to let him think so. But if Harley had in mind an adventure with Eb and the others, he was in for a real shock. In the company of those men, he was going to be more uncomfortable than he dreamed right now. Some lessons, he told himself, were better learned through experience.

WHEN THEY GOT back to the ranch, Eb phoned the number Cy had given him. There was a long pause and then a quick, deep voice giving instructions. Eb was to leave his name and number and hang up immediately. He did. Seconds later, his phone rang.

"You run that strategy and tactics school in Texas," the deep voice said evenly.

"Yes."

"I read about it in one of the intelligence sitreps," he returned, shortening the name for situation reports.

"I thought you were one of those vacation mercs who sat at a desk all week and liked to play at war a couple of weeks a year, until I spoke to Laremos. He remembers you, along with another Jacobsville resident named Parks."

"Cy and I used to work together, with Dallas Kirk and Micah Steele," Eb replied quietly.

"I don't know them, but I know Parks. If you're looking for someone to do black ops, I'm not available," he said curtly, with only a trace of an accent. "I don't do overseas work anymore, either. There's a fairly large price on my head in certain Latin American circles."

"It isn't a foreign job. I want someone to go undercover here in Texas and relay intelligence from a drug cartel," Eb said flatly.

There was a long pause. "I'd find someone with a terminal illness for that sort of work," Rodrigo replied. "It's usually fatal."

"Cy Parks told me you'd probably jump at the chance to do this job."

"Oh, that's rich. And what job would that be?"

"The drug lord I want intelligence on is Manuel Lopez. I'm trying to put him back in prison permanently."

The intake of breath on the other end was audible, followed by a description of Lopez that questioned his ancestry, his paternity, his morals, and various other facets of his life in both Spanish and English.

"That's the very Lopez I'm talking about," Eb replied dryly. "Interested?"

"In killing him, yes. Putting him back in prison… well, he can still run the cartel from there."

"While he's in there, his organization could be suc-

cessfully infiltrated and destroyed from within," Eb suggested, dangling the idea like a carrot on a string. "In fact, the reason we're under the gun in Jacobsville right now is because a friend of our group is protecting the identity of an intimate of Lopez who sold him out to the DEA."

"Keep talking," Rodrigo said at once.

"Lopez is trying to kill a former government agent who coaxed one of his intimate friends to help her get the hard evidence to put him in prison. He's only out on a legal technicality and he's apparently using his temporary freedom to dispose of her and her informant."

"What about the so-called hard evidence?" Rodrigo asked.

"My guess is that it'll disappear before the retrial. If he manages to get rid of the witnesses and destroy the evidence, he'll never go back to prison. In fact, he's already skipped bond."

"Don't tell me. They set bail at a million dollars and he paid it out of petty cash," came the sarcastic reply.

"Exactly."

There was a brief hesitation and a sigh. "Well, in that case, I suppose I'm working for you."

Eb smiled. "I'll put you on the payroll."

"Fine, but you can forget about retirement benefits if I go undercover."

Eb chuckled softly. "There's just one thing. We've heard that you and Lopez had a common interest at one time," he said, putting it as delicately as he could. "Does he know what you look like?"

There was another pause and when the voice came back, it was strained. "No, you can be sure of that."

"This won't be easy," Eb told him. "Be sure you're willing to take the risk before you agree."

"I'm quite sure. I'll see you tomorrow." The line went dead.

EB TOOK SALLY out to dinner that night, driving the sleek new black Jaguar S that he liked to use when he went to town.

"We'll go to Houston, if that suits you?"

She agreed. He looked devastating in a dinner jacket, and she was shy and uneasy with him, after what she'd learned about his fiancée. In fact, she'd told herself she wasn't going to be alone with him ever again. Yet here she sat. Resolve was hard when emotions were involved. His feelings for the woman he'd planned to marry were unmistakable in his voice when he talked about her, and now that she was free, he might have a second chance. Knowing that part of him had never gotten over his fiancée's defection, Sally was reluctant to risk her heart on him again. She kept a smiling, pleasant, but determined distance between them.

Eb noticed the reticence, but didn't understand its purpose. He could hardly take his eyes off her tonight. His green eyes kept returning to linger on her pretty black cocktail dress under the long red-lined black velvet coat she wore with it. Her hair was in a neat chignon at her nape, and she looked lovely.

"Are you sure this is a good idea?" Sally asked him. "I know Dallas will take care of Jess and Stevie, but it seems risky to go out at night with Lopez and his men around."

"He's a vicious devil," he replied, "but he is absolutely predictable. He'll give Jessica until exactly mid-

night Saturday. He won't do one thing until the deadline. At one minute past midnight," he added curtly, "there will be an assault."

Sally wrapped her arms closer around her body. "How do we end up with people like that in the world?"

"We forget that all lives are interconnected in some way, and that selfishness and greed are not desirable traits."

"What good will it do Lopez to kill Jessica and us?" she asked curiously. "I know he's angry at her, but if she's dead, she can't tell him anything!"

"He's going to be setting an example," he said. "Of course, he probably thinks she'll give up the name to save her child." He glanced at Sally. "Would you?"

"I wouldn't have a hard time choosing between my child and someone who's already turned against his own people," she admitted.

"Jessica says there are extenuating circumstances," he told her.

She stared at her fingers. "I know. She won't even tell me who the person was." She glanced at him. "She's probably covering all her bases. If I knew who it was…"

He made a sound deep in his throat. "You'd turn the person over to Lopez?"

She shifted restlessly. "I might."

"Cows might fly."

He knew her too well. She laughed softly. "I wish there was another way out of this, that's all. I don't want Stevie hurt."

"He won't be." He reached across to clasp her cool hand gently in hers and press it. "I'm putting together a network. Lopez isn't going to be able to move without being in someone's line of sight from now on."

"I wish…" she began.

"Don't wish your life away. You have to take the bad with the good—that's what life is. Good times don't make us strong."

She grimaced. "No. I guess they don't." She leaned her head back against the headrest and drank in the smell of the leather. "I love the way new cars smell," she said conversationally. "And this one is just super."

"It has a few minor modifications," he said absently.

She turned her head toward him with a wicked grin. "Don't tell me—the headlights retract and become machine gun ports, the tailpipe leaves oil slicks, and the passenger seat is really an ejectable projectile!"

He laughed. "Not quite."

"Spoilsport."

"You need to stop watching old James Bond movies," he pointed out. "The world has changed since the sixties."

Her eyes studied his profile quietly. He was still handsome well into his thirties, and he glorified evening clothes. She knew that she couldn't look forward to anything permanent with him, but sometimes just looking at him was almost enough. He was devastating.

He caught that scrutiny and glanced at her, enjoying the shy admiration in her gray eyes. "Can you dance?" he asked.

"I'm not in the class with Matt Caldwell on a dance floor," she teased, "but I can hold my own, I suppose. Are we going dancing?"

"We're going to a supper club where they have an orchestra and a dance floor," he said. "A sophisticated place with a few carefully placed friends of mine."

"I should have known."

"You'll like it," he promised. "You'll never spot them. They blend in."

"You don't blend," she murmured dryly.

He chuckled. "If that's a compliment, thank you," he said.

"It was."

"You won't blend, either," he said in a low, soft tone.

She clutched her small bag tightly in her lap, feeling the softness right through her body. It made her giddy to think of being held in his arms on a dance floor. It was something she'd dreamed about in her senior year of high school, but it had never happened. As if it would have. She couldn't really picture Eb at a high school prom.

"You're sure Jess and Stevie will be okay?" she asked as he pulled off the main highway and onto a Houston city street.

"I'm sure. Dallas is inside and I have a few people outside. But I meant what I said," he added solemnly. "Lopez won't do a thing until midnight tomorrow."

She supposed that was a sort of knowledge of the enemy that came from long experience in a dangerous profession. But she couldn't help worrying about her family. If anything happened while she was away, she'd never forgive herself.

THE CLUB WAS just off a main thoroughfare, and so discreet that it wouldn't have drawn attention to itself. The luxury cars in the parking lot were an intimation of what was inside.

Inside, the sounds of music came from a room off the main hallway. There was a bar and a small coffee shop, apart from the restaurant. Inside, an employee in a din-

ner jacket led them into the restaurant, which ringed a central dance floor, where a small jazz ensemble played lazy blues tunes for several couples who were dancing.

"This is really spectacular," she told Eb when they were seated near a small indoor waterfall with tropical plants blooming around it.

"It is, isn't it?" he asked, leaning back to study her with a warm smile. "I have to admit, it's one of my favorite haunts when I'm in Houston."

"I can see why." She searched his eyes in a long, tense silence.

He didn't smile. His eyes narrowed as they locked into hers. She could almost hear her own heart beating, beating, beating…!

"Why, Eb!" came a soft voice from behind Sally. "What a coincidence to find you here, at one of our favorite night spots."

Without another word being spoken, Sally knew the identity of the newcomer. It couldn't be anyone except Eb's ex-fiancée.

CHAPTER EIGHT

"HELLO, MAGGIE," EB SAID, standing up to greet the pretty green-eyed brunette who took possession of his arm and smiled up at him.

"It's good to see you again so soon!" she said with obvious pleasure. "You remember Cord Romero, don't you?" She indicated a tall, dark-haired, dark-eyed man beside her without meeting his eyes. "He and I were fostered together by Mrs. Amy Barton, the Houston socialite."

"Sure. How are you, Cord?" Eb asked.

The other man, his equal in height and build, nodded. Sally was curious about Maggie's obvious uneasiness around the other man.

"Sally, this is Maggie Barton and Cord Romero. Sally Johnson." They all acknowledged the introductions, and Eb added, "Won't you join us?"

Sally's heart plummeted as she saw Maggie's eyes light up at the invitation and knew she wouldn't refuse.

"We may be intruding," Cord said with a pointed look at Sally.

"Oh, not at all," Sally said at once.

"I thought Sally needed a night out," Eb said easily and with a warm smile in Sally's direction. "She's an elementary schoolteacher."

The man, Cord, studied her with open curiosity while Eb seated Maggie.

"Allow me," Cord said smoothly, standing behind Sally's chair.

Sally smiled at the old-world courtesy. "Thank you."

Eb glanced at them with unreadable eyes before he turned back to Maggie, who was flushed and avoided looking at the other couple. "Quite a coincidence, running into you here," he said in a neutral tone.

"It was Cord's idea," Maggie said. "He felt like a night on the town and he doesn't date these days. Better your foster sister than nobody, right, Cord?" she added with a nervous laugh and a smile that didn't touch her eyes.

Cord shrugged broad shoulders indolently and didn't say a word, but his distaste for her reference was there, in those unblinking dark eyes.

Sally was curious about him. She wondered what he did for a living. He was very fit for a man his age, which she judged to be about the same as Eb's. His hands were rough and callused, as if he worked physically rather than sat behind a desk. He had the same odd stare that she'd noticed in Eb and Dallas and even Cy Parks, a probing but unfocused distant stare that held a strange hollowness.

"How are things going at the ranch?" Maggie asked gently. "I heard that you had Dallas out there with you."

"Yes," he replied. "He's doing some consulting work for me."

"Shot to pieces, wasn't he?" Cord asked abruptly, his eyes on Sally's face.

"That happens when a man doesn't keep his mind

on his work," Eb said with a pointed glance at Cord, who averted his eyes.

"One of my friends is hosting a huge party down in Cancún for Christmas," Maggie murmured, drawing a lazy polished nail across the back of Eb's hand. "Why don't you take some time off and go with me?"

"No time," Eb said with a smile to soften the words. "I'm not a man of leisure."

"Baloney," she replied. "You could retire on what you've got squirreled away."

"And do what?" came the dry response. "Do I look like a lounge lizard to you?"

"I didn't mean that," she said, and her eyes searched his face for a long moment. "I meant that you could give up walking into danger if you wanted to."

"That's an old argument and you know what the answer is," Eb told her bluntly.

She withdrew her hand from his with a sad little sigh. "Yes, I know," she said wearily. "It's in your blood and you can't stop." Involuntarily she glanced at Cord.

Eb frowned a little as he watched her wilt. Sally saw it and knew at once that he and Maggie had gone through that very argument years ago when she'd broken their engagement. It wasn't their emotions that had split them up. It was his job that he wouldn't quit, not even for a woman he'd loved enough to marry.

She felt helpless. She'd known at some level that he was carrying a torch for Maggie. She stared at her own short, unpolished nails and compared them with Maggie's long, red-stained, beautiful ones. The difference was like the women themselves—one colorful and flamboyant and drawing attention, the other reclusive and practical and...dull. No wonder Eb hadn't wanted

her all those years ago. Beside the exotic Maggie, she was insignificant.

"What subject is your specialty, Miss Johnson?" Cord asked curiously.

"History, actually," she said. "But I teach second grade, so I'm not really using it."

"No ambition to teach higher grades?" he persisted.

She shook her head and smiled wryly. "I tried it when I did my practice-teaching," she confessed. "And by the end of the day, my classroom was more like a zoo than a regimented place of learning. I'm afraid I don't have the facility to handle discipline at a higher level."

Cord's lean face lightened just a little as he studied her. "I had the facility, but the principal and the school board didn't like my methods," he replied.

"You teach?" she asked, enthused to find a colleague in such an unlikely place.

"I taught high school science for a year after I got out of college," he said. "But it wasn't a profession I could love enough to continue." He shrugged. "I found I had an aptitude in a totally unrelated area."

Maggie's hand clenched on her water glass and she took a quick sip.

"What do you do?" she asked, fascinated.

He glanced at Eb, who was openly glaring at him. "Ask Eb," he said on a brief, deep laugh, with a cold glance in Maggie's direction. "Can we order now?" he asked, lifting the menu. "I haven't even had lunch today."

Eb signaled a waiter and brought Sally's conversation with Cord to an end.

It was the longest and most tense meal Sally could remember having sat through. Maggie and Eb talked

about places and people that they shared in memory while Sally concentrated on her food.

Cord was polite, but he made no further attempt at conversation. At the end of the evening, as the two couples parted outside the restaurant, Maggie held on to Eb's hand until he had to forcibly draw it away from her.

"Can't you come up and have dinner with us again one evening?" Maggie asked plaintively.

"Perhaps," Eb said with a careless smile. He glanced at Cord. "Good to see you."

Cord nodded. He glanced down at Sally. "Nice to have met you, Miss Johnson."

"Same here," she said with a smile.

Maggie hesitated and looked uneasy as Cord deliberately took her arm and propelled her away. She went with him, but her back was arrow-straight and she looked as if she was walking on hot coals and on the way to her own execution.

Eb stared after them for a long moment before he put Sally into the sleek Jaguar and climbed in under the wheel. He gave her a look that could have curdled milk.

"Don't encourage him," he said at once.

Her mouth fell open. "Wh...what?"

"You heard me." He started the car, and turned toward Sally. His eyes went over her like sensual fingers, brushing her throat, her bare shoulders under the coat, the shadowy hollow in her breasts revealed by the low-cut dress. "He has a weakness for blondes. He was ravishing you with his eyes."

She didn't know how to respond. While Sally was trying to come up with a response, he moved closer and slid a hand under her nape, under the heavy coil of hair, and pulled her face up toward his.

"So was I," he whispered roughly, and his mouth went down on her lips, burrowing beneath them, pressing them apart, devouring them. At the same time, his free hand slid right down into the low bodice of her dress and curved around her warm, bare breast.

"Eb!" she choked, stiffening.

He was undeterred. He groaned, overcome with desire, and his fingers contracted in a slow, heated, sensual rhythm that brought Sally's mouth open in a tiny gasp. His tongue found the unprotected heat of it and moved inside, in lazy, teasing motions that made her whole body clench.

He felt her nervous fingers fumble against the front of his dress shirt. Impatiently, he unfastened three buttons and dragged her hand inside the shirt, over hair-roughened muscles down to a nipple as hard as the one pressing feverishly into the palm of his hand.

She was devastated by the passion that had kindled so unexpectedly. She couldn't find the strength or the voice to protest the liberties he was taking, or to care that they were in a public parking lot. She didn't care about anything except making sure that he didn't stop. He couldn't stop. He mustn't stop, he mustn't...!

But he did, suddenly. He held her hands together tightly as he moved a little away from her, painfully aware that she was trying to get back into his arms.

"No," he said curtly, and shook her clenched hands.

She stared into his blazing eyes, her breath rustling in her throat, her heartbeat visible at the twin points so blatantly obvious against the bodice of her dress.

He glanced down at her and his jaw clenched. His own body was in agony, and this would only get worse if he didn't stop them now. She was too responsive, too

tempting. He was going to have to make sure that he didn't touch her that way when they were completely alone. The consequences could be devastating. It was the wrong time for a torrid relationship. If he let himself lose his head over Sally right now, it could cost all of them their lives.

Forcefully, he put her back into her own seat and fastened the seat belt around her.

She just stared at him with those huge, soulful gray eyes that made him feel hungry and guilt-ridden all at the same time.

"I have to get you home," he said tersely.

She nodded. Her throat was too tight for words to get out. She clutched her small purse in her hands and stared out the window as he put the car into gear and pulled out into traffic.

It was a long, and very silent, drive back to her house. He was preoccupied, as distant as she remembered him from her teens. She wondered if he was thinking about Maggie and regretting the decision he'd made that put her out of his life. She was mature now, but beautiful as well, and it didn't take a mind reader to know that she was still attracted to Eb. How he felt was less obvious. He was a man who knew how to hide what he felt, and that skill was working overtime tonight.

"Why did Maggie introduce Cord as a foster child at first and then refer to him as her brother? Are they related?" she asked.

"They are not," he returned flatly. "His parents died in a fire, and she came from a severely dysfunctional family. Mrs. Barton adopted both of them. Maggie took her name, but Cord kept his own. His father was a rather famous matador in Spain until his death. Maggie does

usually try to present Cord as her brother. She's scared to death of him, despite the fact that they've kept in close touch all these years."

That was a surprise. "But why is she scared of him?"

He chuckled. "Because she wants him, although she's apparently never realized it," he returned with a quick glance. "He's been a colleague of mine for a long time, and I always thought that Maggie got engaged to me to put Cord out of the reach of temptation."

She pondered that. "A colleague?"

"That's right. He still works with Micah Steele," he said. "He's a demolitions expert."

"Isn't that dangerous?"

"Very," he replied. "His wife died four years ago. Committed suicide," he added shockingly. "He never got over it."

"Why did she do something so drastic?" she asked.

"Because he was working for the FBI when they married and he got shot a few months after the wedding. She hadn't realized his work would be so dangerous. He was in the hospital for weeks and she went haywire. He wouldn't give up a job he loved, and she found that she couldn't live with the knowledge that he might end up dead. She couldn't give him up, either, so she took what she considered the easy way out." His face set grimly. "Easy for her. Hell on him."

She drew in a sharp breath. "I suppose he felt guilty."

"Yes. That was about the time Maggie broke up with me," he added. "She said she didn't want to end up like Patricia."

"She knew Cord's wife?"

"They were best friends," he said shortly. "And something happened between Cord and Maggie just after

Mrs. Barton's funeral. I never knew what, but it ended in Maggie's sudden marriage to a man old enough to be her father. I don't know why, but I think it had something to do with Cord."

"He's unique."

He glared at her. "Yes. He's a hardened mercenary now. He gave up law enforcement when Patricia died and took a job with an ex-special forces unit that went into freelance work. He started doing demolition work and now it's all he does."

Her eyes softened. "He wants to die."

"You're perceptive," he mused. "That's what I think, too. Hell of a pity that he and Maggie don't see each other. They're a lot alike."

She looked at her purse. "You aren't still carrying a torch for her?"

He chuckled. "No. She's a kind, sweet woman and I probably would have married her if things had been different. But I don't think she could have lived with me. She takes things too much to heart."

"Don't I?" she fished.

He smiled. "At times. But you're spunky, Miss Johnson, and despite the scare you had with your two neighbors, you don't balk at fighting back. I like your spirit. When I lose my temper, and I do occasionally, you won't be looking for a closet to hide in."

"That might be true," she confessed. "But if you were into demolition work, I think I'd run in the opposite direction when I saw you coming."

He nodded. "Which is exactly what Maggie did," he replied. "She ran from Cord and got engaged to me."

That was heartening. If the woman was carrying a

torch for another man, it might stop Eb from falling back into his old relationship with her.

"Jealous?" he murmured with a sensuous glance.

Her heart raced. She moved one shoulder a little and avoided his eyes. Then she sighed and said, "Yes."

He chuckled. "Now that really is flattering," he said. "Maggie is part of the past. I have no hidden desire to rekindle old flames. Except the one you and I shared," he qualified.

Sally turned her head and met his searching gaze. Her breath caught in her throat as she stared back at him hungrily.

"Watch it," he said, not quite jokingly. "When we drive up in your yard, we'll be under surveillance. I don't want an audience for what we were doing in the parking lot at that restaurant."

She laughed delightedly. "Okay."

"On the other hand," he added, "we could find a deserted road."

She hesitated. It was one thing for it to happen spontaneously, but quite another to plan such a sensual interlude. And she wasn't sure of her own protective instincts. Around Eb, she didn't seem to have any.

"Don't make such heavy weather of it," he said after a minute. "There's no hurry. We've got all the time in the world."

"Have we?" she wondered, remembering Lopez and his threats.

"Don't gulp down your life, Sally," he said. "Take it one minute at a time. I'm not going to let anything happen to you or Jessica or Stevie. Okay?"

She swallowed. "Sorry. I panic when I think about how dangerous it is."

"I've been handling danger for a long time," he reminded her. "I have a state-of-the-art surveillance system. Nothing is going to get past it."

She managed a weak smile. "He's very ruthless."

"He's been getting away with murder," he said simply. "He doesn't think the justice system can touch him. We're going to prove to him that it can."

"How do you bring a man to justice when he's rich enough to buy a country?"

"You cut off the source of his wealth," he said simply. "Without its head, the snake can't go far."

"Good point."

"Now stop worrying."

"I'll try."

He reached across the seat for her hand and locked it into his big, warm one. "I enjoyed tonight."

"So did I," she said gently.

"Maggie isn't my future, in case you were wondering," he added in a soft tone.

Sally hoped fervently that it was true. She wanted Eb with all her heart.

His fingers tightened on hers. "I think it might be a good idea if I start driving you and Stevie to school and picking you up in the afternoons."

Her heart leaped. "Why?"

He glanced at her. "Because Lopez wouldn't hesitate to kidnap either or both of you to further his own ends. Even two miles is a long distance when you don't have any sort of protection."

She stared at him worriedly. "Why didn't Jess leave well enough alone?" she asked miserably. "If she hadn't gotten that person to talk…"

"Hindsight is wonderful," he told her. "But try to re-

member that Lopez's operation supplies about a quarter of all narcotics sold in the States. That's a lot of addicted kids and a fair number of dead ones."

She grimaced. "Sorry. I was being selfish."

"It isn't selfish to be concerned for the welfare of people you love," he told her. "But getting Lopez behind bars, and cutting his connections, will help make the world a better place. A little worry isn't such a bad trade-off, considering."

"I guess not."

He brought the back of her hand to his mouth and kissed it warmly. "You looked lovely tonight," he said. "I was proud of you."

Her face flushed at the rare compliment. "I'm always proud of you," she replied softly.

He chuckled. "You're good for my ego."

"You're good for mine."

He kept his eyes on the road with an effort. He wanted to pull the car onto a side road and make passionate love to her, but that was impractical, given the circumstances. All Lopez's men needed was an opportunity. He wasn't going to give them one, despite his teasing comment to Sally about it.

When they pulled up in her driveway, the lights were all on in the house and Dallas was sitting in the front porch swing, smoking like a furnace.

"Have a nice time?" he asked as Eb and Sally came up the steps.

"Very nice," Eb replied. "I ran into Cord Romero."

"I thought he was overseas, helping detonate unexploded land mines?"

"Not now," Eb told him. "He's in Houston. Between jobs, maybe. Why are you sitting out here?"

Dallas stared at the red tip of his cigarette. "Jessica has a cough," he replied. "I didn't want to aggravate it."

"Are the two of you speaking?" Eb drawled.

Dallas laughed softly. "Well, she's stopped trying to throw things at me, at least."

Sally's eyes went enormous. That didn't sound like her staid aunt.

"What was she throwing?" Eb asked.

"Anything within reach that felt expendable," came the dry reply. "Stevie thought it was great fun, but she wouldn't let him play. He's gone to bed. She's pretending to watch television."

"You might talk to her," Eb suggested.

"Chance," Dallas replied, "would be a fine thing. She doesn't want to talk, thank you." He finished the cigarette. "I'll be out in the woods with Smith."

"Watch where you walk," Eb cautioned.

"Mined the forest, did we?" Dallas murmured wickedly.

Eb grinned. "Not with explosives, at least."

Dallas shook his head and went down the steps, to vanish in the direction of the woods at the edge of the yard.

Sally rubbed her arms through the coat, shivering, and it wasn't even that cold. She felt the danger of her predicament keenly and wished that she could have done something to prevent the desperate situation.

"You're doing it again," Eb murmured, drawing her against him. "You have to trust me. I won't let anything happen to any of you."

She looked up at him with wide, soft eyes. "I'll try not to worry. I've never been in such a mess before."

"Hopefully you never will again," he said. He bent

and kissed her very gently, nipping her lower lip before he lifted his head. "I'll be somewhere nearby, or my men will be. Try to get some sleep."

"Okay." She touched her fingers to his mouth and smiled wanly before she turned and walked to the door. "Thanks for supper," she added. "It was delicious."

"It would have been better without the company," he said, "but that was unavoidable. Next time I'll plan better."

She smiled at him. "That's a deal."

He watched her walk inside the house and lock the door behind her before he turned and got back into his truck. Less than twenty-four hours remained before Lopez would make good his threat. He had to make sure that everyone was prepared for a siege.

SALLY PAUSED IN the doorway of the living room with her eyes wide as she saw the damage Jessica had inflicted with her missiles.

"Good Lord!" she exclaimed.

Jess grimaced. "Well, he provoked me," she muttered. "He said that I'd gotten lazy in my old age, just lying around the house like a garden slug. I do not lie around like a garden slug!"

"No, of course you don't," Sally said, placating her while she bent to pick up pieces of broken pottery and various other objects from the floor.

"Besides, what does he expect me to do without my eyesight, drive the car?"

Sally was trying not to smile. She'd never seen her aunt in such a tizzy before.

"He actually accused me of insanity because I won't give up the name to Lopez," she added harshly. "He said

that a good mother wouldn't have withheld a name and put her child in danger. That's when I threw the flowerpot, dear. I'm sorry. I do hope it hit him."

Sally made a clucking sound. "You're not yourself, Jess."

"Yes, I am! I'm the result of all his sarcasm! He can't find one thing about me that he likes anymore. Everything I do and say is wrong!"

"He doesn't seem like a bad man," Sally ventured.

"I didn't say he was bad, I said he was obnoxious and condescending and conceited." She pushed back a strand of hair. "He was laughing the whole time."

Which surely made things worse, Sally mused silently. "I expect it was wails of pain, Jess."

"You couldn't hurt him," she scoffed. "You'd have to stick a bomb up his shirt."

"Drastic surely?"

Jess sighed and leaned back in the chair, looking drained. "I hate arguments. He seems to thrive on them." She hesitated. "He taught Stevie how to braid a rope," she added unexpectedly.

"That's odd. I thought Stevie wanted to beat him up."

"They had a talk outside the room. I don't know what was said," Jess confessed. "But when they came back in here, Dallas had several lengths of rawhide and he taught Stevie how to braid them. He was having the time of his life."

"Then what?"

"Then," she said, her lips compressing briefly, "he just happened to mention that I could have taught him how to braid rope and a lot of other things if I'd exert myself occasionally instead of vegetating in front of a television that I can't see anyway."

"I see."

"Pity I ran out of things to throw," she muttered. "I was reaching for the lamp when he called a draw and said he was going to sit on the front porch. Then Stevie decided to go to bed." She gripped the arms of her chair hard. "Everybody ran for cover. You'd think I was a Chinese rocket or something."

"In a temper, there is something of a comparison," Sally chuckled.

The older woman drew in a long breath. "Anyway, how was your date?"

"Not bad. We ran into his ex-fiancée at the restaurant."

"Maggie?" Jess asked, wide-eyed. "How is she?"

"She's very pretty and still crazy about Eb, from all indications. I think she'd have followed us home if her dark and handsome escort hadn't half dragged her away."

"Cord was there?"

"You know him?" Sally asked curiously.

Jess nodded. "He was a handsome devil. I had a yen for him once myself, but he married Patricia instead. She was a little Dresden china doll, blonde and absolutely gorgeous. She worshipped Cord. They'd only been married a few months when he was involved in a shoot-out with a narcotics dealer. She couldn't take it. When Cord came home from the hospital, she was several days dead, with a suicide note clutched in her fingers. He found her. He was like a madman after that, looking for every dangerous job he could find. I don't suppose he's over her yet. He loved her desperately."

"Eb says he works with Micah Steele."

"He does, and there's a real coincidence. Micah also

has a stepsister, Callie. You know her, she works in Mr. Kemp's law office."

"Yes. We went to school together. But Micah doesn't have anything to do with her or his father since his father divorced Callie's mother. They say," she murmured, "that old Mr. Steele caught Micah with his new wife in a very compromising position and tossed them both out on their ears."

"That's the obvious story," Jessie said dryly. "But there's more to it than that."

"How does Callie feel about Micah's work, do you think?"

"The way any woman would feel," Jessie replied gently. "Afraid."

Sally knew that Jess was talking about Dallas, and how she'd regarded his work as a soldier of fortune. She stared at the darkened window, wondering how she'd feel under the same circumstances. At least Eb wasn't involved in demolition work or actively working as a mercenary. She knew that she could adjust to Eb's lifestyle. But the trick was going to be convincing Eb that she could—and that he needed her, as much as she needed him.

CHAPTER NINE

SALLY FOUND HERSELF jumping at every odd noise all day Saturday. Jessica could feel the tension that she couldn't see.

"You have to trust Eb," she told her niece while Stevie was watching cartoons in the living room. "He knows what he's doing. Lopez won't succeed."

Sally grimaced over her second cup of coffee. Across the kitchen table from her, Jess looked serene. She wished she could feel the same way.

"I'm not worried about us," she pointed out. "It's Stevie…"

"Dallas won't let anything happen to Stevie," came the quiet reply.

Sally smiled, remembering the broken objects in the living room the night before. She drew a lazy circle around the lip of her coffee cup while she searched for the right words. "At least, the two of you are speaking."

"Yes. Barely," her aunt acknowledged wryly. "But Stevie likes him now. They started comparing statistics on wrestlers. They both like wrestling, you see. Dallas knows all sorts of holds. He wrestled on his college team."

"Wrestling!" Sally chuckled.

"Apparently there's a lot more to the professional matches than just acting ability," Jessica said dryly. "I'm

finding it rather interesting, even if I can't see what they're doing. They explained the holds to me."

"Common threads," Sally murmured.

"And one stitch at a time. What did you think of Cord Romero?"

"He's the strangest ex-schoolteacher I've ever met," Sally said flatly.

"He was never cut out for that line of work," Jessica said, sipping black coffee. "But demolition work isn't much of a profession, either. Pity. He'll be two lines of type on the obituary page one day, and it's such a waste."

"Eb says Maggie's running from him."

"Relentlessly," Jess said dryly. "I always thought she got engaged to Eb just to shake Cord up, but it didn't work. He doesn't see her."

"He's in the same line of work Eb was," Sally pointed out, "and Eb said that his job was why she called off the wedding."

"I think she just came to her senses. If you love a man, you don't have a lot to say about his profession if it's a long-standing one. Cord's wife was never cut out for life on the edge. Maggie, now, once had a serious run-in with a couple of would-be muggers. She had a big flashlight in her purse and she used it like a mace." She laughed softly. "They both had to have stitches before they went off to jail. Cord laughed about it for weeks afterward. No, she had the strength to marry Eb—she simply didn't love him."

Sally traced the handle of her cup. "Eb says he isn't carrying a torch for her."

"Why should he be?" she asked. "She's a nice woman, but he never really loved her. He wanted sta-

bility and he thought marriage would give it to him. As it turned out, he found his stability after a bloody fire-fight in Africa, and it was right here in Jacobsville."

"Do you think he'll ever marry?" she fished.

"When he's ready," Jess replied. "But I don't think it will be Maggie. Just in case you wondered," she teased.

Sally pushed back a wisp of hair from her eyes. "Jess, do you know where your informant is now, the one that Lopez wants you to name?"

She shook her head. "We lost touch just after Lopez was arrested. I understand that my informant went back to Mexico. I haven't tried to contact...the person."

"What if the informant betrays himself?"

"You're clutching at straws, dear," Jessica said gently. "That isn't going to happen. And I'm not giving a witness up to the executioner in cold blood even to save myself and my family."

Sally smiled. "No. I know you wouldn't. I wouldn't, either. But it's scary to be in this situation."

"It is. But it will be over one day, and we'll get back to normal. Whatever happens, happens." Jess reminded her niece, "It's like that old saying, when your time's up, it's up. We may not know what we're doing, but God always does. And He doesn't have tunnel vision."

"Point taken. I'll try to stop worrying."

"You should. Eb is one of the best in the world at what he does. Lopez knows it, too. He won't rush in headfirst, despite his threat."

"What if he has a missile launcher?" Sally asked with sudden fear.

Miles away in a communications hot room, a man with green eyes nodded his head and shot an order to a subordinate. It wouldn't hurt one bit to check out the

intelligence for that possibility. Sally might be nervous, but she had good instincts. And a guardian angel in cowboy boots.

MANUEL LOPEZ WAS a small man with big ambition. He was nearing forty, balding, cynical and mercenary to the soles of his feet. He stared out the top floor picture window of his four-story mansion at the Gulf of Mexico and cursed. One of his subordinates, shifting nervously from one foot to the other, had just brought him some unwelcome news and he was livid.

"There are only a handful of men," the subordinate said in quiet Spanish. "Not a problem if we send a large force against them."

Lopez turned and glared at the man from yellow-brown eyes. "Yes, and if we send a large force, the FBI and the DEA will also send a large force!"

"It would be too late by then," the man replied with a shrug.

"I have enough federal problems in the United States as it is," Lopez growled. "I do not anticipate giving them an even better reason to send an undercover unit after me here! Scott has influence with his government. I want the name of the informant, not to wade in and kill the woman and her protectors."

The other man stared at the spotless white carpet. "She will never give up the name of her informant," he said simply. "Not even for the sake of her child."

Lopez turned fully to look at the man. "Because now it is only words, the threat. We must make it very real, you understand? At midnight tonight in Jacobsville, precisely at midnight, you will have a helicopter fly over the house and drop a smoke bomb. A big one." His

eyes narrowed and he smiled. "This will be the attack they anticipate. But not the real one, you understand?"

"They will probably have missiles," the man said quietly.

"And they are far too soft to use them," came the sneering reply. "This is why we will ultimately win. I have no scruples. Now, listen. I will want a man to remove one of the elementary school janitors. He can be drugged or threatened, I have no interest in the method, just get him out of the way for one day. Then you will have one of our men take his place. The substitute must know what the child looks like and which class he is in. He is to be taken very covertly, so that nothing out of the way is projected until it is too late and we have him. You understand?"

"Yes," the man replied respectfully. "Where is he to be held?"

Lopez smiled coldly. "At the rental house near the Johnson home," he said. "Will that not be an irony to end all ironies?" His eyes darkened. "But he is not to be harmed. That must be made very clear," he added in tones that chilled. "You remember what happened to the man who went against my orders and set fire to my enemy's house in Wyoming without waiting for the man to be alone, and a five-year-old boy was killed?"

The other man swallowed and nodded quickly.

"If one hair on this boy's head is harmed," he added, "I will see to it that the man responsible fares even worse than his predecessor. I am a violent man, but I do not kill children. It is, perhaps, my only virtue." He waved his hand. "Let me know when my orders have been carried out."

"Yes. At once."

He watched the man go and his odd yellow-brown eyes narrowed. He had watched his mother and siblings die at the hands of a guerrilla leader at the age of four. His father had been a poor laborer who could barely earn enough to provide one meal a day for the two of them, so his childhood had been spent scavenging for food like an animal, hiding in the shadows to avoid being tortured by the invaders. His father had not been as fortunate, but the two of them had managed to work their way to the States, to Victoria, Texas, when he was ten. He watched his father scrape and bow as a janitor and hated the sight. He had vowed that when he was a man, he would never know poverty again, regardless of what it cost him. And despite his father's anguish, he had embarked very quickly on a path to easy money.

He looked down at the white carpet, a dream of his from youth, and at the wealth with which he surrounded himself. He dealt in drugs and death. He was wealthy and immensely powerful. A word from him could topple heads of state. But it was an empty, cold, bitter existence. He had lived at first only for vengeance, for the ability and the means to avenge his mother and his baby brother and sister. That accomplished, he wanted wealth and power. One step led to another, until he was in over his head, first as a murderer, then as a thief, and finally, as a drug lord. He was ruthless and he knew that one day his sins would catch up with him, but first he was going to know who had sold him out to the authorities two years before. What irony that vengeance had led him to power, and now it was vengeance that had almost brought him down. He cursed the woman Jessica for refusing to give him the name. He had only discovered her part in his arrest six months before. She

would pay now. He would have the name of his betrayer, whatever the cost!

He stared down at the rocks and winced as he saw once again, in his memory, the floating white dress and the equally white face and open, dead eyes of the woman he'd wanted even more than the name of the person who had betrayed him. Isabella, he thought with anguish. He had never loved, not until Isabella came into his home as a housekeeper, the sister of one of his lieutenants' friends. She had talked to him, admired him, teased him as if he were a boy. She had made herself so necessary to him that he told her things that he told no one else. She had made him want to be clean, to give up his decadent life, to have a family, a home. But when he had approached her ardently, she had suddenly wanted no part of him. In a fit of rage when she pushed him away at a party on his yacht, he hit her. She went over the rails and into the ocean, vanishing abruptly under the keel of the boat.

He had immediately regretted the act, but it was too late. His men had searched for her in the water until daybreak before he let them give up the search, only to find her washed up on the beach, dead, when he arrived back at his mansion. Her death had cheapened him, cheapened his life. He was deeply sorry that his temper had pushed him to such an act, that he cost himself the most precious thing in his life. He had killed her. He was damned, he thought. Damned eternally. And probably he deserved to be.

Since that night, two years ago, just before his arrest in the United States for narcotic trafficking, he had no other thought than to find the man who had betrayed him. Nothing made him happy since her loss, not even

the pretty young woman who sang at a club in Cancún just recently. He had taken a fancy to her because she reminded him of Isabella. He had ordered his henchmen to bring her to him one night after her performance. He had enjoyed her, but her violent revulsion had angered him and she, too, had felt his wrath. She had taken her own life, jumped from a high balcony rather than submit to him a second time. Her death had wounded him, but not as deeply as the loss of Isabella. Nothing, he was certain, would ever give him such anguish and remorse again. He thought of the woman Jessica and her son, of the fear she would experience when he had her child. Then, he thought angrily, she would give him the name of her informant. She would have to. And, at last, he would have his vengeance for the betrayal that had sent him to an American prison.

EB HADN'T COME near the house all day. After Stevie was tucked up in bed, Jessica and Sally sat together in the dimly lit living room and watched the clock strike midnight.

"It's time," Sally said huskily, stiff with nerves.

Jessica only nodded. Like Sally, her frame was rigid. She had made her decision, the only decision possible. Now they were all going to pay the consequences for it.

Even as the thought crawled through her mind, she heard the sudden whir of a helicopter closing in.

"Get down!" Jessica called to Sally, sliding onto the big throw rug full-length. She felt Sally beside her as the helicopter came even closer and a flash, followed by an explosion, shook the roof.

Smoke came down the chimney, filling the room. Outside, the whir of the helicopter was accompanied by

small arms fire and the sounds of bullets hitting something hard. Then that sound was abruptly interrupted by a sudden whooshing sound. Right on the heels of that came a violent explosion that lit up the whole sky and then the unmistakable sound of falling debris.

"There went the chopper," Jessica said huskily. "Sally, are you all right?"

"Yes. We have to get out," she said, coughing. "The smoke is going to choke us!"

She helped Jessica to her feet and started her down the hall to the front door while she went to grab Stevie up out of his bed and rush down the same hall with him in her arms. It was like a nightmare, but she didn't have time to count the cost or worry about the outcome. She was doing what was necessary to save them, in the quickest possible time. She could only pray that they wouldn't run out right into the arms of Lopez's men.

She caught up with Jess, who was feeling her way along the wall. Taking her by the arm, with Stevie close, she propelled them to the front door, unlocked it, and rushed out onto the porch.

Eb was running toward them, but an Eb that Sally didn't recognize at first. He was dressed completely in black with a face mask on, carrying a small automatic weapon. Other men, similarly dressed, were already going around the back of the house.

"Come with me," Eb called, herding them into the forest and into a four-wheel-drive vehicle. "Lock the doors and stay put until we check out the house," he said.

He was gone even as the words died on the air. Stevie huddled close to his mother while Sally watched Eb's stealthy but rapid approach toward the house, her

heart racing madly. Even though the attack had been expected, it was frightening.

A tap on the window next to Jessica on the passenger side made them all jump. Dallas pulled off his face mask, smiling as he replaced a walkie-talkie in his belt. "Open the window," he said.

Sally fumbled with the key in the ignition and powered the passenger side window down.

"We got the chopper," he said. "But it's only a smoke bomb in the house, irritating but not deadly. Lopez is a man of his word. He did attack at midnight. Pity about the chopper," he added with glittery eyes. "That will set him back a little small change."

Sally didn't ask the obvious question, but she knew that somebody had to be piloting that helicopter. She felt sick inside, now that the danger was past.

"Is everyone all right?" Jessica asked. "We heard shots."

"The chopper was well-equipped with weapons," Dallas said. "But he wasn't a very good shot."

"Thank God," Jessica said heavily.

Dallas reached in and touched her face gently, pausing to run a rough hand over Stevie's tousled hair. "Don't be afraid," he said softly. "I won't let anything happen to you."

Jessica held his hand to her cheek and choked back a sob. Dallas bent to touch his mouth to her wet eyes.

Impulsively Stevie leaned across his mother to hug the big blond man, too. Watching them, Sally felt empty and alone. They were already a family, even if they hadn't realized it.

Dallas's walkie-talkie erupted in a burst of static. "All clear," Eb's voice came back to them. "I'm phon-

ing the sheriff while the others open the windows and turn on the attic fan to get this smoke out of here. Then I'll lock up."

"What about..." Dallas began.

"We'll take the women and Stevie home with us," he said. "No sense in leaving them here for the rest of the night. Sally?"

Dallas moved the walkie-talkie to her mouth. "Yes?" she said, shaken.

"Come in and help me find what you need in the way of clothes for all three of you. Dallas, take Jess and Stevie back to the house. We'll catch up."

"Sure thing."

Sally got out of the vehicle, still in her jeans and sneakers and sweatshirt, her long hair falling out of its braid. Dallas got in under the wheel as she walked back to the house. She heard the engine roar and glanced back to see the utility vehicle pull out of the yard. At least Jess and Stevie were safe. But she felt shaken to the soles of her sneakers.

Eb was in the smoky living room, having just hung up the phone. His mask was in one hand, dangling along with the small machine gun. He looked tough and angry as he glanced at Sally's white face. He didn't say a word. He just held out his arm.

Sally ran to him, and he gathered her up in his arms and held her tight while she shivered from the shock of it all.

"I'm no wimp, honest," she whispered in a choked attempt at humor. "But I'm not used to people bombing my house."

He chuckled deeply and hugged her close. "Only a smoke bomb, baby," he said gently. "Noisy and fright-

ening, but not dangerous unless it set fire to something. He had to make a statement, you see. Lopez is a man of his word."

"Damn Lopez," she muttered.

"Amen."

Around them, men were pouring over the house. Eb escorted Sally down the hall to her bedroom.

"Get what you need together," he said, "but only essentials. I'd like to get you out of here very soon after the sheriff arrives."

"The sheriff...?"

"It's his jurisdiction," he told her. "I'm sanctioned, if that's what the worried look is about," he added when he saw her face. He smiled. "I wouldn't take the law into my own hands. Not in this country, anyway," he added with a grin.

"Thank goodness," she said heavily. "I had visions of trying to bail you out of jail."

"Would you?" he teased.

"Of course."

She looked so solemn that the smile faded from his lips. He gathered a handful of her thick blond hair and pulled her wan face under his. His grip was a little tight, and the look in his green eyes was glittery. "Danger is an aphrodisiac, did you know?" he whispered roughly, and bent to her mouth.

He hadn't kissed her that way before. His mouth was hard and demanding on her lips, parting them ruthlessly as his body shifted and one arm pushed her hips deliberately into the changing contours of his own.

She felt helpless. Her mouth opened for him. Her body arched up, taut and hot, in the grip of madness. She returned his kiss ardently, moaning when his legs

parted so that he could maneuver her hips between them, letting her feel the power of his arousal.

His tall, fit body shuddered and she could feel the sharp indrawn breath he took.

After a few wild seconds, he dragged his mouth away from hers without letting her move away even a fraction of an inch. He looked down at her with intent, searching her wide, soft gray eyes hungrily. The arm that was holding her was like a steel rod at her back, but against her legs, she felt the faintest tremor in his.

"I've gone hungry for a long time," he whispered gruffly.

She didn't know how to reply to such a blatant statement. Her eyes searched his in an odd silence, broken only by the whir of the attic fan in the hall and the muffled sound of voices as Eb's men searched the house. She reached up and touched his hard mouth tenderly, loving the immediate response of his lips to the caress.

He bent, nuzzling his face against hers to find her mouth. He kissed her urgently, but with restraint, nibbling her lower lip sensuously. Both arms went around her, riveting her to him. Her own slid under his arms and around his hard waist, holding him close. She closed her eyes, savoring the wondrous contact. The fierce hunger he felt was quite obvious in the embrace, but it didn't frighten her. She wanted him, too.

"When I heard the explosion," he said at her ear, his voice tight with tension, "I didn't know what we were going to find when I ran toward the house. We'd planned for any eventuality, but the chopper came in under radar. We didn't even hear the damned thing until we could see it, and then the launcher jammed...!"

She hadn't imagined that Eb would be afraid for

her. It was wonderful. She hugged him closer and felt him shiver.

"We were a little shaken," Sally whispered. "But we're all okay."

"I didn't expect to feel like this," he said through his teeth.

She lifted her head and looked up at his strained face. "Like...this?"

His green gaze met her soft gray one and then fell to her mouth, to her soft breasts flattened against him. "Like this," he whispered and moved deliberately against her while he held her eyes.

She blushed, because it was blatant.

But he didn't smile. "I knew you were going to be trouble six years ago," he said through his teeth. He bent and kissed her again, fiercely, before he put her away from him and stood trying to get his breath.

She was shivering a little in the aftermath of the most explosive sensuality she'd ever felt. She searched his face quietly, despite the turmoil inside her awakened body.

"You've never felt like that before, have you?" he asked in a hushed tone.

She shook her head, still too shaken for words.

"If it's any consolation, it gets steadily worse," he continued. "Think about that."

He turned and went out into the hall with her puzzled eyes following him. She touched her swollen lips gingerly and wondered what he meant.

THE SHERIFF, BILL ELLIOTT, and two deputies pulled up in the yard, took statements and looked around with Eb and the other men. Sally was questioned briefly, and

when the house was secure, Eb drove her back to his house with the rest of his men remaining in the woods.

"I don't think Lopez has any idea of trying again tonight," he said, "but I'm not taking any chances. I've already underestimated him once."

"He does keep his word," she said huskily.

"Yes."

"What do we do now?"

"I take you and Stevie to school and Jess stays at my house. In fact, you all stay at my house," he said curtly. "I'm not putting you at risk a second time."

She was stunned at the emotion in his voice. He was really concerned about her. She felt a warm glow all the way to her toes.

He glanced at her with slow, sensuous eyes. "At least at my own house, I can find one room with no bugs." His eyes went to her breasts and back to her face. "I'm starving."

She knew he wasn't talking about food, and her heart began racing madly.

He caught her hand in his free one and worked his fingers slowly between hers, pressing her palm to his. "Don't worry. I won't let things go too far, Sally."

She wasn't worried about that. She was wondering how she was going to go on living if he made love to her and then walked away.

WHEN THEY GOT to the house, Jessica and Dallas were in the small bedroom Eb's male housekeeper had given Stevie, tucking him in.

Eb had his housekeeper show the others to their rooms and he excused himself, tugging Sally along with him, to Dallas's obvious amusement.

"Where are we going?" Sally asked.

"To bed. I'm tired. Aren't you?"

"Yes."

She supposed he was giving her a room further down the hall, but he didn't stop at any of the closed doors. He led her around a corner and through two double doors into a huge room with Mediterranean furnishings and green and gold and brown accessories. He closed the double doors, locking them, before he turned to the dresser and pulled out a pair of blue silk pajamas.

"You can wear the pajama top and I'll wear the bottoms," he said matter-of-factly.

Her breath escaped in a rush. "Eb…"

He drew her into his arms and kissed her slowly, with deliberate sensuality, making nonsense of her protests with his hands as they skimmed under the sweatshirt and up to find her taut breasts.

She moaned, feeling the fever rise in her as he unfastened the bra and touched her hungrily. Her body arched, helping him, inviting him. Her hands gripped hard against the powerful muscles of his upper arms, drowning in waves of pleasure.

His mouth lifted fractionally. "I won't hurt you," he breathed. "Not in any way. But you're sleeping in my arms tonight."

She started to protest, but his mouth was already covering hers, muffling the words, muffling her brain.

His hands removed the sweatshirt and the bra and he looked at her with quiet, possessive eyes, drinking in the soft textures, the smooth skin, the beauty of her. He touched her gently, smiling as her body reacted to his skilled hands.

His mouth slid down to her breasts and kissed them

slowly, each caress more ardent than the one before. He had her out of her jeans and sneakers and down to her briefs before she realized what was happening.

He moved away just long enough to pick up the pajama top and slip it over her head, still buttoned. He lifted her, dazed, in his arms and paused, balancing her on one knee, to pull the covers back so that he could tuck her into bed. He leaned over her, balancing on his hands, and searched her flushed, fascinated face.

"I'll be in after I've talked to Dallas and reset the monitors."

She didn't bother to protest. Her gray eyes searched his and she sighed a little unsteadily. "All right."

His eyes kindled with pleasure. He smiled, because he knew she was accepting anything he proposed. It was humbling. He kissed her eyelids closed. "Sleep well."

She watched him go, uncertain if that meant he was sleeping elsewhere. She was so tired that she fell asleep almost as soon as the doors closed behind him, wrapped in sensuous dreams.

CHAPTER TEN

SALLY HAD VIOLENT, passionate dreams that night. She moved helplessly under invisible caressing hands, moaning, arching up to prolong their warm, sweet contact. Her body burned, swelled, ached. She whispered to some faceless phantom, pleading with it not to stop.

There was soft, deep laughter at her ear and the rough warmth of an unshaven face moving against her skin, where her heart beat frantically. Slowly it occurred to her that it felt just a little too vivid to be a dream...

Her eyes flew open and blond-streaked brown hair came into focus under them in the pale dawn light filtering in through the window curtains. Her hands were enmeshed in its thick, cool strands and when she looked down, she realized that her pajama top was open, baring her to a marauding mouth.

"Eb!" she exclaimed huskily.

"It's all right. You're only dreaming," he whispered, and his mouth slid up to cover her lips as the hair-roughened skin of his muscular chest slid over her bare breasts. She felt his legs entwining with her own, felt the throb of his body, the tenderness of his hands, his mouth, as he learned her by touch and taste.

"Dreaming?"

"That's right." He lifted his lips from hers and looked down into misty gray eyes. He smiled. "And a lovely

dream it is," he added in a whisper as he lifted away enough to give his eyes a stark view of everything the pajama top no longer covered. "Lovelier than I ever imagined."

"What time is it?" she asked, dazed.

"Dawn," he told her, smoothing her long hair back away from her flushed face. "Everyone else is still asleep. And there are no bugs, of any sort, in here with us," he added meaningfully.

She touched his rough cheek gently, studying him as he'd studied her. He was still wearing the pajama trousers, but his broad chest was bare. Like her own.

He rolled over onto his back, taking her with him. He guided her hands to his chest with a quiet smile. "I was going to let you wake up alone," he murmured. "But I didn't have enough willpower. There you lay, blond hair scattered over my pillows, the pajama top half off." He shook his head. "You can't imagine how lovely you look in the dawn light. Like a fairy, all creamy and gold. Irresistible," he added, "to a man who's abstained as long as I have."

She traced the pattern of hair over his breastbone. "How long have you abstained?"

"Years too long," he whispered, searching her eyes. "And that's why I set the alarm in Dallas's room to go off five minutes from now. It will wake him and he'll wake Jess and Stevie. Stevie will come looking for you." He grinned. "See how carefully I look after your virtue, Miss Johnson?"

She gave her own bare torso a poignant glance and met his eyes again.

He lifted an eyebrow. "Virtue," he emphasized, "not modesty. I don't seduce virgins, in case you forgot."

She couldn't quite decide whether he was playing or serious.

He saw that in her face and smiled gently. "Sally, the hardest thing I ever did in my life was to push you away one spring afternoon six years ago," he said softly. "I had passionate, vivid dreams about you in some of the wildest places on earth. I'm still having them." His hand swept slowly down her body, watching it lift helplessly to his touch. "So are you, judging by the sounds you were making in your sleep when I came to bed about ten minutes ago. I crawled in beside you and you came right up against me and touched me in a way I won't tell you about."

She searched his eyes blankly. "I did what?"

"Want to know?" he asked with an outrageous grin. "Okay." He leaned close and whispered it in her ear and she cried out, horrified.

"No need to feel embarrassed," he chided. "I loved it."

She knew her face was scarlet, but he looked far more pleased than teasing.

He traced her lower lip lazily. "For a few tempestuous seconds I forgot Lopez and last night, and just about everything else of any immediate importance." His eyes darkened as he held her poised above him. "I've lived on dreams for a long time. The reality is pretty shattering."

"Dreams?"

He nodded. He wasn't smiling. "I wanted you six years ago. I still do, more than ever." He brushed back her disheveled hair and looked at her with eyes that were tender and possessive. "I'm your home. Wherever I go, you go."

She didn't understand what he meant. Her face was troubled.

He rolled her over onto her back and propped himself above her. "From what I know of you, my lifestyle isn't going to break you. You've got spirit and courage, and you're not afraid to speak your mind. I think you'll adjust very well, especially if I give up any work that takes me out of the country. I can still teach tactics, although I'll cut down my contract jobs when the babies start coming along."

"Babies?" She looked completely blank.

"Listen, kid," he murmured dryly, "what we're doing causes them." He frowned. "Well, not exactly what we're doing. But if we were wearing less, and doing a little more than we're doing, we'd be causing them."

Her whole body tingled. She searched his eyes with a feeling of unreality. "You want to have a child with me?" she asked, awed.

"Oh, yes. I want to have a lot of children with you," he whispered solemnly.

She laid her hands flat on his broad chest, savoring its muscular warmth as she considered what he was saying. She frowned, because he hadn't mentioned love or marriage.

"What's missing?" he asked.

"I teach school," she said worriedly. "My reputation…"

Now he was frowning. "God Almighty, do you think I'm asking you to live in sin with me, in Jacobsville, Texas?" he asked, with exaggerated horror.

"You didn't say anything about marriage," she began defensively.

He grinned wickedly. "Do you really think I spent so

much time on you just to give you karate lessons?" he drawled. "Darlin', it would take years of them to make you proficient enough to protect yourself from even a weak adversary. I brought you over here for practice so that I could get my arms around you."

Her eyes brightened. "Did you, really?"

He chuckled. "See what depths I've sunk to?" he murmured. He shook his head. "I had to give you enough time to grow up. I didn't want a teenager who was hero-worshipping me. I wanted a woman, a strong woman, who could stand up to me."

She smoothed her hands up to his broad shoulders. "I think I can do that," she mused.

He nodded. "I think you can, too. Can you live with what I do?"

She smiled. "Of course."

He drew in a slow breath and his eyes were more possessive than ever. "Then we'll get Jess out of harm's way and then we'll get married."

She pulled him down to her. "Yes," she whispered against his hard mouth.

Seconds later, they were so close that she wasn't certain he'd be able to draw back at all, when there was a loud knock at the door and the knob rattled.

"Aunt Sally!" came a plaintive little voice. "I want some cereal and they haven't got any that's in shapes and colors. It's such boring cereal!"

Sally laughed even as Eb managed to drag himself away from the tangle of their legs with a groan that was half amusement and half agony.

"I'll be right there, Stevie!"

"Why's the door locked?" he called loudly.

"Come on here, youngster, and let's see if we can

find something you'd like to eat," came a deep, amused adult voice.

"Okay, Dallas!"

The voices retreated. Eb lay shivering a little with reaction, but he grinned when Sally sat up and looked down at him with love glowing in her eyes.

"Close call," he whispered.

"Very," she agreed.

He took a long, hungry last look at her breasts and resolutely sat up and fastened her buttons again with a rueful smile. "Maybe food is a bearable substitute for what I really want," he mused.

She leaned forward and kissed him gently. "I'll make you glad we waited," she whispered against his mouth.

Several heated minutes later, they joined the others at the breakfast table, but Eb didn't mention future plans. He was laying down ground rules for the following week, starting with the very necessary trip Sally and Stevie must take to school the next day.

"We could keep him out of school until this is over," Dallas said tersely, glancing at the child who was sitting between himself and Jessica. "I don't like having him at risk."

"Neither do I," Jessica said heavily. "But it's possible that he won't be. Lopez has a weakness for children," she said. "It's the only virtue he possesses, but he's a maniac about abusive adults. He'd never hurt Stevie, no matter what."

"I'd have to agree with that," Eb said surprisingly.

"Then life goes on as usual," Jessica said. "And maybe Lopez will make a mistake and we'll have him. Or at least," she added, "a way of getting at him."

"What about Rodrigo?" Dallas asked abruptly.

"He phoned me late last night," Eb told him. "He's already in town, in place. Fast worker. It seems he has a relative, a 'mule' who works for Lopez in Houston, a distant relative who doesn't know what Rodrigo really does for a living. He got Rodrigo a job driving a truck for the new operation here." He let out a breath through his teeth. "Once we get Lopez's attention away from Jess," he added, "that operation is going to be our next priority."

"Can't you just send the sheriff over there to arrest them?" Sally asked.

"It's inside the city limits. Chief Chet Blake has jurisdiction there, and, of course, he'd help if he could," Eb told her. "But so far, all we have on Lopez's employees is a distant connection to a drug lord. Unless we can catch them in the act of receiving or shipping cocaine, what would we charge them with? Building a warehouse is legal, especially when you have all the easements and permission from the planning commission."

"That's why we're going to stake out the place, once this is over," Dallas added. He glanced from Jessica to Stevie with worried eyes. "But first we have to solve the more immediate problem."

Jess felt for his hand on the table beside her and tangled her fingers into it. "We'll get through this," she said in a soft tone. "I can't cold-bloodedly give a human being's life up to Lopez, no matter what the cost. The person involved risked everything to put him away. And even then, his attorneys found a loophole."

"Don't forget that it took them a couple of years to do that," Eb reminded her. "He won't be easy to catch a second time. He has enough pull with the Mexican

government to keep them from extraditing him back here for trial."

"I hear DEA's going to put him on their top ten Most Wanted list," Dallas said. "That will turn up the heat a little, especially with a fifty-thousand dollar reward to sweeten the deal."

"Lopez would double their bounty out of his pocket change to get them off his tail, even if we could find someone crazy enough to go down to Cancún after him," Eb said.

"Micah Steele would, in a second," Dallas replied.

Eb chuckled. "I imagine he would. But he's been working on a case overseas with Cord Romero and Bojo Luciene."

"Bojo, the Moroccan," Dallas recalled. "Now there's a character."

Eb was immediately somber. "Okay, tomorrow morning I'll follow Sally and Stevie in to school. Dallas can tail them on the way home. We'll stay in constant contact and hope for the best."

"The best," Dallas replied, "would be that Lopez would give up."

"It won't happen," Eb assured him.

"Have you considered contacting your informant?" Dallas asked Jessica. "If we could get him back to the States, we could arrange around-the-clock protection and get him into the witness protection program, where even Lopez couldn't find him."

She grimaced. "I thought of that, but I honestly don't know how to locate my informant," she said sadly. "The people who could have helped me do it are dead."

Eb scowled. "All of them?"

Jessica nodded with a sigh. "All of them. About six months ago. Just before my accident."

"Rodrigo might be able to dig something up," Dallas said.

"That's very possible," Eb agreed. "Jessica, you could trust him with the name. I know, you don't want to put your informant in danger. But if we can't find him, how can we protect him?"

She hesitated. Then she shifted in her chair, clinging even more tightly to Dallas's big hand. "Okay," she said finally. "But he has to promise to keep the information to himself. Can I trust him to do that?"

"Yes," Eb said with certainty.

"All right, then. When can we do it?"

"Tomorrow after school," Eb said. "I'll get Cy Parks to run into him 'accidentally' and slip him a note, so that Lopez won't get suspicious."

Jessica's head moved to rest on Dallas's shoulder. "I wish I'd done things differently. So many people at risk, all because I didn't do my job properly."

"But you did," Dallas said at once, sliding a protective arm around her. "You did what any one of us would do. And you did put Lopez away. It's not your fault that he slipped out of the country."

Jessica smiled. "Thanks."

"You going to marry my mama, Dallas?" Stevie piped up.

"Stevie!" Jessica exclaimed.

"Yes, I am," Dallas said, chuckling at Jessica's red face. "She just doesn't know it yet. How do you feel about that, Stevie?"

"That would be great!" he said enthusiastically. "You and me can watch wrestling together!"

"Yes, we can." Dallas kissed Jess's hair gently and looked at his son with proud, possessive eyes.

Sally, watching them, knew that everything was going to be all right for Jessica, once they were out of this mess. She'd be free to marry Eb and she'd never have to worry about her aunt or her cousin again. Even more important, Jessica would be loved. That meant everything to Sally.

EB FOLLOWED THEM to school the next morning, keeping a safe distance. But there were no attempts on them along the way, and once they were inside the building, Sally felt safe. She and Stevie went right along to her class, smiling and greeting teachers and other children they knew.

"It's gonna be all right, isn't it, Aunt Sally?" Stevie asked at the door to her classroom.

"Yes, I think it is," she said with a warm smile.

She checked her lesson plan while the students filed into the classroom. A boy at the back of the room made a face and caught Sally's attention.

"Miss Johnson, there's a puddle of something that smells horrible back here!"

She got up from her desk and went to see. There was, indeed, a puddle. "I'll just go and get one of the janitors," she said with a smile.

But as she started out the door, a tall, quiet man appeared with a mop and pail.

"Hi, Harry," she said to him.

"Hard to be inside today when it's so nice outside," he said with a rueful smile. "I should be sitting on the river in my boat right now."

She smiled. "I'm sorry. But it's a good thing for us that you're here."

He started to wheel the bucket and mop away when one of the wheels came off the bucket. He muttered something and bent to look.

"I'll have to carry it. Can I get one of these young-sters to help me carry the mop?" he asked.

"I'll go!" Stevie volunteered at once.

"Yes, of course," Sally said. "Would you rather I went with you?"

He shook his head. "No need. This strong young man can manage a mop, can't you, son?" he asked with a big grin.

"Sure can!" Stevie said, hefting the mop over one shoulder.

"Let's away then, my lad," the man joked. "I'll send him right back, so he won't miss any class," he promised.

"Okay."

She watched Stevie go down the crowded hall behind Harry. It wasn't quite time for class to start, and she didn't think anything of the incident. Until five minutes later, when Stevie hadn't reappeared.

She left a monitor in charge of her class and went down the hall to the janitor's closet. There was the broken bucket, and the mop, but Stevie was nowhere in sight. But the janitor was. He'd been knocked out. She went straight to the office to phone Eb and call the paramedics. Fortunately Harry only had a slight concussion. To be safe, he was taken to the hospital for observation. Sally felt sick. She should have realized that Lopez might send someone to the school. Why had she been so gullible?

Eb arrived at the front office with the police chief, Chet Blake, and two of his officers. They went from door to door, combing the school. But Stevie was no longer there. One of the other janitors remembered seeing a stranger leave the building with the little boy and get into a brown pickup truck in the parking lot.

With that information, the police put out a bulletin. But it was too late. They found the pickup truck minutes later, abandoned in another parking lot, at a grocery store. Stevie was nowhere to be seen.

THEY WAITED BY the telephone that afternoon for the call that was sure to come. When it did, Eb had to bite down hard on what he wanted to say. Jessica and Sally had been in tears ever since he brought Sally home to the ranch.

"Now," the voice came in a slow, accented drawl, "Stevie's mother will give me the name I want. Or her son will never come home."

"She had to be sedated," Eb said, thinking fast. "She's out cold."

"You have one hour. Not a second longer." The line went dead.

Eb cursed roundly.

"Now what do we do?" Sally asked.

He phoned Cy Parks. "Did you get that message sent for me?" he asked.

"Yes. Scramble the signal."

Eb touched a button on the phone. "Shoot."

Cy gave him a telephone number. "He should be there by now. What can I do to help?"

Eb didn't have to be told that the news about Stevie's abduction was all over town. "Nothing. Wish me luck."

"You know it."

He hung up. Eb dialed the other number and waited. It rang once. Twice. Three times. Four times.

"Come on!" Eb growled impatiently.

On the fifth ring, the receiver was lifted.

"Rodrigo?" Eb asked at once.

"Yes."

"I'm going to put Jessica on the line, and leave the room. She'll give you a name. You know what to do with it."

"Okay."

Eb gave the receiver to Jessica and motioned everybody out of the communications room. He closed the door.

Jessica felt the receiver in her hands and took a deep breath. "The name of my informant was Isabella Medina," she said quietly. "She worked as a housekeeper for…"

There was an intake of breath on the other end of the line. "But surely you knew?" he asked at once.

"Knew what?" Jessica stammered.

"Isabella was found washed up on the rocks in Cancún, just before Lopez's capture," Rodrigo said abruptly. "She is long dead."

"Oh, good Lord," Jessica gasped.

"How could you not know?" he demanded.

Jessica wiped her forehead with a shaking hand. "I lost touch with her just before the trial. I assumed that she'd gone undercover to escape vengeance from Lopez. She wasn't going to testify, after all. She only gave me sources of hard information that I could use to prosecute him. Afterward, there were only three people

who knew about her involvement, and they died under rather...mysterious circumstances."

"This is the name Lopez wants?" he asked.

"Yes," she said miserably. "He's got my son!"

"Then you lose nothing by giving him the name," he said quietly. "Do you?"

"No. But he may not even remember her..."

"He was in love with her," Rodrigo said coldly. "His women have a habit of washing up on beaches. The last, a young singer in a Cancún nightclub, died only weeks ago at his hands. There is no proof, of course," he added coldly. "The official cause of death was suicide."

He sounded as though the matter was personal. She hesitated to ask. "You knew the singer?" she ventured.

There was a pause. "Yes. She was...my sister."

"I'm very sorry."

"So am I. Give Lopez the name. It will pacify him and spare your son any more adventures. He will not harm the boy," he added at once. "I think you must know this already."

"I do. At least he has one virtue among so many vices. But it doesn't ease the fear."

"Of course not. Tell Scott I'll be in touch, and not to contact me again. When I have something concrete, I'll call him."

"I'll tell him. Thank you."

"De nada." He hung up.

She went into the other room, feeling her way along the wall.

"Well?" Sally asked.

"My informant is dead," Jessica said sadly. "Lopez killed her, and I never knew. I thought she'd escaped and maybe changed her name."

"What now?" Sally asked miserably.

"I give Lopez the name," Jessica replied. "It will harm no one now. She was so brave. She actually worked in his house and pretended to care about him, just so that she could find enough evidence to convict him. Her father and mother, and her sister, had been gunned down in their village by his men, because they spoke to a government unit about the drug smuggling. She was sick with fear and grief, but she was willing to do anything to stop him." She shook her head. "Poor woman."

"A brave soul," Eb said quietly. "I'm sorry."

"Me, too," Jessica said. She wrapped her arms around herself, feeling chilled. "What if Lopez won't believe me?"

"You know," Eb said quietly, "I think he will."

"Let's hope so," Dallas agreed, his eyes narrow and dark with worry.

Sally put a loving arm around her aunt. "We'll get Stevie back," she said gently. "Everything's going to be okay."

Jessica hugged her back tearfully. "What would I do without you?" she whispered huskily.

Sally exchanged a long look with Dallas. She smiled. "I think you're going to find out very soon," she teased. "And I'll be your bridesmaid."

"Matron of honor," Eb corrected with soft, tender eyes.

"What?" Jessica exclaimed.

"I'm going to marry your niece, Jess," Eb said gently. "I always meant to, you know. And," he added with mock solemnity, "it does seem the least I can do, con-

sidering that she's saved herself for me all these years, despite the blatant temptations of college life…"

"Temptations," Sally chuckled. "If you only knew!"

"Explain that," Eb challenged.

She let go of Jessica and went close to him, sliding her arms naturally around his hard waist. "As if there's a man on the planet who could compare with you," she murmured, and reached up to kiss his chin. Her eyes literally glowed with love. "There never was any competition. There never could be."

Eb lifted an eyebrow. "I could return the compliment," he said in a deep, quiet tone. "You're in a class all your own, Sally mine."

She laid her cheek against his hard chest. "They'll give Stevie back, won't they?" she asked after a minute.

"Yes," he said, utterly certain.

Sally glanced at Jessica, who was close beside Dallas now, leaning against him. They looked as if they'd always belonged together. Things had to turn out all right for them. They just had to. Lopez might have one virtue, but Sally wasn't at all sure that Eb was right. She only prayed that Stevie would be returned when Jess gave up the informant's name. If Lopez did keep his word, and that seemed certain, there was a chance. She had to hope it was a good one.

CHAPTER ELEVEN

IN EXACTLY AN HOUR from the time Lopez hung up, the phone rang again. Eb let Jessica answer it.

"Hello," she said quietly.

"The name," Lopez replied tersely.

She took a slow breath. "I want you to understand that I would never have given up my informant under ordinary circumstances. But nothing I say can harm her now. I only found out today that she's beyond your vengeance. So it doesn't matter anymore if you know who she was."

"Who…she was?" Lopez asked, his voice hesitant.

"Yes. Was. Her name was Isabella…"

His indrawn breath was so harsh that Jessica almost felt it. "Isabella," he bit off. There was a tense pause. "Isabella."

"I lost touch with her before your trial," Jessica said curtly. "I assumed that she'd gone away and taken on another identity to escape being found out. I didn't know that she was dead already."

Still, Lopez said nothing. The silence went on for so long that Jessica thought the connection was cut.

"Hello?" she asked.

There was another intake of breath. "I loved her," he spat. "In my life, there was no other woman I trusted so

much. But she wanted nothing to do with me. I should have known. I should have realized!"

"You killed her, didn't you?" Jessica said coldly.

"Yes," he said, and he didn't sound violent. He sounded oddly subdued. "I never meant to. But I lashed out in a moment's rage, and then it was too late, and all my regrets would not bring her back to life." He drew another breath. "She was close enough to me that she knew things no one else was permitted to know. It occurred to me that she was asking far too many questions, but I was conceited enough to believe she cared for me." There was another brief pause. "The boy will be returned at once. You will find him at the strip mall in the toy store in five minutes. He will not be harmed. You have my word. Nor will you ever be threatened by me again. I...regret...many things," he added in an odd tone, and the line went dead abruptly.

Jessica caught her breath, still holding the receiver in her hand, as if it had life.

"Well?" Dallas asked impatiently.

She felt for the instrument and replaced the receiver with slow deliberation. "He said that Stevie would be in the toy store in the strip mall, in five minutes, unharmed." Her eyes closed. "Unharmed."

Eb motioned Dallas toward Jessica.

"Let's go," he said tersely.

"What if he lied?" Jessica asked as Dallas escorted her out to the big sports utility vehicle Eb drove.

"We both know that Lopez is a man of his word, regardless of his bloody reputation," Dallas said tersely. "We have to hope that he told the truth."

Jessica nibbled on her fingernails all the way to the mall, which was only about six minutes away from Eb's

ranch. She sat close beside Dallas in the back seat, holding his hand tightly. Sally glanced back at them, silently praying all the way, worried for all of them, but especially for little Stevie. Her hand felt for Eb's and he grasped it tightly, sparing her a reassuring smile.

The minutes seemed like hours as they sped into town. Eb had no sooner parked the vehicle in the parking lot than Jessica was out the door, hurrying with Dallas right beside her to guide her steps.

Eb and Sally followed the couple into the small toy store, and there was Stevie, sitting on the floor, playing with a mechanical elephant that walked and lifted its trunk and trumpeted.

"It's Stevie," Dallas said huskily. "He's...fine!"

"Where? Stevie!" Jessica called brokenly, holding out her arms.

"Hi, Mom!" Stevie exclaimed, leaving the toy to run into her arms. "Gosh, I was scared, but the man taught me how to play poker and gave me a soda! He said I was brave and he admired my courage! Were you scared, Mom?"

Jessica was crying so hard that she could barely speak at all. She hugged her child close and couldn't seem to let him go, even when he wiggled.

"Let his dad have a little of this joyful reunion," Dallas murmured dryly, holding out his arms.

Stevie went right into them and hugged him hard. "I don't have a real dad now," he said, "but you're going to be a great dad, Dallas! You and me will go to all the wrestling matches and take Mom and describe everything to her, won't we?"

"Yes," Dallas said, his voice husky, his eyes bright

as he rocked his child in his arms with mingled relief and affection. "We'll do that."

Jessica felt her way into Dallas's arms with Stevie and pressed there for a long moment. Beside them, Sally held tight to Eb's hand and smiled with pure relief.

"I had an adventure," Stevie said when his parents let go of him. "But it's nice to be home again. Can I have that elephant? He sure is neat!"

"You can have a whole circus if I can find one for sale," Dallas laughed huskily. "But for now, I think we'll go back to the ranch."

They paid for the elephant and got into the truck with Eb and Sally.

"Can you drop us off at our house?" Jessica asked Eb.

There was a hesitation. She heard it and smiled.

"Lopez said that he had no more business with me," Jessica told him. "He didn't even question what I told him," she added. "He said that Isabella was always asking him questions and pretending to care about him. He knew she didn't. He did sound very sorry that he killed her. Perhaps the small part of him that's still human can feel remorse. Who knows?"

"One day," Dallas said curtly, "we'll catch up with him. This isn't over, you know, even if he is through making threats toward you and Stevie. He's going to pay for this. And, somehow, we're going to stop him from setting up business in Jacobsville."

"We have Rodrigo in place," Eb agreed, "and Cy watching the progress of the warehouse. It won't be easy, but if we're careful, we may cut his source of supply and his distribution network right in half. Cut off the head and the snake dies."

"Amen," Dallas replied.

DALLAS GOT OUT of the sports utility vehicle with Jessica and Stevie, waving the other couple off with a big smile.

"You really believe Lopez meant it when he said he was quits with Jessica?" Sally asked, still not quite convinced of the outlaw's sincerity.

"Yes, I do," Eb replied, glancing at her with a smile. "He's a snake, but his word is worth something."

Sally turned her head toward Eb and studied his profile warmly, with soft, covetous eyes.

He glanced over and met that look. His own eyes narrowed. "A lot has happened since last night," he said quietly. "Do you still mean what you told me at dawn?"

"That I'd marry you?" she asked.

He nodded.

"Oh, yes," she said, "I meant every word. I want to live with you all my life."

"It won't bother you to have professional mercenaries running around the place at all hours for a while?" he teased.

She grinned. "Why should it? I am, after all, a mercenary's woman."

"Not quite yet," he murmured with a wry glance. "And very soon, a mercenary's wife."

"That sounds very respectable," she commented.

"I'm glad you waited for me, Sally," he said seriously.

"So am I." She slid her hand into his big one and held on tight. It tingled all the way up her arm.

"We've had enough excitement for today," he said. "But tomorrow we'll see about getting the license. Do you want a justice of the peace or a minister to marry us?"

"A minister," she said at once. "I want a permanent marriage."

He nodded. "So do I. And you have to have a white gown with a veil."

Her eyebrows arched.

"You're not just a mercenary's woman, you're a virtuous mercenary's woman. I want to watch you float down the aisle to me covered in silk and satin and lace, and with a veil for me to lift after we've said our vows."

She smiled with her whole heart. "That would be nice. There's a little boutique…"

"We'll fly up to Dallas and get one at Neiman Marcus."

She gasped.

"You're marrying a rich man," he pointed out. "Humor me. It's going to be a social event. Let me deck you out like a comet."

She laughed. "All right. I'd really love a white wedding, if you don't mind."

"And we'll both wear rings," he added. "We'll get those in Dallas, too."

Her eyes were full of dreams as she looked at her future husband hungrily. There was only one small worry. "Eb, about Maggie…"

"Maggie is a closed chapter," he told her. "I adored her, in my way, but she was never in love with me. I stood in Cord's shadow even then, and she never realized it. She still hasn't." He glanced at her and smiled. "I love you, you know," he murmured, watching her eyes light up. "I'd never have proposed if I hadn't."

"I love you, too, Eb," she said solemnly. "I always will."

His fingers curled tighter into hers. "Dreams really do come true."

She wouldn't have argued with that statement to save her life, and she said so.

IT WAS THE society event of the year in Jacobsville, eclipsed only by Simon Hart's wedding with the governor giving Tira away. There were no major celebrities at Eb and Sally's wedding, but Eb did have a conglomeration of mercenaries and government agents the like of which Jacobsville had never seen. Cord Romero was sitting with Maggie on the groom's side of the church, along with a tall, striking dark-haired man with a small mustache and neat brief beard. Beside him was a big blond man who made even Dallas look shorter. On the pew across from him, on Sally's side of the church, was a blue-eyed brunette who avoided looking at the big blond man. Sally recognized her as Callie, the stepsister of the big blond man, who was Eb's friend Micah Steele.

A number of men in suits filled the rest of the groom's pews. Some were wearing sunglasses inside. Others were watching the people on the bride's side of the church, which wasn't packed, since Sally hadn't been back in Jacobsville long enough to make close friends in the community. Jessica was there with Stevie and Dallas, of course.

Sally walked down the aisle all by herself, since she hadn't contacted either of her parents about her wedding. They had their own lives now, and neither of them had written to Sally since the breakup of their family when she moved in with Jessica. She didn't really mind going it alone. Somehow, under the circumstances, it even seemed appropriate. She wore a dream of a wedding gown, with yards and yards of delicate lace and a train, and a veil that accentuated her blond beauty.

Eb stood at the altar waiting for her, in a gray vested suit with a white rose in his lapel. He turned as she

joined him, and looked down at her with eyes that made her knees weak.

The ceremony was brief, but poignant, and when Eb lifted the veil to kiss her for the first time as her husband, tears welled up in her eyes as his mouth tenderly claimed hers. They held hands going back down the aisle, wearing matching simple gold bands. Outside the church, they were pelted with rice and good wishes. Laughing, Sally tossed her bouquet and Dallas intercepted it to make sure it landed in Jessica's hands.

They climbed into the rented limousine and minutes later, they were at Eb's ranch, pausing just long enough to change into traveling clothes and rush to the private airstrip to board a loaned Learjet for the trip to Puerto Vallarta, Mexico, for their brief honeymoon.

The trip was tiring, and so was the aftermath of the day's excitement. Sally climbed into the huge whirlpool bath while Eb made dinner reservations for that evening.

She didn't realize that she wasn't alone until Eb climbed down into the water with her. He chuckled at her expression and then he kissed her. Very soon, she forgot all about her shock at the first sight of her unclothed bridegroom in the joy of an embrace that knew no obstacles.

He kissed her until she was clinging, gasping for breath and shivering with pleasure.

"Where?" he whispered, stroking her tenderly, enjoying her reactions to her first real intimacy. "Here, or in the bed?"

She could barely speak. "In bed," she said huskily.

"That suits me."

He got out and turned off the jets, lifting her clear

of the water to towel them both dry. He picked her up and carried her quickly into the bedroom, barely taking time to strip down the covers before he fell with her onto crisp, clean sheets.

She knew that first times were notoriously painful, embarrassing, and uncomfortable, but hers was a notable exception. Eb was skillful and slow, arousing her to a hot frenzy of response before he even began to touch her intimately. By the time his body slid down against hers in stark possession, she was lifting toward him and pleading for an end to the violent tension of pleasure he'd aroused in her.

Her breath jerked out at his ear at the slow, steady invasion of her most private place in a silence that magnified the least little sound. She heard his heartbeat, and her own, increase with every careful thrust of his hips. She heard his breathing, erratic, rough, mingling with her own excited little moans.

She felt one lean hand sliding up her bare leg as he turned and shifted his weight against her, and when he touched her high on her inner thigh in a rhythm like the descent of his body, she arched up toward him and groaned in anguish.

He laughed softly at her temple while he increased the rhythm and caressed her in the most outrageous ways, all the while whispering things so shocking that she gasped. Tossed between waves of pleasure that grew with each passing second, she found herself suddenly suspended somewhere high above reality as she went over some intangible cliff and fell shuddering with ecstasy into a white-hot oblivion.

She felt him there with her, felt his pleasure in her body, felt his own release even as hers threatened to last

forever. She wondered dimly if she was going to survive the incredible delight of it. She shivered helplessly as pleasure washed over her and she clung harder to the source of it, pleading for him not to stop.

When she was finally exhausted and barely able to catch her breath, he tucked her close in his arms and pulled the sheet over them.

"Sleep now," he whispered, kissing her forehead.

"Like this?" she asked unsteadily.

"Just like this." He wrapped her closer. "We'll sleep a little. And then…"

"And then."

The dinner reservations went unclaimed. Through the long night, she learned more than she'd ever dreamed about men and bodies and lovemaking. For a first time, she told her delighted husband, it was quite extraordinary.

They had breakfast in bed and then set out to explore the old city. But by evening, they were exploring each other again.

A WEEK LATER, they arrived back home at Eb's ranch, to find a flurry of new activity. A local undercover DEA agent, whose wife Lisa Monroe lived on a ranch next door to Cy Parks, had been found murdered. Apparently he'd infiltrated Lopez's organization and been discovered. Rodrigo was still undercover, and Eb was concerned for him. The warehouse next door to Cy was in the final stages of construction. Things were heating up in Jacobsville.

"At least we had a honeymoon," Eb murmured dryly, hugging his new wife close.

"So we did," she agreed. She looked up at him lovingly. "And now you're back off adventuring."

"Well, so are you," he pointed out. "After all, isn't teaching second-graders a daily adventure as well?"

She hugged him close. "Being married to you is the biggest adventure, but you have to promise not to ever get shot at again."

"I give you my word as a Girl Scout," he murmured dryly.

She punched him in the stomach. "And if you wade into battle, I'll be right there beside you holding spare cartridges."

He searched her eyes. "You really are a hell of a woman," he murmured.

She grinned. "I'm glad you noticed."

"Lucky me," he said only half facetiously, and bent to kiss her with unbridled passion. "Lucky, lucky me!" he added while he could manage speech.

Sally wrapped her arms around him and held on tight, as intoxicated with pleasure as he was. There would always be the threat of danger, but nothing that the mercenary and his woman couldn't handle. But for the moment, she had her soldier of fortune right where she wanted him—in her gentle, loving arms.

* * * * *

Also by Delores Fossen

Harlequin Intrigue

Saddle Ridge Justice

The Sheriff's Baby
Protecting the Newborn
Tracking Down the Lawman's Son
Child in Jeopardy

Silver Creek Lawmen: Second Generation

Targeted in Silver Creek
Maverick Detective Dad
Last Seen in Silver Creek
Marked for Revenge

The Law in Lubbock County

Sheriff in the Saddle
Maverick Justice
Lawman to the Core
Spurred to Justice

Visit her Author Profile page
at Harlequin.com for more titles.

SAFETY BREACH

Delores Fossen

CHAPTER ONE

THE MOMENT THAT Gemma Hanson opened her front door, she heard something she didn't want to hear.

Silence.

There were no pulsing beeps from the security system. No flare of the bead of red light on the panel, warning her that she had ten seconds to disarm it or the alarms would sound. That meant someone had tampered with it.

The killer had found her.

The fear came, cold and sharp like a gleaming razor slicing through her, and it brought the memories right along with it. Nothing though, not even the fear, was as scalpel sharp as those images that tore into her mind.

She dropped the bag of groceries and the gob of keys she'd been holding, and Gemma grabbed the snub-nosed .38 from her purse. Just holding the weapon created a different kind of panic inside her because in the back of her mind, she knew that it wouldn't be enough to stop *him*.

No.

This time the killer would get to her. This time, he would finish what he'd started a year ago and make sure that the ragged breaths she was dragging in and out were the last ones she would ever take.

She forced herself to go as still as she could. Tried

to steady her heartbeat, too, so she could listen for any sound of him in the small house. It wouldn't do any good to run. She'd learned that the hard way the last time he'd come after her—because running had been exactly what he'd expected her to do.

Maybe even what he'd *wanted* her to do.

It had been a game to him, and he'd been ready. Good at it, too. That's how he'd been able to fire three bullets into her before she'd barely taken a step.

"Where are you?" Gemma asked, still standing in the doorway. A whisper was all she could manage with her throat clamped tight, but the sound still carried through the quiet house. Too quiet. As silent as the grave.

He didn't answer, no one did, so Gemma tried again. This time, though, she used his name.

"Eric?"

She got out more than a whisper with that try. Her voice actually sounded a whole lot stronger than she felt, but any strength, fake or otherwise, wouldn't scare him off. If Eric Lang had any fears, Gemma had never been able to figure them out, and uncovering that sort of thing was her specialty.

Had been her specialty, she mentally corrected.

These days, she didn't teach criminal justice classes and didn't assist the FBI with creating criminal profiles for serial killers like Eric. Instead, she input data for a research group, a low-level computer job that the marshals had arranged for her. The only talent she had now was getting easily spooked and having nightmares.

And speaking of being spooked, every nerve inside her went on full alert when she heard the sound of the engine. Gemma automatically brought up the gun as she'd been trained to do. She forced herself not to pull

the trigger though. Good thing, too, because it wasn't Eric. However, it was someone who shouldn't be here.

Sheriff Kellan Slater.

Gemma instantly recognized him even from this distance and behind the windshield of the unfamiliar blue truck. Of course, it would have been hard not to notice Kellan. The cowboy cop was tall, lanky...unforgettable. Gemma knew because she'd had zero success in forgetting him.

Kellan got out of his truck, but he stopped when he spotted her .38, and he pulled out his gun in a slick, fluid motion. "Is Eric Lang here?" he called out.

That didn't ease her thudding heartbeat. Even though she hadn't seen Kellan in the year since her attack, Gemma hoped this was his version of a social visit. Not that they had any reason to be social, now that the hurt and blame was between them. However, if he hadn't come here to find out how she was, then perhaps he'd tell her that she was imagining things. That her WIT-SEC identity hadn't been compromised, that no one had actually tampered with her security system and that she was safe.

But Kellan wasn't giving her much of a reassuring look.

With his gaze firing all around them, he hurried onto the porch, automatically catching on to her arm and pushing her behind him. Protecting her. Which only confirmed to her that she needed to be protected.

"Is Eric here?" Kellan repeated.

Gemma knew this was going to make her sound crazy. "I haven't actually seen him since the night he attacked me, but someone turned off my security system." She swallowed hard before she added the rest.

"I sensed he was here. And I think he's been watching me. He found me."

Those last three words had not been easy to say, and they'd had to make their way through the muscles in her throat that felt as if they were strangling her.

Even though Kellan hadn't given her much reassurance before, she waited for some now. But he didn't give her any. "Are you sure you just didn't forget to set the alarm when you went out?"

Gemma wanted to laugh, but it definitely wouldn't be from humor. "I'm positive."

Even though she was living her fake life with a fake name that the marshals had given her, all the steps didn't mean she was safe. Gemma knew that, and it was why she was obsessive about taking precautions. Not just with arming the security system but carrying the .38.

"Do you know for sure if anyone's actually inside the house?" Kellan pressed.

Gemma shook her head, and she was about to explain that she'd stopped in the doorway. No explanation was necessary though. Because that's when Kellan glanced down at the floor where she'd dropped her groceries and keys. It was the kind of sweeping glance that cops made, and while Kellan didn't exactly look like most cops, he was a blue blood to the core. A third-generation sheriff of Longview Ridge, Texas—their hometown.

Of course, he'd only gotten that sheriff's badge after his own father had been murdered, and she knew Kellan would have gladly given it up to have his father back.

"Stay right next to me," Kellan insisted, and he stepped into the small entry. The moment they were both inside, he motioned for her to shut the door.

Gemma did, and while she kept a firm grip on her

gun, they stood there, listening. With her body sand-wiched between Kellan and the door. The back of him pressed against the front of her.

It stirred different kinds of memories.

Of the heat that had once simmered between them. Of the long, lingering looks that he'd once given her with gunmetal eyes. Of the way his rough hands had skimmed over her body. Years ago, they'd been lovers but had drifted apart when she'd left for college. They'd found their way back to each other and likely would have landed in bed again if Eric hadn't struck first. After that, well, Kellan no longer wanted her that way.

Because he blamed her for his father's death.

Of course, he blamed himself, too, which had put an even bigger wedge between them. Kellan would never be able to forgive himself for what'd happened, and Gemma wasn't sure she could forgive him for not being able to stop it.

All that lack of forgiveness was why she knew some-thing was horribly wrong. This was the last place Kel-lan would have wanted to come, and she was the last person he'd want to try to protect.

"Wait here while I have a look around," Kellan in-sisted. "And lock the door. If you hear anything, and I mean anything, get down on the floor." He glanced back over his shoulder at her, and she saw that his jaw had tightened even more than it had been when he'd first arrived. "Understand?" he added.

There was a lot of anger and old baggage in that *un-derstand*. The last time she hadn't listened to a sheriff, she'd nearly been killed and two people had been mur-dered. Maybe three since one of the possible victims,

Caroline Moser, was still missing and presumed dead. She would definitely listen this time.

Kellan stepped away from her, heading first to the kitchen, where he checked the pantry. Since the living room, dining room and kitchen were all open, she had no trouble seeing him, but that changed when he went into the bedrooms. First hers and then the guest room. Gemma just stood there, waiting and praying. If Eric was indeed inside, she didn't want him claiming another victim.

Especially a victim who was trying to protect her.

That's what Kellan's father, Buck, had been doing the night Eric had gunned down him and his deputy. Then Eric had escaped and hadn't been seen in the past year. But unlike the people he'd murdered that night, Eric was very much alive. Gemma could feel that all the way down to her breath and bones.

It seemed to take an eternity or two, but Kellan finally came out from the bedrooms, and he shook his head. "He's not here, but your bedroom window was open. I'm guessing you didn't leave it that way?"

The air stalled in her throat, and it took her a moment to answer. "No. I've never opened that window." Heck, the only times she'd ever opened the curtains was to make sure the window was closed and locked.

He nodded, and the grunt he made let her know that it was the answer he'd expected. "So, someone's been here. Maybe Eric." He went to the keypad for the alarm, brushing against her arm as he walked by her. It was barely a touch, but she noticed.

So did Kellan.

Their gazes connected for a split second before he mumbled some profanity and looked away. He sounded

disgusted with himself. Maybe because he didn't want to feel that quick punch of attraction. Gemma didn't want to feel it, either. It was a distraction, and something like that could get them both killed.

Kellan took out his phone and texted someone. Perhaps one of his brothers who were all in law enforcement. Gemma took out her phone, too, ready to call her handler, Marshal Amanda Hardin, but Kellan shook his head.

"Don't involve your handler yet," he said. "There's been a leak, and I haven't discovered the source."

Gemma lost what little breath she'd managed to regain, and because she had no choice, she leaned against the wall for support. Kellan helped, too. Well, he did after he muttered more of that profanity. He took hold of her arm, marched her to the sofa and had her sit before he went to the window. Keeping watch.

"What happened?" she asked. "Tell me about the leak."

He glanced back at her, his tight jaw letting her know she should brace herself, that what he was about to say would be bad news. "There's been another murder."

Gemma was glad she was sitting down, but she had to shake her head. Kellan was a sheriff, and while Longview Ridge wasn't exactly a hotbed of crime, murders did happen there. That was something that Kellan and she both had too much experience with. However, Gemma couldn't figure out why a murder there would have brought Kellan here to her WITSEC house in Austin, a good ninety miles from Longview Ridge. Unless...

"Did Eric kill someone else?" she managed to say.

Kellan's hesitation confirmed that that was indeed

what had happened. "We found the body about two hours ago."

Two hours. That meant Kellan had left the crime scene and come straight to her. "Who was killed?" she snapped.

Judging from the way his forehead bunched up, he didn't want to tell her. But then she knew it was connected to her, or Kellan wouldn't be here. "Iris Kirby," he finally answered.

That felt like the slam of another bullet into her. Oh, God. Iris. Gemma knew her, of course. She knew almost everyone in Longview Ridge. Iris had been her favorite teacher in high school.

Gemma wasn't sure she could stomach hearing the answer to this, but it was a question she had to ask. "You're sure she was murdered? And how do you know it was Eric?"

Without taking his attention from the window, he pulled up a photo on his phone and handed it to her. "That was left at the crime scene. And as for how we know it's murder, Iris died from three gunshot wounds to the torso."

The slams and punches just kept coming, and each of them brought one more wave of the nightmarish images. That's because Eric had shot both Gemma and Kellan's father three times. She supposed Eric considered that his signature. One of them anyway. Leaving notes at the crime scenes was the other. And the picture on Kellan's phone was that of a note.

"'Too late again, Sheriff Slater,'" she read aloud. "'Tell Gemma that Iris didn't suffer. I made it fast as a favor to her. And then tell Gemma that she's next. I

know where to find her. Three-twenty-three East Lane, Austin. Our girl didn't go too far, did she?'"

As hard as it was to read those words, Gemma tamped down the rising fear and tried to view this as a profiler. The note was meant to taunt Kellan and her.

And it had.

Along with twisting her insides into knots. Judging from the tight muscles in Kellan's body, it had done the same to him. However, this wasn't proof there had been a breach in WITSEC.

"How would Eric have gotten access to WITSEC files?" she mumbled.

Gemma waved it off though before Kellan could even speculate. Eric was smart, and he was a whiz with computers. He'd even joked once that he would have made a fairly decent hacker, and then had added to the joke that Caroline and she would have made even better ones. Eric wouldn't have needed help from anyone in WITSEC to get into the files because he could have done it himself.

"So, Eric knows where I am," she concluded. "He killed Iris to…what? Send me into a panic? A rage, maybe? To hurt me by murdering someone I knew? Because panicked, angry people don't always think straight, and they make mistakes."

Kellan huffed. "Best to save your criminal analysis for Eric. When the FBI was looking for him, he was right under your nose, and you didn't even know it."

Because Kellan glanced at her again when he said that, she saw the glare in his eyes. She saw it soften, too, when he regretted giving her that jab.

But in this case, it was true, and she deserved any jab he might send her way. That's because Eric had been

her student in a criminal justice class before she'd made him her intern. He'd worked side by side with her, case by case, and until the night he'd tried to murder her, she hadn't known he was a serial killer.

That was the ultimate taunting.

"I believe Eric was here," Kellan continued a moment later. "He killed Iris last night so he had plenty of time to get from Longview Ridge to Austin. Plenty of time to watch you and wait for you to leave so he could break into your house."

Yes, but why hadn't Eric just stayed and waited for her? Had he found out Kellan was coming, and Eric hadn't wanted to deal with a lawman? Especially one who wanted him dead.

Still, that didn't feel right.

Of course, she'd learned the hard way that it was a mistake to trust her feelings when it came to Eric.

"There's Owen," Kellan said, his voice shattering the silence.

Owen, as in his brother Deputy Owen Slater. And he was yet someone else who would want to face down Eric.

"Owen's been working with Austin PD to set up spotters on the road," Kellan added. "Don't worry, Owen didn't tell the local cops who you really are. He said you're a witness in an upcoming trial and that we need to get you back to Longview Ridge."

Her legs suddenly felt like glass, but she forced herself to stand. Gemma also glanced out the window. Owen was indeed out there, sitting behind the wheel of a black car.

"Are you really taking me to Longview Ridge?" she asked.

"Best not to say where we're going in case Eric bugged the place."

Oh, mercy. She hadn't even thought of that. But she should have. Eric had succeeded in rattling her, and he had likely figured that was the first step in getting to her.

"Don't bring anything with you," Kellan instructed when she reached for her purse.

Yes, because Eric could have planted tracking devices on clothes or anything else in the house. She'd had her purse with her when she'd gotten groceries, but maybe Eric had managed to put a tracker on it before that quick shopping trip. Or even while she was at the store. She couldn't take her phone either because he could use it to pinpoint her location. Then, he could follow wherever Kellan was taking her.

Kellan motioned toward his brother, and Owen got out of the car. Like Kellan, he already had his weapon drawn, which meant any of her neighbors could see that and become alarmed. Maybe alarmed enough to come outside and try to figure out what was going on. No one had shown much interest in her in the nine months she'd been there, and now wouldn't be a good time to start.

"Move fast," Kellan said, and that was the only warning she got before he took hold of her, positioning her right next to him. He opened the door and got them moving.

"Aww, don't be that way," someone said.

Eric.

The voice came from behind them, from inside the house, and Kellan must have recognized it, too, because he dragged her to the ground next to the concrete steps.

"Don't leave before we have time to play," Eric joked.

And the killer laughed just as the shot blasted through the air.

CHAPTER TWO

HELL. KELLAN WANTED to kick himself for not getting to Gemma sooner so this wouldn't happen.

But he hadn't been sure who he could trust, hadn't known how the info about Gemma's location had been breached. His brother Jack was a marshal and would have been his normal contact for something like this, but Jack was in Arizona escorting a prisoner. That's why Kellan had tried to handle this himself.

Now none of that mattered because they could both be gunned down by a serial killer.

Kellan scrambled over Gemma, pushing her all the way to the ground so he could cover her with his body. It wasn't an ideal position, nothing about this was. They were literally out in the open with only the steps for cover. That wouldn't do squat to protect them if Eric came around the side of the house and through a back door. Of course, if he did that, then Owen would see him.

"Were either of you hit?" Owen called out.

Kellan shook his head and hoped that was true. Beneath him, Gemma was trembling. No doubt reliving a boatload of memories, too. But he couldn't tell if she'd been injured, and Kellan didn't want to risk moving off her to find out.

While Owen made a call, no doubt to get them

backup, his brother had taken up cover behind the door of the unmarked cruiser. It was bullet resistant, which meant if Kellan could get Gemma to it, she'd be a whole lot safer than she was here. But there was a good twenty feet of space between them and Owen. That was twenty feet that Eric could use to gun them down.

Well, maybe.

When Kellan had searched Gemma's house, Eric hadn't been inside. And Kellan had shut and relocked the open window along with checking to make sure no other locks had been tampered with. So, how had Eric gotten in?

Or had he?

There was something else off about this. The angle of the shot seemed to have been all wrong. It was hard to tell, but instead of coming from inside the house, the bullet had been fired more to the left side of it. If that's indeed where the shooter was, then he and Gemma wouldn't have been able to see him. Neither would Owen—which could be the exact reason the shot had been fired from there.

And that led him to something else that didn't fit.

Eric himself.

There was no reason for Eric to put himself in the middle of what could turn out to be a gunfight. Way too risky. No, he was more the lay-in-wait type, and if he'd truly wanted Gemma dead, he would have just waited inside and shot her when she'd opened the door. That would have given him a minute or two to flee before Kellan had even arrived.

So, who'd fired the shot? And where the hell was Eric?

"I think the voice we heard could have been a recording," Kellan whispered to Gemma.

She went still, obviously giving that some thought, then nodding. A recorder wouldn't have been that hard to hide if Eric had indeed managed to come in earlier through the window. Also, it would give Eric an advantage if they thought he was inside the house. That's where they would be pinpointing their focus when the real danger could be at the side of the house. Or even across the street from them.

That sent Kellan snapping in that direction. "Get down!" he yelled to Owen. Kellan hadn't actually seen anything, but a year of chasing Eric had told him to expect the unexpected when dealing with the snake.

Owen did drop down, putting his body behind the door. Just as another shot came. And just as Kellan had thought, this one came from a house directly across the street. This time, he got a glimpse of the shooter who'd fired out the second-story window. A bulky guy dressed all in black, and he was using a rifle with a scope. If Owen hadn't ducked when he had, he'd be dead.

Which might have been Eric's intent all along.

In addition to being a snake, Eric also liked to torment his victims, and killing Owen would have definitely accomplished that. Along with adding another huge layer of guilt and grief they were already feeling because of his father's murder.

"Hold your position," Kellan instructed Owen. "How long before the local cops get here?"

"About five minutes," Owen answered. "I've texted them to let them know about the gunfire."

That meant Austin PD wouldn't come in with guns blazing. They'd stay back, evaluating the situation while trying to figure how to get Gemma safely out of there. Kellan and Owen would be doing the same thing. Be-

cause Kellan didn't want anyone dying today. Eric had already claimed enough lives.

Another shot came—again from the second floor of the neighbor's house. The bullet blasted into the stone steps just inches from where he and Gemma were. Owen pivoted and returned fire. It worked because the gunman ducked out of sight. That didn't mean he was leaving, but the guy might think twice before appearing in the window again.

"I need to stop this," Gemma whispered, and she mumbled something else he didn't catch. "One of my neighbors could be hurt."

That could have already happened. The shooter could have harmed or killed anyone else who happened to be in that house just so he could use the window to launch the attack. However, it was also possible that her neighbor was working for Eric. Or maybe Eric had simply hired some thug to break into the house and fire the shots. Either way, Kellan wasn't seeing how Gemma would be able to do anything to put an end to this.

However, Gemma must have thought she could do something because she moved, levering herself up on her arms and lifting her head. "I'll try to bargain with Eric. It's me he wants."

Kellan put her right back down on the ground. "You don't know that. Don't get Owen and me killed because we're trying to protect you."

Yeah, it was harsh, but it worked because Gemma stayed put. Besides, it was partly true. He didn't wear a badge for decoration, and that meant he'd do whatever it took to keep her safe.

Even though Kellan seriously doubted that it was possible to negotiate with Eric, he took out his phone.

He was about to shout out for Eric to call him, but before he could do that, his cell rang, and he saw Unknown Caller pop up on the screen. He hit the answer button and put it on Speaker so he could keep his hands free in case he had to return fire.

"Want to talk, do you, Sheriff?" Eric asked.

Just hearing the sound of the killer's voice caused the anger to roar through Kellan. He hated this man for what he'd done, and Kellan wished he could reach through the phone line and end this piece of slime once and for all.

"Call off your hired thug," Kellan warned him.

"I will…in about four minutes, give or take some seconds. That's about when the city cops will get there."

Kellan wasn't sure if Eric had heard Owen say that, but it was just as possible the shooter across the street had relayed that info to him. Not just that info, either, but every move they were making. It was highly likely that Eric wasn't anywhere near Gemma's house.

"Why are you doing this? Why now?" Kellan demanded while he continued to keep watch around them.

That included keeping watch of Gemma.

Her breathing was way too fast now, and it was possible she was about to have a panic attack. God knew what kind of psychological damage had been done to her because of what had happened a year ago. Of course, she was hearing the voice of the man who'd nearly killed her, so Kellan doubted she was going to have much luck reining in her fear.

"Why now?" Eric repeated. "Well, duh. Because it's nearly the anniversary of your daddy's death. Which I'm sure you remember in nth detail. I'll bet Gemma remembers it, too."

They did. It was impossible to forget that in only three days, it would be a year since their lives had been turned upside down. And apparently Eric was going to make sure they recalled it by giving them a new set of grisly memories to go along with it.

Kellan tried to fight off the images from that night, but they came anyway. The storm with lightning slicing through the sky. Ironic that it was the lightning that had given him glimpses of what was going on. Just flashes of the horror that had started before Kellan had even gotten on the scene.

When Gemma had figured out too late that Eric was a serial killer the FBI had been after for years, she'd called the sheriff, Kellan's father, Buck, and he'd told Gemma to wait, not to confront Eric until he got there. Instead, she'd attempted to stop Eric when he tried to leave. Eric had then taken Gemma and her best friend/research assistant, Caroline Moser, hostage. Kellan's father, Buck, and another deputy, Dusty Walters, had gone in pursuit, only minutes ahead of Kellan who'd gotten the call after them.

His dad and Dusty had come upon Eric's vehicle that had skidded off the road because of the storm. The accident had happened in front of an abandoned hotel with the mocking name of Serenity Inn. A crumbling Victorian mansion with acres of overgrown gardens and dark windows that had looked like darkened eye sockets. Eric had forced the women at gunpoint onto the grounds, and Dusty and his father had followed.

That's when Kellan had arrived.

Just in time to hear the crack of the gunfire, and then seconds later, he'd seen his father lying, bleeding—dying—on the weed-choked, muddy ground.

Kellan had ordered Dusty to call for an ambulance and stay with Buck while he went in pursuit of Eric who had slipped into the house with the women. Because of more of those flashes of lightning, Kellan had seen Eric shoot Gemma in the shell of what had once been the grand foyer. He'd seen her collapse, and while he was saving her life by stopping the blood flow, Eric had escaped with Caroline in the dark maze of rooms, halls and stairs. Kellan hadn't even managed to get off a shot for fear of hitting Caroline.

For all the good that'd done.

While Kellan had been saving Gemma, Eric had shot through one of the windows at Dusty, killing the deputy instantly. Kellan hadn't known it then, but his father was already dead.

Later, they'd found Caroline's blood in one of the rooms. No body though. No Eric, either. Just a dead sheriff and deputy who'd been doing their jobs and an injured profiler who hadn't done her job nearly well enough.

"You screwed up the investigation," Eric went on. "You didn't get things right when it came to solving your father's murder."

"What the hell are you talking about? You killed him. I got that right," Kellan snapped. Then, he reminded himself, again, that Eric liked playing the tormenter, and what better way to do that than by implying that Kellan had botched something as important as the investigation that followed the murder and Gemma's attack?

"You need to take a second look at the details of your father's case. The devil is in those details," Eric went on. "That's what this warning is all about."

"Warning?" Kellan questioned. "You had someone shoot at us. That's more than a warning."

"My man didn't hit you, did he?" Eric said, his voice dripping with sarcasm.

In the distance, Kellan heard a welcome sound. Sirens from the responding police officers. Now, he had to hope that the cops' arrival didn't cause the gunman to open fire again.

"Time's running out," Eric added, which meant he'd likely heard the sirens, too. "Gotta go."

Of course, he wasn't staying around for this. And his hired gun must have felt the same way because Kellan saw him run from the window.

Getting away.

That was better than trying to gun them down again, but Kellan hated that the shooter would escape. Kellan wanted to chase down the idiot and make him pay for what he'd done. But that would mean leaving Gemma— and she'd then be an easy target for Eric.

"One more thing," Eric said. "My advice would be for you to run because things are about to get very… loud."

Eric ended the call, and it didn't take Kellan long, just a couple of seconds, for him to realize what was about to happen.

"Cover us," Kellan shouted to his brother.

He hooked his arm around Gemma's waist, dragging her to her feet, and with her in tow, Kellan started running toward the unmarked cruiser. Good thing, too.

Because behind them, Gemma's house exploded into a fireball.

CHAPTER THREE

GEMMA CLUTCHED HER hands into fists to try and stop herself from shaking. It didn't help, but maybe it made it less noticeable to Kellan who kept glancing at her while he carried on his phone conversations.

She hated feeling like this—with the nerves and fear all tangled in her stomach. But what she hated even more was that Eric and his hired gun had gotten away. She had no doubts, none, that they'd be back.

And this time, they might actually kill them.

"You need to put some distance between us," she told Kellan.

It wasn't the first time she'd said it, either. She'd repeated variations their entire time at the Austin Police Department. However, Kellan was doing the opposite of distancing himself, because he and Owen were taking her to Longview Ridge. Something she'd been opposed to the moment Kellan had told the Austin cops what he had planned for her.

Gemma agreed with him about her needing protective custody while the Justice Department figured out how her WITSEC identity had been breached, but going "home" had enormous risks. Still, here they were on the interstate, heading to the very place Eric would expect them to go.

Owen was behind the wheel of the unmarked cruiser,

and Kellan was next to her on the back seat. Both were keeping watch while they got updates on the investigation. There was also an Austin patrol car with two cops behind them just in case things turned ugly. Eric likely wouldn't be able to set explosives along this route, but he could perhaps cause a car accident.

"Eric will keep coming after me," Gemma repeated when Kellan finished his latest call.

Just saying that caused the sound of the blast to echo through her head. And she could feel the effects of it, too, since the debris flying off the explosion had given Kellan and her plenty of nicks and cuts. None serious, but they stung, giving her a fresh memory of how close they'd come to dying.

Everything she owned was gone, of course. Not that she'd had anything of value. The place had felt, well, sterile. A lot like her life had for the past year. The only real loss of her personal things was her purse and phone. Now she had no cash or credit cards—which meant she had to rely on Kellan to help her. At least for a little while. But once the marshals were cleared of having any part in the WITSEC leak, Gemma needed to call Amanda to see about arranging a safe place she could go.

If there was such a place, that is.

Since Kellan didn't even react to her reminder about Eric not stopping, she gave him another one. "You could get caught in crossfire, or worse, the way you did at my house."

That got a reaction. He gave her a look that could have frozen El Paso in August, and he tapped the badge he had clipped to his belt.

"That badge didn't save your father," she snapped,

but she instantly regretted the mini outburst. There were enough bad memories floating around them without her adding that one. "I'm sorry."

He was back in no-reaction mode and turned his lawman's gaze to keep watch out the window. Gemma watched, too. Not out the window but at Kellan.

Mercy, that face. It still got to her. Still tugged and pulled at her in all the wrong places. Sculptured with so many angles and tinted with just a hint of amber from his long-ago Comanche bloodline. Those bloodlines had blessed him with that thick black hair that he'd probably never had to comb. It just fell into a rumpled mane that he hid beneath his cowboy hat.

There was nothing rumpled about his body. It was toned from the endless work he put in on his family's ranch and the rodeo competitions he still did. Once, she'd seen him take down an angry bull that he'd roped. All those muscles—both the bull's and Kellan's— locked in a fierce battle. Dust flying. Hooves and feet digging and chopping into the ground. The snorts from the bull, the grunts of exertion from Kellan.

Kellan had won.

He had literally taken the bull by the horns, brought it down and then calmly walked away. Gemma thought that was the way he handled lots of things in his life. Not women, of course. He did take what he wanted from them. But never forced or even coerced. He took simply because it was offered to him.

Gemma knew plenty about that because once she'd offered herself to him. And he'd taken.

He glanced at her again, maybe sensing that she was playing with memory lane, and she got a flash of those incredible eyes. That had been the first thing she'd ever

noticed about him. Sizzling blue or stormy gray, depending on his mood. Right now, his mood was dark and so were his eyes, but she'd seen them heat up not from anger but from the need that came with arousal.

Arousal that she had caused.

It hadn't been one-sided back when they'd been eighteen, and she'd willingly surrendered her virginity to him on the seat of his pickup truck. She had no idea who'd been on the receiving end of his virginity, but she'd been thankful for whomever had given him enough practice to make that night incredible for her. One that had become her benchmark. She was still looking for someone who could live up to him.

His eyebrow came up, and for one humming moment, they stared at each other until his mouth tightened. It was as if he'd gotten ESP issued with that badge, and he was giving her a silent warning to knock off the sex thoughts. He was right, too, as he usually was. But it had been much easier to slip into those memories than the things she needed to face.

Things she needed to piece together.

Like why Eric had waited a year to come after her? But that could be as Kellan had suggested—because it had taken him that long to find her. However, there were the other things that Eric had said.

You need to take a second look at the details of your father's case. The devil is in those details. That's what this warning is all about.

"Do you believe you could have missed something in your father's murder investigation?" she asked, knowing it could earn her another of those frosty glares.

It didn't though. Instead, Kellan took a deep breath. "Maybe."

There was doubt, but that could have nothing to do with the way Kellan had handled the case. It could be the guilt over not being able to save his father.

"Eric's never said anything like that before," she went on.

Kellan shifted his position, their gazes colliding. "You've had other contact with him over the past year?"

"No." And she was thankful she hadn't, either. Not just because she hadn't wanted to deal with Eric, but also because she was betting Kellan would have been riled to the core if her answer had been yes. He would have wanted to know why he hadn't been told everything that pertained to Eric since he was looking for the killer.

"Eric left messages for me when I was still in the hospital, remember?" she continued. Gemma hadn't actually spoken to him since she'd been first in surgery and then recovering from her injuries. But the hospital staff had recorded the calls and turned them over to Kellan.

"Yeah, I remember." The muscles in his jaw went tight again. "He threatened you."

She nodded, hoping that he didn't repeat the actual words. Gemma didn't need to hear them again to recall that Eric had been enraged that she'd lived and could therefore testify that he'd been the one to shoot her.

Except she couldn't.

Gemma had some memories of that horrible night, but because of the storm and the darkness, she hadn't seen much. About the only thing she could say for sure was that Eric had taken Caroline and her from Gemma's house in Longview Ridge, and that later there'd been a gunfight.

"I'll take another look at the investigation," Kellan assured her, though it wasn't necessary for him to say that. From the moment she'd heard Eric toss that out there, she'd known that Kellan would dig back into the files despite the fact that he likely knew every single detail in them.

"The Austin cops weren't able to trace the call Eric made to you, and there's been no sign of the shooter," Owen relayed to them when he got off the phone.

Neither piece of information was a surprise. Eric had no doubt used a burner or disposable phone. And as for the shooter, the guy hadn't been in the house when Austin PD had searched it. The home owners hadn't been there when the shooter had broken in, so they hadn't seen him, either.

Now the hope was that there was some kind of trace evidence or prints that the CSIs could use to ID him. Gemma doubted though that he'd been that careless, and if the shooter had slipped up, then Eric would just kill him rather than allow him to be captured and interrogated. Heck, the man could already be dead. Eric didn't like leaving loose ends. It was the whole reason he was so angry with her. So, why had he issued just a warning and not finished her off? Maybe he wanted to torment her first. An easy kill might not be as much fun for him.

"What about my neighbors?" Gemma asked. "Were any of them hurt?"

Owen shook his head and made eye contact with his brother in the rearview mirror. "Were you able to get any details on the bomb?"

"They haven't been able to find the detonator and until they do, they won't be able to start figuring out

who built it. Eric doesn't have bomb-making experience. Or at least he didn't a year ago, so he likely hired
someone or spent some research time on the internet."

Gemma had heard Kellan talking with the bomb
squad, but she'd only heard his end of the conversation. Which hadn't been much. Obviously, Kellan hadn't
liked that there hadn't been much progress in the investigation. Then again, it'd only happened six hours ago,
and the CSIs were still processing the scene.

Kellan's phone rang again, something it'd been doing
throughout the drive, and he mumbled some profanity when he saw the name on the screen. For a heart-
stopping moment, Gemma thought it might be Eric, but
then she saw her handler's name on the screen. Amanda
had already called once when they'd still been at the
police station, and Kellan had let it go to voice mail, but
he answered it now, and he put it on Speaker.

"Have you figured out who leaked Gemma's location?" he greeted.

"No, but it wasn't me," Amanda answered without
hesitation. However, she did sound as frustrated and
annoyed as Kellan. "Where's Gemma?" she snapped.

"She's safe." Kellan looked at her and put his index
finger to his mouth in a stay-quiet gesture. "I need you
to find the source of the leak and prove to me that you
fixed it. Then I'll give you Gemma's location."

"That's not the way this works, *cowboy*," Amanda
argued. "I'm the one in charge here, not you."

Gemma winced because she could feel Kellan bris-
tling from the marshal's cowboy label and sharp tone.
Amanda had never been a warm and fuzzy kind of person, and she was even less so right now.

"Gemma's in WITSEC," Amanda went on, "and that puts this under the jurisdiction of the marshals."

"Only if the marshals can protect her, and you've just proven that you can't." Kellan huffed. "Eric killed another woman last night and left a note for Gemma with her address. He's coming after her, and I'd rather make sure that no one wearing a badge is feeding Eric info to help him do that."

That silenced Amanda for a couple of seconds. "Is this about Rory?" Amanda came out and asked.

It was a question Gemma had expected. Rory was Marshal Rory Clawson, and Kellan's then fellow deputy, Dusty Walters, had been investigating the marshal for the murder of a prostitute whose body had been found in Longview Ridge. Dusty hadn't been able to find any evidence other than hearsay before Eric had gunned him down.

"Why would it be about Rory?" Kellan challenged.

"Because I figure you're holding a grudge against Rory because you weren't able to pin bogus charges on him. You still haven't been able to pin those charges on him," Amanda emphasized. "Or maybe you've got a wild notion that he aided Eric in some way."

Kellan didn't waste any time firing back. "Did he?"

Amanda made a dismissive sound. "This isn't over. You will turn Gemma over to me," the marshal added before she ended the call.

It sounded like a threat, and Gemma was certain they'd be hearing from her again soon. Maybe though, Amanda wouldn't try to put her in a new WITSEC location until they had some answers about this latest attack.

"Do you trust her?" Kellan asked when he put his phone away.

Gemma opened her mouth to answer yes, but she stopped. The truth was, she didn't know Amanda that well at all. They'd only met twice in the months that Amanda had been her handler.

"I don't have any reason *not* to trust her," Gemma settled for saying.

"Other than someone compromised your location, a location that only a handful of people knew, and Amanda was one of them." Kellan paused, and then he huffed even louder than he had when he'd been talking to Amanda. "I just don't want to make another mistake."

Gemma could have said those same words to him. If she'd just lived up to her reputation of being a top-notch profiler, she could have stopped him.

"I owe you," Kellan added a moment later.

That got her attention, and Gemma turned in the seat to face him. "You owe me?" she repeated.

Again, that was something she could have said to him. She'd been the one to mess up, not Kellan. But before she could press him on that, his phone rang again, and this time it wasn't Amanda. It was Unknown Caller on the screen.

"Eric," she whispered on a rise of breath.

Owen must have thought it was him, too. "I'll try to trace it while he's on the line." Owen quickly handed his brother a small recorder, and Kellan clicked it on before he hit the answer button.

"So, I guess you're both still alive and kicking?" Eric asked the moment he was on the line. "If Gemma had died, my little bird would have told me."

"And who exactly is that little bird?" Kellan snapped.

"Someone in a very good seat for birds." Eric chuckled.

Maybe a marshal or a cop. But Gemma tried not to react to that because this could be just another of Eric's taunts. The word was probably already out that she'd survived, and he could have heard about it through any means from gossip to even a news report. Then again, maybe he knew she wasn't dead because he'd had no intentions of killing—yet. Not until he'd made her suffer.

"Sorry, but I need to keep my bird's name to myself for now," Eric added a moment later. "Might need him…or *her* again."

Kellan's eyes narrowed. Obviously, he also hated these games that Eric loved to play. "I'm guessing you blew up Gemma's house just in case there was any evidence left behind. That tells me you were actually in it."

"I was," Eric admitted, causing her skin to crawl. "It was fun to see how she's living her life these days. So much security! You could practically feel the worry when you stepped into the house."

Three bullets could do that, and it twisted away at her that just by hearing his voice, he could pull that old fear from her.

"I left that little microphone so I could talk to you," Eric admitted.

"You mean so you could try to make us believe you were still inside," Kellan snapped. "But you weren't. No way would you have risked getting blown up, because you're a coward."

"Sticks and stones," Eric joked, but there was just enough edge to his voice that made Gemma wonder if Kellan had hit a nerve.

At one time Eric had wanted to be an FBI agent. Or so he'd led her to believe. And maybe that was true. If so, that coward insult would have stung.

"Too bad you didn't blow up her neighbor's house where you had your hired thug shoot at us," Kellan went on. "It wasn't very smart of him to leave a spent shell casing behind. Sometimes there are fingerprints on those."

It was a bluff. If the CSIs had indeed found something like that, they would have mentioned it in the calls Kellan had made to them. Still, it got a reaction from Eric.

Silence.

She doubted this would send Eric into a rage or panic, but maybe it would rattle his cage enough for him to make a mistake.

"If there really is a casing," Eric said, his words clipped, "then I suppose we'll just have to wait and see."

"Oh, there's a casing all right," Kellan assured him, "and if we use it to ID the shooter, then there'll be a trail to you."

"No, there won't be. But good luck wasting your time with that."

"It might not be a waste of time," Gemma reminded him. And it earned her a glare from Kellan. But she finished what she intended to say, and she made sure her voice was as steeled up as she could manage. "You believe you covered your tracks, but maybe you didn't. You're not perfect. You were in a panic the night Caroline and I found out what you were, and you took us hostage, remember? That wasn't the well thought out actions of a cocky killer."

Eric paused for a long time. "I remember," he snapped. "And I'm sure you do, too. All that research we did together on Geo-Trace, and you didn't have a clue."

She hadn't. She, Eric and Caroline had worked for

two years on Geo-Trace, the name of their project for profiling and predicting specific areas of cities where violent crimes were most likely to occur. It could have helped law enforcement if Eric hadn't been manipulating the data. He'd done that by murdering his victims in those predicted areas.

"Why did you do it? Why did you kill all those people?" Gemma asked Eric, earning her another glare from Kellan.

Yes, those were questions that could wait, and Eric likely wouldn't even give her an honest answer, but maybe by keeping him on the line, Owen would be able to trace the call.

"That's a conversation for another time," Eric snarled.

"Not really. My guess is that you were in love with me and wanted to impress me."

"Don't flatter yourself, sweetheart. I never loved you. It was never about you."

There'd never been any hints that Eric had indeed had any romantic interest in her, but it twisted away at her to think that Eric could have done those monstrous crimes because of feelings that she hadn't picked up on. That was yet another layer of guilt she could add to her life.

"Sheriff Slater, are you going to let Gemma do all the talking?" Eric pressed. "I wouldn't if I were you. After all, if it wasn't for Gemma, your daddy and that deputy would still be alive."

"If it weren't for *you*, they'd be alive," Kellan corrected.

"Oh, but you're wrong about that," Eric quickly answered.

Kellan cursed. "Quit playing mind games and tell me what the hell it is you want."

"Always did enjoy your direct approach. So, here's the deal. Now that I'm back on my feet, I'm looking for Caroline. And you should be, too."

"I have been looking for her," Kellan assured him. "Plenty of people have been. Did you kill her?"

"No. Last I saw her, she was very much alive."

Gemma found herself gripping on to the seat, but she shook her head. Eric could be lying, though she wanted that to be true. She had enough blood by association on her hands.

"I've killed a dozen or so people," Eric went on, "but Caroline isn't one of them. Neither was your father or the deputy. Dusty Walters. As much as I'd like to take credit for their deaths, I can't."

Gemma nearly laughed, and it wouldn't have been because that was funny but because it was ridiculous.

Wasn't it?

"What the hell are you talking about?" Kellan snarled. "I saw you shoot Gemma, and the bullets that killed my dad came from the same gun."

"Because I found it on the floor inside the house. I picked it up and used it. I didn't, however, use it on Deputy Walters. You know that because he was shot with a different weapon."

"You had two guns on you," Gemma murmured. At least that had been the most logical theory. For now, she scoffed, "So, you're saying you're innocent?" Gemma didn't bother to take the sarcasm out of that.

But still, something inside her turned a little.

"No, I shot you, all right," Eric admitted, and he sounded so pleased about that. "Wish I'd put the bul-

lets in your head, but that's what do-overs are for. You can have your own do-over, too, Kellan. But here's my advice—find Caroline because she's the one who can tell you who really killed Deputy Walters and your father."

CHAPTER FOUR

KELLAN WASN'T ABLE to shut out Eric's words. They knifed through his head, a violent steady assault that was screwing around with his concentration.

Gemma wasn't helping with his concentration, either, and since they'd arrived at his office, Kellan had been silently cursing her almost as much as he was Eric.

Almost.

Eric was a sociopathic lying snake, and he loved batting around people's emotions. Like a cat playing with a half-dead mouse. That didn't mean Kellan could dismiss what Eric had said, but he also wasn't going to accept it as gospel truth.

So far, there'd been nothing about Gemma he could dismiss. Damn her. He wanted something to make himself immune, and common sense and bad blood sure as hell weren't doing it. It riled him that his body hardened whenever she looked at him. Like now, for instance.

Gemma was in a corner of his office, and their gazes connected when he finished his latest call to the techs who'd tried to trace Eric's call. Kellan had to shake his head. As expected, they'd had no luck with that. Also as expected, she sighed, lowered her head and got back to work.

She was working on a laptop that Owen had gotten for her so she could start researching some angles about

where Eric might have been for the past year. Kellan had warned her to have no contact with her handler, had issued other warnings about hacking—something she was darn good at—or exchanging any communications with anybody. Since Gemma was scared and feeling guilty about Iris's murder, she would probably stick to that, and maybe she'd even be able to find something that would help.

Now that I'm back on my feet... Eric had said.

Maybe that meant he'd been out of commission. That would explain his nearly one-year absence. He hadn't been in jail. Kellan had combed the records for that, just in case Eric had been picked up under an assumed name. He'd investigated any and all possibilities for that and had come up empty.

So, maybe Eric had been hurt and physically unable to kill? Of course, this could be about finances, too. With every law enforcement agency in the state looking for him, he would have needed funds to move around.

Kellan's phone rang again, and he answered it right away when he saw that it was Austin PD. That caused Gemma to send another look his way. Caused Kellan to issue another round of that silent profanity for the bronc-kick of heat he felt behind the zipper of his jeans. Thankfully, it didn't affect his hearing.

"Just wanted you to know that there's still no sign of the shooter," Sergeant Alan Gonzales said. "Or Eric Lang. We'll keep looking though." The update, or rather the lack of it, had probably come because Kellan had left the sergeant two messages to call him.

Kellan was still stewing over the gunman's getaway, and nearly peppered the sergeant with questions about why the gunman hadn't turned up on highway cameras

or why no one had spotted him or someone matching his description, but he knew Gonzales. He was a good cop. Still, if Kellan had thought it would get him answers, he would have peppered a good cop with those questions and more. But it was obvious Gonzales had nothing to give him.

He ended the call, taking some of his frustration out on the button on his phone that he jabbed too hard, and he got up to pour himself his umpteenth cup of coffee. Of course, Gemma was looking at him, waiting.

While he gathered his thoughts—and pushed other thoughts aside—he studied her a moment over the rim of his cup. She was as wired as he was, and she'd chewed on her bottom lip so much that it was red and raw. Her fidgeting hands had plowed through her long brunette hair, too. Another sign of those nerves.

She was normally polish and shine with that flawless face and mouth that had always made him think of sex. Today though, her mussed hair tumbled onto her shoulders as if she'd just crawled out of bed, and the only shine came from those ripe green eyes that shimmered from the fatigue of staring too long at the computer screen.

Kellan thought of sex again, cursed again, and forced himself to tell her what she was no doubt waiting to hear. The info he'd just learned from that phone call.

He went across the room toward her. Close enough to see that her pulse was already skittering against the skin of her throat.

"They didn't find Eric or the shooter." He said it fast, knowing there was no type of sugarcoat that would make it better. It'd left a bitter taste in his mouth, all right. Because it meant Gemma was in just as much

danger now as she had been when they'd escaped from her house.

A weary sigh left her mouth, causing her breasts to rise and then fall. If they'd never been lovers, he might have put a comforting hand on her arm. But that was dangerous. Because even though he doubted either of them wanted it, there was a connection between them that went beyond the pain and the hurt of what'd happened a year ago.

"Why did you say you owed me?" she asked.

The question came out of the blue and threw him, so much so that he gulped down too much coffee and nearly choked. Hardly the reaction for a tough-nosed cop. But his reaction to her hadn't exactly been all badge, either.

Kellan lifted his shoulder and wanted to kick himself for ever bringing it up in the first place. Bad timing, he thought, and wondered if there would ever be a good time for him to grovel.

"I didn't stop Eric from shooting you that night." He said that fast. Not a drop of sugarcoating. "You, my father and Dusty. I'm sorry for that."

Her silence and the shimmering look in her eyes made him stupid, and that was the only excuse he could come up with for why he kept talking.

"It's easier for me to toss some of the blame at you for not ID'ing a killer sooner," he added. And he still did blame her, in part, for that. "But it was my job to stop him before he killed two people and injured another while he was right under my nose."

The silence just kept on going. So much so that Kellan turned, ready to go back to his desk so that he wouldn't continue to prattle on. Gemma stopped him

by putting her hand on his arm. It was like a trigger that sent his gaze searching for hers. Wasn't hard to find when she stood and met him eye to eye.

"It was easier for me to toss some of the blame at you, too." She made another of those sighs. "But there was no stopping Eric that night. The stopping should have happened prior to that. I should have seen the signs." Gemma silenced him by lifting her hand when he started to speak. "And please don't tell me that it's all right, that I'm not at fault. I don't think I could take that right now."

Unfortunately, Kellan understood just what she meant. They were both still hurting, and a mutual sympathy fest was only going to make it harder. They couldn't go back. Couldn't undo. And that left them with only one direction. Looking ahead and putting this son of a bitch in a hole where he belonged.

She nodded as if she'd reached the same conclusion he had, and Gemma swiveled the screen so he could see it. It was a collage of photos of the crime scene at the Serenity Inn. He'd wanted to give her some time to level her adrenaline and come down from the attack, but it was obvious she was ready to be interviewed.

"I've been studying this," she said, "and Eric could have been telling the truth about some things." She paused. "I hope he's telling the truth about Caroline, that he left her alive."

Yeah. But if she was alive, did that mean she'd been with a serial killer this whole time? That twisted the knot in his stomach. There were things worse than death.

"I know you didn't get a good look at everything in the inn where Eric had you that night. Eric said he

picked up the gun from inside the inn. Did he?" Kellan asked.

"It's possible. He'd drugged me by then so everything was blurry around the edges. But, yes, he could have done it. When he stepped into the house, he had his arms crooked around mine and Caroline's necks. Caroline hadn't been drugged so she managed to elbow him as he was backing up with us. She fought like a wildcat."

Kellan nearly smiled. That sounded like Caroline. "If he was telling the truth, the gun would have been on the floor. Eric would have had to reach down to get it."

She stayed quiet a moment, and he could almost see the images replaying in her head. "He staggered when Caroline was clawing at him." Another pause, her forehead bunched up. "They both fell, I think. But only for a few seconds."

He hadn't thought that knot in his stomach could get any tighter. It did. Because a few seconds was plenty enough for Eric to have grabbed a gun and used it to shoot Gemma just as Kellan had been walking through the door. If that had happened though, and if by some miracle Eric had been telling the truth, then that left Kellan with a big question.

Why was the gun there?

Kellan looked at the photos again, letting it play out in his mind, too. "There are some *inconsistencies*." He hated that blasted word, so sterile and detached from the emotion. Still, it was better than saying that there were things that had caused him a year of living hell and to not have a single full night of sleep.

"Dusty was shot with a different gun than my father and you," Kellan said, spelling it out, again, with the

hopes the inconsistencies might go away. "We always assumed Eric had two weapons and had possibly even run out of ammo in the one he'd used on Dad and you and that's why he shot Dusty with another one."

She cleared her throat just a little as if trying to clear her head, too. "Neither gun was found at the scene, which means Eric could have taken them with him. I don't suppose either have turned up in a pawn shop or someplace like that?"

"No." He'd been keeping tabs on that because a gun could possibly still have trace or fiber evidence even after a year. "I did put in a request, though, to have the CSIs go through the Serenity Inn again. They'll head there first thing in the morning."

For the first time today, he saw some kind of amusement in her eyes. He doubted it was from actual humor but rather because Gemma would know how that played out. "I'll bet they weren't happy about that. How many times have you had them go through it?" she asked.

"Three." He'd lost count of how many visits he'd made himself. "That hotel was once a house, built in 1880, and people had hidey-holes all over. It has twenty-eight rooms and nearly fifteen thousand square feet. And as if that weren't enough, it sat empty for a decade before Eric got near it. The squirrels and mice could have added even more holes. Easy to miss something in all that space."

Gemma made a sound of agreement, pushed her fingers through her hair again. She opened her mouth, but then closed it as if she'd changed her mind. "Sorry. I was about to attempt a profile. We both know how reliable I am with those."

That bite to her voice was drenched in regret and

pain, things he knew plenty about. And while he didn't want to go the profile route, either, he did want to run something past her.

"Rory Clawson," he threw out there. "I know you've been doing hypnosis and therapy to help you remember more of what happened after Eric drugged you, and just wondered if you recalled him being there that night."

"No. No recollection of that," she said without hesitation but then paused. "How did you know about the hypnosis and therapy?"

"I've been getting updates on any and every aspect of this investigation—in case any new evidence came to light." Kellan didn't intend to apologize for it, either. "I want my father's killer caught."

Gemma continued to stare at him as if trying to figure out if that was all there was to it, but she didn't press it. "I've been searching computer records, too, for updates. In case there's any new evidence," she added, emphasizing his own words.

Of course, she had. Because his father's killer was also the same person who'd put three bullets in her. Well, probably. Unless Eric was telling the truth and Gemma had been the only person he'd shot that night.

"I can't hack into Rory's records," she went on. "And, yes, I just tried."

Again, no surprise, but he gave her a warning glare because she'd just confessed to committing a crime. He was ornery enough to consider arresting her but secretly wished he'd had the "moral flexibility" to do the hacking himself. Yes, he wanted the truth, but the badge meant something to him, and it had meant something to his father, too. Buck wouldn't have wanted Kellan

or his other sons bending the law even when it was for the sake of finding his killer.

Gemma must have had no trouble interpreting his glare or the way *his* forehead was now bunched up. While looking him straight in the eye, she lifted her hands, palms up, wrists exposed, as if waiting for him to cuff her.

Kellan's glare deepened, and using his free hand, he braceleted those exposed wrists to push them back down. Unfortunately, that involved the touching that he'd been trying to avoid. Touching, that seemed to bother Gemma, too, because her breath hitched a little, and her gaze finally darted away.

"I'm sorry," she said when his grip melted off her. "That put you in a tough position, but I'm not sorry for trying to get to the truth. Eric is out there, *killing*." Now she shuddered, gave her bottom lip another bite until her mouth stopped trembling. "And he found out where I was, how to get to me. It bothers me that Rory's a marshal and therefore could have gotten access to my WITSEC location."

"That's not the only thing that bothers me about him, but yeah, that's part of it. What bothers me just as much is that I haven't been able to solve the murder of Lacey Terrell, the prostitute Dusty was investigating. He was convinced that Rory was behind that somehow."

Kellan didn't add more because his phone rang again. This time it was Jack, and Kellan went back across the room so he could have at least a little privacy when he talked to his brother.

"Owen just told me what Eric said," Jack blurted out the moment he was on the line. "Did he really say he didn't kill Caroline?"

None of this was a surprise. Not the question and certainly not the desperate emotion that went with it. Jack loved Caroline, and even though all the signs had pointed to her being dead, Jack would never give up, never heal, until they found her body.

"For just a second, think with your badge and no other part of you," Kellan insisted. "Eric is a liar."

Kellan glanced at Gemma to see if she was listening. Maybe she was, but she was also back to working on the computer. Hopefully, not hacking into anything.

"Yeah," Jack snapped. "But there's no reason for him to lie about that."

Sure there was, and it was going to slice Jack, and himself, to spell out what his brother already knew. "If we're focused on finding Caroline, then we'd be looking in the wrong direction—for Eric. No way would he leave her alive if she could be found and lead us back to him."

"Maybe she escaped," Jack insisted.

"Maybe." This was going to slice, too. "But then, she would have found a way to get in touch with you."

His brother's groan was the worst slice of all. Jack was his kid brother, and it hurt to feel him hurting like this.

"I want to talk to Gemma," Jack snarled several moments later. "I want to work this latest murder investigation with you."

Kellan had anticipated that, too, and had no intention of refusing. "It might hit close to home," Kellan warned him. "The marshals might be involved."

"Rory?" Jack immediately asked.

"Maybe. But also Amanda Hardin. Any idea how and why she became Gemma's handler?"

His brother paused a moment. "No. I would have done it, but I wasn't exactly at my best."

No, because Jack had been in love with Caroline, and she was still missing. His brother had gone a little crazy when they'd found Caroline's blood and then no sign of the woman.

"You're asking if I trust Amanda?" Jack concluded. "I don't really know her that well, but I soon will. Let me see what I can find out, and I'll get back to you."

Kellan thanked him, and he turned, ready to face Gemma's questions about what Jack had said regarding her handler. But it was obvious from her widened eyes that he had his own question.

"What happened?" Kellan demanded.

"Eric," she said, a new kind of quiver in her voice. "I know where he's been for the past year, and I think I know how to find him."

CHAPTER FIVE

THE FEAR WAS gone now. Or at least it had been stomped down for a while and replaced by the relief of what Gemma had found in her computer search.

Now that I'm back on my feet.

Eric probably hadn't even given it a thought about saying that to her and Kellan. It'd been simply a way of starting his latest taunt. But it had opened a big, wide door for Gemma.

She caught on to Kellan's arm, pulling him closer so she could show him what was on the laptop. For just a split second he went stiff, maybe because she'd touched him, but it was possible that she looked a little crazy. He might have thought she was losing it.

And then he saw the screen.

The records from a hospital in Mexico City.

"I started doing hospital searches for the last year. Looking for anyone who fit his description. And, yes, some hacking was involved," she added.

With his eyes fixed on the data, Kellan waved that off, moved out of her grip and went even closer to the screen.

"I figured you'd searched the jails so I excluded those," Gemma added and waited for Kellan to nod. "So, I decided to go for medical records. Eric obviously

used an alias, but that's him." She pointed to the name on the file. Joe Hanson. "The SOB used my last name."

That irritated her, but she pushed it aside, knowing that Eric would have done that with the hopes of her noticing and feeling the sting. Gemma wasn't going to give him the satisfaction.

"Everything fits," she went on. "The age, height, weight and the small sun tattoo on the inside of his right wrist." The tat he'd told her that he'd gotten for his eighteenth birthday. To celebrate, he'd said. But now she wondered if it had a sinister meaning, maybe even to mark his first kill.

Kellan sat down, scrolled through the lengthy record. The notes were in Spanish, which he clearly had no trouble translating. "He went in with a gunshot wound," Kellan said. "Temporary paralysis due to the bullet being lodged in his spine." He looked up at her. "Someone shot him."

She nodded, and even though there were other things she wanted to show him in the hospital records, Gemma pulled up the next file. The police report.

"Eric claimed he had no idea who'd shot him and gave them that fake name, Joe Hanson. He said someone had abducted him and a woman he'd been traveling with. Cassie Marlow."

"The same initials as Caroline. Maybe she shot him," he mumbled, and he continued scrolling. Gemma hadn't gone beyond this point in the file but fully intended to do that as soon as Kellan had skimmed through it.

"Eric didn't give the cops much info," Kellan went on. "Claimed he was blindfolded for the two weeks he'd been held by the so-called kidnapper." The details he had given though eerily mimicked what he'd done to

Gemma. Arm around the throat. The drugging. And being shot.

"Eric's too vain to have shot himself," Gemma said. "And even if he had thought this was a good plan, to hide out in a hospital until the heat died down, he wouldn't have risked paralysis."

The sound of agreement Kellan was making came to an abrupt stop. His finger went still on the keyboard, and almost frantically Gemma followed his gaze to see what'd put that stark expression on his face.

"Hell," he said.

Gemma saw it then, too. The detailed report of the Mexican police finding a decomposed body in a car where they'd also found Eric wounded and bleeding. The body of a woman whose throat had been slit.

"Oh, God." Gemma's legs gave way, and if she hadn't sat on the edge of the desk, she would have fallen.

Because the body in the car matched Caroline's description.

Kellan didn't give her any reassurances that it might not be Caroline. No cop's words about needing to wait and see. He simply took her hand and held it.

"That's how Eric murdered his victims before he took Caroline and me hostage and did the shootings at the inn," she mumbled, not able to stop the flow of words that came with the rush of sickening dread. "God, he cut her throat."

Gemma had to fight to keep hold of her breath, had to fight just so she wouldn't scream and pound her fists on the wall. Eric had killed her. He'd killed Caroline.

The tears came, hot and bitter, and the grief was just as fresh as it had been a year ago. "I'm responsible for

this. I hired Caroline and Eric. Their paths would have never crossed if I hadn't hired them."

Kellan stood, staring at her, and the grip he put on her shoulders was far from gentle. "Stop it," he said, his voice a low, dangerous warning. No gentleness there, either. "This is exactly what Eric wants. He wants you crying and broken so you'll be an easier target."

Gemma hated to admit that Eric might have succeeded. He couldn't have hurt her more if he'd ripped out a piece of her heart.

Kellan got right in her face. "Don't give in to this. Help me find him." He punctuated each word with anger that had tightened every muscle in his face and turned his eyes to the color of a violent storm. "You said you thought you knew how to find him. Tell me. *Now.*"

Well, he certainly wasn't taking the approach of handling her with kid gloves. Not that she wanted it. Kid gloves weren't going to fix this.

Her hands were shaking when she moved back to the keyboard, and she pulled up the medical files again. The tears were still there, but she tried to blink them away so she could see. She didn't want to miss any of the details here.

"He stayed a month in the hospital in Mexico and then was transferred to a nursing and rehabilitation center here in the States where he learned to walk again." Gemma had to swallow before she could continue. "The center isn't cheap, so he must have gotten his hands on some money. Eric was a trust fund baby, and that wasn't touched, but he could have had other accounts stashed under other names."

"Like Joe Hanson," Kellan mumbled almost absently. He'd put his attention back on the screen now, and he

saw the very name that had given her that jolt of excitement. A jolt that was no longer there because it'd been
replaced by an emotion of a different kind.

From the bombshell news of the body in Eric's car.

"Maylene Roth," Gemma read. "She's the private
nurse Eric hired while at the center. When he was dis-
charged from there *two weeks ago*, the medical staff
turned over his care to Nurse Roth. The doctor noted
the nurse was very attached to the patient and would
stay with him indefinitely."

"*Attached*," Kellan repeated on a heavy sigh. "Either
his lover or a groupie."

Gemma agreed, and with every part of her still trembling, she pulled up the final document. "That's the address on record for Maylene." It was in San Antonio.
"Eric won't be there, of course, but we can try to track
him through her."

She held her breath when Kellan gave her his cop's
look, and Gemma figured he was on the verge of giving
her a lecture about there being no "we" in the tracking-
down process, that this was something only for him
and his fellow cops. No lecture though. He stepped
out into his squad room and had a short conversation
with Owen.

"I ordered a background check on Maylene and
will have the cops go to her address," Kellan told her
when he came back into his office. "Not a quiet, just-
checking-on-you approach, either. Full sirens and
SWAT gear. The chances are slim to none that either
of them will be there, but it'll send a message to Eric
that we're on to him and that I'm willing to use his
friend to get to him."

Good. It was exactly the kind of game that Eric

would play, and if Eric had any "attachment" to Maylene, it might rattle him. Then again, Gemma had to
wonder if Eric even had enough normalcy inside him
to rattle. As a profiler, she'd interviewed dozens of serial killers, but none of them had had such a perfect
cold mask as Eric did.

Kellan took out his phone. "I'll make arrangements
for you to go someplace safe," he said. "But first I want
to work on getting whatever info I can on the body that
was found in Eric's car."

"I can probably access autopsy records—"

"No. Let me do it. And don't mention this to Jack.
Not yet."

She wouldn't, not until they had more info. Proof, she
amended. Best not to give Jack a double dose of grief,
one from hearing about the body and another when Kellan managed to get an ID. Then, Gemma could grieve
right along with him.

"Where did you have in mind for me to go?" she
asked.

Kellan didn't get a chance to answer because of the
voices that came from the squad room. Not Owen, but
it was someone Gemma immediately recognized.

Marshal Amanda Hardin was walking straight toward them. "Have you lost your mind?" Amanda immediately snapped.

Since Amanda was volleying glances at her and Kellan, Gemma thought the question was aimed at both of
them. Amanda was clearly upset, her posture stiff, her
mouth in a flat line. Like the other times Gemma had
seen the woman, she was wearing black dress pants,
white shirt and her marshal's badge. Unlike the other

times, Amanda looked frazzled with her hair mussed and the dark circles under her eyes.

"I'm busy," Kellan answered, and in the same slick way she'd seen him draw his weapon, he closed the laptop, no doubt so that the marshal wouldn't see what they'd been researching, and he positioned himself between Amanda and her.

That told Gemma loads. That Kellan wasn't going to trust Amanda. Good. Because Gemma didn't, either.

Kellan's response and the protective move certainly didn't improve Amanda's mood, and her narrowed gaze flew to Gemma's. "I didn't think I'd need to spell this out for you, but you're acting like an idiot," the marshal said. "You're in grave danger. Eric Lang is at large, and yet here you are in the very place that Eric will expect you to be. And you're with a town sheriff who has no authority to interfere with WITSEC."

Amanda flicked a glance at Kellan.

"Guess you're the idiot and I'm the interfering local cop," Kellan grumbled to Gemma. Despite everything, she had to fight back a smile.

Amanda noticed that, too, and shot them both glares. The marshal paused several moments, obviously trying to rein in her temper. It worked, sort of. When she spoke again, her voice was slightly more level.

"I've already arranged for a safe house," Amanda told Gemma. "You need to come with me. I'm not giving you a choice about that. I'm not going to allow you to stay here where you'll be an easy target."

In the past year, Gemma had thought she'd lost the backbone and confidence that she'd once had. Eric had done that to her. But now she felt a little of that back-

bone return, and Gemma stepped out to Kellan's side
to face the marshal head-on.

"No," Gemma said.

There were plenty of emotions that zinged through
Amanda's eyes. Concern might have been in there, but
Gemma saw a lot of anger. "No?" Amanda repeated
like a challenge.

"No," Gemma repeated like a declaration. "I'm not
going with you. I voluntarily placed myself in WITSEC,
and now I'm removing myself. That means you're no
longer my handler, and you can go."

The color drained from Amanda's face, and Gemma
had no idea what emotions she was witnessing now.
What the heck was this about?

It took the marshal a hard breath before she recovered enough to look at Kellan. "If she stays here, Eric
will kill her."

Kellan didn't jump to deny that, probably because
he knew that Eric would indeed come after her again.

"*You* could get her killed if she stays with you,"
Amanda added.

Kellan lifted his shoulder, but Gemma thought there
was nothing casual about that shrug. "Eric got to the
last safe house you set up for Gemma. The one *you* had
set up for her," Kellan reminded the marshal. "It's up
to Gemma if she wants to take a risk like that again."

"I have no intention of going anywhere with you,"
Gemma told Amanda.

Amanda's now hard gaze lingered on her a couple of
seconds before it slid to Kellan. "Are you two sleeping
together again? Because it's obvious you're not thinking
with the right parts of your bodies right now."

Kellan's glare and huff weren't casual, either. He

merely looked past Amanda and at Owen. "Escort Marshal Hardin out of the building." Kellan stepped back and closed the door in Amanda's face.

Kellan then turned to Gemma. "If you want to change your mind and go with her—"

"No." She didn't have to think about that, but she did want to give some thought to the way Amanda had gone pale when Gemma had told her she was leaving WITSEC.

Gemma had heard some snippets of Kellan's conversation with Jack, and Kellan had asked his brother something about why Amanda had become her handler. Gemma very much wanted to know what Jack had had to say.

The door opened, and for a moment Gemma thought that Amanda had returned to continue an argument that she stood no chance of winning, but it wasn't the marshal. It was Owen. One look at his face, and Gemma knew something was wrong.

A moment later, Owen confirmed just that.

"There's been another murder."

CHAPTER SIX

MILTON OSWALD.

An hour ago, the name had meant nothing to Kellan, but it sure as heck had some meaning now. That's because from everything found at the scene, he was their missing shooter, the very person who'd tried to gun Gemma and him down.

According to the preliminary report he'd just pulled up, the man was basically a thug with a mile-long record.

And now he was dead.

Oswald's body had been found just inside the Longview Ridge jurisdiction, and Kellan figured that was intentional. Now he had a murder investigation that would tie up not only a team of deputies and himself but also the CSIs.

It wasn't just the stretch on the manpower and resources though. It was the emotional toll of it, and the note left at the scene was certainly a whopping big toll. Not just for Kellan but for Gemma.

From the sound that Gemma made when she looked at the report on Oswald, she tried to bite back a groan. She failed. Kellan cursed and wished he hadn't viewed the photo that the deputies had just sent him with their initial report. The gruesomely clear picture of the man sprawled out on the ground in front of the Serenity Inn.

In that photo, Oswald's skin was already white, indicating he'd been dead at least a half hour. His lifeless eyes had started to sink back in his skull. With the blood, it made it seem as if he was wearing some kind of sick Halloween mask.

In contrast, Gemma's eyes were filled with life. And probably the same dread and disgust that he was feeling as her gaze skirted over the screen.

Kellan tried to close the file, but Gemma caught on to his hand, stopping him. "This is Eric's doing," she said, touching her fingers to the image of the man's neck and the slit that had almost certainly been his cause of death.

Yeah, that was his signature, all right. But they hadn't needed the cut to confirm that it was indeed Eric. That's because the snake had left them a note pinned to Oswald's shirt.

Here's your missing shooter, Sheriff Slater. Now Gemma and you can sleep better tonight knowing he's not out there to harm you. Sweet dreams.

Kellan knew that the only one who'd sleep better was Eric. That's because Oswald was no longer a loose end.

"Who found Oswald's body?" Gemma asked. "How did they find it?"

"An anonymous 911 call. One of my deputies lives close to there and was on his way to work. He went to the scene and had no trouble spotting it."

Judging from the volume of blood, Eric had killed him there, maybe by luring the guy to the scene with the promise of payment. Kellan should have considered that Eric would go back there.

Kellan eased her hand away from the keyboard, and

this time he managed to shut down the file. She wasn't as pale as the dead guy, but seeing the picture wasn't helping her color any.

It occurred to Kellan that the paleness worried him. Maybe more than it should. Because that kind of concern meant his focus was shifting away from Eric and on to her. Something that he knew could have the worst consequences.

Because that's what'd happened the night his father had been killed.

He'd been so homed in on saving Gemma that he had almost certainly missed signals that could have saved his father. Maybe saved her, too, from getting shot.

Doing something to correct that focus shift, Kellan stood to get yet more coffee. And put some distance between Gemma and himself.

"There's a recording of the person who called in Oswald's death?" she pressed, though he figured she'd noticed his not subtle shift of position.

Kellan nodded. "It was a woman. She refused to identify herself when the dispatch operator asked for her name."

"Maylene," Gemma concluded in a rough whisper.

That was his guess, too, and Kellan had passed that on to the deputy team who'd be primary on this case. Since this was now a homicide investigation, that would make the woman a person of interest. Of course, it might make her dead because Eric might think of her as another loose end who should be permanently silenced, but there was nothing Kellan could do about that now.

However, there was something he could do about Gemma.

Something she wasn't going to like. Hell, he didn't

248 DELORES FOSSEN

like it, either, but no scenario he could come up with would be ideal.

He stepped out of the office first, to have a quick chat with Owen in order to set things in motion, and then Kellan went back in to lay things out for her.

"I'm going to take you to the ranch," he said, and he just continued despite the head shaking. "We'll be there in about ten minutes."

She went still. There'd been no need for him to tell her how far away the place was. Gemma knew because she'd been there.

And she'd been in his bed.

Gemma didn't ask if that was a wise decision. It wasn't. But it was the best of the worst options they had. He couldn't turn her over to the marshals, and a safe house would stretch the manpower of the sheriff's office to the breaking point—which would please Eric to no end.

Kellan made a quick check over his shoulder where Owen gave him a nod. "Come on," he told Gemma, picking up the laptop and putting it into the small suitcase that Owen had gotten for her.

Owen had also managed to get her a replacement phone along with some clothes and toiletries. Kellan handed her the bag so it'd free up his hand in case he needed to use his weapon.

Gemma started walking with him, but she shook her head again. "Doesn't Owen live on the grounds with his daughter? You can't take me there. This could put her in danger—"

"It's fine," Owen volunteered. "She's going away with her nanny for a few days."

That couldn't be easy on Owen. His brother's wife

had died in childbirth, crushing him, and Kellan believed the only reason Owen had made it through that darkness was because of his little girl. Owen would miss her, desperately, but he wouldn't do anything to risk her safety and neither would Kellan. That's why he'd sent a reserve deputy with the nanny. Owen was too valuable to lose, but if things heated up, Kellan would have no choice but to send him to guard the child.

However, Kellan was certain that Eric wasn't after a child. Eric's target was standing right next to Kellan.

When they reached the front door, both Owen and Kellan glanced around the area and drew their guns despite it only being a few feet to the cruiser. Kellan didn't see anything, but there were plenty of places for someone to hide on Main Street.

After Kellan gave him a nod, Owen went out ahead of them, throwing open the back door of the cruiser before he hurried to get behind the wheel. Kellan hurried, too, pressing his hand on Gemma's back to keep her low until they were both in the back seat. As soon as they were in, Owen drove off.

Kellan didn't let down his guard. The cruiser was bullet resistant, but he was also concerned about someone following them. Eric had to consider that Kellan would take Gemma to the ranch, but there was no need to hand Eric that info on a silver platter.

"The hands are putting down the strip spikes on the road like you asked," Owen said when they reached the end of Main Street. "Eli is on the way there, too. Once he's in place, I can go back to the office and help with the murder investigation."

Eli was a Texas Ranger and would do just fine as backup without Kellan having to tie up any more of his

deputies. There was the added benefit of having three lawmen brothers. Too bad he couldn't use Jack for this, but he might be having his own demons to face when they ID'd the body in Eric's car.

"I'm having the CSIs put up two surveillance cameras at the Serenity Inn," Kellan went on, mentally going through the list of things he'd need to check on once he had Gemma settled. Then he could focus on finding Eric before he struck again. "It's a long shot that Eric would go back there, but he could if he's in the mood to play more games."

Of course, that would also mean another dead body.

"I'll keep doing computer searches on Maylene to find out anything I can about her," Gemma added, obviously going through her to-do list, too. "What about the raid on her house? When will that happen?"

Kellan checked his watch. "Any minute now." It was anyone's guess though as to how long it'd be before the cops found anything. If Maylene wasn't there, then the entire house would have to be processed to find any evidence of not only Maylene's link to Eric but any proof that he'd actually been to her house.

Gemma turned to look out the window when Owen took the turn to the ranch. Even though the sun was just starting to set, there was still plenty of light for her to see the stretch of pastures and the Angus cattle that grazed there. It looked peaceful, and Kellan wanted to keep it that way.

She dragged in a long breath when Owen came to a stop in front of the house. Maybe preparing herself for the run inside or maybe because of the jolt of memories she was about to face.

Kellan got out ahead of them, unlocking the door to

the house and checking to make sure there were no signs of a break-in. None. The security system immediately triggered, and he entered the code before he motioned for Owen to get Gemma inside. He reset it as soon as they were inside with the door locked.

Gemma came to a halt in the foyer, her attention going straight ahead to the large framed picture that hung on the wall facing the door. His parents. It was one of the last photos they'd taken of them together before his mom had gotten cancer and passed away ten years ago. It wasn't a posed shot but one of them standing by the corral, their hands linked while they watched Jack working with a new horse. All three were smiling.

"It's nice," she said, her voice barely a whisper. "Very nice."

The picture hadn't been there a year ago when he and Gemma had been lovers and his father had still been alive. It was possible it brought back memories of that night. Sometimes, it did for Kellan, but in his case, it brought on more good than bad.

Owen volleyed a few glances at them, and Kellan didn't think it was because of Gemma's reaction to the picture. It was probably because the foyer was zinging with emotion, and while it wasn't the blasted heat between Gemma and him, emotion of any kind could lead to trouble.

"I need to grab a shower so I'll be ready to go back to work when Eli gets here," Owen said, heading up the stairs.

Kellan shot him a scowl and hoped that this wasn't Owen's way of giving them some privacy.

"I'll put your suitcase in the guest room," Kellan told her, taking the bag from her. She'd had it clutched

in front of her like a shield. "If you're hungry, just help yourself to whatever you find in the fridge."

Gemma nodded and released a quick breath and dragged in another one as if she'd been holding it too long and was suddenly starved for air. Just a breath, Kellan assured himself. Not the meltdown, adrenaline crash he'd been expecting from her. Still, instead of just heading up the stairs, he set down the suitcase and looked at her.

"I need a truce with you," she said, surprising him.

Even though he wasn't sure what she meant, he nodded and was ready to point out that a truce was already in place. She was in his house, under his protection, and they were working together to find Eric. Yes, there were still plenty of bad feelings between them stemming from both of them sucking at their jobs and that in turn causing his father's death. Still...

Gemma stepped right into his arms, her body landing against his. He got that quick jolt of heat that was mixed with, yes, those emotions. Talk about a lethal combo.

"I take meds," she whispered with her mouth close to his ear. "Some of them are to stave off panic attacks, and I'm due a dose very soon." Her voice trembled when she added that. "I'm not telling you this so you'll feel sorry for me or baby me, but I can't take them right now because they fog my head and I won't be able to work. So, you might hear me tonight...when the nightmares come."

Well, hell. Kellan would have had to be a coldhearted bastard not to react to that, and before he could even try to come up with a different solution, his arms went around her.

"If you hear me tonight," she went on. "Don't come in the room. I'll be okay."

He seriously doubted the okay part or that she wouldn't need meds to get her through the night. Kellan considered having Owen pick her up a prescription and then he could demand that she take the damn pills, but he knew that wouldn't do any good. Nightmares couldn't kill, but Eric could, and she was as determined to find him as Kellan was.

"Can I do anything to help?" he asked, easing back from her so he could see her.

She gave him a slight smile, but it didn't make it to her eyes, and she stepped out of his grip. "You're doing it. I need this truce." She hiked up her chin then, clearly trying to look a lot stronger than she felt, and she picked up her bag. "I can put this in the guest room. I know the way." She did. In fact, Gemma probably knew every inch of his house.

Every inch of him, too.

Not exactly the right thought to settle the nerves jangling just beneath his skin. Those nerves caused him to jolt a little when the sound of his ringing phone shot through the foyer. Gemma immediately stopped and waited for him to look at the screen.

"Rory Clawson," Kellan told her.

While he didn't especially want to talk to the marshal, this could be related to the investigation. More likely though, Rory was going to try to browbeat Kellan into persuading Gemma to go back into WITSEC. As far as Kellan was concerned, there was zero chance of that happening until he knew every single detail of how Eric had found Gemma.

Kellan took the call, putting it on Speaker, and he

immediately heard Rory's greeting. "Sheriff Slater. Kellan," Rory amended.

Over the past year, Kellan had had several conversations with the marshal, and unlike Amanda, Rory's attitude was laid-back, just as it was now. Kellan had no intention of aiming for laid-back.

"What do you want?" Kellan asked, and he thought he heard Rory make a heavy sigh.

"Amanda said she'd gone by your office, that she saw Gemma and that Gemma looked shaken up."

"What do you want?" Kellan repeated. He kept his tone just one notch short of being hostile, but that wouldn't last if Rory was wasting his time.

"Please tell Gemma how sorry I am about Eric finding her. I'm glad you were there to get her out."

"Yeah, she's glad about that, too." And that had more than a smidge of sarcasm. "How did Eric find her?" Kellan snapped.

"Maybe through Oswald, the dead triggerman."

Kellan certainly hadn't expected Rory to say that, even if it was a possibility. Judging from Gemma's suddenly wide eyes, she felt the same.

"Why Oswald?" Kellan pressed.

"I'm sure it'll come up when you're deeper into the murder investigation, but he was a criminal informant for the Austin cops," Rory explained. "And he was also a hacker. I'm betting that's the reason Eric hired him."

Kellan bet the same thing. Well, if this was true. He doubted Rory was lying to him about something that would be easy to verify, but Kellan intended to verify it anyway. Maybe the marshal was innocent and had had no involvement with the dead prostitute and sex trafficking that Kellan's father had been investigating,

but Kellan had always felt in his gut that there was a connection.

"If I find out anything else about Oswald or Eric, I'll call you," Rory said. There seemed to be some weariness in his voice now. "Keep Gemma safe," he added as he ended the call.

Kellan stared at the phone a moment before he looked at Gemma to get her take on that conversation. "You think Amanda and Rory could be playing a version of good cop, bad cop?" she asked.

"That's possible. Or maybe Rory just knows there's nothing he can say that will make me trust him. Not right now, anyway." Kellan tipped his head to the stairs. "Why don't you go ahead and get settled. I'll make a pot of coffee and start a deeper background check on Oswald."

This time, Gemma hadn't even had time to take a step before his phone rang again. Kellan thought it might be Rory calling to add something he'd forgotten. But it said Unknown Caller on the screen.

"Eric," Gemma said, pressing her hand to her heart and moving closer.

Since there was a high probability it was indeed Eric, Kellan hit the record function on his phone and took the call, again on Speaker. He didn't say anything though. He just waited for the caller to say something.

"Sheriff Slater?" a woman asked.

Definitely not Eric. "Who is this?"

"I can't stay on the line," she said without answering his questions. "Eric could find me."

That got his attention. "Eric's after you?"

"Yes, and I can't risk him finding me. He'll kill me, Sheriff Slater. He'll murder me like he did the others."

Her voice broke, and she made a hoarse sob. "I need to get away, and I want your help to do that. I'll call you again."

"Tell me where you are, and I'll send deputies to you. I can keep you safe."

The woman only sobbed again. "I'll call you when I can," was her answer.

"Wait," Kellan said before she could hang up. "Who are you?"

"I'm Maylene Roth. God. Oh, God. I should have never trusted Eric."

And the line went dead.

CHAPTER SEVEN

Oh, God. I should have never trusted Eric.

Maylene's words went through Gemma's head, repeating along with the ache that pulsed at her temples. Actually, she was aching everywhere, but the pain in her head was making it especially hard to think. Still, she forced herself—again—to concentrate while she paced the floor of the guest room.

The woman had sounded terrified. And maybe she was. But it was just as possible that Eric had put her up to making that call and that anything she told them would be a lie to cover for him. After all, the medical report had said Maylene was *attached*.

She glanced at the door that she'd purposely kept slightly ajar. She'd done that in the hopes that if Maylene called back, then she'd either be able to hear Kellan's phone ringing or that he would come and get her. Since his bedroom was just across the hall, it wouldn't be a long trip for him to make.

But there'd been no phone ringing. No other whispered cop conversations like the earlier ones in the evening between Owen and Eli after he'd shown up to relieve his brother. There was only the dull, throbbing silence and the fatigue.

Gemma shifted her attention to the laptop on the nightstand. It was still running a probability program

to help her narrow down possible locations for Eric. Even if it gave her results though, she wasn't holding out hope that it would be in any place where they could get to Eric in time to stop him from killing again. Still, they didn't have a lot of options.

Sighing and silently cursing, Gemma dropped down on the bed. Her legs were just too tired to keep pacing, something she'd been doing for the past two hours since she and Kellan had finally called it a day and put aside the investigation to get some rest.

As many steps as she'd taken, she was surprised she hadn't put ruts in the hardwood floor. She'd certainly put a huge dent in her already drained energy levels, and her body couldn't keep going like this. It was already past midnight, and she had to try to sleep.

As much as she dreaded the thought of it.

Maybe, just maybe, the dreams would give her some peace tonight.

Gemma snapped to a sitting position when she heard a phone ring, and she stood when Kellan came hurrying into the room. He had his phone extended for her to hear.

"Maylene," he said to the caller. "Where are you?"

"It's not safe. I can't tell you." The woman sounded even more terrified than she had before.

"If I don't get to you, Eric could kill you." In contrast, Kellan's voice was calm. Nothing calm about his face though. The muscles in his jaw were at war.

"Yes, Eric can kill. He killed that woman in Mexico."

That caused Gemma to go even closer to the phone, though she could hear Maylene just fine.

"What woman?" Kellan asked.

Maylene made the same sobbing sound she had with the earlier call. "He called her Caroline."

Gemma had thought she had steeled herself up enough to hear that. She hadn't. And she had to sit down on the bed. Kellan kept his cop's face, but Gemma knew that beneath his tough exterior, that had to hurt because of his brother Jack.

"I could end up like Caroline if I stay with him," Maylene went on. "That's why I have to get away from him. That's why I need your help."

"Just tell me where you are," Kellan insisted.

"I can't. Not until I'm sure it's safe, and I can't stay on the line in case someone's trying to trace this. I just want you to be ready when it's time for you to help me. I'll call you right back."

"No. Wait," Kellan snapped, but he was talking to the air because Maylene had already ended the call.

Kellan cursed, squeezed his eyes shut and then scrubbed his hand over his face. Gemma totally understood that frustration because it could be hours before Maylene spoke to them. If at all.

"Unknown number," he said, adding more profanity. "Even if Maylene's using a burner cell, she's not staying on the line long enough for me to trace it."

No, and Gemma doubted that was by accident. Maylene wasn't going to let them find her until she was ready for that to happen. Maybe that wouldn't be too much longer.

Kellan turned off the recorder function on his phone, walked closer to the bed and looked down at her. Well, actually he looked at her clothes. She was still wearing the same outfit she'd had on earlier. So was he, but his shirt was unbuttoned,

He took hold of her chin, angling her face to examine her eyes. "Will it do any good if I tell you to try to get some sleep?" he asked, but he immediately pulled back his hand and waved that off. "How are you holding up?"

Maybe this concern was part of the truce they'd reached. Or because he was worried about her having a panic attack that she'd warned him about.

Gemma considered saying that she was okay, but she wasn't that good of a liar. "My stomach is in knots because of what happened to Caroline. I'm scared for Maylene. For us. For anyone who crosses Eric's path. I'm upset. Tired. And…" She certainly hadn't meant to go quiet when she looked up at Kellan, but her attention landed on his bare chest.

Really? She was feeling this now? Gemma gave a hollow smile, a sigh and shook her head.

Kellan could have pretended he didn't know what she meant, but maybe he wasn't in the mood for lies, either. "Tempting," Kellan said. "But I think we both know if I put my arms around you right now, it won't stop there."

It wouldn't. The sex between them had been good. Darn good. And coupled with the spent adrenaline, fatigue and worry, it wasn't wise to add attraction to that mix. That's why it surprised her when he eased down on the bed next to her. Definitely not a good idea, but at least they were not face-to-face, no longer making that deep eye contact that only lovers could make. Instead, they were looking straight ahead.

He reached out again, this time not touching her chin but running his thumb over her bottom lip. As much as Gemma knew she should stop this and guard her heart, she felt herself leaning right into that touch. She would have done more than lean, too.

If Kellan's phone hadn't rung.

He snapped away from her, his expression as surprised and frustrated as hers, and then Gemma saw Unknown Caller on the screen. As he'd done with the other calls, he hit the recorder before he answered.

"Sheriff Slater," Maylene said. She said something else that Gemma couldn't understand. That's because the woman was sobbing. "Meet me tomorrow at noon. Serenity Inn. Please come because that's where I plan to lure Eric. Kill him for me. Please. Before he kills all of us."

KELLAN TRIED TO shut out the chatter and noise in the squad room so he could volley his attention between the live feed from the surveillance camera at the Serenity Inn and the medical examiner's report for Oswald.

He'd printed out the report to free up his computer so he could use full screen for the surveillance camera. He wanted to see something—in either the report or at the inn. To find something. He wanted a blasted smoking gun that would give them Eric on a silver platter.

There sure as heck was nothing in the report or on-screen that would do that.

But maybe Maylene would come through for them four hours from now as she'd said. Maybe she could indeed lure Eric there at noon. However, it was just as possible that this was a trap or a wild-goose chase. Still, a trap could yield them Eric if they played this right.

Kellan had started the "playing right" by already having three deputies in position near the inn. When it got closer to noon, he'd go out there, as well. Wearing Kevlar and armed to the hilt. And if he got lucky, this would all come to an end today.

He got up from his desk to pour himself another cup of coffee but decided against it. He was already a tangle of nerves, and coffee wasn't going to fix that. Nothing was, except for bringing both Eric and Maylene into custody.

Gemma looked at him when he sank back down behind his desk, and she raised an eyebrow. "What, eight cups is your limit?" she asked. She managed a slight smile to go with that.

"Trying to cut back." No smile for him, but it was light enough to ease just a bit of that tension.

The strain on her face wasn't easing anything though. Gemma had likely gotten as little sleep as he had, and she had passed on the coffee, making him wonder if she'd given up caffeine because it interfered with her usual meds.

Meds that she still hadn't taken.

Maybe once this situation with Maylene was resolved, he'd be able to coax her into taking not only the meds but also a nap. *Alone.* He made sure he mentally repeated that to his body.

His body didn't seem to be listening though. And that was the reason he forced his attention off her and back to the report.

"I got some more info on Maylene," she said, sipping the herbal tea that she'd ordered from the diner. "She and Eric were classmates at an expensive private high school. Maylene flunked out."

Gemma turned the computer screen so he could see a picture of Maylene when she'd been a teenager, and he mentally compared it to more recent ones that he'd pulled up from DMV records and high school tran-

scripts. She hadn't changed much. A plain face with no makeup and straight brown hair.

"I can see if they actually had classes together," Gemma went on, "but it wasn't a large school."

So, the pair had known each other for a while and came from similar backgrounds. Well, other than the fact that Eric had never flunked out of anything and likely wouldn't have with his high IQ. But Maylene wasn't stupid. After all, she had a nursing degree, so maybe there was some other reason she'd left the school. Maybe that reason was Eric.

Kellan was still mulling that over when Jack came in, a tray of take-out cups in one hand and a huge box of doughnuts in the other. The box was open, and the deputies flocked to it like a mini-swarm, each of them snagging one or two as Jack said, "Help yourselves." Once they were done, he set the box on the small table where Gemma was working.

"Woman does not live by herbal tea alone." Jack flashed her a smile and plucked another cup of tea from the holder. "There's an apple fritter in there with your name on it."

He hadn't been joking about that. The apple fritter did indeed have a napkin placed over it, and Gemma's name was written on it.

"Thanks." She rose to brush a kiss on Jack's cheek.

Such a simple gesture caused Kellan's stomach to clench. He didn't especially want a chaste peck from Gemma, but it was a reminder that she no longer had that ease with him. No longer felt it was her right to kiss him whenever she wanted.

And vice versa.

"Is this some kind of bribe?" Kellan asked him when Jack put the coffee and drinks on the edge of Kellan's desk.

"No. Just lucky timing. As I was coming in, I saw Amanda pull into the parking lot. I figured a chocolate-glazed doughnut might make the visit easier to tolerate."

No. It wouldn't. And Kellan had one thought about the woman's visit—what the heck did she want now? He wouldn't have long to find out because at that moment, Amanda came through the front door, her attention going straight to him.

"If the subject comes up," Jack added, "Amanda pressed to become Gemma's handler. In fact, she called in a couple of favors to make sure it happened."

Interesting and not actually a surprise since Amanda seemed to have taken the duty personally and with more than the usual fervor. The question was, why had she done that? Was it because of Rory?

Jack glanced at the computer screen with the feed from the Serenity Inn. "Want me to keep an eye on that while you tell the marshal to go to hell?"

Kellan debated his options and nodded for Jack to take a seat behind his desk. "This won't take long. And don't let her see the screen." He glanced at Gemma to tell her the same thing, but she was already closing her laptop.

"I'm busy," Kellan snapped the moment Amanda came in.

She nodded, and there was none of the raw anger that'd been on her face the previous day. In fact, the look she gave both of them seemed to be some kind of apology, but if so, Kellan wasn't going to buy her "good cop" act.

"This won't take long." Amanda turned her attention to Jack as if she might ask him to leave, but then she reached behind her and shut the door.

"I'm busy," Kellan repeated, his voice sharp.

She nodded but stayed put. "There are some things I need to tell you. Things that may or may not come up during your investigation."

Kellan hadn't thought there was anything the marshal could say that would allow this meeting to go on, but he'd been wrong.

Amanda dragged in a long breath, shoved her hands into her pants' pockets. "I volunteered to be Gemma's handler. That'll come out sooner or later."

"It already has come out," Kellan assured. He didn't ask her why, something he very much wanted to know, but instead gave her a moment to flick a glance at Jack.

Jack looked up from the computer screen and smiled at her.

Amanda's expression seemed slightly less apologetic when she shifted back to Kellan. Maybe because she thought revealing that detail herself would earn her some brownie points. It wouldn't, and Kellan made a circling motion with his finger for her to continue.

The marshal did, after another long breath. "Rory and I are lovers, but I suspect you already knew that."

Kellan tried not to look surprised, though Gemma's eyes widened. Jack obviously hadn't known, either, or he would have already spilled a tidbit like that.

"Yes, I let my feelings for Rory get in the way of how I handled myself yesterday. I was angry that you *might* have a vendetta against Rory because of what happened to your father."

Her body language and the way Amanda had said that *might* let him know that she did indeed believe there was a vendetta.

"Is there a point to all of this?" Gemma asked. "Did you think if you stayed close to me that I'd tell you if Kellan found evidence to prove that Rory murdered the prostitute?" She was both impatient and tough.

Good. Kellan figured it was all an act, but he liked having the marshal taken down a notch. And no, it wasn't because of the power play that she'd tried to make by forcing Gemma back into WITSEC. It was because he simply didn't trust Amanda.

"Yes, there's a point," Amanda continued. "It's not about Kellan. It's not even about Rory." She paused, muttered some profanity. "It's about Eric."

Again, Amanda had surprised him. "What about him?" Kellan pressed.

Amanda didn't jump to answer, and her forehead bunched up. "First of all, I didn't withhold evidence. I wasn't even sure if it all connected." She paused before her eyes went to Gemma's. "I believe Eric murdered a dear friend of mine. Her name was Callie Wellman."

That obviously meant something to Gemma because Kellan saw the spark of recognition even as she shook her head. "Callie Wellman is a missing person I tried to link to Eric. I couldn't."

"Neither could I," Amanda said quietly.

Kellan knew there was a long list of missing women that the FBI, and obviously Gemma, had researched to try to find out if they were part of Eric's body count. Kellan had studied that list, but there had been dozens of names, and he hadn't committed them to memory.

"Why do you think Eric killed her?" Kellan asked Amanda, and depending on how she answered, he'd decide if she'd withheld evidence.

Amanda took her hands from her pockets so she could drag one through her hair. "Callie told me that she'd met someone. He was a student at the college. She said he was some hotshot criminal justice guy and that she was going to meet him for coffee. That was two years ago and also the last I heard from her." Another pause. "She was...*is* like a sister to me."

Kellan wanted to point out that there were hundreds of criminal justice students, and that the odds were slim of it being Eric. But if Amanda had the instincts to go along with her badge, then this could be one of those unexplainable gut feelings that had pointed him in the right direction too many times to count.

Of course, that hadn't worked the night his father had been murdered.

Nor had it worked for Gemma when Eric was working right next to her.

"I'm sorry," Amanda went on, still talking to Gemma. "I became your handler so I'd get first dibs at finding Eric. I figured that eventually he'd try to come after you, and I could catch him."

A bad feeling immediately flashed through Kellan's head. "Did you leak the location of Gemma's WITSEC house so Eric would be able to get to Gemma?" He had to speak through clenched teeth.

There was steel and ice in Amanda's eyes when she looked at him. "No. Of course, not." It sure seemed as if she wanted to add more. Probably something that included some curse words, but instead she turned and stormed out.

Kellan would have gone after her, to grill her about that, but his phone dinged with a text message, and he saw it was from Gunnar Pullam, one of the deputies he had posted in the woods near Serenity Inn.

A woman just arrived in a four-door sedan. The license plates are smeared with mud. Can't confirm if it's Maylene or not, but she'll soon be in camera range.

Kellan hurried to the desk. Gemma, too, and along with Amanda, they looked at the camera feed. Despite the meeting still being three and a half hours away, a woman walked into view.

It was hard to see her face because she was wearing huge sunglasses, and her hair was tucked beneath a baseball cap. Actually, it was hard to see her body, too, since she was wearing baggy pants and a loose men's shirt.

With slow, cautious steps, the woman went closer to the inn. Closer to the camera, too, and when she looked up, Kellan had no doubt who this was.

It's Maylene, he texted to Gunnar. Kellan had studied the woman's picture enough to know her despite the attempts to hide her hair and face. "Hold your position, but stop her if she tries to leave."

"You're hoping she was able to lure Eric there," Gemma said in a hoarse whisper.

Kellan risked glancing at her. She certainly didn't look so strong and tough now, and that herbal tea didn't stand a chance against nerves like this. He would have liked to have given her some kind of reassurance, but Kellan had no idea how to manage that. Maybe, though, Eric would show up, and he could end this.

While he continued to watch the screen, Kellan took the Kevlar vest from the small closet behind his desk. That certainly didn't ease Gemma's nerves, but she had to have known that he would go there.

"What's your plan?" Jack asked him.

"You'll stay here with Gemma. I'll go to the inn and park nearby on that old ranch trail." No need to tell Jack which one because they both knew that area like the backs of their hands. "If Eric shows, I'll arrest him. If he doesn't, I'll arrest Maylene and get her to tell me where Eric is."

It was simple enough, but all three of them—and the deputies on scene—knew that plenty could go wrong.

"Keep your eye on Maylene and call me if there's any change in her position," Kellan added, and he headed for the door.

"Wait," Jack called out.

Jack motioned for Kellan to come back over to the computer screen. When he did, he saw Maylene looking directly up at the camera that was on the roof of the front porch.

Kellan cursed, expecting her to run, but she didn't. With her attention as fixed on the camera as he was fixed on her, she caught on to the bottom of her shirt and lifted it.

"Something's on her stomach," Gemma immediately said.

Yes, there was, and Jack used the computer keys to zoom in on it. And Kellan soon saw the words written there in bold letters.

Don't come here. It's a trap.

OF COURSE, KELLAN went anyway.

From the moment Gemma had seen Maylene's message, she had known that Kellan would go to the Serenity Inn. There was no way he would stay tucked away in the sheriff's office while his deputies risked a trap by bringing the woman into custody.

Unlike Gemma.

He'd had no trouble tucking her away, and with a repeated warning for Jack to "watch her," Kellan and Owen had hurried out of the squad room. There'd been no verbal goodbyes, but Kellan had given her a quick glance from over his shoulder. Eye-to-eye contact. Coming from Kellan, it was almost as potent as a kiss.

Even after the cruiser was out of sight, Gemma stood in the doorway and tried to rein in her fears. Impossible to do, and she might have stood there indefinitely if she hadn't felt the hand on her shoulder. Jack. With the gentlest of touches, he eased her back into the office and shut the door. Probably so that she wouldn't be in the line of sight of the windows.

Only then did Gemma realize this could be a reverse trap. Eric and/or Maylene could have planned to get Kellan and as many deputies out of the building so that Eric or one of his henchmen could come after her.

"Anything new on the investigation?" Jack asked her. He immediately went back to checking the computer screen.

Gemma doubted there was something about the case that he didn't already know. Well, with the exception of Maylene saying the body in Eric's car was Caroline's. But that info wasn't going to come from Gemma. That meant Jack's question was to distract her.

"No." She went to the computer to watch.

Maylene was still on the screen, but she was no longer looking up at the camera. She had moved to the side of the porch and had crouched down next to an overgrown shrub. Not exactly concealed, but at least she wasn't out in the open.

"Maybe she's waiting for Eric," Gemma said. Or she could just want it to look that way. Ditto for her "trap" warning. It could be real or just part of a sick plan to kill Kellan, and a Kevlar wasn't going to save him from a head shot.

With that thought eating away at her, the minutes crawled by, making her wish that she could hear the conversation on the police radio. If she did that though, she wouldn't be able to watch what was happening on the screen.

"If it bothers you to look at the place, you can wait on the other side of the room and I'll tell you what happens," Jack offered.

He was thinking that the inn would trigger the bad memories of her own shooting. And it did. But right now, it was triggering more concerns about the present than the past.

"I can do the same for you," Gemma said. "It has to bother you to see this place, too."

Jack made a sound of agreement. "I could say that about the entire town." He shrugged. "But home is home."

Yes, and despite everything that'd happened, she'd missed living here. Missed the people.

And she'd missed Kellan.

God, had she missed him.

She checked the time. Only three minutes had passed. But since the inn wasn't that far from town, it

wouldn't be long now before Kellan and Owen got to the trail. After that, it would be a short walk to the inn itself.

"Are you still in love with Kellan?" Jack's question came out of the blue.

Gemma took her eyes off the screen a moment to flash him a flat look. "*Still?* That implies I was in love with him before things…well, just before."

"Yeah, it does. Are you still in love with him?" Jack flashed a cocky grin to go along with that repeated question, and Gemma wasn't sure if he truly wanted to know or if he was again trying to distract her. She suspected the latter.

The distraction wasn't working. Worse, the flashbacks were coming, and they were blending with the thoughts of Kellan being there. Of Maylene being there, too. Because if the woman was truly innocent and on the run from Eric, then she could be in grave danger.

Jack's phone dinged with a text message. "Kellan's on the trail and heading to the inn," he relayed after reading it. "Owen's about to call. He'll keep his phone on so we'll have audio."

His phone immediately rang, and even though Owen didn't say anything, she could hear the sounds he made while he moved. Could hear his already heavy breathing, too.

Gemma automatically moved closer to the screen. "Kellan and Owen will be coming from this direction?" she whispered, tapping all the way to the right.

"Probably. I doubt he and Owen will split up. They'll probably try to use the trees for cover until they make it to Maylene." Jack moved closer, too, until they were huddled together. "I couldn't tell if she was armed."

Neither could Gemma. Nor did she know if the

baggy clothes were usual for the woman or if she was using all that bulk to hide a weapon. The way Maylene had hunkered down, she could have already drawn that weapon and been ready to try to use it on Kellan and his brother.

When her lungs started to ache, Gemma released the breath she didn't even know she'd been holding, and she got just a slight jolt of relief when she saw Kellan at the bottom of the screen. Owen was only about five feet away, and both of them were firing glances all around.

Maylene must have seen them, too, because she levered herself up just a little. She shook her head. Frantically shook it.

"Get down!" Maylene shouted.

That was the only warning Kellan and Owen got before the explosion ripped through the yard.

CHAPTER EIGHT

KELLAN HEARD MAYLENE'S SHOUT, and he instantly dropped down into the shallow ditch on the side of the walkway that led to the Serenity Inn. Good thing, too, because the blast came just seconds later. It was deafening, the sound roaring through him; beneath him, the ground shook.

He immediately glanced over at Owen and said a quick prayer of thanks when he saw that his brother was shaken but okay. Now he had to make sure the same was true for his other deputies. And Maylene.

"I don't see anyone," Owen said, coughing from the dust and debris that the explosion had kicked up.

Neither did Kellan. Not even Maylene. Maybe since the woman had given them that warning, she'd managed to get away from the blast, but it was too risky for Kellan to go looking for her.

He made the calls to the deputies while Owen phoned for a bomb squad. God knew how long it would take them to get there, but in the meantime he could seal off the area as much as possible in case there was a second bomb.

"We're both okay," Kellan heard Owen say several long moments later. *It's Jack*, he mouthed to let Kellan know who was on the other end of the line.

Kellan was about to curse when he realized the

explosion would have been on the camera feed and Gemma would have seen it. But before he could get out a single word of profanity, his phone dinged with a text message. It was from Unknown Number.

You might want to check on Gemma, the message said. Poor thing. She's at your office with only a deputy and your brother to protect her. Think that'll be enough to stop me from getting to her?

Eric. The snake was going after Gemma.

"Come on," Kellan told Owen. His brother didn't question it. He just started running back toward their vehicle while Kellan barked out orders to the other deputies to secure the area and call the Texas Rangers for backup. Like the bomb squad though, the Rangers wouldn't be there for a while.

Kellan didn't have to tell Owen to keep watch. They both did. Because Kellan was well aware that this threat to Gemma could be a trap.

The moment they were back in the cruiser, Kellan got them moving while he stayed on the phone with Gunnar to spell out to the deputy that he didn't want him or anyone else going near the inn. Again, it could be another trap with yet more explosives. It was also the reason he'd turned on the security alarm for the cruiser before he'd ever started on the ranch trail. That way if Eric or someone else had tried to tamper with the vehicle, the alarm would have sounded.

"Jack knows there could be trouble at the sheriff's office," Owen relayed when he finished the latest call with their brother.

Kellan didn't doubt that Jack would be ready, but he wanted to kick himself for letting things come to this. He should have anticipated that Eric would do some-

thing so he could try to get to Gemma. She was the target.

"Still no sign of Maylene," Owen added after reading a text that had almost certainly been sent by one of the deputies on scene. "But she could be under the debris."

Yeah. She could be dead. In fact, she probably was. Kellan didn't know the exact spot where the explosion had been planted, but it might have been impossible for Maylene to get away. And it wasn't hard to figure out why Eric would want her dead. The woman was just another loose end for him.

Thankfully, there was no traffic on the rural road that led into town, but Kellan didn't let down his guard. He continued to keep watch, along with sending up some prayers that he wouldn't be too late.

The miles crawled by, and it seemed to take an eternity before he finally reached the sheriff's office. Kellan braked to a quick stop, and with his gun still drawn, he hurried inside with Owen right behind him. He also hit the button on his keypad to activate the security on the cruiser. He didn't want anyone trying to tamper with it, and someone might try even though it was parked directly in front of the eyes of cops.

Kellan's heart skipped a couple of beats when he found the place empty, but then he spotted Jack peering out from his office. His brother was in there with Deputy Clarie McNeal, and Kellan immediately knew they had positioned themselves in front of Gemma.

"No Eric and no hired thugs," Jack quickly let him know.

Kellan felt the jolt of relief, but it didn't last because he saw Gemma. She was pale and shaking. Ready to lose it. Jack and Clarie must have realized the same

thing because they both stepped out, moving back into
the squad room so that Kellan could go into his office. Before he could even get the door shut, Gemma
launched herself at him, landing in his arms.

She didn't speak. Didn't cry as far as he could tell.
Gemma just buried her face against his neck and held
on. Now he felt the trembling even more. Her breath
was coming out in short shallow bursts, and her heart
thudded against his chest. Definitely not the concern
of someone who was a casual friend, but there'd never
been anything casual between Gemma and him.

"I'm all right," he assured her, because he had no
idea what else to say. It wasn't enough. Nothing would
be enough. "So are the deputies."

He eased back to finish the update about Maylene
and maybe come up with the right thing to say, but Kellan made the mistake of meeting her eyes. He saw the
tears she was blinking back and the concern—for him.
But there was only a flash of that before the air changed
between them, and his gaze drifted lower, to her mouth.

Hell.

They were practically wrapped around each other.
Her breasts were pressing against him—which meant
other parts of them were pressing, too. Not good with
the emotions zinging around them. Especially not good
with that whole change-in-the-air thing. Everything
went still, as if waiting for something to happen.

And what happened was the kiss.

Before he could talk himself out of it, his mouth went
to hers, not a gentle gesture of comfort. Not this. It was
fast, hard and filled with heat and need. Much too hungry, considering they were both coming down from

the shock of the explosion—and that they shouldn't be doing this.

Kellan mentally repeated that *hell* several more times, but he didn't stop. In fact, he made things worse by cupping the back of her neck so he could angle her and deepen the kiss. Yeah, he was stupid, all right. Stupid and worked up.

She made a sound that came from deep within her throat, not exactly from pleasure, either. It was need, raw and edged, and it knifed through him. Kellan was certain it was doing the same to her.

Her fingers, no longer trembling, pressed into his sides, gripping hard as they moved up his back and into his hair where she fisted a handful. Holding on to him. While the kiss raged on.

When she finally broke for air, Gemma kept her face against his, and he could feel the muscles of her forehead bunched up. Her breath gusted against his neck, and with a voice with hardly any sound, she said his name.

"Kellan."

He'd heard her say it that way before. It'd been on that slick rise of heat that came with sex. So much emotion. Too much, and she must have sensed that because she pulled back, putting some space between their bodies. Slowly, she released the grip that she had on his hair. Then her hand brushed across his shoulder and down the length of his arm before she stepped back.

"We can't pretend this doesn't matter," she whispered.

For just a handful of words, they packed a punch. And while they were true, Kellan figured this was the worst time possible for him to admit that he'd just

crossed a huge line. She wasn't a job. Heck, maybe she never had been. But if he said that to her now, then he was going to have to tell her something else. That he was too involved with her to be objective, that he should turn her and this investigation over to someone else.

But that wasn't going to happen.

The truth was, even with the line crossed, he didn't trust anyone else. She kept staring at him, no doubt waiting for him to say that, but the moment ended when there was a knock at his door. Both knew this could be critical information, maybe even news of an impending attack. That's why Kellan quickly threw open the door, but it wasn't Jack, Owen or Clarie.

It was Rory.

Since Kellan was so not in the mood for this, he was ready to tell the marshal to get lost, but Rory spoke before he could say anything.

"I think I just saw Eric," Rory blurted out. The man was out of breath, and he put his hands on his hips as if steadying himself.

"Where?" Kellan snapped.

"He was just up the street. I was on my way here, and I saw a man in the alley next to that antiques store. I stopped, and the guy started running. I went after him, but he had too much of a head start on me." Rory shifted his attention to Gemma then. "I'm sorry. But it was Eric, and he was only a few blocks from here."

Kellan wasn't surprised, but he was riled. Not just because he'd figured Eric would come here but also because he hadn't gotten Gemma some place safe. There were too many buildings crammed onto Main Street. Too many places for Eric to hide and launch an attack. Heck, he wouldn't even have to get close to the sheriff's

office because he could possibly get one of his henchmen to set explosives as he'd done at the inn.

"I can help you move Gemma if you like," Rory offered.

Kellan gave him a flat look. "No thanks," he said at the same time that Gemma simply said, "No." And she moved to stand next to him, arm to arm.

Rory nodded as if that were the answer he'd expected. "I do have something that might help with your investigation," he added a moment later. "Or it could be just white noise." He paused. "Your dead gunman, Oswald, was once lovers with Lacey Terrell."

Beside him, Kellan felt Gemma's arm muscles tighten. Kellan had a similar reaction. There was no need for Rory to explain who Lacey Terrell was. She was the dead prostitute Kellan's father and Dusty had been investigating at the time of their own murders. Dusty's top suspect was none other than Rory.

"Like I said, it could be white noise," Rory continued, "but knowing how Eric operates, he could have picked Oswald because he knew it would stir up the connection with Lacey."

That was possible, anything was when it came to Eric. The same might be true of Rory though.

Or Amanda.

If either of them had anything to do with Gemma's attack, they could have reasoned that using Oswald might make them look innocent. After all, they wouldn't be stupid enough to use someone who could go back to the very heart of Buck's and Dusty's murders. But, of course, Rory and/or Amanda could have done it to throw a monkey wrench in the investigation.

"I'll keep looking for any other connections to Os-

wald," Rory went on. He checked his watch. "I plan to call Lacey's friend Tasha Murphey and find out if she's recently seen or heard anything from Oswald."

Tasha Murphey was someone else who didn't need an explanation. That's because as Lacey's best friend, Kellan had interviewed the woman several times over the past year, but Tasha hadn't been able to give him anything new. Still, that didn't mean he was going to nix Rory talking to her. Even though Kellan didn't trust Rory, the marshal might uncover something they could use.

"Thanks for the info," Kellan told Rory, and he made sure his tone had a definite goodbye to it.

Rory got the message, though he did give one pleading look to her before she shook her head. The marshal finally walked away, and Kellan kept his eyes on him until he was out the door.

"Once we're sure that Eric's out of the immediate area, I want to move you back to the ranch," Kellan immediately told her. "You can say no, but—"

"I'm not saying no," she interrupted. "I don't want to stay here, not with Eric so close."

Good. They were on the same page, and Kellan motioned for Jack. "Rory said he spotted Eric up the street. He also told me that Oswald and Lacey were lovers."

That got a raised eyebrow from Jack. "You believe him?"

"Yeah. On both counts. That's why I'm taking Gemma back to the ranch. You're driving."

Jack nodded without hesitation. "What about Owen?"

"He'll stay here with Clarie." Kellan checked the time. "The Rangers should be here soon to help with the

team out at the inn. Maybe help here, too. I'll alert the ranch hands to make sure everything is secure there."

Since the cruiser was still parked right by the front door where Kellan had left it, he motioned for Gemma to stay back while he went to the door. Jack came, too, and together they looked out, up and down the street. Most of the buildings were one-story so that helped, but Kellan knew there could be a gunman on one of the roofs. That's why he took several moments to check for any glints of metal or any other sign that something wasn't right.

"I'll get in the back seat with Gemma," Kellan told his brother.

That earned him another of Jack's famous raised eyebrows. Jack could carry on a good chunk of conversation with that particular expression.

"Keep that thought to yourself," Kellan grumbled.

Which, of course, only caused Jack to smile. The smile faded, however, when Kellan got Gemma moving. Jack suddenly became all lawman, and Kellan knew he'd do whatever it took to keep Gemma safe.

His brother went out first, unlocking the cruiser and getting it started. Kellan went next. He opened the door, rushing Gemma inside, all the while bracing himself for shots. But no one fired at them, thank God.

Jack took off, going in the opposite direction of the inn and where Rory had last spotted Eric, but Kellan had no way of knowing if they were heading toward trouble or away from it. That's why he kept watch, along with ignoring the glances Jack was giving him in the rearview mirror. His brother no doubt knew that things were heating up again between Gemma and him. Jack

probably had some worries, too, as to how this would affect not only the investigation but Kellan himself.

Kellan was wondering the same thing.

We can't pretend this doesn't matter, Gemma had told him after that scorching kiss. And she was right. But dropping the pretense wasn't going to help when it came to keeping his focus.

"There's a truck ahead," Jack said, causing Kellan's attention to shift from the side window to the front windshield.

Kellan immediately saw it. An older model with the red paint blistered and rusted in places. It wasn't unusual for a truck to be out here. After all, this was ranch land, but it wasn't a vehicle he recognized. Plus, Kellan didn't like the way it was just creeping along, going a good thirty miles under the speed limit.

Jack didn't have a choice but to slow down. This was a road with plenty of curves and blind spots, and this stretch was the worst part of the trip. His brother couldn't risk a head-on collision by trying to pass the truck.

With his gun still in his hand, Kellan took out his phone and texted Owen to run the license plate. While he waited, Kellan glanced at Gemma to make sure she was okay, and in that glance he saw her eyes widen, causing his attention to snap back to the truck.

Hell. What now?

There was the flash of brake lights, the sound of tires screeching on the asphalt as the truck came to a stop. Jack hit his brakes, too. Almost immediately, the driver of the truck threw open his door, barreled out and ran toward the ditch.

"Get out of here now!" Kellan shouted to his brother.

But Jack was already doing that. He threw the cruiser into Reverse and hit the accelerator just as the driver scrambled into the ditch. Kellan didn't have time to figure out why he'd done that.

Because the blast tore through the truck.

CHAPTER NINE

EVERYTHING SEEMED TO happen at once. The ear-splitting blast, immediately followed by the blazing pieces of the truck raining down on them and the road. The safety glass on the windshield held, but it cracked and webbed so that it was impossible to see.

"We got company," Jack belted out. He jammed on the brakes again, slamming all three of them in their seats.

Gemma's heart was already in her throat, already pounding, but that only got worse when she looked behind them and spotted the SUV. It, too, had come to a stop, not directly behind them but sideways so it was blocking the road. Two men got out, one from the front seat and the other from the back. Both aiming guns at the cruiser.

The first of the shots slammed into the glass.

Cursing, Kellan pushed her down on the seat. "Call for backup," he told Jack. "And if you can manage it from cover, keep an eye on the guy in the ditch."

Gemma certainly hadn't forgotten about him, but the full impact of what could happen hit her like a fist to the stomach. That man was no doubt a hired gun, and he could also start shooting, trapping them in the cross fire. It would take a while, but the bullets could

soon rip the cruiser to shreds, and then she, Jack and Kellan would be killed.

That twisted away at her heart.

"It's me they want," she reminded Kellan. "I could try to negotiate with them and stop them."

Kellan gave her an icy glance that could have frozen the sun. "Not a chance. You're staying put."

He sounded exactly like the cop that he was, but Gemma wasn't giving up. She would do whatever it took to save Kellan and his brother. After all, they were only in danger because of her, and she had enough blood on her hands.

Gemma was ready to try again when her phone rang, and she saw Unknown Caller on the screen. She showed it to Kellan, hit the answer button and put the call on Speaker.

"Gemma," Eric immediately greeted. "In a bit of a fix, are you?"

She gathered every ounce of breath and courage that she could manage. "Call off your thugs."

Eric chuckled. "I think not. They're not done playing with you yet. Are you scared?" he taunted.

"Of course, I am. I'd be stupid not to be scared, but at least I'm not a coward...like you," she added a heartbeat later. "But then being brave was never your strong point, was it?"

Gemma knew that would hit a nerve. And it did. Definitely no more laughter from him, and she didn't need to see Eric's face to know there would be a flash of hot anger in his eyes.

"I don't need to be the one to actually pull the trigger to end you," Eric spat out. "Or your lover. How is Kellan, by the way?"

She hated her own flash of anger, hated even more that he could carry through on this. A coward's bullet could still be deadly.

Gemma looked up at Kellan, but he had his attention focused on the gunmen behind them. Jack's attention was ahead, and he automatically flinched when a shot blasted into the front windshield.

"That came from the guy in the ditch," Jack relayed.

So, the cross fire had begun.

"Kellan is fine," Gemma said to Eric. It was a lie, of course, but she refused to give Eric the satisfaction of knowing that he had just orchestrated her greatest fear. Not her own death. But Kellan's.

Eric laughed again. "I doubt that. Tell me, will you kiss him goodbye before he bleeds to death in your arms?" He didn't wait for an answer. "I told my men to save you for last. Wouldn't want you to miss anything."

With that, Eric ended the call.

If Kellan had any reaction to what he'd just heard, he didn't show it. His voice wasn't the only thing that was all lawman now. So was his expression and every iron-hard muscle in his body.

The shots continued, each of the bullets eating their way through what was left of the glass. Now, Kellan glanced at her. "Stay down," he repeated, and in the same breath, he made eye contact with Jack in the rear-view mirror. "Hit the accelerator and aim for the men. When they scatter, I'll deal with them."

Gemma felt a new slam of fear, as she had no idea if it was a good plan or not. Maybe it was the only plan they had.

"No!" she said when Kellan lowered his window.

But he ignored her. "I'll take care of the one in the ditch first," he told Jack. "Move now."

Jack did. The tires on the cruiser squealed as it sped backward. She immediately heard the shouts from the men who'd been in the SUV. Shouts and more gunfire. Kellan didn't even look back at them. He took aim and fired, sending three shots ahead.

"Got him," Kellan growled.

Just as Kellan said that, she heard, and felt, the thud on the back of the cruiser. There was a screech of pain, and the shots stopped. So did Jack, but it was so he could throw the cruiser into gear and get them turned around. Kellan fired again, only one shot this time, and it was followed by his raw profanity.

"Want to go after him?" Jack asked.

Kellan shook his head. "No. Get us out of here. I'll send someone after him."

So, one of them had gotten away, but it was hard for Gemma to be sorry about that right now because of the relief flooding through her. Cautious relief. Because Eric could have set another trap for them along the way.

Kellan looked at her, their gazes connecting, and things silently passed between them. She could see that he was already blaming himself for this. She was doing the same, but apologies and reassurances would have to wait. He pushed the button to raise his window, and then he called Owen.

From the front seat, she heard Jack breaking more of the glass. No doubt because that was the only way he could see through the windshield. Once he'd done that, he sped up, hurrying them back toward town. She doubted Eric was still there, but Gemma prayed there weren't any other gunmen. With the shape the cruiser

was in, they wouldn't have much protection against bullets.

"The Rangers will come out and assist," Kellan relayed to Jack once he'd finished his call with Owen. "I want them to take over processing this crime scene, too. And the one at the inn."

Good. She didn't want Kellan out in the open to do something like that. Also, the Rangers had more men and resources to get it done faster. Info gathered from those scenes could help them piece all of this together.

"Eric will use you to get to me," Gemma said to Kellan, but she had to clear her throat and repeat it because her voice cracked and was practically soundless.

"He'll use whatever he can," Kellan argued. "He's desperate, and that means he'll make a mistake."

She prayed that was true, but he'd literally gotten away with murder for too long. The best way to stop him would be to set some kind of trap, where she'd be bait, but she doubted it was the right time to bring that up to Kellan.

"You know the drill," Kellan said to her several minutes later. "Move fast and go straight to my office and stay away from the windows."

Yes, she did know, and while she was thankful they were all in one piece, it twisted at her insides to know that this wasn't the end.

The moment Jack stopped the cruiser, Kellan had her out and running through the door that Owen had already opened. Like Jack and Kellan, Owen also had his gun drawn, and there was plenty of concern on his face.

"We have a visitor," Owen told them the moment they were inside. "I searched her and put her in the interview room."

"Who?" Kellan asked, taking Gemma by the arm so he could lead her into his office.

Owen dragged in a long breath before he answered. "It's Maylene, and she says that she can help you catch Eric."

KELLAN SUDDENLY HAD a dozen questions, but he started with the simplest one first. "You're sure it's Maylene?"

Owen nodded. "It's the same woman who was on the security camera footage from the inn. She's not hurt," he added, obviously anticipating what Kellan would ask next. "Just a few nicks and cuts on her face and hands. She refused medical treatment."

Kellan couldn't force her to see a doctor, but the minor injuries were a surprise. The last time he'd seen Maylene, she'd been plenty close to that blast.

"Please tell me you checked her for weapons," Gemma said. She was no longer shaking, not on the outside anyway, but Kellan figured she was about to have a whopper of an adrenaline crash. It certainly felt as if he was.

Owen nodded again. "And I have Clarie standing guard outside the interview room so that she doesn't try to leave." He volleyed glances at Kellan and Gemma. At Jack, too, who'd already moved across the room to start the string of calls and follow-ups that would need to be done. "Are all of you okay?"

"We weren't hurt," Kellan settled for saying. "I had to shoot two men. A third one got away."

"Yeah, Jack told me that when he called for backup. The Rangers should be out at the scene any minute now. They'll look for him."

Kellan didn't doubt that, but finding the gunman

probably wasn't going to happen. The guy had too much of a head start on them. But maybe they wouldn't need a hired thug if they had Maylene. Of course, there were no guarantees that the woman was actually there to help.

"How did Maylene get away from Eric and get here?" Kellan asked.

"She said she managed to run and hide until she thought it was safe to come out. Sam Willard gave her a lift. He picked her up when he saw her walking near his place."

That was possible. Sam's horse ranch wasn't that far from the inn, but it put a knot in Kellan's stomach to think that the elderly man could have given a lift to a killer. Or at least a killer's accomplice.

"While you were out, you got a call," Owen went on. "From Tasha Murphey. It's small potatoes in the grand scheme of things, but she said she needed to talk to you, that she was upset about Rory contacting her."

Kellan hadn't forgotten about Rory saying he would call Tasha about her possible connection to Oswald, but he didn't have time to deal with her now. Once he'd gotten what he could from Maylene, then he needed to figure out a safe way to get Gemma back to the ranch.

"I want to see Maylene," Gemma insisted. "I want to talk to her."

Kellan had been expecting this, and Gemma was no doubt expecting his response. "I can't let you sit in on the interview. You know that. It could compromise anything she says, and I don't want her slipping through any loopholes."

"Neither do I, but I need to see her," Gemma blurted out, but then she stopped and steadied herself with several deep breaths. When her eyes came to his again,

she wasn't exactly calm, but it was better. "You'll have cause to hold her."

"Yeah," Kellan assured her. "At minimum she's a person of interest in the attacks. She's not going anywhere."

"Actually, I'd like to say the same for you," Owen spoke up, and he looked straight at Kellan. "Just minutes ago someone tried to murder you, and you had to kill two men. I don't think it's a good idea for you to try to interview a woman who might have had some part in that."

Kellan opened his mouth to argue with him. He was the sheriff, and it was his job, period. But then Owen made another glance at Gemma, and Kellan thought his brother might be telling him that he should be making sure that she didn't fall apart. She wouldn't. Stubbornness alone would keep Gemma on her feet, would keep her pushing in this investigation. But she was human, and soon, very soon, she was going to come down from the attack.

"You take the interview with Maylene," Kellan told Owen, "but I want to introduce myself, and I'll watch from the observation room."

"I'm watching, too," Gemma insisted.

Kellan didn't even try to nix that. Yes, there was a good chance that Maylene would say something to upset Gemma even further, but at least she would be with him so he could keep an eye on her. He doubted that Eric would send gunmen into the sheriff's office, but Kellan didn't plan on taking any chances. He didn't want to let her out of his sight. And no, it didn't have anything to do with that kiss.

He hoped.

Kellan stayed ahead of Gemma as they walked to the interview room, and when they reached it, Clarie stepped aside and went back into the squad room. Maylene immediately got to her feet, and Kellan saw the nicks and cuts Owen had mentioned. Her shirt and hair also had smears of dirt and soot.

"Sheriff," Maylene said, but she barely spared him a glance before her attention went to Gemma. "I'm so sorry."

Maylene's voice was barely louder than a breathy whisper, and she went to Gemma as if she might hug her or something. Kellan didn't let that happen. He stepped to the side, blocking Maylene from getting closer. The woman looked up at him, her shoulders slumping as if disappointed that he hadn't trusted her to get near Gemma.

"Deputy Slater will interview you," Kellan said, keeping his tone as official and as devoid of emotion as he could. That was hard to do though, since part of him wanted to get to the truth.

"I don't want to talk to your brother," Maylene protested. "I want to talk to Gemma and you." But it seemed to Kellan that she added him as an afterthought. "I can help you get Eric."

"So you said. How?" Kellan asked.

Maylene certainly didn't jump to answer. She pushed her hair from her face, made a low sobbing sound and pressed her hand to her mouth for a moment. "Eric wants me dead now. The explosion proves it."

No, it didn't. Eric could have had multiple reasons for setting that blast, and he wouldn't have cared what kind of collateral damage he caused. That included Maylene being blown to bits.

"Eric knows I betrayed him," Maylene said several moments later. "He won't forgive me for that. He'll try to kill me again, and when he does, when he comes after me, you can catch him."

"And how do you suggest that I make him come after you?" Kellan asked, but he immediately waved that off. Even if Maylene allowed herself to be used like that, it didn't mean she wouldn't be leading them into a trap. "Where's Eric?" he demanded.

She looked him straight in the eyes. "I honestly don't know. That's the truth," Maylene quickly added. "He doesn't trust me, and he's not going to tell me where he is."

"You were a fool to trust him," Gemma muttered. "So was I."

Maylene nodded. "And I regret it as much as you do. He'll kill us both if he gets the chance."

Finally, Maylene had said something that had Kellan in complete agreement. "Give your statement to the deputy," Kellan repeated.

"Are you arresting me?" Maylene asked before he could walk away.

"Have you committed a crime?" Kellan fired right back at her.

Maylene frantically shook her head. "Eric tricked me. I didn't know what he was. I swear I didn't. But I know now, and even though I haven't done anything wrong, I want you to arrest me. That will stop him from getting to me until I can figure out how we can catch him."

Kellan gave the woman no assurances of an arrest, protective custody or something else. That would be

up to Owen, depending on what he learned in the interview.

He and Owen changed places in the doorway, and Kellan led Gemma to the observation room so they could watch behind the two-way glass. Thankfully, someone had put a chair in there because he immediately had Gemma sit.

"I'm okay," she said as if defending herself.

Kellan just gave her a flat look. "You're not. You look ready to collapse, but a chair is the best I can do right now. You want a drink of water?"

She shook her head, and he got a little suspicious when she dodged his gaze. When he shifted his position, he saw the reason she was avoiding eye contact. She was blinking back tears.

"Hell." He reached for her, but she moved away from him.

"Touching's a bad idea right now. A hug wouldn't stay just a hug."

True, and that was the only reason he didn't pull her into his arms. That and if he was holding Gemma, it would make it darn hard to concentrate on what Maylene was saying.

Which wasn't much.

The woman was still arguing that she wanted him and not Owen to do the interview. If she kept it up, Kellan would have to go back in there, but he was hoping Maylene would settle down and spill whatever there was to spill.

When Kellan heard the footsteps in the hall, he stepped in front of Gemma again and put his hand over his weapon. No threat though. It was Clarie.

"We have another visitor," Clarie said. "Tasha Murphey."

Kellan groaned softly. Obviously, the woman hadn't waited for him to return her call which he wouldn't have done for a while. He'd wanted to deal with Maylene and the explosion before talking to Tasha.

"She said it's important," Clarie added, "but she's not here to see you. She claims that Maylene called her and told her to come. She's here to see her."

"Maylene?" he and Gemma said in unison.

Clarie shrugged and nodded. "If we play connect the dots, Tasha and Lacey were friends. Lacey was murdered but was also lovers with Eric's gunman Oswald. You think it's a coincidence that Tasha knows Maylene?"

There was an easy answer to this. No. It wasn't a coincidence, and Kellan headed toward the squad room so he could have a chat with Tasha.

CHAPTER TEN

GEMMA DIDN'T ASK for permission to go with Kellan. She just followed him, and it didn't take her long to spot Tasha even though she'd never actually met the woman. Gemma had done a background check and saw photos of Tasha. She'd also read the statement she'd given to Kellan's father and Dusty when they'd been investigating Lacey's murder.

Tasha was still by the reception desk where Clarie had no doubt left her, and unlike Maylene she stayed put as if she wanted to be as close to the door as possible. With her police record for prostitution, theft and drug possession, it was highly likely that the woman wasn't comfortable in a police station.

Also highly likely that Tasha was still turning tricks.

Gemma hated to judge a person by their clothes, but Tasha's micromini leather skirt, bloodred cropped top and sex-against-the-wall heels definitely looked more suited for seedy bars and dark street corners than a *voluntary* visit to a small-town sheriff's office.

Jack was near the reception desk, too, but he must have sensed this conversation would go better without him, because he went into Kellan's office. He didn't shut the door though, and Gemma suspected he was not only listening but that he was also ready to come to back up if this visit turned bad.

"I called you," Tasha snapped the moment Jack was gone, and she aimed that comment and a stony look at Kellan. "Why did you set Rory on me?"

Kellan held his ground, giving her that cold cop's stare in return. "I didn't. It was his idea to get in touch with you so he could ask you about Oswald." He paused. "Do I need to clarify who Oswald is?" Now there was a touch of sarcasm in his voice.

"No. He was Lacey's man for a while." A muscle twitched in Tasha's heavily made-up jaw. Actually, several muscles were twitching, and the wild almost unfocused look in her eyes made Gemma wonder if the woman needed a fix. "But Rory would have known I didn't have anything on Oswald. He would have known I hadn't seen Oswald in months."

"And how would Rory have known that?" Kellan said.

"Because the marshals have been spying on me, that's why," Tasha said without hesitation.

Kellan went a step closer. "Why would they do that? And why would Maylene call you to come here?"

Tasha huffed as if the answer was obvious. It wasn't, and that's why Gemma stared at the woman. Tasha noticed the stare, too, and she narrowed her eyes.

"I know who you are," Tasha spat out. "You're spying on me, too?"

Gemma shook her head. "I have no reason to do that."

Tasha glanced around, then scrubbed her hand over her face, smearing her mascara and makeup even more than it already was. "I'm just punchy, that's all. Look, I don't want to get involved in this."

When she didn't add anything else, Kellan made a

circling gesture with his finger to indicate he wanted
her to continue.

"Maylene," Tasha clarified after more of those
glances around. "I don't want to get involved with her."

"How do you know her?" Kellan pressed.

Now there was some hesitation, and Tasha chewed
on her bottom lip before she went on. "We grew up together. Our mothers were friends. And no, I don't want
a lecture about squandering away my life and not living up to potential."

Gemma knew that Tasha's parents were wealthy, but
she certainly hadn't come across any connection between Maylene and her. Of course, she hadn't been
looking for that, not with so many other threads of information to investigate.

"Eric and you grew up together, too?" Gemma asked.

"No." Tasha couldn't say that fast enough. "Maylene
met him when she went to the private high school. By
then I was...on a different path."

Yes, to juvie for drug possession and shoplifting,
followed up by repeated trips to rehab. "Maylene and
you have stayed in touch though," Gemma pointed out.

Tasha lifted her shoulder. "She only calls me when
something's wrong." She rolled her eyes, huffed. "Well,
I've got my own problems, and I want you to get Rory
and the marshals off my back." Her voice got louder
with those last words, and she directed her anger at
Kellan.

Kellan studied her a moment. "What do you think
the marshal wants with you?"

Again, Tasha made an "isn't it obvious" sound. She
opened her mouth, closed it, and she was clearly trying to figure out how much, or how little, to say. When

her gaze came back to Kellan's, there was some fire in her eyes.

"Get Rory and that she-bitch marshal off my back, and I'll tell you," Tasha bargained.

"You mean Amanda?" Kellan questioned. "What does she have to do with this?" he included when Tasha nodded.

"Amanda would do anything to protect her man, wouldn't she?" Her expression was both cold and flat. "They're lovers. You know that."

Kellan didn't deny it, but he did take a couple of seconds before he responded. "I'll call Rory and Amanda and tell them not to contact you again."

"I want more." She aimed her red polished finger at Kellan. "I want you to threaten Rory and his marshal cronies. I want you to do whatever it takes to get them to back off. I mean *really* back off. I don't want them following me or prying into my life."

That was a whole lot of emotion in her voice, and Gemma didn't think it was her imagination that the woman was scared. Maybe she had a reason for that if Rory and Amanda were dirty.

"All right," Kellan finally agreed. "I have plenty of friends who are Texas Rangers. I'll have them work through some of their contacts and make sure Rory or any other marshals don't hassle you again. Now, tell me why it's so important that I do this?"

Tasha took her time answering. "Because I don't want to end up dead like Lacey."

Gemma and Kellan exchanged glances. "You think Rory or the marshals had something to do with that?"

A burst of air left her mouth, a sick laugh that wasn't from humor. "You're a cop. You figure it out."

"It'd be easier to do that if you tell me why you're so afraid." Kellan's voice wasn't so sharp now, and he stooped down a little to be on the same eye level as Tasha. "Has Rory ever threatened you?"

"No." Tasha glanced away again, looking at everything but Kellan. "He wouldn't have to. I know that tangling with him could get me killed."

Tasha turned as if she might walk out. Or rather might try to do that. Gemma was certain Kellan wasn't going to let her go. He stepped forward, but Tasha whirled back around.

"By the way, you didn't hear this from me, and if you press it, I'll deny I said it," Tasha added, her hard eyes now drilling into Kellan's. "But Rory was having sex with Lacey. No, not just sex," she amended. She blinked back tears. "Lacey was in love with him, and I think… I *thought* he had feelings for her, too."

Gemma choked down the groan that nearly escaped from her throat and then reminded herself that this could all be the delusions of a drug addict. Or a flat-out lie. But those tears that slid down Tasha's face certainly looked like the real deal.

Kellan didn't have much of a reaction, either. There was only a slight change in his lawman's expression. "When did this affair happen?"

Tasha glanced away again. "It was still going on right up until the time Lacey was murdered."

Now there was a change in Kellan. He cursed under his breath. "You have proof?"

"Nothing that a cop would call proof, but Lacey told me, and I believe her. She had no reason to make up something like that, and I could see her feelings for him. It's hard to hide it when you love someone that much."

That hung in the air for several uncomfortable moments.

"Does anyone else know about this?" Kellan asked.

Tasha lifted her shoulder. "Maylene found out. I'm not sure how, but she thought you should hear about it. Lacey didn't spread it around, because she didn't want to hurt Rory. She knew something like sleeping with a confidential informant could cost him his badge."

It could, but it could do more than that right now. It could cost him his freedom if he was arrested. And that could happen. Well, it could if Tasha was telling the truth, because as a minimum it would mean that Rory had withheld evidence in a murder investigation.

"Was Lacey afraid of Rory?" Kellan went on.

"No." Tasha didn't hesitate. She blinked and stared at him. "You don't get it, do you?" Tasha shook her head. "It wasn't Rory who killed her. I can't prove it, but it was Amanda who killed Lacey."

KELLAN COULDN'T IGNORE his dull, throbbing headache any longer. As soon as he finished his shower and dressed, he popped two ibuprofens and chased them down with water that he drank straight from his bathroom faucet. A good night's sleep would no doubt do more than the pills, but he figured the best he would be able to manage was some catnaps.

It was Amanda who killed Lacey.

Those were the words that kept going through his head, and they sliced through with the images of Gemma's too pale face and her fear when they'd been under fire in the cruiser. He'd seen more of that fear when he and Clarie had finally driven Gemma back to the ranch. This time without incident, thank God. He doubted

though that their safe arrival at his house would help her sleep any better than he would.

No.

And he'd gotten proof of that before his shower. That's when he'd heard her stirring in the guest room across the hall. Pacing was his guess. Worrying. Trying to figure out what they were going to do now that they had not one but two marshals as suspects.

Jack would help them with that. *Was* helping, Kellan silently amended. Shortly after Tasha's bombshell, Jack had driven back into San Antonio so he could start looking into the woman's allegations.

His brother wouldn't take the bull in the china shop approach. Jack would use some of his charm and finesse to try to get to the bottom of it, but word would eventually get back to Rory and Amanda that Jack was asking questions. And if they didn't get wind of it, the pair would soon know when Kellan dragged their butts in for questioning. Just because a person wore a badge, it didn't put them above the law, and in this case, those badges could have been the reason his father and Dusty were murdered.

One of the reasons, anyway.

Eric could have been solely responsible, and since the snake was still at large, that meant yet more precautions had to be taken. Maylene was in a holding cell at the sheriff's office, officially as a material witness, but if the woman was telling the truth about being on the run from Eric, then she had a Texas-sized target on her back.

Tasha probably had a target on her, too, but she'd refused protective custody. She'd also refused to stay at the sheriff's office after telling him about Amanda. Probably because she didn't trust him. Or any other cop

for that matter. Now he needed to figure out if Tasha was lying...or if she'd just blown his investigation wide-open. To do that, he'd need to bring the woman back in for a full interview, but first he wanted to see how far Jack could get with this through his own sources.

Still toweling his hair dry from his shower, Kellan came out of his bathroom and stopped. Gemma was obviously no longer pacing in the room across the hall because she was now sitting on the foot of his bed. Her hands were in her lap, one of her bare feet tucked behind the ankle of her other, and the long look she gave him held far more interest than it should have.

"I started to call out to you to let you know I was in here," she said. "Just in case you were going to walk out here naked."

Well, he wasn't naked, but he wasn't fully dressed, either. He'd pulled on jeans and a shirt, but the shirt wasn't buttoned, and his jeans weren't zipped the whole way. He didn't fix that now because it seemed like closing the barn door after the horse was already out. Besides, Gemma had seen him all the way naked before.

And he had also seen her without a stitch of clothes.

Probably not something he should recall right now, especially not with such detailed memories of all the interesting parts of her. The most interesting though, was that face, but he had no intentions of admitting it.

"I didn't come in here for sex," she added a moment later.

Man, she had a way of off-balancing him. She always had. "Did you need to borrow my toothbrush?" he asked, just to try to keep things light. But it was a losing battle because being light didn't stand a chance around them.

"I, uh, just didn't want to be alone." Gemma frowned and then glanced away from him.

Yeah, he got that. He didn't especially want that, either, but it wasn't exactly safe having them together like this. No bullets flying. No open laptop, jammed with the details of the investigation. No other people in the room.

And then there was the bed.

It was a huge temptation, but that didn't stop Kellan from going to her and sinking down next to her. "Will you get some sleep if I'm in the bed next to you?" he bargained.

"Maybe." Her gaze came back to his and then slipped lower to his chest—which she had no trouble seeing because his shirt was still unbuttoned. "No," she amended. She plowed her hands through the sides of her hair and groaned. "I honestly didn't come in here for sex. We never had that kind of relationship, and I couldn't use you like that. No friends with benefits for us."

No. Neither one of them was the casual-sex type. There'd been feelings and emotions. There'd been lots of caring for each other. And that had all gone to hell in a handbasket after his father's murder and her nearly dying.

"I could give you a pass and just say—use me," he joked. Well, it wasn't completely a joke. Kellan was sure the smile that he flashed didn't quite make it to his eyes.

Her smile didn't make it to her eyes, either. She stared at him as if trying to figure out what to do, and then she surprised him when she lifted her top. Not in some "come and get me" sexual gesture. She only exposed her stomach.

Which was plenty enough.

The scars were there. The ones from her surgery to remove the bullets that Eric had fired into her.

"I just need to get this out in the open," she said, studying him. "I need to see in your eyes that this isn't going to keep tearing us apart."

Kellan wasn't sure what she saw when she looked at him, but he seriously doubted it was an expression that could make her believe the scars didn't matter. They did. They mattered *a lot*. Not because they marked her otherwise perfect body. He could deal with that, but he would always know that he'd been unable to stop it from happening.

"Yes." Her voice was a whisper now, and she looked away. "Eric got past you to do this, and he got past me to kill God knows how many people. Maybe your father. Maybe Dusty. But even if he didn't kill them, there are plenty of others, and I didn't stop it."

She blinked hard, and Kellan knew the tears were just seconds away from falling. Knew, too, the risk of pulling her into his arms, but he did it anyway, and he brushed a kiss on her forehead. That was possibly the biggest mistake he could have made. Because a gentle kiss like that wasn't fueled by heat but by the very emotions that had first landed them in bed for the noncasual sex.

"Is this too much for you?" she asked, her voice shaking.

"It will be if you put your hand inside my shirt." Kellan thought he did a better job of smiling that time, because she laughed.

Gemma eased back, their eyes connecting. "I know your hot spots, and this isn't one of them." She eased her hand to his arm and gripped lightly.

She was wrong. Every part of him was ready to be aroused right now. Even that arm she touched. But she was right about knowing the prime ones.

"You used your profiling skills on me when you found my hot spots," he reminded her. It was stupid to discuss this with her, with the air starting to crackle between them and that shimmer on her face. "You identified possible target areas, then narrowed them down by trial and error."

Even the "errors" had felt darn good.

She made a sound of agreement, lifted her shoulder, and he was glad using the word *profiler* hadn't put the shadows back in her eyes.

Gemma reached up, brushed her fingers against the base of his ear. "Here."

Yeah, that would indeed become a hot spot if her mouth got involved in this. Kellan considered just letting her take this to the next level. That's what his body wanted him to do, but he knew his body rarely made good decisions about this sort of thing. That's why he gave her another of those chaste kisses. This time on her cheek. Then, he gathered her into his arms and moved her farther up the bed and to the pillows.

"I want you to get some sleep," Kellan said. "Let's see if we remember how to spoon."

Her eyebrow came up, letting him know that spooning wasn't going to do squat for this ache that was spreading through both of them. But it might give her a chance to get some much-needed rest. He'd rest better, too, knowing that she was right there in case something went wrong. Well, he would rest better that is if he managed to forget that this was his former lover next to him.

Kellan risked pulling her against him, her back to his

front, and he felt the immediate protest from that stupid part of him that wanted this to be a whole lot more. Before he could even have an argument with himself, his phone buzzed, and just like that, he went on full alert when he saw Jeremy Cranston's name on the screen. Jeremy was not only one of his top hands, Kellan had put him in charge of security for the ranch.

"Boss, I'm by the cattle gate, and I think you need to get out here and check this out," Jeremy said the moment that Kellan answered. "A woman just came walking up the road, and before she passed out, she insisted on seeing you." He paused. "She had a gun, but I took it from her."

That was not what Kellan had been expecting to hear. "A woman? Did she say her name was Tasha Murphey?" If so, she could be in danger.

"No, sir. This woman claimed she didn't know what her name was, but I sure know it." Jeremy paused. "Boss, it's Caroline Moser, the woman we all thought was dead. But she's alive, all right. Well, for now anyway. I've already called for an ambulance, but you need to get down here fast because I think she's hurt real bad."

CHAPTER ELEVEN

GEMMA WAS PLENTY close enough to Kellan to hear exactly what his ranch hand had said. The shock hit her first and then the words sank in.

"Caroline," Gemma repeated. "She's hurt. I need to go to her." And she would have run out the bedroom door if Kellan hadn't stopped her.

"This could be a trap," Kellan calmly reminded her. He kept hold of her hand while he continued to speak to Jeremy. "You're positive it's Caroline?"

"Yes, sir. I've seen her plenty of times when your brother used to bring her here to the ranch."

Jack had indeed brought Caroline here, because they'd been in love. But then Eric had taken Caroline hostage, and no one had seen her for the past year. Maylene had told them about the body in Eric's car, but if Caroline was here, that meant she was very much alive.

But maybe not for long.

"How bad is she hurt?" Gemma blurted out. "Has she been shot?"

"I don't think so," Jeremy answered. "She's got a bunch of cuts and bruises all over her, like somebody beat her up, and she was talking, well, crazy before she passed out. Something's wrong, no doubt about that. Should I put her in my truck and drive her up to your house?"

"No. Don't move her. I'll come down in the cruiser."

"I'm going with you," Gemma insisted the moment Kellan ended his call.

He let go of her so he could put on his boots and holster, but he looked at her, his mouth set in a hard line. She knew he was about to tell her no, that he wanted her to stay safely tucked away while he took all the risks.

"Please," Gemma added. "Caroline's my friend. I'm the reason Eric kidnapped her." And God knew what the monster had put her through if he'd actually had her all these months.

Kellan stared at her, huffed, and then he nodded. Gemma didn't give him a chance to change his mind. She hurried across the hall to the bedroom, put on her shoes and then raced down the stairs right behind him.

"Clarie, you'll drive us," Kellan told his deputy once they'd reached the foyer. "Gemma will stay in the cruiser with you while I see what's going on down at the cattle gate."

Kellan had to disengage the security so they could leave without setting off the alarms, and then he re-armed it when they were on the porch. Probably because he didn't want anyone using this as a chance to sneak in the house while they were gone. But if that was the plan, then Caroline wasn't in on it. No way would she help Eric. Well, unless Eric had managed to brainwash her or something.

Gemma quickly pushed that thought aside.

No need to borrow trouble when they already had enough of it. It was best just to speak to Caroline and try to figure out what was going on.

It was already past midnight, but there were plenty enough security lights on the property that Gemma

saw the three trucks that were by the cattle gate that stretched across the road. Clarie pulled right in the middle of the other vehicles, probably so that Gemma would have even more protection. A sniper would have to get through lots of metal to get to her.

"Stay here," Kellan warned Gemma. He drew his gun and stepped out, walking toward the trio of hands who were crouched down around the woman who was lying on the ground.

Gemma moved to the edge of her seat, and thanks to the cruiser headlights, she saw her. Her heart slammed against her chest and her breath went thin.

God, it *was* Caroline.

But Jeremy had been right about the cuts. There was blood on Caroline's too pale face, and she was moving her head from side to side, the way a person did when they were in pain.

"Put down the window for me," Gemma instructed Clarie. Gemma couldn't do it herself because the windows and locks were controlled from the front.

Clarie obviously wasn't happy about that, but the deputy knew that Caroline was Gemma's friend. That's probably why she lowered the window just a fraction.

"Caroline?" Gemma called out to her.

Caroline's eyes went wide, and when she looked at the men surrounding her, she tried to scramble away from them. Kellan stopped her from doing that by taking hold of her arm.

"Stay away from me," Caroline yelled on a gasp. "I'll hurt you if you touch me."

Gemma pressed her fingers to her mouth. Mercy, she sounded terrified, and Caroline was certainly in no shape to fight back. Kellan moved back from her,

and the other hands didn't touch her. However, they did
corral her in with their bodies so that she couldn't run.

"Who are you?" Caroline asked, volleying wild
glances at them.

"You know who I am." Kellan kept his voice calm.
"I'm Sheriff Kellan Slater. You came here to see me,
remember?"

Her eyes widened again, and while her gaze fired all
around, Caroline shook her head as if baffled by that.
When she moved, Gemma could see what appeared to
be a scar on her head along with some fresh bruises. It
was possible Caroline had some kind of injury that was
affecting her memory.

"She had this in her pocket with the gun," Jeremy
explained, and he passed a piece of paper to Kellan.

Kellan looked at the note and then held it so that
Caroline could see it. "You have my name written here.
See, it says Sheriff Kellan Slater."

Not simply Kellan. That caused the knot in Gemma's
belly to go hot. Because Caroline wouldn't have used his
title. Kellan was her friend, and she would have called
him by his first name.

"Why did you want to see me?" Kellan asked Caroline. "Where have you been all this time? And where's
Eric?"

Each question seemed to confuse Caroline even
more, and she looked on the verge of panicking until
her attention landed on Gemma. "Help me, please,"
Caroline said to her.

"Unlock this door," Gemma ordered Clarie.

Clarie muttered some profanity, but she didn't disengage the locks until Kellan gave her the go-ahead nod.

As soon as she had the door open, Gemma scrambled to her.

"You'll be okay," Gemma assured her. She took Caroline's hand and tried not to react to all the injuries she was seeing on her friend. She stayed quiet a moment, giving Caroline some time to settle. "What happened to you?" Gemma asked.

Caroline opened her mouth, closed it, and this time when she shook her head, it wasn't a frantic, panicked motion. There was confusion and pain, and a hoarse sob tore from her mouth.

Clarie hurried to the cruiser and came back with two plastic evidence bags. One for the note and one for the gun that Jeremy had taken from Caroline. Gemma took a quick look at both. She didn't recognize the gun, but the writing on the note appeared to be Caroline's. It had not only Kellan's full name and title but also his address—an address that Caroline knew well. Or at least she had a year ago. She shouldn't have had to write it down.

"Can you tell us anything about what happened to you?" Gemma whispered to her.

"I don't know," Caroline said. "I don't know." She just kept repeating those three words while she collapsed into Gemma's arms.

In the distance, Gemma heard the ambulance siren, and she knew she only had a couple of minutes before the medics whisked Caroline away. It was obvious her friend needed medical attention, obvious, too, that she'd experienced some kind of extreme trauma, but Gemma knew this might be her last chance to say anything to Caroline before the doctors, and then Kellan, took over. Kellan was going to want to question her.

"I'm so sorry," Gemma told her. She felt the tears threaten, and she tried to blink them back. "I didn't see Eric for who he was. How bad did he hurt you?"

Caroline pulled her hand away from Gemma and studied her. Or rather she tried. From the rapid blinking of her eyes, she could tell Caroline was having trouble focusing. "I know you?" she asked, and yes, it was a question.

Gemma nodded. "We're friends."

There was nothing on Caroline's battered face to indicate she believed that. "Someone wants me dead. Is it you?" This time it was a question, and it was aimed at Kellan.

He tapped his badge. "I'm a cop, and no, I don't want you dead. I want to protect you."

Again, there was no hint that Caroline believed him. The stare she gave him was long and hard, but her gaze fired away when the ambulance turned onto the ranch road and came toward them. Gemma expected Caroline to fight the medics as she'd done with Kellan and the hands, but she kept her attention on Kellan while they put her on a gurney and then into the ambulance.

"I want to go to the hospital with her," Gemma told Kellan.

"Not in the ambulance," he said as if he'd been expecting her to make that demand. "We'll follow it to the hospital." He took her by the arm and got her in the cruiser, and as soon as the ambulance took off, Clarie pulled out right behind it.

Gemma tried to keep it together, but this time when the tears threatened, she wasn't able to hold them back. Nor was she able to stop the sound in her throat when the sob broke.

"No, you're not responsible for this," Kellan snapped. His voice was tough, all cop, but he was gentle when he wrapped her in his arms.

But she was responsible, and just like that, all the memories came flooding back. Not just of Caroline's kidnapping but her own shooting. And Buck's and Dusty's murders.

"Once she heals, Caroline will be able to give us answers," Kellan said. "She saw things that went on that night."

Yes, she had. In fact, Caroline was their best bet at finding out the truth, but Caroline's repeated words came back to haunt Gemma.

I don't know.

Kellan eased her away from him. "I need to call Jack."

Gemma's stomach tightened because she knew it would be a mixed bag. Jack would be beyond relieved that Caroline was alive, but it was going to crush him when he saw her injuries. He would blame himself for not being able to protect her.

Kellan took out his phone. However, he almost immediately tossed it aside and drew his gun. Gemma felt the instant punch of adrenaline, but it was dark and she didn't know what had put that alarm all over Kellan's face.

Then she saw the SUV.

It was parked on the side of the road with its lights off. It didn't stay that way. Once the ambulance sped past it, Gemma heard the roar of the engine.

And the SUV came right at them.

"Look out!" Kellan shouted to Clarie.

His warning hadn't come in time, but thankfully

Clarie jerked the steering wheel to the right to avoid a head-on collision.

The SUV still bashed into them though, ramming into the side of the cruiser. The slash of metal against metal, and the impact was enough to send them exactly where Kellan didn't want to go.

To the ditch.

He could tell from the way the cruiser sank that their tires on the passenger's side were now bogged down. Clarie threw the cruiser into Reverse, trying to get them out, but Kellan wasn't holding out hope that would happen. After all, the SUV hadn't gone in the ditch with them.

"Call Owen and tell him what's happening. Then, call Jeremy," Kellan said, passing Gemma his phone. "I need their help. Tell him I want the hands to approach with caution."

That last reminder was a necessity because Kellan figured this was going to be another attempt to kill them. Later, he'd curse himself for that and try to figure out if Caroline had been bait to draw them out. If so, it'd worked because here he was on an open road with Gemma once again in danger.

Beside him, Gemma made the calls, and while Kellan knew that Jeremy and the others would come right away, it would still take about five minutes for them to get there. Too long, and he doubted whoever was in the SUV would wait that long to make a move.

He was right.

The SUV turned around and came at them again from behind, ramming into the driver's side door again. It was the only saving grace in this. Gemma was on the other side of the cruiser, and if bad turned to worst, she

could be able to get out and take cover in the ditch. In case that happened, he passed her his backup weapon.

In the near darkness, her eyes met his. She was scared, of course, but he saw a whole lot more. "If they get past us, they could go after the ambulance." Her voice was a ragged whisper. "They could kill Caroline."

Yeah, and Kellan figured that was the plan. Of course, there could be other hired thugs waiting ahead to intercept the ambulance. That's why he'd wanted Gemma to call Owen. His brother would respond from the other direction and might be able to stop another murder from happening. In the meantime, Kellan had to do the same here.

"Get down on the floor," he told Gemma when the SUV started turning around, no doubt to come at them again. It'd be an attack from the front this time. "Clarie, lower my window."

Both Gemma and the deputy did as he ordered, and Clarie put down her window, too. She'd obviously given up on getting out of the ditch and took his cue about trying to stop whomever was behind the wheel of the SUV.

When the SUV sped forward, Clarie ducked down so that it would give Kellan a clear shot, but the deputy fired, too. Together, they sent double rounds straight into the SUV windshield, cracking the glass into a spiderweb, and then they immediately pulled back when the SUV crashed into them. The SUV stopped, side by side with the cruiser.

The moment seemed to freeze.

Kellan could see the driver. The bulky shouldered guy had blood on his head, but his hands were firmly on the wheel. But it wasn't the driver that caused the moment—and Kellan's heart—to stop. Judging from

Gemma's gasp, she saw it, too. Their reactions were for the man in the back seat.

Eric.

Kellan certainly hadn't expected Eric to be personally involved in an attack, but it was him, all right. He'd seen that face enough in his nightmares. However, Eric wasn't sporting his usual cocky grin.

He looked...afraid.

But that couldn't be right. Eric wasn't the *afraid* type, but Kellan didn't have time to consider what else might be on the killer's mind. That's because the driver let go of the wheel and drew a gun. Someone on the other side of Eric, someone who Kellan couldn't see, thrust a gun into Eric's hand, too.

Kellan didn't let either of them get off any shots. "Take out the driver," Kellan barked to Clarie, and she fired, her bullets slamming into the man.

But not killing him.

Groaning in pain, the man hit the accelerator.

All of that happened in the blink of an eye. Kellan had already taken aim at Eric, and he double tapped the trigger.

Just as Clarie's shots had done, the bullets crashed through the passenger's side window, and Kellan didn't miss, either. Before the SUV sped away, the last thing Kellan saw was the blood as Eric slumped back on the seat.

CHAPTER TWELVE

Gemma was doing everything possible to rein in her emotions. Kellan already had enough to worry about without being concerned she might fall apart. She wouldn't, but it was going to take an effort to tamp everything down.

Caroline was being examined so Gemma didn't know how bad things were with her friend, but even if she made a full physical recovery, it didn't mean she would be okay. But she was alive, and Gemma latched on to that as a much-needed silver lining in all of this.

She took several long, steadying breaths while she sat in the private waiting room of the Longview Ridge Hospital. Kellan wasn't sitting though. He was at the door, keeping watch, while he was talking on the phone with a Texas Ranger who was in pursuit of Eric and the men in the SUV.

Well, hopefully he was in pursuit.

Maybe the Ranger had even managed to capture them. Or better yet, maybe Eric was dead.

Gemma had seen the blood and the shock on Eric's face after Kellan had shot him. What she hadn't seen was the last flicker of life as death claimed him. And since Eric was like a cat with nine lives, he might have figured out a way to survive two bullets to the chest. After all, she'd survived three.

Kellan ended his latest call, but when he didn't turn to her right away, she knew the news wasn't good. "The Rangers didn't find Eric," she said.

Now he turned sideways so that he could keep watch in case anyone came up the hall toward them. "Not yet. They're calling in another team to help them. In the meantime, I'll keep a deputy with Caroline."

Yes, because if Eric was indeed alive, he might try to kill her. Of course, it was possible that Caroline had served his purpose by drawing Gemma out—a thought that sickened her. It would sicken Caroline even more if and when she realized that was what had happened.

Gemma stood when she heard the footsteps. Her first thought was this was the doctor, coming to update them, but the person was running, and since Kellan didn't draw his gun, she figured it wasn't a threat.

It was Jack.

"I want to see Caroline," Jack immediately blurted out. "Where is she?" His breath was gusting, and there was a sheen of sweat on his face.

"You can't see her. Not yet." And as Kellan had done to Caroline earlier, he took hold of his brother's arm.

Jack cursed, slung off his grip and started back down the hall. Kellan only sighed and motioned for Gemma to follow him. He didn't move out of the doorway until she was by his side, and he didn't run. But then he had an advantage over Jack because he knew where Caroline was. Since Jack didn't, he raced down the hall, opening every door. By the time he made it to the last examining room, she and Kellan had caught up.

Clarie was in the room, and she was in midreach for her weapon. However, she stopped when she saw them. The deputy was next to the door, and Caroline was on

the bed with a doctor and nurse hovering over her. Both snapped toward them, and the doctor scowled.

"I told Kellan that the patient couldn't have visitors yet," the doctor said. Gemma knew him. He was Dr. Michael Gonzales, and while he didn't look very happy about being interrupted, he must have realized that he wasn't going to be able to stop Jack. Good thing, too, because Jack merely pushed him aside and went straight to the bed.

"Caroline." That one word was heavy with emotion, and for a moment she thought Jack might scoop Caroline up in his arms. And he probably did want to do that, but there was no place on her body that wasn't bruised or cut. "Caroline," he repeated.

Jack picked up her hand, gently lacing his fingers through hers, but Caroline shook her head and tried to recoil. Since the bed was narrow, she couldn't go far.

"Who are you?" she asked.

Jack stared at her and then threw a glance over his shoulder at Kellan and Gemma to see if they had an explanation. However, it was Dr. Gonzales who spoke.

"Caroline has a head injury," he told Jack. "Two of them actually." He pointed to the scar on her forehead. "That one's healed, but she has another on the back of her head."

The healed one was likely given to her by Eric, when he'd taken Caroline and Gemma hostage. Heck, Eric had probably given her the most recent one, too.

"My guess is the blunt force trauma caused memory loss," Dr. Gonzales went on, "but I'll need to run some tests on her to see what's going on."

Because Jack was now the one who looked ready

to lose it, Gemma went to him and put her hand on his arm.

"She didn't know who we were when she got to the ranch," Gemma whispered.

Apparently, Caroline still didn't remember, judging from the wild, frightened look in her eyes.

Jack stood there, casting uncertain looks at all of them before his attention settled on Caroline. "I'm Jack. Marshal Jack Slater," he added. "Remember?"

Caroline's reaction was to back even farther away from him, and she might have fallen off the bed if the nurse hadn't caught her.

Gemma saw the hurt all over Jack, and she knew this wasn't about the things that Caroline might not be able to tell them about the attack. This was personal because he was in love with her.

"I don't know," Caroline said, and just as she'd done at the ranch, she repeated it.

Kellan stepped closer. "A serial killer named Eric Lang took you hostage. Do you remember anything about that?"

Caroline volleyed more of those glances at them, and Gemma couldn't tell if she was actually trying to remember or if her memories were so horrific that she had pushed them away—permanently.

Find Caroline because she's the one who can tell you who really killed Deputy Walters and your father, Eric had said. Well, they had found her, and it was obvious that Caroline wasn't going to be able to give them any answers. Not tonight anyway.

"Do you remember anything?" Kellan tried again. He tipped his head to Gemma. "Anything about when you worked with her?"

Caroline studied her again but only for a few seconds. "I don't know. I don't know." Except this time, she got louder with each word. More agitated, too, and she batted away both the doctor and nurse when they tried to settle her down.

"Wait outside," the doctor snapped to Jack. "After I've finished my exam, I'll come out and talk to you."

Jack wouldn't have gone on his own, and that's why she and Kellan got on each side of him and led him out the door. Even then he kept looking back at Caroline, kept muttering and swore under his breath.

Once they were in the hall, Jack's cursing turned to groans, and he put a hand on each side of his head and squeezed hard. "What the hell happened to her? How'd she get to the ranch?"

"I don't have the answers you want, but it's my guess that Eric brought her there. When he called yesterday, he said he was looking for her, so that could be when she escaped. Or else he lied about that and has had her this whole time. Eric could have dumped Caroline at the end of the road by the ranch because he thought it'd lure out Gemma."

Jack lowered his hands and looked at her. "And it worked."

Gemma shook her head. "Whatever happened, Caroline didn't do it voluntarily."

She wouldn't mention the possible syndromes a person could go through after being held captive a long time. Especially captive by someone like Eric. As a lawman, Jack could no doubt fill in the blanks on his own.

"Besides," she went on. "I don't think Eric was lying about that. I believe Caroline had indeed gotten away

from him." She paused. "I know that doesn't explain the note she had with her."

"What note?" Jack snapped.

Gemma shook her head. "Kellan's name and address. Caroline's alive," Gemma reminded Jack. Reminded herself, too. "She'll heal. She'll get back her memory." And she prayed that wasn't wishful thinking.

Jack scrubbed his hand over his face, and she could practically see the thoughts firing through his head. "I'm not leaving her here alone, and no, I don't want Clarie to stay with her," he added when Kellan opened his mouth to say something. "I'll stay here with her until she's released from the hospital, and then I'll have her moved to WITSEC."

"The danger might be over," Kellan explained. "Eric could be dead."

Jack paused as if considering that. "I'm still staying with her. I can't leave her."

Kellan didn't argue with that, probably because he knew it wouldn't do any good. Gemma wasn't sure she believed in actual soul mates, but if it existed, that's what Jack and Caroline were. That's why it had to eat away at him that she didn't remember him.

The door to Caroline's room opened, and Dr. Gonzales stepped into the hall. "I don't think her injuries are life threatening," he said right off. "My biggest concern right now is the head injury. It could have caused some swelling on her brain, and that in turn could be the reason for her memory loss."

"So, it could all come back." Jack sounded relieved and cautious.

"Too soon to tell. The good news is there are no signs

of sexual assault, and she's been well fed. Slightly dehydrated, but the IV will fix that."

The no sexual assault wasn't a surprise to Gemma. Eric hadn't been into that. He'd been satisfied enough to commit murder,

"She has defensive wounds," Jack pointed out. "Her hands are cut and bruised."

The doctor nodded. "Yes, I would say that she managed to fight her attacker, but she took some licks, too. There are bruises on her stomach and ribs."

Some of the color drained from Jack's face.

"Probably punches from one of Eric's thugs." Gemma hated that she'd said that aloud, but when all three men looked at her, she continued. "Eric couldn't beat Caroline in a fight. Not a fair one anyway. She's had self-defense training." She turned to the doctor. "Was she drugged?"

He nodded. "I don't know with what yet, but I've drawn blood, and it'll be tested." The doctor checked his watch. "I don't want you to question Caroline tonight. My advice is all of you should go home, get some rest and come back in the morning. *Late* in the morning," he emphasized.

"Jack's staying," Kellan said before his brother could.

The doctor's eyebrow came up. "Caroline got agitated when she saw you. I think she'd be more comfortable with Clarie in the room."

"Then I'll wait here outside her door so that she won't see me," Jack insisted.

Dr. Gonzales made a suit-yourself sound and strolled away while making notes on a tablet.

"I'll have Gunnar go with Gemma and me back to the ranch," Kellan said, taking out his phone.

Gemma nearly protested, but she wasn't sure exactly what she wanted him to do differently. They couldn't question Caroline, and she didn't especially want to go to the sheriff's office. It was late, nearly three in the morning, and like her Kellan was probably feeling the bone-weary fatigue from the adrenaline crash.

"Call me if there's any change or if you need anything," Kellan added to Jack.

They exchanged a glance that could only pass between brothers before Kellan took out his phone. While he made the call to Gunnar, he took her back to the private waiting room where they'd been earlier. Even though Gemma couldn't hear the conversation he was having with his deputy, she guessed from the way Kellan's forehead bunched up that it wasn't going well.

God, she hoped it wasn't more bad news because Gemma was afraid she wouldn't be able to take it. Her body suddenly felt as if it were made of glass, the kind of glass that would break with a touch.

Kellan finished his call, cursed and put his phone away. "Maylene's family sent in a team of lawyers. They convinced a judge to spring her from jail so she can have a psychiatric evaluation. We have no choice but to release her."

Gemma's mind was whirling, and it took her several moments to see the big problem with that. "Eric. If she's working with Eric, she can go to him. And since she's a nurse, she can help him. If she's not working with him, it'll be easier for him to have her killed."

Kellan nodded and gave a sigh of acceptance. She saw the fatigue then. Even more than there had been just minutes earlier. "Gunnar's on his way and will go

with us to the ranch. I'm not sure how long I can spare him though."

She understood. So many irons in the fire. And Gemma was about to tell him that when she heard the voice. Not Gunnar. But rather Amanda. Gemma wasn't sure whose groan was louder—Kellan's or hers.

"What kind of game do you think you're playing?" Amanda snapped when she appeared in the doorway. A doorway that Kellan kept blocked because he didn't step aside.

"You don't want to get in my face right now, Amanda," Kellan warned her.

"Funny that you should say that, because getting in my face is exactly what you're doing." Amanda's mouth was in a flat line. "You're having your people investigate me. How dare you!"

Gemma knew this was tricky territory for Kellan because he probably wasn't going to want to spill what Tasha had told. Plus, there was no proof of it. That's why Jack had been looking into things. Obviously though, Amanda had gotten wind of what was going on. Or at least she was aware that someone was digging into her personal life.

Kellan dragged in a long breath, put his hands on his hips. "I'm having you investigated because you withheld information about Eric murdering your friend. By your own admission, you manipulated the system to become Gemma's handler, only to have her WITSEC location breached. I tend to get testy when things like that happen."

Gemma didn't miss what Kellan *hadn't* told the marshal. Nothing about the possibility that Amanda might have murdered Lacey because she'd been jealous of her

lover—Rory—having sex with the prostitute. Gemma would have liked to know how Amanda would react to that, but it would be a risky ploy to bring it up.

Because it might send Amanda or Rory after Tasha.

"I didn't have anything to do with the leak at WIT-SEC," Amanda practically shouted at Kellan, but then Gemma immediately saw her trying to rein in her temper. And then she saw why.

Rory came up the hall and appeared in the doorway.

Great. Now they had to deal with two marshals. Two marshals that neither Kellan nor she trusted.

"Amanda," Rory said. Definitely not a shout, and he aimed a sympathetic glance at Kellan. "Are you and Gemma okay? I heard you were attacked again. I got concerned when I called your office, and a Texas Ranger answered and told me that you two were at the hospital."

"We're fine," Kellan said, but there was nothing about his tone to indicate that was true. He was as riled as Amanda was.

"Kellan's trying to pin something on us," Amanda snarled, but her voice was much lower now. "He believes we've broken the law." She spun back toward Kellan. "We didn't have anything to do with your father's murder."

"What about Lacey's murder?" Kellan fired back.

Amanda went stiff before even more anger flashed in her eyes. "Not hers, either. We're not criminals."

Kellan made a sound that could have meant anything. "You'll hear this soon enough, but Caroline Moser's resurfaced. She's alive."

Gemma moved closer so she could watch their expressions. If either Rory or Amanda had indeed had

something to do with killing Lacey, Dusty or Buck, Gemma figured they wouldn't be happy about a potential new witness. Rory's eyes widened, but if Amanda had a reaction, she kept it to herself.

"How did Caroline get away from Eric?" Rory asked. "And what about that body that was found in Eric's car in Mexico? If that wasn't Caroline, then who was it?"

Kellan shook his head. "I can't answer any of that."

"Can't or won't?" Now it was Rory who snapped.

"Both," Kellan readily admitted. "Caroline was injured. I'm not sure how yet, but because Eric is still at large, she's in protective custody, and I haven't been able to question her."

Rory and Amanda exchanged glances, and Gemma figured they were trying to figure out a way around Kellan so they could get to Caroline. That wasn't going to happen because Jack wouldn't let either of them get near her.

"Eric," Rory repeated on a frustrated sigh. "I called a Texas Ranger friend on the way over here, and he said there was no sign of the SUV. You're positive it was Eric?"

"Yes," Gemma answered before Kellan.

Rory stayed quiet as if waiting for more, but Gemma followed Kellan's cue and didn't add anything.

"The Ranger told me you thought you'd shot Eric," Rory went on, looking at Kellan.

Either that was news to Amanda or else she thought it was a good time to fake surprise. "You shot him? Is he dead?"

Kellan lifted his shoulder. "I won't know until they find the SUV."

And even then, they might not. Yes, the CSIs would

be able to measure blood loss, but unless Eric's actual body was in the vehicle, it didn't mean he was dead. Or alive, for that matter.

Another of Eric's hired help could have gotten Eric to a doctor or hospital. That was the reason that one of the calls that Kellan had made was to get out the word to inform him of any patient showing up with gunshot wounds. Gemma also made a mental note to do some computer searches to see if she could figure out how Eric was paying for all this "help."

"Instead of investigating me, we should be working together to find Eric," Amanda threw out there. "I want to talk to Maylene. Please." Amanda's mouth was still tight when she added that last word. "You know why it's important for me to find Eric."

"I do," Kellan admitted. He didn't mention Amanda's dead friend, but Gemma suspected that Rory knew all about it. "But even if you could talk to Eric, that doesn't mean he'd tell you the truth."

"He would," Amanda insisted. "He'd want to brag about it."

Yes, Gemma had to agree with the marshal on that, and that's why it niggled away at her that Eric had denied killing Kellan's father and Dusty. And that Eric had been so adamant that Caroline knew the truth.

Maybe Eric hadn't been the only killer at the inn that night. One who might be more dangerous than Eric simply because they didn't know who he or she was. One who could hide behind a badge. At least Eric had been forthcoming that he had committed murder.

"Better the devil you know than the one you don't," Gemma muttered. She certainly hadn't expected to say that aloud. Or for it to get Amanda's and Rory's attention.

Rory obviously picked up on the meaning because now there was some anger in his eyes. "Amanda's not dirty," he assured her. Which, of course, assured her of nothing—especially when Rory brushed a loving hand down Amanda's arm.

"I'm going to help the Rangers look for Eric," Rory said to no one in particular. "You need a ride?" he added to Amanda.

The marshal shook her head and kept her attention fixed on Rory as he walked away. She only returned her attention to Gemma when Rory was out of sight.

"You're in love with him," Gemma concluded.

"Yes." Amanda said it quietly and with what Gemma thought might be some regret. "I hadn't intended for it to happen." But she immediately waved that off as if she'd just admitted too much.

Kellan must have picked up on that, too, and he obviously wasn't going to let Amanda off the hook. "It must have hurt you when you found out Rory was having sex with Lacey."

The surprise flashed through Amanda's eyes, but she quickly recovered. "Yes," Amanda repeated. "How did you find out?"

"A source," Kellan settled for saying.

"A source," she muttered, already turning to leave. She said the rest of it as she walked away. "Yes, it hurt when I found out."

Just as Amanda had done with Rory, Kellan kept his eyes on the marshal, and he cursed under his breath. "She just gave herself motive for murder."

CHAPTER THIRTEEN

CONSIDERING EVERYTHING THAT had gone on, Kellan figured he should count it as a major achievement that he'd finally gotten Gemma safely back to the ranch. He'd managed that without anyone firing a single shot at them or trying to blow them up.

Too bad it wouldn't last.

That was the thought that kept repeating in his head as he paced across his bedroom floor while he waited for updates. *Any* updates. He had so many threads of this investigation going on right now that sooner or later something was bound to break. Maybe it would break in Gemma's and his favor. Caroline's and Jack's, too.

Jack was mentally in bad shape, what with Caroline not remembering who he was or what'd happened the night their father had been murdered. But at least Caroline was alive, so there was hope that her memory would return. Kellan just hoped when it did that she'd be able to deal with whatever the hell she'd been through all these months.

He'd left his bedroom door open so he could hear Gemma in the guest suite or Gunnar if he called out to him from downstairs. Kellan didn't hear a sound from either of them, but he considered going across the hall to check on Gemma.

He groaned.

It wasn't a good idea for a man to lie to himself, and if he went to her, it would be for sex. That reminder was enough for him to stay put and sink down onto the foot of his bed. He wasn't the only one with too many "threads." Gemma had them, too, and she didn't need the added complication of rolling around on the sheets with him.

He knew he wouldn't get any sleep, so Kellan didn't even try that. Instead, he took his laptop from the nightstand so he could see if there were any answers to his emails about Amanda.

Now that the marshal with the constant bad attitude had confessed that she knew about Rory's affair with Lacey, it meant Kellan needed to find anything to prove that Amanda had killed the prostitute. He'd have to do an interview with her and check her alibis, not just for the night of Lacey's murder but also his father's and Dusty's. It was a mountain-sized understatement that Amanda wasn't going to like that much.

Of course, there wasn't much about any of this Kellan liked, either, so they'd be in the same boat. Still, he didn't have a choice about what he had to do. If there was a link, he had to find it. Ditto for Maylene. The woman's lawyers might have convinced a judge to free her, but there were lots of unanswered questions. Including the big one.

Was Maylene a killer?

Better the devil you know than the one you don't, Gemma had said about Amanda and Rory, and Kellan agreed. He could add Maylene in there, too, of suspects who possibly hadn't been up-front with them. Maylene seemed vulnerable and innocent, but he needed to backtrack and see if it was all just an act. If so, that

made a very dangerous woman. Even more dangerous than Amanda or Rory because Maylene could team up with Eric.

Kellan had silenced his phone, but it dinged with an incoming call, and when he saw Jack's name on the screen, he put his laptop aside and went to his bedroom door to close it before he answered.

"I don't have anything new on Caroline," Jack immediately volunteered, and Kellan could hear that the no-change was worrisome for his brother. "I'm calling about the missing SUV."

Before Kellan could respond to that, his door opened, and Gemma stepped in. "I heard your phone," she blurted out.

Obviously, she hadn't been asleep if she'd heard such a soft sound. "It's Jack," he let her know. "I'll put the call on Speaker so you can hear him." It was a risk because this could be bad news, but one way or another Gemma would have to know. He couldn't keep even the god-awful stuff from her since she was the target.

"I called the Rangers to ask for an update, and I learned they just found an SUV matching the description of the one that crashed into you." Jack paused. "It's *the* SUV," he added a moment later. "The driver's dead. No ID on him yet. And no signs of Eric, either. However, there was blood in the back seat."

Kellan's stomach clenched. It would have made things so much safer if Eric had been dead, though part of Kellan didn't want the man to have such an easy way out. He wanted Eric locked up in a cage for the rest of his life. That could still happen, but now they'd have to find him—again.

He looked up at Gemma to see how she was han-

dling this. Not well. The worry was right back on her face, and she looked exhausted. With a heavy sigh, she sat down next to him and buried her face in her hands. Because there was nothing Kellan could say to her to make this better, he just slipped his arm around her.

"There have been no reports from hospitals about anyone showing up who matches Eric's description," Jack continued a moment later. "Nor are there any un-accounted-for doctors or nurses or ones who've been reported missing."

Yes, Kellan had checked for that, too, because Eric had kidnapped before and would likely do it again. Still, it was possible a kidnapping had happened, and no one had noticed that the person was gone. If Eric needed medical attention, he would figure out a way to get it even if he had to kidnap, and then kill, again.

"Caroline's having an EEG and some other tests done now," Jack went on. "I'll call you when I have the results." He hesitated again, then cursed. "She called me *Marshal Slater.*"

Kellan knew that had to be hard to hear since Jack and Caroline had been lovers. *Marshal Slater* definitely wasn't intimate. He was about to remind Jack, though, that it could all be temporary, that Caroline might regain her memory before the night was out, but he didn't like lying to his brother any more than liked being lied to himself. So, Kellan settled for saying, "I'm sorry."

It wasn't nearly enough, but just as it had been with Gemma, there was nothing Kellan could say that would ease Jack's pain.

"Thanks," Jack mumbled before he ended the call.

Other than to drop her head on his shoulder, Gemma didn't move when he slipped his phone back into his

jeans pocket. He steeled himself up in case she was about to go through all the things that had gone wrong. Or worse, all the things that *could* still go wrong.

But she didn't.

When she looked up at him, he saw the stillness in her eyes. Behind that stillness, though, was no doubt a whole lot of worry, but she somehow managed to tamp it down.

"You obviously weren't sleeping if you heard my phone beep," he said and risked brushing a kiss on the top of her head.

"No." She lifted her shoulder. "I was debating if I should come over here and have sex with you."

Oh, man. That wasn't a good thing for him to hear, not with his body in knots and his nerves humming. Gemma's shrug let him know that she understood it wasn't a good thing for her to say.

However, it was the truth.

"Sex won't fix anything," she added, her voice a breathy whisper. "And I don't want to settle for kissing or just spooning."

She didn't dodge his gaze. Didn't look embarrassed or uncertain about the moment. Or about anything else. She just looked at him as if waiting for him to make the next move.

Kellan had a short debate with himself. A totally unnecessary debate. Gemma was offering him sex, and he wouldn't turn it down, period. She was right. It wouldn't fix anything except maybe the most important thing of all. It would ease this need that was clawing its way through him. It would dull the ache. And it would remind him that she was everything that he'd ever wanted.

Kellan didn't make her wait long. He pulled her to him and set things into motion with a kiss.

GEMMA HADN'T EXACTLY been subtle with her offer of sex so it wasn't a surprise when Kellan took her up on it. But what was a surprise—a shock, actually—was that something as simple as a kiss could heat her in an instant from head to toe. But then, Kellan had always managed to do just that.

She wound her arms around him, already fighting to get closer. Already needing the kiss to be so much more. She wanted him hot and fast. Something rough that would do a quick cooldown of this scalding heat.

Something where she wouldn't have to think.

But she did think. And she knew that Kellan would regret this because for him it would mean a loss of focus. A complication. Sex would do that for her, too, but resisting was no longer an option.

Her body burned against his. Her mate. That's what the primal pulse inside labeled him, but her heart was telling her that he was so much more.

Gemma made a sobbing sound when she broke for air, and it must have alerted him that something was wrong because he stopped and pulled back. He brushed her hair from her face, but what he didn't do was ask her if she wanted to put an end to this. Well, he didn't ask with words, but the question was there in his gun-metal-gray eyes.

She took in that look in his eyes. His face. Yes, his face could always do it for her even if the need hadn't already been at the surface.

"I want you," she settled for saying.

Still, he continued to study her for several moments.

Things passed between them. It was like those unspoken conversations he'd had with his brothers, but this was a different kind of chat.

The kind of chat between lovers.

When Kellan lowered his head and kissed her again, it wasn't that urgent, out-of-control fire as the other one had been. This was long, slow. Thorough. Surprisingly gentle. She didn't think he was giving her a chance to change her mind, either. No. This was what he wanted from her, and she was going to give it to him. Or rather let him have her this way.

He slipped his hand into her hair, easing her head to an angle so he could deepen the kiss. He touched his tongue to hers. Also gently. Still no urgency. And that caused the taste of him to slide right through her.

The heat slid up a notch when his hand went to the front of her shirt. Gemma tensed only a second when she remembered her scars. But Kellan had already seen them. In fact, he'd seen all the worst things about her, and yet he was still kissing her. Still giving her this gentleness when there'd been no such gentleness in her life for a long, long time.

With that same gentle coaxing he was doing with his mouth, his hand went under her top. Over those scars. And into her bra. He pushed it down and ran very clever fingertips over her nipples.

He knew the sensitive things about her, too, and he was doing an incredible job of stoking the heat higher and higher. Still, Gemma resisted the onslaught until his hand went in the other direction. With that same slow ease, his hand trailed up her thighs. He didn't even put those clever fingers inside her panties. He just brushed against them, and she was toast.

The restraint inside her snapped, and the next sound she made definitely wasn't a sob. It was a throaty groan. She caught the flash of his smile—yes, a smile—before she claimed his mouth and pushed him back on the bed.

Now she was rough and couldn't help herself. Everything inside her was past the simmering and had gone to a full boil. She had to have him now.

Kellan didn't resist when she pinned his wrists to the bed and used her other hand to go after the buttons on his shirt. Her own hands were shaking so it wasn't a graceful effort, but the moment she had his shirt open, she went after his chest. And she showed no long, lingering restraint that he had with her mouth.

He let her take him as she kissed her way down his body, but when her mouth made it to the front of his jeans, she felt the same snap that had just gone through her. He groaned, too. Then he cursed, mixing her name in with that profanity.

And in a flash, he had her on her back and was on top of her.

Now she saw it. His eyes had a storm in them and he was as hard as stone, his erection straining against her. His grip was far from gentle when he shoved up her skirt and rid her of her panties.

Gemma felt his jeans brush against the inside of her thighs and considered getting them both naked so she could feel even more of him. She quickly discarded the idea, though, when he put his fingers inside her and nearly caused the climax to come on like a flash fire.

She fought it, wanting to hang on to this for as long as she could. Which wouldn't be long. That's why she battled against his clever touches to get him unzipped and freed from his boxers. Then, she was the one curs-

ing when he stopped to grab a condom from his nightstand drawer.

The moment he had it on, he plunged into her, filling her until she thought that she might burst. The pleasure came—rough and raw. *Thorough.* That was the one word that kept repeating in her head as he thrust into her.

Her mate. *Hers.*

She rose as he lowered himself. Again and again. The rhythm, primal now. And fast. Then, even faster. Until the coil inside her was so hot, so vicious, wound so tight that she couldn't hold on any longer.

Kellan kept his eyes on her. They were blue and narrowed now. Sizzling like fire created by some warrior pagan god. And he watched her, doing exactly what he wanted to do while he sent her crashing right over the edge.

He watched her do that, too.

Her vision blurred. And dazed and quivering, with her body closing like a fist around him, she could only hold on as he emptied himself into her.

CHAPTER FOURTEEN

KELLAN HAD BEEN certain that he wouldn't sleep, not after Gemma had come to him with her *offer*. But he'd been wrong about that. Maybe it was just sheer fatigue, great sex or the combination of both, but he'd closed his eyes and drifted off.

With Gemma curled up next to him.

Hours later, she was still there with her face pressed to the curve of his neck. She was naked now though. They'd managed to get their clothes off for the second round of sex that'd been just as great as the first, and then she'd obviously managed to sleep, too.

Kellan didn't want to wake her, but it was nearly six, and despite having gotten barely an hour of sleep, he had to get his day started. There were phone calls to make, persons of interest to interview and paperwork to complete. All of which he wanted to ditch when he looked down at Gemma.

A sensible man would kick himself for taking her as he'd done. But he hadn't been anywhere near sensible. Taking her a second time was proof of that. The fact that he wanted her again was more proof that he didn't need.

He eased away from her, surprised that the movement didn't cause her to stir and wondered if it had. It was possible she was actually already awake and was

puzzling over what'd happened as much as he was. Also like him, she could use some time to think.

Kellan took his phone and gun, choosing to do his thinking in the shower, but with everything else he had to do, he kept it short, and he didn't find any answers in the scalding hot water. Of course, that was asking a lot of a mere shower.

He spent less than five minutes total, managing to change into some fresh clothes and brush his teeth. Then, he checked his emails on his phone, scanning through the sparse updates that he found there before he went back into the bedroom. He figured it was time to wake Gemma so they could go to his office, but the bed was empty.

Alarm shot through him.

He drew his gun, but then he heard the shower running in the guest room across the hall, and he released the breath that he'd sucked in. Even though it was highly likely that nothing was wrong, he glanced into the guest room anyway. She'd left open the adjoining bathroom door, and he saw Gemma's silhouette behind the opaque glass of the shower stall.

His body clenched, and it wasn't alarm that shot through him this time. It was need, and Kellan might have done something stupid and acted on that need if his phone hadn't rung. Jack's name popped up on the screen so Kellan went back into his bedroom to take the call.

"Is everything okay?" Kellan immediately asked.

Jack greeted him with a groan, and for such a simple sound, Kellan still heard the weariness. "No one tried to kill us, so that's good," Jack said.

It was indeed good. "You're still at the hospital?"

"Yeah. I sent Clarie home so she could get some rest."

Kellan wanted to point out that Jack needed rest, too, but it wouldn't do any good. If their positions had been reversed, Kellan would have stayed at the hospital, as well.

"The doc got back some of the test results," Jack went on. "There's no sign of brain swelling, which means the memory loss is from mental or emotional trauma rather than the injury."

Kellan was thankful that there wasn't that kind of physical damage because it meant Caroline could recover, but the trauma told them that she'd been through hell and back. There was no way to give Jack any comfort about that so Kellan didn't even try.

"There were traces of drugs in her system," Jack continued. "Barbiturates, and there were two recent needle marks so Dr. Gonzales thinks that's how the drugs were administered." He paused. "Along with other defensive wounds, there was bruising around the injection sites."

Which likely meant someone had administered the drugs by force. Not a surprise, but it added to an already gruesome picture. Caroline had tried to fight whomever had done this to her, but she'd lost. Partially anyway. Yes, the person had managed to drug her, but she'd gotten away.

"If you find Eric, I want a shot at him," Jack added a moment later.

There was a thick layer of anger coating the exhaustion and worry. Not a good combination. But Kellan was pretty sure that his brother didn't mean an actual shot as in putting a bullet in the snake. Still, with Jack's emotions running this high, it was too big of a risk to take.

"I'd rather you stay with Caroline. She needs you just in case there are any more hired thugs out there." It was playing dirty, but Kellan knew it had worked when Jack cursed.

"Catch the bastard," Jack growled, and he ended the call.

As Kellan put his phone away, Gemma hurried into the room. She was toweling dry her hair, and he could tell from the way the side of her top was hiked up that she'd dressed in a hurry.

"Anything?" she asked, tipping her head to his phone.

"No brain damage for Caroline." He kept it at that and hoped she wouldn't press for details. To help his chances with that, he went to her and brushed a kiss on her mouth.

There was suspicion in her eyes when she met his gaze. "I figured you'd be trying to put up a wall between us. Conflict of interest, loss of focus, etc."

"I tried," he admitted, and when he lingered a moment with the next kiss, Kellan forced himself to step back. He cursed, something he'd been doing too much of lately, and it wasn't helping. "I need to wrestle a bull," he grumbled.

Her eyebrow lifted, and amusement flirted with the bend of her mouth. "Is that a metaphor?"

He shook his head. "Taking down a bull would burn off some of this...restlessness." That wasn't anywhere near the right word for it, but Gemma knew what he meant.

"I watched you do that once," she said. "Years ago." More of the amusement came, this time to her eyes, and he was glad to see it. If talking about the past lessened

her fear and worry, then he was all for it. "It was...*interesting.*"

He got the feeling that wasn't the actual word she meant, either. That maybe what she'd seen had been arousing. Or maybe that was just what a certain part of his anatomy wanted him to believe.

Thankfully, he didn't have to deal with the temptation because his phone rang. He pulled the cell from his pocket, and just like that, he became all cop again. That's because of what he saw on the screen.

Unknown Caller.

There'd only been two people who'd recently shown up on screen that way—Maylene and Eric. Gemma obviously knew that, too, because of the soft gasp she made. She moved closer to Kellan, but he went ahead and put the call on Speaker after he hit the record function on the phone.

"Sheriff," the caller immediately said. The voice was weak, more breath than sound.

"Eric?"

"Who else?" Despite the weakness, the killer still managed some cockiness in his tone. "I guess you thought you'd killed me. You nearly did," he added with a cough.

"Don't expect me to feel sorry for you," Kellan snapped. "Where are you?"

"I'll get to that." Eric cleared his throat. "First, tell me about Caroline. I've heard you found her."

"Who told you that?" Kellan countered.

"Oh, you're trying to protect her. How sweet," Eric cooed. "I'm sure your brother appreciates your valiant effort to save the love of his life."

Kellan tried to not let Eric egg him on, but it was

hard to hold on to his temper when he wanted to kill this piece of slime. Gemma no doubt felt the same, and she slid her hand down his arm as if to help settle him.

"Caroline was an unfortunate problem," Eric went on. "She got away from me in Mexico."

"Then who was the dead woman we found in your car?" Kellan pressed.

"I'm not sure. She was just some woman who recognized me from the news, and she was going to call the cops. She had a gun, and the bitch actually shot me before I could tackle her. I killed her," he added as if discussing the weather. "Around that same time is when I lost Caroline. That was nearly a year ago, and I didn't know where she was. Not until yesterday when one of my *associates* spotted her right in Longview Ridge." He paused. "She didn't even know who I was."

Kellan had to get his teeth unclenched so he could speak. "So, you drugged her, beat her up and dumped her near the ranch to lure Gemma into the open."

"That's only partly true. I didn't dump her. She got away from us. And as for beating her up, she got in some punches of her own. Our Caroline is no fragile little flower, but she can be beaten down like the rest of us."

The leash snapped on Kellan's rage. "You son of a bitch. So help me God, I will put you in the grave."

Gemma's gentle touch turned into a hard grip, and she yanked Kellan around to face her. Her eyes held both sympathy and a warning. A warning that he knew he needed when he heard Eric laugh.

"Temper, temper," Eric taunted.

"Say another word about beating up Caroline, and I'll let Jack come after you," Kellan taunted right back.

Silence. Then a restrained "yes" from Eric. "I suspect I'd stand a better chance with you than I would with your brother. Though come to think of it, the doctor did have to dig *your* bullets out of me."

So, Eric had seen a doctor. That was a thread that Kellan needed to pull a little harder if he could find out where Eric was.

"And then there's the problem with Gemma," Eric continued. "I'm betting you're not happy with me because of the associates I hired to take care of her."

Kellan didn't fall for the jab this time. "Do you have a reason for calling, or do you just have too much time on your hands?"

"Oh, I have a reason, all right." And this time, it seemed as if Eric's temper was flaring. "After I got the medical attention I needed to stay alive, one of my associates decided to splinter off and conduct some business of his own. He kidnapped me."

Gemma and Kellan exchanged glances, and he wasn't sure who had more doubts about that.

"I figured you wouldn't believe me, but you can check things out for yourself. That associate, Marvin Hiatt, should be at the Longview Ridge Bank right about now. He forced me to give him the key to a safety-deposit box that's loaded with some of my emergency funds."

Kellan was about to ask Eric why he would keep money right up the street from the sheriff's office. But there was no need. This had been another way of toying with them.

Gemma waited until Kellan gave her the nod, and she hurried out in the hall, no doubt to call one of his deputies to check the bank.

"It's hard to get good help these days," Kellan continued with Eric. "But there are holes in your story. Why would a hired-gun-turned-kidnapper leave you with a cell phone?"

"A mistake on his part. I had three phones with me, and he only found two. He missed the one I had in my boot. I managed to take it out, but I haven't had any luck getting out of the ropes he used to tie me up. Nor is Maylene answering when I try to call her. That leaves you, Sheriff."

"What the hell do you want me to do? Come and rescue you?"

"Yes." Eric let that answer hang in the air. "I popped some stitches when I was fighting with the ropes, and I'm bleeding. A lot. I considered calling 911, but I decided to go right to the source. Unless some of my other sources magically come through to help me, I'm all yours. You just have to come and get me."

A lot of thoughts went through Kellan's head. None good. But first and foremost was that this was a trap.

"Where exactly should I come and get you?" Kellan asked.

"I'll call you back in fifteen minutes. After you've captured Hiatt. I'll tell you. Then, Sheriff, I'll be yours for the taking."

GEMMA HAD HAD no trouble hearing what Eric had just told Kellan. She had no trouble, either, believing this was another sick game. That's why she wasn't holding her breath, waiting for a report from the deputy and Texas Ranger that were on their way to the bank to locate the so-called associate that Eric had told them about.

Judging from Kellan's expression, he felt the same way. Ditto for Gunnar, who was keeping watch from the kitchen window.

Kellan poured himself another cup of coffee while he finished off a piece of toast that he'd started eating as soon as it'd popped up from the toaster. He didn't look overly tense, but she could see the strain in his eyes. A conversation with Eric could do that, leaving you angry and drained at the same time.

"Eat," Kellan told her again. "This could take a while."

She tried a bite of her own piece of toast that had already gotten cold, but she figured it wasn't going to sit well in her stomach. Hearing Eric had drained her, too, along with leaving her muscles tense. Everything inside her twisted and churned, and it only got worse with each passing second.

"Maybe he'll just die," she said, causing Gunnar to make a quick sound of agreement.

But even if Eric did die, Gemma wanted proof of it. She wanted to see his body so that she wouldn't spend the rest of her life looking over her shoulder.

Even though she'd been expecting it, the sound of Kellan's ringing phone still caused her to gasp. He hit answer and put it on speaker.

"This is Griff," the caller said. Griffin Morris, the Texas Ranger that had gone to the bank. "We've got Hiatt."

No gasp this time for Gemma. But the shock caused her to get to her feet and move closer to Kellan and his phone.

"He resisted, at first," the Ranger explained. "But we caught him coming out of the vault room at the bank

where they have the safety-deposit boxes. He had a large amount of cash on him."

"Did he actually confess?" Kellan asked.

"He's volunteered a few things and is claiming he didn't actually kill anyone. He's asking for a plea deal. He wants immunity and in exchange he'll tell us where he left Eric. Said he kidnapped him and tied him up because he knew Eric had a lot more money than he was paying him."

"It could be a trap," Gemma blurted out.

Kellan nodded, stayed quiet a moment. "Have Owen call the DA," he finally said to the Ranger. "No immunity for him, but I want Hiatt offered a lighter sentence contingent on him leading us to Eric. Let me know what the DA says."

Kellan ended the call and looked at her. She figured he was going to try to console her, to reassure her that this could be exactly what they needed to put an end to the danger. But he didn't say anything. On a heavy sigh, he just pulled her into his arms. She might have taken in some of the silent comfort he was giving her if there'd been time. But he had to pull away from her when his phone rang again.

"Unknown Caller," he relayed to her when he saw his screen.

Gemma dragged in a long breath, steeling herself up for another encounter with Eric. But it wasn't him.

"Sheriff Slater," Maylene said the moment he answered. "I just got a phone call from Eric. He told me he was hurt and that he needed my help."

So, Eric had managed to get in touch with her. Or maybe Maylene had been in on this all along. Gemma didn't trust Maylene any more than she did Eric.

"Did Eric say where he was?" Kellan asked.

Maylene wasn't quick to answer that. "I hate him. He ruined my life, and I'm going to kill him."

"Hell," Kellan spat out. "No, you're not. You're going to tell me where he is so I can arrest him."

Maylene made a raw sob. "He won't stay in jail. He'll just get out and ruin other people's lives. He'll kill again. I have to stop him."

Kellan cursed even more. "Where are you, Maylene? And where's Eric?" he demanded.

Again, Maylene took her time answering. "He's in a hunting cabin off Davidson Road, and I'm heading there now. You can't stop me."

"Maylene, wait. Don't do this," Kellan snapped, but he was talking to himself because the woman had already ended the call.

Gemma knew what Kellan was going to do before he even put his phone away. "Get some of the ranch hands to come in the house so they can stay with Gemma and you," he immediately said to Gunnar.

She shook her head and was ready to beg Kellan not to go, but Gemma knew it wouldn't do any good.

"Owen and at least one of the Rangers will go with me," Kellan said, already heading for the door. "I won't try to take Eric alone."

That didn't give her much consolation. "Eric could be armed and waiting for you to show up."

Kellan didn't confirm that, not with words anyway, but he knew it was a possibility. "I know where this cabin is. It's by the creek with a lot of trees around it. We can use the trees for cover while we close in on him."

She shook her head again. "He could have set explosives."

"I'll call in the bomb squad," he said, and he disarmed the security system to let in the two hands who were there to guard her. "Just stay put."

He opened his mouth, closed it and then pulled her to the other side of the foyer. Kellan stared at her, and she saw in his eyes what he had been about to say. Gemma nipped that in the bud.

"Don't you dare tell me you love me, because you'd be just saying that instead of goodbye," she warned him. "I'm not saying goodbye to you."

Despite everything that was going on, he smiled at her. "All right. I don't love you."

The corner of her mouth lifted; that was as much as she could manage. "Thank you." She caught on to handfuls of his shirt, yanking him to her, and she kissed him. "Swear to me that you'll come back to me."

"I swear," Kellan said, looking her straight in the eyes. "I swear."

He brushed a kiss on her cheek and headed out the door.

CHAPTER FIFTEEN

KELLAN PULLED THE cruiser to a stop at the end of Davidson Road and eyed the cabin that was in a small clearing just ahead. It'd been a while since he'd been in this neck of the woods, but it was just as he remembered. Lots of trees with a small creek coiling around the property. It was normally a quiet, serene place.

Not at the moment though.

Since Kellan didn't trust Eric or anyone connected to him, the bomb squad was already on scene. He'd called them as he'd driven away from the ranch and then had gone to the sheriff's office to pick up Owen and Ranger Griff Morris.

The two men of the bomb squad had made good time getting there. They were dressed in bulky gear and were examining the grounds with equipment. They weren't Kellan's men but rather were from the county and responded when the locals needed help. In this case, they'd responded quickly because they knew there could be a serial killer inside.

Gemma knew it, too.

Her image popped into Kellan's head. The stark fear on her face when he'd said his non-goodbye. There'd been nothing he could say to give her any reassurance, and that would continue. Because Kellan knew Gunnar would be monitoring both their cruiser radio and

the bomb squad's, which meant it was highly likely that Gemma would be hearing it, too. Kellan wished he could shelter her from that, but he couldn't. However, maybe he could put a quick end to this once the area and cabin were cleared.

"No vehicle other than the bomb squad van," Owen relayed. "No sign of anyone else, either, including May-lene." He handed Kellan the binoculars he'd been using.

Kellan zoomed in on the cabin windows. The morning sun was reflecting off the glass, making it impossible to see inside, but the sunlight gave him an ample view of the grounds.

"Either of you been inside the place?" Ranger Morris asked from the back seat. He, too, had binoculars.

"Once," Owen answered, surprising Kellan. His brother shrugged. "Cal Davidson had a party here when I was in high school."

Cal was Owen's friend, and the cabin belonged to Cal's grandfather, a crotchety man who almost certainly hadn't approved of a party. But the grandfather had passed now, and the place belonged to Cal.

"The only room closed off is the bathroom," Owen explained. "But there are two small storage closets."

Eric, if he was indeed there, could be shut up in one of those. Of course, maybe Hiatt hadn't taken the trouble to hide his captive since he'd perhaps figured he wouldn't be gone that long.

"I don't see any signs that anyone has trampled around the perimeter of the cabin," Griff added.

Neither did Kellan. There was a mix of shrubs and weeds by the windows, and if someone had stepped on them, it would have shown. But he couldn't see the back of the place. Thankfully, there wasn't enough room to

park a vehicle back there, but Hiatt or Eric could have left a hired thug there to keep watch. If they'd done that though, the bomb squad would have likely flushed them out.

The minutes crawled by as the bomb squad did their job, and while Kellan knew it was necessary, everything inside him was raring to go. If Eric was in there, he wanted him.

"Hell," Owen grumbled, and Kellan pulled the binoculars from his eyes to see what had gotten his brother's attention.

Maylene.

She was getting out of a small blue car that was parked just up the road from them. He couldn't see a gun, but Kellan had to assume that if she'd managed to get a vehicle, she had also gotten hold of a weapon.

Maylene froze when she spotted them, and even though Kellan couldn't get a good look of her face from the distance, he didn't think she was pleased about him being there.

Welcome to the club.

"You want me to arrest her?" Griff asked.

Kellan was debating how to handle it when Maylene jumped back in her car and sped off. Part of him was glad she hadn't stayed around to complicate things, but that didn't mean she wouldn't be back. In fact, as crazed sounding as the woman had been, she might just go farther up the road, park and make her way here on foot. Kellan would have to keep an eye out for her.

One of the bomb squad guys gave them a thumbs-up, and a moment later Kellan got a text. All clear on the outside. We're heading in now.

Good. That was Kellan's cue to pull the cruiser even

closer to the cabin. Close enough that he could easily watch without the binoculars. He got out, keeping behind the cruiser door. Owen did the same on the passenger's side, and Griff got out behind Kellan. All of them already had their weapons drawn.

The bomb squad went on the porch, each of them peering through the windows that flanked the door. Both men shook their head, indicating they didn't see anyone inside.

Kellan cursed and hoped this wasn't all a wild-goose chase.

He waited, watching and holding his breath when the squad checked the front door. They didn't go in that way though. They broke the window and took another look inside.

"There's blood on the floor," one of them relayed to Kellan. "A lot of blood. It looks as if someone got dragged."

That meshed with what Eric had said, but it didn't mean it was true. The blood could belong to another of his victims.

Thankfully, things moved a lot faster then. One of the guys went in through the window, dropping down out of sight. Several minutes later, the front door opened.

"Call an ambulance," the guy shouted to Kellan. "There's a man up in the bathroom. Can't tell who he is 'cause there's blood on his face."

Kellan hurried away from the cruiser and barreled onto the porch. With his gun ready, he made a beeline for the bathroom.

And he saw Eric.

Just as the killer had said, his wrists were tied with a rope to the sink, and yes, there was blood. Not just

on Eric's face where it appeared he'd been beaten, but it was also on his shirt and on the floor. He still had his cell phone clutched in his hand.

At first Kellan thought he was dead since he wasn't moving, but then Eric's eyes fluttered open. "Sheriff, you came." Even now there was a touch of cockiness to his voice. "I trust that you caught Hiatt. And yes, he did this to me."

As much as it twisted at him, Kellan checked for weapons—there were none—and he yanked open Eric's shirt so he could try to slow down the bleeding. It was his job, but sometimes, like now, his job sucked.

"You're wasting your time, you know," Eric said, his eyelids drifted back down, and he dragged in a thin breath. "I'm dying. Funny that it should end this way. Me in a bathroom. You, trying to save me."

Kellan didn't trust himself to comment on that when all he wanted to do was finish beating Eric to a pulp.

"Just in case there is a hereafter, I'll settle up with you," Eric went on. "I didn't kill your father nor that deputy."

"And we're to believe you?" Owen snapped. Only then did Kellan realize his brother was right behind him.

"It's the truth." With his eyes still closed, the corner of Eric's mouth lifted into a smile. "I don't want to take credit for something I didn't do, and I didn't do either of them. In fact, they weren't even killed by the same person."

Nothing could have kept Kellan quiet after hearing that. Maybe this was just another load of bull, but if Eric was clearing his conscience, then Kellan wanted to hear what he had to say.

"Who killed them, then?" Kellan demanded.

Eric opened his mouth, then grimaced. Kellan heard the death rattle in the man's throat and chest. "I'm not the only monster on your turf, Sheriff," Eric said in a ragged whisper. "Save yourself. Save Gemma."

And the moment he'd gotten out those words, Eric Lang took the last breath he would ever take.

GEMMA DIDN'T EVEN try to tamp down the fear that was spiking through her. And she hated that she was tucked away at the ranch while Kellan was out there facing down a killer.

Or walking into a trap.

Either one of those could be deadly.

Eric might be injured. Heck, he might even have been kidnapped by one of his own hired thugs. He could even be dying. But that didn't mean Eric wouldn't use his last seconds on earth to deliver one final blow to her. Killing Kellan would be the ultimate blow. Eric could destroy both Kellan and her by doing that.

That thought hit her so hard that Gemma had to sink down in the chair at the kitchen table. Gunnar was already seated, and he was monitoring the scanner for reports from the cabin. At first, he'd tried to do the "monitoring" through headphones, but Gemma had put a stop to that. As hard as it was for her—she had to hear what was going on.

So far, not much.

Kellan, Owen and Griff were in a holding pattern, and it was as if time had stopped. Just to give herself something to do, Gemma forced herself to her feet and went to the kitchen window to keep watch. She also slipped her hand over the gun that she'd tucked in the back waist of her jeans. That was yet something else

she'd talked Gunnar into doing. She doubted that Eric could get to the ranch, but she didn't want to be unarmed if that happened.

When she got to the window, she immediately spotted the ranch hand on the back porch. He was armed with a rifle—as was the one on the front porch. They'd stay in those positions, guarding her, until Kellan returned.

"The bomb squad gave the all clear," Gunnar relayed to her a split second before she heard that static-laced info come through on the scanner.

That was a relief, but Gemma knew this only put Kellan one step closer to going into the cabin and facing, well, whatever he would face there. Maybe Eric. Maybe one of his uninjured henchmen.

When her lungs started to ache, she released the breath she'd been holding and moved to the other side of the window so that she'd have a different angle for keeping watch.

She could see the barn, but there wasn't anyone about. That was because Kellan had put hands on the road to stop anyone from just driving up. It wasn't foolproof though, and they all knew it. There were ranch trails that coiled and cut all around the property, and someone could have parked on the main road and used those trails to get close to the house.

"Kellan's going inside," Gunnar said.

The deputy was watching her now, volleying those cautious glances at her, probably making sure she wasn't about to have a panic attack. She wouldn't. Even though there was plenty of panic inside her, she would keep it together for Kellan's sake. It might cause him to lose focus if he heard she was having trouble.

The conversation she'd had with Kellan started playing in her head. The *l*-word had been part of that, and while it hadn't exactly sent Kellan running, she wouldn't hold him to anything he'd said to her in that moment.

Well, nothing except that "I swear."

He had sworn to her that he'd come back safe, and she latched on to that like a lifeline.

"Kellan's in with Eric," Gunnar told her. "Owen said Eric's bleeding out. Dying."

So, that was true, too. Part of her wanted to be there so she could look the snake in the eyes, so that he could see that he hadn't beaten her, after all. Another part of her just wanted him to go ahead and die, and then Kellan could come back to her.

The static hissed and crackled, and she caught bits and pieces of Eric and Kellan's conversation. Eric said something about Hiatt and settling up. Then, it was as if the static cleared for her to hear—clearly—what he said next.

"I didn't kill your father nor that deputy."

Yes, that was Eric's voice all right, but it wasn't exactly a news flash. He'd said something similar during one of his phone calls. Gemma didn't believe him. Or rather she didn't want to believe him. But if he'd indeed killed them, then this would have been a time for him to brag. After all, he was dying.

"I'm not the only monster on your turf, Sheriff," Eric muttered. "Save yourself and Gemma if you can."

That alone could have put her heart in her throat, but Gunnar drew his gun and hurried to the window. He pushed her aside, but she could still see the barn.

"Do you think that means Eric sent another gunman?" she asked.

"Maybe." Gunnar didn't take his attention off the backyard. "Or it could be Eric's parting shot."

Yes, with just those handful of words, he could rob them of any peace and have them looking over their shoulders.

That might have given her some relief. If Gemma hadn't seen the movement by the side of the barn. For just a split second she thought maybe someone had peered out, so she watched, holding her breath again.

But nothing.

Obviously, every nerve was zinging inside her, and it wouldn't take much for her to see a bogeyman. Not Eric though. He was dead. She wasn't mistaken about Gunnar saying that, but instead of feeling any relief or celebration, Gemma could sense that something was indeed wrong.

There was a strange sound. As if something had smacked against the side of the house. The ranch hand shifted in that direction. So did she and Gunnar, and again, they waited.

Not long this time though.

She felt the jolt of adrenaline as smoke started billowing out from the side of the house. Gemma didn't think this had come from a fire. No. It was pure white and thick, and even though she was no expert, she thought it might be from some kind of smoke bomb. That would explain the strange sound she'd heard just seconds earlier.

Oh, God.

There was no good reason for someone to do something like this. But there was a bad one. Someone had gotten onto the ranch, and that someone was about to launch an attack.

Gemma got confirmation of that when she heard the next sound. One that she had no trouble recognizing.

It was a gunshot.

CHAPTER SIXTEEN

KELLAN TRIED NOT to think. He just drove as fast as he could and hoped if Eric was telling the truth, that he would get to the ranch in time to stop anything bad from happening to Gemma.

I'm not the only monster on your turf, Sheriff.

Of course, Kellan had known that, but he had no idea which monster Eric meant. Or if the man was just blowing smoke during his last seconds alive. Still, Kellan couldn't discount pieces that just didn't add up.

"If Eric didn't kill your father and his deputy, who did?" Griff asked. He was familiar with the case, anyone in the area was, but he probably didn't know the details like Kellan.

"Maylene, maybe," Owen answered. Like Kellan and Griff, he was keeping watch around them on the drive back because one of Eric's assassins could be waiting along the road to do one last bidding for a dead boss. "It'd be a lot easier if it was Maylene," his brother added in a grumble.

Yes, it would be, considering their other two suspects were both marshals who could be hell-bent on covering up the murder of a prostitute. Rory could be doing that because he'd been the one to commit the murder. Amanda, because she wanted to protect Rory or because she'd been so jealous of his affair that she'd

murdered Lacey in cold blood. Whatever their motive, if it was either of them—or both—it could mean the danger wasn't over.

Hell, it could be just beginning.

Kellan had already texted one of the hands to let him know to stay vigilant. He hadn't sent the same message to Gunnar though, but that's because it would have alarmed Gemma even more than she already was. Besides, if the hands saw anything, they would alert Gunnar, and his deputy could take things from there.

His phone rang, and when he saw Jack's name on the screen, Kellan took the call and put it on Speaker. "Is it true? Is Eric really dead?" Jack asked the moment he was on the line.

"It's true. But he didn't confess to killing Dad or Dusty."

That caused Jack to curse, something Kellan considered doing. He wanted this tied up in a neat little package, too, but more than that he needed to make sure Gemma was okay.

"I'm on my way to the ranch now and am only a few minutes out," Kellan added. There wasn't any way to tell Jack that Eric had left him with a bad feeling in his gut. Especially since Eric always made him feel that way. "Something's wrong," he admitted. "I have to get to Gemma."

That didn't help Jack's profanity. "You'd better have backup with you."

"I do. You stay there with Caroline. Eric might have left some orders from the grave, and he could have sent someone after Caroline."

"No one will get near her." Jack's voice was low and

dangerous, exactly how Kellan felt. "Make sure you do the same for Gemma."

"I will. Gotta go. There's another call coming in." And his heart skipped some beats when he saw Gunnar's name on the screen.

"We've got a problem," Gunnar immediately said.

Yeah, and the deputy didn't have to explain exactly what that problem was. Kellan heard the gunshot.

"Is Gemma all right?" Kellan snapped.

"For now. Just get here as fast as you can," Gunnar insisted, but not before Kellan heard a second shot.

Obviously, Griff and Owen heard the shot, too, because both of them drew their weapons. Getting ready for whatever they were about to face. Kellan readied himself, too, and he pressed down hard on the accelerator, trying to eat up the distance between Gemma and him.

Gunnar didn't stay on the line with Kellan. Probably because the deputy was trying to move Gemma somewhere out of the line of fire. That steadied Kellan, some. Gunnar was well trained, an experienced deputy, but Eric's hired guns had likely honed their "craft," too.

"What the hell?" Owen grumbled when they took the turn to the ranch, and they saw the thick white smoke billowing around the house.

Kellan's first thought was an explosion. There'd certainly been enough of those after Eric had turned up in Longview Ridge. But this was no explosion. Someone was trying to smoke Gemma and Gunnar out of the house.

Ahead of him, the hands that Kellan had left at the gate were already in their trucks, heading for the house.

Good. That meant he'd have plenty of backup. Unfortunately, the hands might not be a match for professionals.

"Call them," Kellan instructed Owen. "Tell the hands to hold back until I get ahead of them."

Kellan didn't slow down while his brother did that. He just kept speeding toward the cattle gate, then past it. Thanks to Owen's call, the trucks pulled off the side, and Kellan sped by them.

There was no sign of Gunnar or Gemma. Also, no sign of the hand who should have been on the front porch. Of course, with that thick cloud of smoke, it was hard to see anything.

Kellan pulled up closer to the house, and he cursed when he spotted the hand. Facedown. Maybe dead. And again, he mentally kicked himself for not being here. He'd let Eric lead him into a trap, after all. It just hadn't been the trap that Kellan had been expecting.

The anger boiled through him, and Kellan wished Eric was alive only so he could kill the bastard.

"Stay in the cruiser," Kellan instructed Griff and Owen.

It took everything inside him to give that order for them to stay put. He needed to get to Gemma—but if they got out, a hired gun could pick them off one by one. That wouldn't help Gemma, and it could get someone else killed.

Kellan pulled off the driveway, crashing the cruiser through the fence and across the yard. Once he got to the side of the house, it was like driving blind because the smoke was so thick. He prayed that he wouldn't run into Gemma or Gunnar, and that's why he pressed down on the horn. Yes, that would alert a gunman, but the odds were the thug already knew they were there.

In fact, that could be the thug's plan.

Eric's plan.

It twisted at him to think that the killer wasn't done with them yet.

Kellan finally made it past the smear of smoke, and he caught sight of the back porch. Again, what he saw there wasn't good. There was another ranch hand lying in a crumpled heap. Worse, there was a second wave of smoke, and this time it wasn't coming from the yard but rather the house. It was billowing out the back door.

Kellan's phone dinged with a text message, but since he didn't want to take his attention off the house, he handed it to Owen.

"It's from Gunnar," Owen relayed. "Gemma and he are coming out the front and they need cover."

Kellan didn't waste a second. He threw the cruiser into Reverse, plowing back through the yard until he reached the front porch. This time he didn't stay inside. He threw open his door. Griff and Owen did the same, clearing the way for Gunnar and Gemma to hurry into the cruiser once they got out.

His heartbeat was thudding in his ears, making it hard to hear, and the smoke was stinging his eyes. Still, Kellan kept watch, waiting—and praying—for Gemma and Gunnar to appear.

The front door finally flew open, and Gunnar came out. The moment he spotted Kellan, he reached back, taking hold of Gemma's arm.

Gunnar had her.

That caused both relief and adrenaline to slam through Kellan, and he ran onto the porch so he could help get her to safety. However, when he reached the steps, Kellan saw something else.

Or rather someone.

A beefy man came up behind Gunnar and Gemma. And with the smoke billowing around her, the guy hooked his arm around Gemma's neck, snapping her back against his chest and out of Gunnar's grip.

And the man put a gun to her head.

FOR JUST A BREATH of a second, Gemma thought she would be able to get to Kellan. She thought they would all be okay and get out of this nightmare. But that all changed—first when she saw the fresh look of terror on Kellan's face.

Then, she'd felt the arm around her throat.

And the gun.

A thousand thoughts and feelings hit her at once, but the one that pierced through that frenzied whirl was that this could get Kellan killed. But Kellan dove for cover. So did Owen, Griff and the hands. Kellan landed on the side of the stone steps, but he immediately shifted his position, levering himself up and bringing his gun.

"Wouldn't do that if I were you, Sheriff," the man behind her growled, causing Kellan to freeze. "That'd be a real bad idea."

Gemma didn't recognize the voice, but then this was probably one of the thugs that Eric had hired. A way of tying up all those loose ends and she was the ultimate prize because she was the one who'd gotten away.

Caroline, too.

And it sent another layer of sickening dread over Gemma that at this very moment one of Eric's goons might be doing the same thing to Caroline as this one was doing to her. At least she could fight back, but Caroline wasn't in any shape to do that.

"Let her go," Kellan snapped. His eyes were narrowed to slits, and every muscle in his body looked primed and ready for a fight. A fight that couldn't happen as long as this snake had a gun to her head.

Gemma needed to figure out what to do about that.

"Not gonna happen," the hit man answered Kellan. "But here's what we're gonna do instead. All of you and any other hands you've got stashed nearby will put down your weapons and back up. If you do that, nobody dies."

Kellan didn't budge. Neither did Gunnar, Owen or Griff. There were also four ranch hands who were behind cover at the backs of their trucks.

"And I'm to believe you about no one dying?" Kellan fired back. "There are two men down, one on the back porch and another just a few feet from you."

"They're not dead. Just stunned and drugged. My boss didn't want any unnecessary collateral damage."

That was laughable. Eric didn't care who was killed in this as long as he got Caroline and her. Maybe Kellan, too. Gemma didn't know how deep Eric's hatred for Kellan went, but Eric could have included him in this cleanup detail.

"My boss only wants the lady here," the thug added. "I'll be taking her for a little ride. I'm to show her something and then let her go."

No one hearing that believed it. Especially not Gemma.

"Guns down," he repeated. "Then, put your hands up so I can see them."

The man jammed the gun even harder against her head. So hard that Gemma couldn't hold back a wince and a soft groan of pain. Then she felt the blood from where the barrel of the gun had dug into her skin.

Kellan saw the blood, too.

He cursed, his grip tightening on his gun. Gemma kept her gaze on him, silently pleading with him not to do anything. Not like this. The thug could literally gun Kellan and the rest down while using her as a human shield.

She felt the blood trickle down the side of her face, and Gemma figured that was the tipping point for Kellan. He couldn't save her, not here anyway. Like her, he had to wait for some kind of opening and pray that this jerk made a mistake. The other hired guns for Eric certainly had.

"Frank, you can come out now," the goon said. "I'm gonna need a little help here."

Gemma cursed softly when she heard the footsteps, coming from behind her, and even though she couldn't see *Frank*, she felt it when he reached in and put a pair of plasticuffs on her wrists.

"Don't make me hurt her to get you to obey," the thug warned Kellan. "I can start putting bullets in her. It won't kill her, but it'll hurt—bad."

Gemma had firsthand experience what it felt like to be shot. And it did hurt. But not as much as seeing that look in Kellan's eyes. He was blaming himself for this. He was reliving the other nightmare of when she'd been held at gunpoint.

With his eyes still locked on hers, Kellan tossed his gun to the side, lifted his hands. One by one, the others followed suit. Almost immediately, her captor started moving with her. Frank was likely watching their backs.

"I'm gonna need a vehicle and keys," the goon said when he reached the steps with her. "I'll take that red truck." Other than the cruiser, it was the one nearest

to the house. "And remember, if any of you tries to shoot me, the bullet could go through me and into her. Plus, I'm sure my own finger would tense and I'd end up shooting her in the head. Wouldn't want that, now, would we?"

Gemma tuned him out. Tried to tune out the flashbacks, too, and with each step she took, she tried to figure out how to stop this. She tested the man's reaction by dropping down her weight a little.

"That'd be a good way to get the sheriff killed," he whispered in her ear. "Despite what I just told them, he's the one I'll shoot if you don't cooperate. He's the only one who'll die. I doubt you'd be able to live with knowing you killed him."

She wouldn't, and that's the only reason she stopped. It was best to get away from Kellan and the others. Yes, they would go in pursuit, but once she was in the truck with this snake and Frank, she might be able to cause them to wreck if she threw her body against the steering wheel. It was risky, but anything she did would be.

"Back up," Frank yelled out to the hands. And they did.

When they reached the truck, Gemma heard the engine still running, and the man didn't waste any time shoving her inside through the driver's door. He followed her, shutting the door, and Frank got in from the other side, trapping her in the middle. Only then did she get a look at their faces.

Strangers.

Frank was thin and wiry, and he was loaded down with assorted weapons. The one who'd snatched her was bulky and built like a wrestler, which meant she wouldn't be able to hold her own physically with him.

Maybe, though, she wouldn't need to do that if she could send the truck into the ditch.

Gemma tried to get out of the plasticuffs, more as a distraction since she knew they would hold. She wiggled her shoulders.

And the pain exploded in her head.

She hadn't seen the blow coming from the butt of Frank's gun, but she certainly felt it. It blurred her vision and knocked the breath out of her.

"Settle down," Frank warned her. "I don't have orders to kill you, but that doesn't mean I won't."

Despite the searing pain, Gemma latched on to those words. "You expect me to believe Eric didn't leave orders to kill me?"

Frank lifted his shoulder. The gesture was casual enough, but there was concern, or something, in his dull blue eyes when he glanced behind them. Kellan was no doubt already in pursuit.

"I'm supposed to give you a message from Eric Lang," Frank said. "Just carrying out a man's dying wish. I'm to tell you that Eric was telling a fib when he said he didn't kill the sheriff's dad and that deputy. That's the word Eric told me to use—*fib*." Judging from Frank's oily smile, that amused him.

It didn't amuse Gemma, but it was definitely something Eric would have said. "Why did he *fib*?"

"How the hell should I know?" Frank snapped. "The guy was a couple of cards short of a deck if you know what I mean. He said he killed them both and that I should tell you, that you should call the sheriff and let him know, too."

With that, he took out a phone and pressed the button for a number that was already programmed into the

phone. Her vision still wasn't clear, and her head was throbbing like a bad tooth, but Gemma had no doubts that Frank was calling Kellan. A moment later, she got confirmation of that.

"Sheriff Slater," he said, his voice as fierce and clipped as she figured his expression would be.

"Tell him what Eric said." Frank passed the phone to her.

"Kellan," Gemma managed after she cleared her throat. She wanted to sound strong with the hopes of making this easier for Kellan. If that was possible.

"Gemma." Not fierce and clipped this time when Kellan spoke. But there was so much worry.

Frank rammed his elbow into her side, obviously his way of reminding her to get on with the message. "Eric apparently told these men that he had indeed killed your father and Dusty."

"Eric wanted to set the record straight," Frank added in a snarl loud enough for Kellan to hear.

"And why would Eric want to do that?" The fierceness was back. "Why would he care what I know or don't know when he's dead?"

"Don't know, don't care," Frank answered. "I'm just the messenger here."

"Yeah, one who kidnapped a woman from my home."

Frank chuckled. "I guess that had to get your goat, what with you being a lawman and all. Don't worry, Sheriff, you'll get her back in one piece. More or less," Frank added, sneering at her. "My advice would be for you and your fellow badges to back off and let this play out."

There was nothing Kellan would want to play out when hired thugs and Eric were involved.

"You need to make sure Caroline is okay," Gemma blurted out, knowing it could earn her another bashing. Or worse. Still, she had to try. But Frank didn't hit her again. He merely ended the call and put his phone away.

"We're almost there," the driver said, causing Gemma to glance around to see where they were.

And the chill rippled like ice over her skin.

Because this was the road to Serenity Inn.

Oh, God. The last time she'd been here, Eric had nearly killed her.

While she fought to hang on to her breath, Gemma reminded herself that Eric was dead. That didn't help, though, because he wasn't the only one who could murder her and Kellan. Hired guns could do that, too.

The inn came into view, and even though it was daylight, it looked spookier than it had the night Eric had taken her there. Most of the windows had been boarded up, and the ones that hadn't been were just dark holes of broken glass. They reminded her of eye sockets.

The driver went through the side of the yard, or rather what was left of it after the explosion, and as if they'd rehearsed it, both men got out, the driver dragging her after them. A man got on each side of her, and they ran with her into the inn. The moment they were inside, they padlocked the door from within. Since the lock looked new, she guessed they'd been the ones to put it there.

Gemma forced herself to breathe. Hard to do because the stale air inside was clogged with dust, mold and other smells she didn't want to identify. Even in the barely there light, she could still see the foyer floor. And the bloodstains that were there.

Hers.

Outside, she heard vehicles braking to noisy stops. Kellan and the others, no doubt. Frank took out his phone, and she saw him press Kellan's number again. He didn't put the call on Speaker, but she was close enough to him to hear when Kellan answered.

"Tell me what it'll take to get you to release Gemma," Kellan demanded.

"I haven't been paid to negotiate with you, but you should keep yourself and your men back, Sheriff. One more step, and you could all go *kaboom*."

Gemma shook her head, not wanting to believe that, but Frank took out a small device. It was the size of a cell phone and looked like the remote control for a toy car. It had two switches, one labeled Arm, and the other, Execute, was about two inches below it.

When Frank hit the switch and a green light flared on, her stomach went to her knees. But Frank smiled.

"All ready to go now," he said, his thumb moving to hover over the second button. *Execute*. "If I press this, it's gonna be too late for all of us."

The man had just armed a bomb.

CHAPTER SEVENTEEN

KELLAN IMMEDIATELY MOTIONED for Owen, Griff and the hands to stop in their tracks. This could be a bluff, but if Eric was involved in this, then he could have hired someone to set another bomb.

But Kellan was beginning to think that was a big *if*.

Something about all of this wasn't right. If Eric wanted revenge against Gemma, why hadn't his thugs just killed her at the ranch? Of course, maybe Eric just wanted it all to end here, like a sick full circle.

Another possibility came to mind, too. Eric could have left instructions to use Gemma to draw out Caroline so he could finish her off, as well. It wouldn't work. Gemma wouldn't lure out Caroline even if it meant saving herself. Besides, Caroline had no memory of her anyway.

"Why bring Gemma here?" Kellan snapped. He wasn't even sure the hired gun was still on the line, not until he responded.

"Just following orders. And speaking of orders, here's one for you, Sheriff. Start walking toward the inn. Just you. None of your little helpers. I've got my hands on a controller for the bomb, and the light is blazing green. That means it's ready to go, and I've got my thumb over the button that could put you in a lot of pieces."

Kellan looked at the window on the bottom right. It was boarded up, but there was a gap in between two of the boards, and Kellan saw someone peering out at him.

"You said there were explosives," Kellan reminded him. That wouldn't stop him. One way or another he was getting inside so he could try to save Gemma.

No. Not try. He *would* save her. Kellan refused to think differently.

"Oh, there's a boomer out there all right, but you can follow what's left of the stone walkway to the side of the porch. Remember that part about only you coming. If not, the blast goes off and your girl might get hurt. These walls aren't that thick."

That kicked up his pulse several notches, and he felt the slick layer of fear slide over him. It wasn't the first time he'd felt it, but the stakes felt higher than they ever had before.

"You know this could be a trap," Owen warned him. His brother and the rest were behind the cover of their vehicles—where Kellan wanted them to stay.

Kellan nodded, and without ending the call, he slipped his phone in his shirt pocket to free his hands. He started walking. He'd picked up his gun from the yard at the ranch before he left, and he still had it out of his holster. If he got the chance to use it, he would.

With each step, his heart beat faster. His chest went fist tight. And it took everything inside Kellan to fight away the flashbacks from that other night.

He didn't look down at the ground. Didn't want the distraction of remembering the spots where his father and Dusty had died. Kellan just kept walking, and once he made it to the side of the porch, he climbed up.

"What now?" Kellan snapped to the caller.

"Come on in." The welcome was coated with the same kind of mockery that Eric favored, and Kellan heard what he thought was someone disengaging a lock on the front door.

He knew in his gut that if he went, he'd be gunned down.

Kellan slowed, taking a closer look at the gap in the window. No one was peering out at him now, but he could see inside.

Gemma.

She was there in the foyer, much as she'd been the night Eric had taken her. Her hands were still cuffed behind her, and like the big bulky guy next to her, her attention was nailed to the front door. She opened her mouth as if to call out to him, but the thug said something to her. Something probably meant to make her stay quiet. She didn't.

"Kellan, no!" she shouted.

The thug backhanded her, and Gemma's head snapped back. Something else snapped, too. The leash Kellan had on the rage inside him. He took aim through the crack and fired.

Two bullets slammed into the thug's chest.

Kellan didn't wait for him to drop. He ran to the front door, kicking it open and then moving quickly to the side so that the second man couldn't shoot him. But the guy was already running toward the back of the house.

"He was going to shoot you," Gemma said. "And he's got some kind of device. I'm almost positive it's to set off a bomb. There's a button labeled 'Execute.'"

Kellan didn't have a lot of knowledge about explosives, but Eric had clearly found someone who knew how to blow things up. The proof of that was in the

front yard of the inn where there was a gaping hole and debris.

"Owen, tell everyone to stay put," Kellan called out to his brother, and he went to Gemma.

Hell, her face was bleeding, and she was shaking. But she also looked riled to the core. That was good. Much better than a panic attack.

The skinny second man disappeared into a room off a long, dark hall, but Kellan didn't go after him. The thug on the floor was still alive, moaning in pain.

And he was armed.

Kellan did something about that. He snatched up the thug's gun, putting it in the back waist of his jeans, and he moved Gemma away from the man in case he tried to grab her. He didn't want one of the goons getting their hands on her again.

"You came," she said, her breath gusting. "That wasn't very smart."

He nearly smiled. "I swore I'd come back to you, and here I am."

This time when he looked at her, there were tears shimmering in her eyes. Kellan wanted to kiss her, to hold her, but there wasn't time. He used his pocketknife to cut the plasticuffs and then handed her the thug's gun.

"There's really a bomb?" he asked.

"I think so, but it must be outside because I didn't see Frank bring it inside." She tipped her head to the hall. "That's his name, and he said Eric hired him." She paused. "I'm not sure I believe him."

"Neither do I."

But that left Kellan with a huge question—who had done this? And what was he going to do about it? He couldn't take Gemma back outside, not with the pos-

sible bomb, and he didn't want to leave her alone with the injured thug. If he wanted to catch this Frank and get answers, then he'd have to go after him and take Gemma with him. Not that he could have talked her into doing otherwise.

While keeping watch around them, he took out his phone to see if Frank was still on the line. He wasn't. So Kellan sent a text to Owen to let him know that Gemma was okay, more or less, and that he should call the bomb squad to get them out there.

Kellan wouldn't have backup until they cleared the place, and by then Frank could be long gone. If there was a bomb, Frank would know where it was and get around it.

"Watch our backs," Kellan told Gemma. He hated to rely on her for that. She'd just been through a horrible ordeal. A kidnapping. And she was probably having some horrible flashbacks, but he didn't have a lot of options here.

With his gun still gripped in his hand, Kellan started moving. There was a large staircase to his right, but that was boarded off. Not that it would stop someone from going up there, but he didn't see any footprints in the thick layer of dust on the floor. All the footprints led to the hall so that's where Kellan went.

Kellan had been in this hall before, but he cursed when he saw all the doors. At least a dozen of them. The other times he'd been in this part of the inn, it had been weeks and even months after his father's murder. There hadn't been the threat of a hired gun ready to strike.

Unfortunately, the hall was even darker than the foyer, and it made it much harder to see the floor. There were dim pockets of light coming from the doors that were open, but most were closed. He didn't know if

they'd been that way before Frank's attempted escape or if the thug was hiding behind one of them.

Of course, since each room had windows, it was also possible the man was long gone. Because of the thick shrubs and trees around the place, Owen and the others might not have even seen him.

When Kellan reached the first door, he kicked it open, and waited a heartbeat to make sure he wasn't about to be gunned down. No sound. Nothing. He glanced inside and didn't see a single footprint in the dust so he moved to the next one.

Behind him, he could hear Gemma's still uneven breathing, and when her back brushed against his, he could feel her tight muscles. Maybe she wouldn't hate him too much for putting her through this kind of hell.

Kellan kicked in another door. Nothing there, either. Ditto for the next two. He was about to bash in the door of the fourth when there was some movement at the end of the hall. Someone peered out from one of the rooms, and Kellan automatically took aim at the person.

"Don't shoot," someone said.

Maylene.

Hell, what was she doing here? He didn't like the way she kept turning up where she shouldn't.

Kellan didn't fire, but that was only because the woman didn't appear to be armed. However, he did make sure he was in front of Gemma.

"Eric's dead," Maylene said, her voice trembling. She seemed to be trembling, too, but Kellan knew that could be faked. "You killed him. Good. I didn't want him alive after what he did. He did horrible, horrible things." Maylene sounded as if she were about to lose it.

"How did you get in here?" Kellan asked her.

"Through the back." She made a vague motion behind her. "Not all the windows are boarded up or locked. I came here because I wanted to see the place where he tried to kill me. He nearly blew me up in that explosion."

"And he still could. There's a bomb nearby. Did you see the man who set it?"

Even in the darkness, he could see Maylene's eyes widen. "No. I didn't see anyone." Her gaze fired around. "We need to leave. We have to get out of here."

The woman turned as if ready to bolt, but someone reached out from behind her and put her in a choke hold. Just as the thug had done to Gemma back at the ranch.

Seeing that felt as if someone had slugged Kellan in the gut, but he kept his hand steady. Took aim. But he didn't have a clean shot, not with Maylene in the way.

Maylene shrieked, but the sound was strangled, no doubt because the man was already cutting off her oxygen.

"Let her go!" Kellan tried, and he sent a warning shot at the man, aiming the bullet into the ceiling above the guy's head.

The man was behind Maylene, but Kellan saw his gun snake out. And the man fired.

Kellan pulled Gemma into the room in the nick of time because the bullet slammed into the doorjamb.

"Help me," Maylene called out on the tail of another of those shrieks.

Kellan wasn't sure if this was a trap or not, but he couldn't just let the woman be murdered in front of him. He leaned out to send off another warning shot, and that's when he saw the face of the man who was holding her. Not Frank.

Rory.

EVERYTHING SUDDENLY WENT so still that Gemma thought it was as if everything, including her body, had simply stopped. Her breath. Her heart. Even her thoughts.

The moment just froze.

Rory stood there, his arm curved around Maylene's throat, his gun aimed at Kellan and her. And in that moment she knew why it'd come to this.

"You killed Lacey," Gemma said, her voice carrying like a whispered echo in the empty inn.

"Then you murdered my father and Dusty to cover it up." Kellan's voice wasn't exactly a whisper. More a dangerous growl.

"No. Not your father." Rory spoke calmly. He didn't sound especially angry despite the fact he was on the verge of killing a woman. "But Dusty, yes. I'm sorry about that. Sorry it had to go down that way."

Strange that he would admit to one murder but not the other. But if Rory hadn't murdered Buck, then who had? Eric had denied it, as well.

"The only thing you're sorry about is getting caught," Kellan spat out.

"Yes," Rory admitted. He was calm. Too calm. And that was even more chilling. He wasn't killing in some crazed haze like Eric. This was ice-cold and calculated.

There was only a thin thread of light in that part of the hall, but Gemma caught Maylene's eyes and saw the terror in them.

"Is Maylene part of this?" Gemma asked.

"No. She's not what you'd call an organized thinker. Eric used her."

Gemma glared at him. "And you didn't?"

Rory certainly didn't deny that, so maybe he'd lured Maylene here. It wouldn't have taken much. She wasn't

just an unorganized thinker, the woman was almost certainly mentally unstable.

"Amanda's helping you." Gemma threw it out there, hoping it would hit a nerve. By God, she wanted to know who was involved in this so they could be punished.

"No. Not Amanda." Rory didn't hesitate, but the moment he answered her, he shoved Maylene forward, took aim at her.

And he fired.

The bullet slammed into Maylene. She screamed, a hoarse pitiful sound that told Gemma the shot hadn't killed her. Not yet anyway. But she was in pain. Worse, that scream might send Owen, Griff and the hands running into the inn, and they could set off the explosives. If that happened, they could all be killed.

Rory didn't wait around. The moment Maylene hit the floor, he turned and ran back into the room where he'd been hiding.

"He's not getting away." Kellan took off after him, the sound of his cowboy boots slamming against the hardwood floor.

Gemma went with him, keeping watch behind them in case they were ambushed. After all, Frank could still be around, and if so, she needed to get that remote control from him and try to deactivate the bomb.

"Stay behind me," Kellan warned her as they reached Maylene.

The woman was moaning and had her hand over her shoulder, and while there was blood, Gemma prayed it wasn't life threatening. There was no way they could get an ambulance out there, not until they'd secured the area. Whenever that would be.

"Put some pressure on the wound," Gemma instructed the woman. It wasn't enough, but at the moment it was all she could do. She needed to make sure Kellan wasn't about to be ambushed.

Kellan peered into the room where Rory had disappeared, and he immediately cursed. Gemma soon saw why. The window in this room wasn't boarded up.

It was wide-open, the tattered remains of old white curtains fluttering in the breeze. It looked like a ghost.

Since there was some light here, she could also see the footprints in the dust. A lot of them, making her wonder if this was how Frank had escaped, too. But she soon saw that he hadn't. Frank was on the floor, in one of the shadows in the corner of the room.

"Stun gun," Rory said, causing Gemma to snap to attention, and she frantically tried to pick through the darkness and find him.

Rory was in the opposite corner from Frank. Sitting there, his back wedged against the wall. He had his gun in his right hand, and it was pointed directly at Kellan. The remote control for the bomb was in his lap, the fingers of his left hand hovering over the button with that sickening label.

Execute.

Gemma's first instinct was to shoot him, but she couldn't do that, not with him holding that remote.

He could blow the place up.

"You did more than stun him," Kellan said.

Gemma had a closer look, and she saw the syringe sticking out of Frank's neck. It had been rammed into him like a knife, and she thought maybe it had killed him. She couldn't see any signs that he was breathing.

It was impossible for her to feel sorry for the mon-

ster on the floor who'd kidnapped her and brought her to this place. Not under Eric's orders, either. But Rory's. However, seeing him sprawled out on the floor like that was proof that Rory was capable of killing. He'd already admitted to that, but it turned her stomach for it to be right in front of her.

"He was about to escape out the window, and he saw me. I could see it in his eyes that he knew what was going on, I couldn't leave him alive. He would have eventually blackmailed me the way Eric did." Rory's forehead bunched up, and he winced as if the impact of what he'd done was hitting him hard.

Good, Gemma thought. She didn't want any of Eric's insanity or cockiness. She wanted Rory to understand every bit of the misery he'd caused.

Misery that wasn't over yet.

She nearly reminded him that his other henchman was still alive. Well, maybe he was. But hearing something like that might send Rory even farther over the edge. If that was possible.

From out in the hall, Maylene moaned, but it sounded as if the woman hadn't moved. Maybe if Maylene put some pressure on the gunshot wound, it would be enough until the medics could get to her.

"You need to put down your gun and that controller," Kellan told the marshal. "You're not going to get out of this alive."

"No," Rory readily agreed. He kept his eyes locked with Kellan's. "It was never supposed to go this far. I don't expect you to understand, but it was never supposed to go this far."

Kellan cursed. It was raw and mean. "You son of a bitch. You killed people. You just shot a woman out

in the hall. And you brought Gemma here to kill her. Why? She had nothing to do with Lacey."

But Kellan stopped, went still. "You were going to pin all of this on Eric. His sick orders from the grave. Mop up. You were going to stand back with blood on your hands and let Eric take the fall."

Rory made a sound of agreement. "Both Frank and his partner thought they were working for Eric. They told you exactly what I instructed them to tell you. I figured if you believed Eric was behind this, that he had killed your father and Dusty, that you'd let it go."

"Never," Kellan assured him. "I would have kept digging."

"Yes, I know." Rory dragged in a long breath. "You and Gemma just wouldn't let it go. Dusty, your father and you kept digging and digging, Eric, too."

"Eric?" Gemma challenged.

No sound of agreement that time. It was more of a quick hollow laugh. "A year ago, Eric contacted me a few hours before he kidnapped you, said that he'd worked it all out. That he knew I'd killed Lacey and tried to cover it up so Amanda wouldn't find out. But it wasn't like that. I didn't plan to kill her. It just happened when she tried to blackmail me."

"You think that excuses what you did?" Kellan snapped. "It doesn't."

"No. It doesn't. But Eric used it. He said he'd go to you with some so-called proof. Something that I left behind at the scene of Lacey's death. Eric lured me here to the inn that night, and that's when I shot Dusty. I thought I was shooting Eric." His gaze came to Kellan's again. "But not your father. I swear on Amanda's soul that I didn't kill him."

388   DELORES FOSSEN

Kellan certainly didn't jump to say he believed him.
Neither did Gemma. But he hadn't sworn on his own
soul but rather Amanda's. So, maybe Rory didn't have
that death on his head.

Gemma glanced at the syringe in Frank's neck and
wondered if the drugs inside it had been meant for her.
Re-creating the scene of what Eric had done to Caroline
and her a year ago. Just one more piece of a pretense put
together so a killer could get away with what he'd done.

"Eric had given Dusty proof of my affair with
Lacey," Rory continued. His eyes were blank, the look
of a man who'd been defeated. "That's how Eric lured
me here that night. He wanted me to kill you, your father and Dusty." He glanced at Gemma. "He was going
to save Caroline and you for himself."

That wasn't a surprise. Eric loathed her. Caroline,
too, because they'd been the ones to expose him for the
monster that he was. Still, he was no more of a monster
than Rory. Because Rory had sworn to uphold the law,
and here he was taking it into his own dirty hands. In
that moment, she despised him more than she did Eric.

"You didn't have to involve Maylene in this," Gemma
said, glancing over at the woman.

"Yes, I did, because I couldn't be sure what Eric had
told her." Rory looked up at Kellan then. "I didn't kill
Eric, but I wanted to. God, I wanted to. It's a nice touch
that he got betrayed by one of his own men."

Yes, it was. If Eric had lived though, she doubted he
would have been amused by it. He would have murdered
Hiatt in a brutal way.

"You gave Eric the location of my WITSEC house?"
Gemma asked. Not that it mattered, but it would tie up
that one loose end in her mind.

Rory nodded. "*I* was the breach in WITSEC. Whatever you do, don't try to pin any of this on Amanda."

"That's exactly what I'm going to do," Kellan replied. "That's why you're going to put down the remote and your gun so I can take you into custody. You can confess to everything and by doing so, you clear your girlfriend's name. If not, I'll go after her and find a way to connect her to your crimes. I'll put her behind bars for the rest of her life."

Gemma could see what Kellan was doing. He was trying to goad Rory into making sure Amanda didn't get hurt in this.

But she would anyway.

If Amanda loved Rory as much as she claimed, this was going to destroy her. And when Gemma looked in Rory's eyes, she saw that he knew exactly that.

"Please don't do that to her. Please," Rory said. "Tell her I'm sorry." He moved both of his hands.

In the same motion, Kellan lunged at him. But it was too late. Rory hit the button on the remote just as he fired a bullet in his own head.

CHAPTER EIGHTEEN

KELLAN'S HEART STOPPED DEAD. He automatically lunged at Gemma, wrapping his arms around her waist and pulling her to the floor so he could try to use his body to protect her.

They hit, hard, the jolt of the impact slamming through him, but Kellan shoved aside the pain and braced himself for the explosion.

It didn't come.

He held his breath, waiting, wondering if the bomb was on a timer. Maybe. If so, the threat was still there, and it was possible that the sound of the last gunshot would cause Owen and the others to come closer. Kellan took out his phone, to call them and tell them to stay back, but then he saw the controller still on Rory's lap.

Rory was clearly dead, his head now slumped to an obscene angle against the wall, and his eyes blank and lifeless. There was blood spatter everywhere, including on the controller, but it didn't cover the lights.

The green light was off.

Kellan had a closer look, and he realized that Rory hadn't executed the bomb. He'd turned it off.

The breath of relief swooshed out of him, but there'd be no real relief until he had Gemma safely away from this place. There could be another way to set off the bomb, one that didn't involve the controller.

A marshal—especially a dirty one—would have seen to that. Rory had obviously changed his mind about blowing them up, but there could be other hired guns out there waiting to do the job. They wouldn't have gotten the "memo" that their boss had just offed himself.

Kellan pulled her to her feet, and that's when their eyes met. Definitely not relief, either. Or shock, something he had expected.

"We have to get out of here," she said.

He wasn't going to argue with that, but when he glanced at Maylene who was lying in the doorway, he knew leaving wasn't going to be easy. The woman was bleeding, and unlike Gemma, there was some shock.

"Frank was going to leave out the window," Kellan reminded her.

Or rather that's what Rory had told them. Kellan didn't like to put any stock in anything Rory had said, but judging from the position of Frank's body, it made sense. And if it was a safe enough way for him to escape, then they could use it, too.

"Are you hurt?" Kellan asked Gemma, and it twisted at him that he hadn't already asked, or checked for himself. He'd soon remedy that when he had her safe.

"I'm okay. Let's get Maylene out the window."

Kellan figured the okay wasn't anywhere close to the truth. Her face was bleeding, and the bruises were already forming on her cheek. Still, Gemma moved fast when they went into the hall, got on each side of Maylene and hoisted the woman up.

He kept watch because the hired thug was still in the foyer, but Kellan didn't see the man as he and Gemma made their way to the window. It was a risk because he could end up hurting Maylene more than she already

was, but they couldn't stay inside. Thankfully, Maylene cooperated, but she did let out a long whimpering sob when she saw Rory.

"He shot me," Maylene said. "Why? I never did anything to him."

Since Kellan didn't have an answer for that, he just stayed quiet and eased Maylene out the window. "Don't move," he told the woman. "There could be explosives out here."

In hindsight, he should have figured out a gentler way of telling her that because he had to latch on to Maylene to keep her from running. Kellan held on to her while he climbed out. Gemma was right behind him, and she landed on her feet right next to him.

"Kellan?" he heard Owen shout. There was plenty of concern in his brother's voice.

Kellan sat Maylene on the ground and took out his phone. Owen answered on the first ring. "We're out of the house, and in the backyard. Gemma and I are... fine." He used Gemma's answer only because he didn't want to get into the truth.

"Good." Owen blew out a breath. "Stay put. The bomb squad just got here to do a scan. There's an ambulance here, too."

Since Kellan hadn't heard any sirens, it must have made a silent approach, but he was glad it was there. Maylene's injuries didn't appear to be life threatening, but she needed help. That's why it was so damn hard to stand there and wait.

"There's another hired gun in the foyer," Gemma said, leaning in closer to the phone. Closer to Kellan, too. He wanted to pull her into his arms. Wanted her against him. But he needed to keep his hands free in

case he had to defend them. "Maylene's also been shot, and she's in the backyard with us."

"I can try to get to you," Owen offered.

"No." Kellan couldn't say that fast enough. "Make sure the grounds are clear first. The thug Frank said the walls of the inn weren't that thick, meaning that the bomb was outside." Well, unless there were others.

Owen didn't sound relieved now. He cursed. "How bad did things get in there?"

Bad. But Kellan didn't say that aloud, either. "It was Rory. He killed Lacey and Dusty. Rory did that to cover up his affair with Lacey." Kellan had to pause. "Rory just killed himself."

Silence. Followed by more profanity that was raw and punched up with emotion. "And Dad? Did Rory kill him, too?"

"He said he didn't." Kellan hated to add this next part. "And I believe him."

The words had hardly left his mouth when Kellan heard the footsteps behind them. He immediately turned, putting Gemma behind him, and he saw Amanda making her way toward them. She had drawn her gun, but she held it down by her side.

Kellan's first thought was that she'd come there to finish the job that Rory had started, but then he saw her eyes. They were red from crying, and there were fresh tears on her cheek.

"Is Rory here?" Amanda asked, her voice trembling. "I tapped into the GPS, and I know he came here. I found his car on a trail." She made a vague motion to the right, but she never took her gaze off Kellan.

"Put down the gun, Amanda," Kellan warned her.

She shook her head as if not understanding. Aman-

da's gaze fired from Maylene, to Gemma and then back to Kellan.

"If you tapped into his GPS, then you knew something was wrong," Kellan said. "You knew what he'd done to Lacey and Dusty? You knew he was a killer and was ready to kill again to cover his tracks?"

More tears came, and this time her head shakes became frantic. The moment the gun slipped from her hand and fell, Kellan hurried to her to restrain her. He doubted she was an actual accessory to Rory's crimes. Not before the fact anyway. But he wasn't taking any chances. When he put plasticuffs on her, Amanda sank to her knees on the ground.

"Rory's dead," she muttered. It wasn't a question.

"Yes, he killed himself."

Kellan steeled himself to give her details, but he didn't get a chance because he heard a new wave of footsteps.

"It's me," Owen said, and Kellan spotted his brother coming up the trail Amanda had taken. "I saw Amanda making her way back here, and since she didn't set off any explosives, I figured I'd come back and lend a hand."

As Amanda had done, Owen glanced around as if piecing things together, and he cursed softly. Not because of Amanda or even Maylene but when his attention landed on Gemma. "You've been taking some punches lately."

Gemma nodded. "But I'm okay now."

Unlike her earlier assurance that she was okay, Kellan thought this one might be closer to the truth.

"I didn't see any other gunmen," Owen went on, and he looked at Amanda. "Is she under arrest?"

"No," Kellan answered, and since he had his brother's help, he risked slipping his arms around Gemma's waist. "Just being cautious."

Owen made a sound of agreement. "Come on. We can use the trail to get Maylene to the ambulance. To get you and Gemma to the cruiser, too. I'll handle Amanda while Griff deals with the bomb squad."

"There's an injured man in the foyer," Gemma reminded him. "And Frank's in the room."

"Yeah. We'll take care of him once the building and grounds are cleared." Owen went to Maylene, lifting her so he could support her weight. Kellan did the same to Gemma so they could start walking.

Kellan continued to keep watch, but he no longer felt that sinking feeling in the pit of his stomach. Eric and Rory were dead. For now, the danger had passed.

"Jack called," Owen said as they walked. "No change in Caroline's condition. He said he'd call you after you were at the sheriff's office."

Good. Because they needed to talk.

"Caroline will have to stay in protective custody," Gemma muttered.

And Kellan had to nod. Caroline was the only person who could possibly ID his father's killer. That meant she was in danger. Well, maybe she was. Maybe like Rory and Eric, his father's killer was dead, too. Still, it was too big of a risk to take not to keep Caroline under protection. Then, once her memory returned... well, then they'd have to deal with whatever was now trapped in her head.

When they made it back to the front road, Owen handed off Maylene to a medic who immediately whisked her into the ambulance.

"You should let the medics check you," Owen added to Gemma.

She shook her head. Kellan nodded. He compromised by adding, "Soon."

And the look Kellan gave her let Gemma know that he wouldn't budge on that. He'd come close to losing her, and he had to make sure she was truly all right. First though, he wanted to get her off her feet before she fell flat on her face.

Kellan threaded his way through the medics, bomb squad, Griff and the hands who were still around, and he led Gemma to the cruiser. He got her in the front seat but didn't drive. That's because he wasn't sure he was steady enough to do that. Not yet. She wasn't the only one who was shaken.

He reached for her, to pull her into his arms, but he was surprised when she stopped him.

"You're not going to apologize," Gemma said, and she sounded a lot stronger than he'd expected. "Eric was a bastard. Rory was a bastard. And they both failed."

She put her hands on the sides of his face, forcing eye contact even though he had no intention of looking anywhere else. "You swore to me that you'd come back, and you did." Her breath shuddered now, the nerves showing. "You did," she repeated, the shudder making it to her voice.

He nodded. "I have this thing about keeping my promise to a woman I've seen naked." It had the intended effect.

It made her smile.

Kellan smiled, too, when he eased his hand around the back of her neck, pulled her to him and kissed her. There it was. That kick of both comfort and heat. It slid

right through him, healing all the raw parts of him. She probably wouldn't believe him if he told her the effect she had on him, so he went in a different direction.

"I love you," he said. "And, no, that's not a goodbye," he quickly added. "I have this thing about saying 'I love you' to a woman whom I, well, love."

Gemma stared at him. And stared. Before she smiled again. "I love you. And I have this thing about making sure it lasts a lifetime."

He felt another surge of comfort and heat, this one like an avalanche. It was exactly what Kellan wanted. "You swear?" he asked as he pulled her to him for another kiss.

"I swear," Gemma answered, and her mouth met his.

* * * * *